J. M. Coetzee

KV-648-865

J. M. Coetzee

Countervoices

Carrol Clarkson

UNIVERSITY OF WINCHESTER
LIBRARY

© Carrol Clarkson 2009

All rights reserved. No reproduction, copy or transmission of this
publication may be made without written permission.

No portion of this publication may be reproduced, copied or transmitted
save with written permission or in accordance with the provisions of the
Copyright, Designs and Patents Act 1988, or under the terms of any licence
permitting limited copying issued by the Copyright Licensing Agency,
Saffron House, 6-10 Kirby Street, London EC1N 8TS.

Any person who does any unauthorized act in relation to this publication
may be liable to criminal prosecution and civil claims for damages.

The author has asserted her right to be identified as the author of this
work in accordance with the Copyright, Designs and Patents Act 1988.

First published 2009 by
PALGRAVE MACMILLAN

Palgrave Macmillan in the UK is an imprint of Macmillan Publishers Limited,
registered in England, company number 785998, of Houndmills, Basingstoke,
Hampshire RG21 6XS.

Palgrave Macmillan in the US is a division of St Martin's Press LLC,
175 Fifth Avenue, New York, NY 10010.

Palgrave Macmillan is the global academic imprint of the above companies
and has companies and representatives throughout the world.

Palgrave® and Macmillan® are registered trademarks in the United States,
the United Kingdom, Europe and other countries.

ISBN: 978–0–230–22156–7

This book is printed on paper suitable for recycling and made from fully
managed and sustained forest sources. Logging, pulping and manufacturing
processes are expected to conform to the environmental regulations of the
country of origin.

A catalogue record for this book is available from the British Library.

A catalog record for this book is available from the Library of Congress.

10 9 8 7 6 5 4 3 2
18 17 16 15 14 13 12 11 10

Printed and bound in Great Britain by
CPI Antony Rowe, Chippenham and Eastbourne

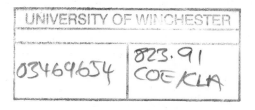

UNIVERSITY OF WINCHESTER

03469654   823.91
            COE KLA

For Jacques Berthoud

Contents

Acknowledgements

Jacques Berthoud (to whom this book is dedicated) supervised my doctoral thesis on Charles Dickens at the University of York. It is to Jacques that I am indebted for developing a way of writing about literature.

In relation to the present project, my first and ongoing thanks go to David Attwell. His extraordinary intellectual generosity and verve have resulted in my writing a much better book than the one I'd initially proposed.

Two conferences have played a vital role in my work on Coetzee: the colloquium organized by Mark Sanders and Nancy Ruttenberg at New York University in March 2007, and the conference organized by Lucy Allais of the philosophy department at the University of the Witwatersrand in Johannesburg in March 2009. I've benefited immensely from papers presented at these conferences, and from conversations with the other participants. Thank you to Jakob Lothe, who invited me to be the co-supervisor of Kjetil Enstad's doctoral thesis, and to give postgraduate classes on Coetzee at the University of Oslo in February 2008; it's during my preparation for the Oslo visit that I refined important parts of my thinking.

Thank you to the Coetzee student-scholars (both visiting and resident) at the University of Cape Town. Their intellectual energy and enthusiasm is at the core of our discussion group, the Coetzee Collective, which in turn provided me with the motivation to write this book. I would especially like to mention Kjetil Enstad, Donald Powers, Arthur Rose, Karen Jennings and Lance Herman. Sue Buchanan (who compiled the index) has been a sustained source of encouragement throughout the project. My sincere thanks also go out to my colleagues at UCT and to the visiting speakers who have supported and participated in our Coetzee Collective meetings. Lyn Holness and John De Gruchy of UCT's Research and Innovation Centre have given me invaluable practical advice and support – not least when I first set out on this project.

Several people have read my essays and reviews (sometimes even before I myself knew that I'd be writing a book), and earlier drafts of chapters. I've gained a great deal, in different ways, from exchanges with Peter Fitzpatrick, Drucilla Cornell, Derek Attridge, Raj Mesthrie, Mark Sanders, Andrew van der Vlies, Bernhard Weiss, Elisa Galgut, Mike Marais and Gail Fincham. I've gained more than it is possible to say, and more than I myself probably realize, from nearly two decades of conversation with my husband, Stephen Clarkson, who reads my work with challenging and inspiring philosophical insight.

A big thank you to Jacob and Christopher: like Elizabeth Costello's two children, they've been left to their own devices more often than I feel pleased to admit, but unlike Helen and John, they've never resorted to making 'tiny whining sounds' at my door while I'm trying to write.

The image on the cover is a detail from the *Book of Speaking in Tongues* (ink and gold on bone) by Pippa Skotnes. Thank you, Pippa, for permission to use this image, and for taking such an engaged interest in the book.

Chapter 2, 'You', has its beginnings in a review essay, 'Derek Attridge in the Event', *Journal of Literary Studies* 21.3/4 (December 2005) 379–386.

Chapter 4, 'Voiceless', is based on an article, ' "Done because we are too menny": Ethics and Identity in J.M. Coetzee's *Disgrace*', *Current Writing* 15.2 (October 2003) 77–90.

An earlier version of Chapter 5, 'Names', appears as an essay in a book: 'Remains of the Name', *Literary Landscapes from Modernism to Postcolonialism*. Eds. A. de Lange, G. Fincham, J. Lothe and J. Hawthorn (Palgrave, 2008), pp. 125–42.

Introduction

'I don't think or act in sweeps', says Coetzee to David Attwell in one of the interviews in *Doubling the Point*. 'I tend to be rather slow and painstaking and myopic in my thinking' (Coetzee, *Doubling the Point* 246). A cursory perusal of the titles of some of Coetzee's critical essays bears testimony to the measure of his statement: 'The Manuscript Revisions of Beckett's *Watt*'; 'The First Sentence of Yvonne Burgess' *The Strike*'; 'The Rhetoric of the Passive in English'; 'The Agentless Sentence as Rhetorical Device'; 'Time, Tense and Aspect in Kafka's "The Burrow"'... These linguistic analyses may not at first seem pertinent to the deeply ethical concerns that have attracted the interest of much Coetzee scholarship, yet one of my leading arguments is that sustained attention to Coetzee's preoccupation with a grammar that limits linguistic and aesthetic choices provides a way of appreciating the complexity of Coetzee's ethical engagements. Clearly, I am using the term 'grammar' in a slightly special sense here – in the sense of what the structures of language within a work of literature enable the writer to say.[1] More specifically, my discussion throughout the book constitutes an extended thinking through of the ethics and aesthetics of literary address: that is to say, in what ways do seemingly innocent linguistic choices on the part of the writer have ethical consequences for the position of the speaking or writing self in relation to those whom one addresses, or in relation to those on whose behalf one speaks, or in relation to a world one attempts to represent or create in writing?

Underwriting these questions throughout my book is a sustained exploration of what we might understand as constituting 'ethics' in

1

Coetzee's work. If, in Coetzee's terms, '[s]eriousness is, for a certain kind of artist, an imperative uniting the aesthetic and the ethical' (Coetzee, *Giving Offense* 73), it is worth pursuing just what that seriousness might consist in. In several of his interviews, reviews, critical essays – and also his fiction, we witness Coetzee responding (in different ways) to other writers, thinkers and artists with a critical and creative acuity that leads to a searing self-interrogation, and it is within this context of seriousness that I shall be using the term 'ethics' in the discussions to follow. I take my cue from Coetzee's own reflections throughout his writing about what the term 'ethics' might entail – reflections perhaps most deftly summarized in his response to a question posed by David Attwell in the 2003 Nobel Prize interview:

> I would say that what you call 'the literary life,' or any other way of life that provides means for interrogation of our existence – in the case of the writer fantasy, symbolization, storytelling – seems to me a good life – good in the sense of being ethically responsible. (Coetzee and Attwell, 'An Exclusive Interview with J.M. Coetzee' 3)

Throughout his work, both fictional and non-fictional, Coetzee develops what one might call a philosophy of writing. But to date, Coetzee scholarship has not paid sustained attention to the *link* between Coetzee's explicit preoccupation with language from the perspective of the linguistic sciences on the one hand, and the ethical force of his work, from a literary-philosophical perspective, on the other.[2] Using the linguistico-philosophical underpinnings of his fiction and critical essays as a starting point, the book explores Coetzee's ethics of writing, which is perhaps most striking in its consideration of the grammar of subject positions: what is ethically at stake in the use of proper names, or in recourse to a first-person plural 'we', or in the projection of an implied second-personal 'you' through the very logic of literary address? What authorial commitments arise by writing in the first person, or in the third? Grammatical choices such as these frequently arise in Coetzee as having profoundly ethical ramifications – especially in relation to questions about the authority, and hence the responsibility, on the part of the writer.

An engagement with questions raised by the linguistic sciences is at the core of Coetzee's writing; the fiction and critical essays bear testimony to that, as do Coetzee's own statements on the matter. In response to a question posed by Jean Sévry in 1985, for example, Coetzee speaks about the continuity between his interest in linguistics, and his 'activities as a writer': 'in many ways I am more interested in the linguistic than the literary side of my academic profession', says Coetzee;

> I think there is evidence of an interest in problems of language throughout my novels. I don't see any disruption between my professional interest in language and my activities as a writer. (Coetzee and Sévry 1)

And in his opening address at the 'Linguistics at the Millennium' conference held at the University of Cape Town in January 2000, Coetzee expresses the wish to acknowledge, 'in some way', the debt he owes to the linguistic disciplines: 'although I cannot any longer call myself an active linguist, my own approach to language has been shaped more deeply than I know by immersion in ways of thinking encouraged by linguistic science' (Coetzee, Opening address at the 'Linguistics at the Millennium' conference 1). In taking this interdisciplinary continuity seriously, my discussion throughout the book considers Coetzee more broadly as a *writer*, rather than exclusively as a novelist. In his sustained attention to problems of language across his novels and his critical essays (so my argument goes), Coetzee makes an active and original contribution to contemporary literary-critical thinking; his novels do not simply serve as allegories of an extraneous and *given* theoretical or philosophical frame.

In the remarkable series of essays and interviews with David Attwell in *Doubling the Point*, Coetzee speaks in some detail about his preoccupations as a writer of fiction and as a literary critic. In many of the discussions to follow I use these essays and dialogues as my starting points, thinking in the tracks of Coetzee as critic, to ask what insights his linguistic investigations may have to offer to a reader of his fiction. *Doubling the Point* thus provides the impetus for the present project, but this is not to say that I read the novels as straightforward illustrations, within a fictional framework, of ideas delineated in Coetzee's critical writing. As I hope to show, and as even a preliminary reading of his entire oeuvre must testify, the relation between Coetzee's critical writing and his fiction is far more subtle and complex than such a reading would allow.

In this introduction, I place emphasis on a particular moment in Coetzee's intellectual biography, namely, the ten years or so leading up to the writing of his first novel, *Dusklands*, which was published in 1974. In this time Coetzee wrote his MA dissertation on the novels of Ford Madox Ford (he defended his dissertation at the University of Cape Town in 1963) and his doctoral thesis on Samuel Beckett, which he completed at the University of Texas at Austin in 1969. Thus Coetzee begins developing his own literary-critical discourse, but in ways that would prepare the ground for his own distinctive projects in prose fiction.

His doctoral thesis, *The English Fiction of Samuel Beckett: An Essay in Stylistic Analysis* is an important resource, since it provides invaluable insight into Coetzee's preoccupation with narrative as a form of rule-bound play; the thesis also draws attention to, and sheds light on, comments elsewhere in Coetzee's interviews and critical essays that one might otherwise easily overlook. Perhaps most importantly, though: Coetzee's generative interest in linguistically based stylistic analysis as *part of* his enterprise as a writer of fiction is clearly visible throughout his life of writing, and we see the beginnings of this in the thesis on Beckett, which 'treat[s] style [so the abstract tells us] as linguistic choice within the economy of the work of art as a formal whole'. In the course of the argument the thesis explores, but ultimately questions the value, for literary analysis, of statistical methods of stylistic description.[3] By the time he wrote his thesis, Coetzee found himself at an unusual intellectual confluence of mathematics, computational logic, linguistic science and English literature. He had his BA Honours degrees in English literature and linguistics – and in mathematics. He completed his MA on Ford Madox Ford at the same time that he was working as a mathematician and computer programmer in England (between 1962 and 1965). Of Ford Madox Ford's *The Good Soldier*, Coetzee writes in his MA dissertation that it is 'probably the finest example of literary pure mathematics in English' (Coetzee, *The Works of Ford Madox Ford* x). Speaking to David Attwell in 1992 about his work on Beckett, Coetzee remarks that he set out writing his doctoral thesis at a time when there seemed to him 'to be something in the air, a possibility that linguistics, mathematics, and textual analysis might be brought together in some way' (*Doubling the Point* 25–6). Even though the project, *in these terms*, did not seem to warrant further exploration on Coetzee's part, the work that he did on Beckett is pivotal in terms of the development of his own craftsmanship as a writer:

> The essays I wrote on Beckett's style aren't only academic exercises, in the colloquial sense of that word. They are also attempts to get closer to a secret, a secret of Beckett's that I wanted to make my own. And discard, eventually, as it is with influences. (*Doubling the Point* 25)

Coetzee's immersion in linguistics[4] enabled him to appreciate more clearly (with 'a degree of consciousness', he says (*Doubling the Point* 25)), the effects of Beckett's writing on his own, and an understanding of style in terms of the author's linguistic choices which, in turn, are at least in part determined by the overall structure of each literary work. Despite his final disaffection with the spiritless mechanics of a numerical analysis of style ('What do the figures tell us? and, specifically, What do the measures measure?' (*The English Fiction of Samuel Beckett* 159)), Coetzee's approach stresses the materiality of writing; style is a matter of observable linguistic phenomena and, by extension, it is the complex sequence of empirical linguistic choices on the part of the writer that produces certain literary-aesthetic effects. In Michael Riffaterre's terms, 'In the sender-receiver function which actualizes the poem, the receiver's behavior may be subjective and variable, but it has an objective invariable cause' (Riffaterre, 'Criteria for Style Analysis' 419). In the attempt to get closer to Beckett's secret *as a writer* the emphasis of the thesis is not so much on the thematic or philosophical content of the works under discussion ('Dante and the Lobster', *Murphy* and *Watt*) as it is an attempt to identify patterns in Beckett's linguistic choices, and to analyse the stylistic effects of these patterns and rhythms within the structure of the literary work. I shall be considering Coetzee's fiction in a related way – as *experiments* with the effects that can be generated by putting certain linguistic structures into the field of narrative play. The young John of Coetzee's fictionalized autobiography, *Youth* (published in 2002), speaks about his first attempt at writing prose in precisely these terms: 'He sets aside a weekend for his first experiment with prose' and

> The story that emerges from the *experiment*, if that is what it is, a story, has no real plot. (Coetzee, *Youth* 61, my emphasis)

It is worth noticing the way in which this anecdote is phrased. 'The story that emerges from the experiment' does not cede syntactical – or subjective – agency to the writer. It is as if a story (if it is that!) surfaces in the writing, independently of authorial control. Here, then, are markers of Coetzee's early leanings towards structuralism, which recall especially the Roland Barthes of 'The Death of the Author' and 'To Write: An Intransitive Verb?'[5] Indeed, it is with rare enthusiasm in an interview (this time with Stephen Watson in 1978) that Coetzee speaks about Roland Barthes as a source of literary-critical inspiration:

> I have the greatest admiration for Barthes as someone who has experienced what I regard as the fundamental movements in modern criticism in a very intense and very intelligent way, and really has much to say to practising writers. (Coetzee and Watson, 'Speaking: J.M. Coetzee' 24)

Here, as elsewhere throughout his interviews and critical essays, Coetzee's engagement with a literary-philosophical figure is distinctive: whether he is speaking about other novelists, or about poets, or linguists, or literary critics, or even scientists or philosophers, Coetzee treats them as *fellow-writers*. As a *writer*, each thinker confronts specific, if complex, challenges in the activity of working with language. Coetzee identifies these challenges and then proceeds to analyse their implications with all the rigour that his own linguistic background affords. At the same time, though, Coetzee himself is an artist, and his literary-critical engagements with novelists, scientists, philosophers... carry the freight one would expect from someone practising the creative arts: 'what linguistic challenges did Kafka face? or Newton? or Celan? or Descartes? How might these challenges best be understood, and how might I learn from these challenges in my own writing? What challenges of my own do I face?' In an interview about Kafka, Coetzee speaks of 'the kind of writing-in-the-tracks one does in criticism' (*Doubling the Point* 199). If the distinction that is being drawn here is between creative writing and literary criticism, where criticism comes off second-best, it is also, importantly, a distinction between reading and *writing*. Taking proper heed of this second distinction means that great value is placed on the activity of critical writing *as part of* a creative exercise – and the initial assumption about the secondary order of criticism is tempered in an important way. It is worth the trouble to consider this carefully. First, here is the part of the discussion that gives a sense of the subtle and intimate relations of artistic creativity and literary criticism through the activity of writing:

> I work on a writer like Kafka [Coetzee says] because he opens for me, or opens me to, moments of analytic intensity. And such moments are, in their lesser way, also a matter of grace, inspiration. Is this a comment about reading, about the intensities of the reading process? Not really. Rather, it is a comment about writing, the kind of writing-in-the-tracks one does in criticism. For my experience is that it is not reading that takes me into the last twist of the burrow, but writing. (*Doubling the Point* 199)

A similar kind of response can be seen when Coetzee writes about Beckett in his doctoral thesis, or about Lacan in his essays on censorship, or about Celan in the *New York Review of Books*, or about nineteenth-century English travel writers in *White Writing*, and in his own fictionalized autobiography, *Youth*. The strong (if implicit) message that comes across is that Beckett, Lacan, Celan and Burchell are all writers themselves, and it is in their capacity *as writers*, with Coetzee writing in their tracks, that the author's own creative activity is sparked.

This brings me to the title of my book, which comes from a passage where Coetzee writes of writing, setting it against the 'monologic ideal' of the straitjacketed interview. This is not to say that writing is under the absolute control of the author (Coetzee speaks of an author's '*phantasmatic* omnipotence' (my emphasis)) or that writing is free; in fact, quite the contrary, and in an intricate way:

> Writing is not free expression. There is a true sense in which writing is dialogic: a matter of awakening the countervoices in oneself

and embarking upon speech with them. It is some measure of a writer's seriousness whether he does evoke/invoke those counter-voices in himself, that is, step down from the position of what Lacan calls 'the subject supposed to know.' (Coetzee, *Doubling the Point* 65)

It is as if Coetzee's critical engagement with the writing of others – already an explicit dialogue – proceeds to raise countervoices within himself, so that each word that he writes becomes *dialogic* in Bakhtin's specific sense of the term. 'Imagine a dialogue of two persons', writes Bakhtin,

> in which the statements of the second speaker are omitted, but in such a way that the general sense is not at all violated. The second speaker is present invisibly, his words are not there, but deep traces left by these words have a determining influence on all the present and visible words of the first speaker. We sense that this is a conversation, although only one person is speaking, and it is a conversation of the most intense kind, for each present, uttered word responds and reacts with its every fibre to the invisible speaker, points to something outside itself, beyond its own limits, to the unspoken words of another person. (Bakhtin, *Problems of Dostoevsky's Poetics* 197)[6]

A serious author, playing up this dialogic potential of writing, instead of trying to suppress it, raises a countervoice, producing a discourse inflected by an invisible interlocutor. An ultimate and unitary authorial voice is thus no longer assured. Clearly, Coetzee's engagement with other writers is one of intellectual *involvement*. It is not the case, I would argue, that Coetzee merely illustrates, or presents by way of allegory in his own fiction, a theory or philosophy developed by someone else. Instead, throughout his work, Coetzee is responsive to other writers and to practitioners and philosophers of different branches of the linguistic disciplines, but in ways that enable him to develop a refined literary-critical discourse of his own, and to conduct experiments in prose fiction himself with a heightened degree of consciousness about that process. In Bakhtin's terms:

> For the prose artist the world is full of other people's words, among which he must orientate himself and whose speech characteristics

he must be able to perceive with a very keen ear. He must intro-
duce them into the plane of his own discourse, but in such a way
that this plane is not destroyed. He works with a very rich verbal
palette, and he works exceptionally well with it. (Bakhtin, *Problems
of Dostoevsky's Poetics* 201)

Coetzee writes about Bakhtin at several important junctures in his
own critical writing – in the essay, 'Confession and Double Thoughts:
Tolstoy, Rousseau, Dostoevsky' (an essay Coetzee would later identify
as pivotal in his career in its turn to a more philosophical engagement with his situation in the world),[7] in the essay on Breyten
Breytenbach in *Giving Offense*, and in a review of Joseph Frank's five-
volume biography of Dostoevsky (in *Stranger Shores*). In this last-
mentioned essay, Coetzee speaks about the critical currency of
Bakhtin's concept of dialogism – a dialogic novel is one in which
there is no central claim to truth or authority since there is no dominating authorial consciousness; instead the reader is presented with
a number of competing voices and discourses. But Coetzee goes on
to make an interesting observation: 'what is missing in Bakhtin', says
Coetzee, is the acknowledgement that dialogism in Dostoevsky is
not reducible to a question of ideological positioning, or even novelistic technique. Ultimately, 'Dostoevskian dialogism grows out of
Dostoevsky's *own* moral character, out of his ideals, and out of his
being as a writer' (*Stranger Shores* 145–6, my emphasis). In this discussion of Bakhtin and Dostoevsky (which I revisit in some detail in
Chapter 3, 'Voice'), we see in Coetzee an attentiveness and a return
to the idea of authorial consciousness – and the ethical implications
attendant upon that. These preoccupations constitute a break with
more programmatic structuralist conceptions of authorship, authority and authorial consciousness.

At the time of doing his doctorate, Coetzee is concerned to meet
the rigour demanded by a linguistically based stylistics, but simultaneously, to 'evolve a linguistic stylistics with some kind of critical
penetration' (*Doubling the Point* 197) – or, in the terms of his thesis,
'to present non-trivial critical conclusions based on empirically
verifiable stylistic features' (Coetzee, *The English Fiction of Samuel
Beckett* 156). It is within this distinctive context that I think
Coetzee's thesis on Beckett can be read as a sustained critical
engagement with the work collected in a book called *Essays on the
Language of Literature*, most especially with the essays in Part Five,

'Style and Stylistics'. More specifically still, the thesis seems to me to be in direct conversation with contributions by W.K. Wimsatt, Richard Ohmann and the two essays by Michael Riffaterre. Riffaterre is careful to acknowledge the importance of linguistics in stylistic analysis, but also recognizes the risk of conflating style and language:

> Linguistic, structural description of style [...] requires a difficult adjustment: on the one hand, stylistic facts can be apprehended only in language, since that is their vehicle; on the other hand, they must have a specific character, since otherwise they could not be distinguished from linguistic facts. (Riffaterre, 'Criteria for Style Analysis' 412)

In his thesis Coetzee takes this problem to the next level. Where Riffaterre is preoccupied with the relation between linguistics and stylistics, Coetzee is interested in integrating linguistic stylistics within a meaningful *literary* analysis.[8] Coetzee explicitly states his 'focal points of disagreement with positivist stylistic linguistics':

> (a) The experience of a work of literature is not necessarily linear in time, i.e. the analogy of reader to decoding device is misleading [Riffaterre draws this analogy in his essay, 'Criteria for Style Analysis'].
> (b) Stylistic features are not necessarily more primitive than larger-scale structural or formal features, i.e. the program of stylistic description followed by critical analysis may sometimes be misguided. (Coetzee, *The English Fiction of Samuel Beckett* 18)

What Coetzee hopes to demonstrate is that linguistically based stylistics 'do[es] not, and seemingly cannot, integrate the study of style into overall literary study' (Coetzee, *The English Fiction of Samuel Beckett* 7). Yet in much of his own writing, Coetzee explores further the possibility of just such an integration, which means that his discourse falls beyond the generally accepted reach of linguistic stylistics. Coetzee discusses several of the writers with whom he engages (Kafka, Newton, Beckett, Celan, the Dutch poet, Achterberg – to name a few) as pressing the boundaries of their respective languages. Coetzee, in order to speak with justice about these writers, in turn hopes to 'push at the limits of the linguistic disciplines' (*Doubling the Point* 197).

Let me demonstrate this briefly by tracking (reconstructing?) just one of Coetzee's many intellectual paths, which has to do with his fictional account of his own emergence as a writer – and his engagement with structuralism. A variant of Barthes' conception of the 'death of the author' occurs to the John of *Youth*: 'might it not be argued that the invention of computers has changed the nature of art, by making the author and the condition of the author's heart irrelevant?' (Coetzee, *Youth* 161).[9] It is at this time that Coetzee was experimenting with computer-generated poetry. In the brief explanatory essay that he attached to one of these poems ('Computer Poem', published in 1963 in the University of Cape Town student journal, *The Lion and the Impala*),[10] Coetzee goes so far as to suggest that even most of his editing of the poem could have been done by a more sophisticated computer program; not only the author, but even the editor cedes ground to the writing generated by the machine. In the abstract of his doctoral thesis, Coetzee understands style to be a question of linguistic choice within the structure of the work of art as a formal whole – and it is interesting to see that it is in related terms that he speaks about the program that he wrote for his computer poems. The poem (Coetzee tells us) is structured on a paradigm of eight statements (action-present, place, manner, action-past, action-present, place, manner, manner). 'I', 'you' and 'they' – are added later at random, 'and then', Coetzee goes on to say, '(somewhat cynically) statements of Nature-description are inserted randomly' ('Computer Poem' 12–13). The computer generated 2,100 poems, within the programmed structure, using a vocabulary bank of about 800 words. Coetzee then chose one of these poems and edited it:

```
        Poem (ex computer)
             Dawn Birds Stream
             Calm-Morning
        You)  Stand-Among
             Forest
             Alone Tense
        You)  Cry
        You)  Spend-The-Nights
```

> 1)   Away-From
>   Terrified Rapt
>   Owls Blackmen
> You)   Hope Violence
>   (Coetzee, 'Computer Poem' 12)

And:

> Poem (edited)
> Dawn, birds, a stream, a calm morning.
> You stand among the trees alone and tense.
> You have cried.
> You spend the nights away from me,
> Terrified, rapt,
> Among owls and black men,
> Hoping for violence.
>   (Coetzee, 'Computer Poem' 12)

An experiment then, in which the final outcome challenges complacent assumptions about the attribution of authorship to a text. But what is at stake in the notion of 'experiment' itself? This question is crucial in my approach to Coetzee's writing, not least because I take it to serve as a conceptual hinge between Coetzee's preoccupation with linguistics (especially structuralist linguistics, and transformational-generative grammar)[11] on the one hand, and his attentiveness to the potential – but not entirely predictable – ethical impact of a literary artwork on the other. It is the idea of experiment that seems to me to precipitate Coetzee from literary criticism towards the practice of writing fiction. 'The *feel* of writing fiction', he says,

> is one of freedom, of irresponsibility, or better, of responsibility toward something that has not yet emerged, that lies somewhere at the end of the road. When I write criticism, on the other hand, I am always aware of a responsibility toward a goal that has been set for me not only by the argument, not only by the whole philosophical tradition into which I am implicitly inserting myself, but also by the rather tight discourse of criticism itself. (*Doubling the Point* 246)

Even though Coetzee openly expresses his appreciation of structuralism, and the work of Barthes in particular, it is clear that Coetzee's own development of a literary-critical discourse goes well beyond what a mainstream structural analysis would afford. In its most deductive form, structuralism considers *any* narrative (in a sense broad enough to include paintings, cinema, news items, conversation, stained-glass windows, theatre...) to 'share [...] with other narratives a common structure which is open to analysis' (Barthes, 'Introduction to the Structural Analysis of Narratives' 253). The focus of attention in this strict and early phase of Barthes' structuralism is on the technical and entirely predictable interrelation between the parts of the posited structure. Yet if an 'experiment' has do with objective physical phenomena of empirical science, it is, at the same time, a 'test', a 'trial' a 'procedure adopted in *uncertainty* whether it will answer the purpose', an 'action or operation undertaken in order to discover something *unknown*' (*OED*, my emphasis); the approach in an experiment is not deductive in the way that the structuralist enterprise so explicitly announces itself to be; the results of an experiment, by definition, are not known *a priori*.

In his own fiction Coetzee goes on to experiment with the possibilities that are at once limited, and opened up by linguistic structures. Just as philosophers develop thought-experiments, Coetzee develops formal and literary ones, setting up various conditions of possibility within language for aesthetic play and therefore, contingently, for historical and ethical awareness.[12] It seems to me that this is a central preoccupation in Coetzee's activity as a writer – a negotiation of the tension between the material stuff of the words that have to be written, and the uncertainty of the more elusively abstract impact of a work of art on the other. Structuralism, in its own terms, and versions of stylistics rooted in structural linguistics, stop short of a discussion of the ethical effects of the work of art. But it is this interplay of physical medium and abstract effect that inspires Coetzee's own thinking about art, both as a writer and as a reader, in the broadest possible sense of this latter term. Thus the *impetus* of Coetzee's discussions about art – while taking into account all the implications of the linguistic turn in stylistics and in approaches to narrative – is very different from that of an orthodox structuralist approach. At least some of the complexity of Coetzee's aesthetics is evoked in an incident in *Youth*, when the protagonist encounters a painting by Robert Motherwell, *Elegy for the Spanish Republic 24*. The painting consists of 'no more than an elongated black blob on a white field'. Nevertheless, the John of *Youth*

> is transfixed. Menacing and mysterious, the black shape takes him over. A sound like the stroke of a gong goes out from it, leaving him shaken and weak-kneed.
>
> Where does its power come from, this amorphous shape that bears no resemblance to Spain or anything else, yet stirs up a well of dark feeling within him? It is not beautiful, yet it speaks like beauty, imperiously [...] Does *Elegy for the Spanish Republic* correspond to some indwelling shape in his soul? (Coetzee, *Youth* 92)

The painting 'speaks' to its viewer in a singularly complex and intimate way, and yet one can imagine that at the time of creating this work, the painter may well have been experimenting with black blobs on a white ground. Coetzee often speaks about the scene of writing along similar lines: the writer experiments by placing words on a page, without knowing what the effects will be, and even without quite knowing what it is that he wanted to say. It is only once the words have been written and read (and once the words are written, the writer, too, becomes a reader) that something will have been said, and that we can begin to appreciate the dynamic and protean force-field of the work of art as it takes singular effect in each reader's or viewer's response.[13] The program that Barthes sets up in his 'Introduction to the Structural Analysis of Narratives' is clearly not intended to take on an aesthetic discussion of this kind, and if we are to accept that there are sympathetic resonances between the young John of *Youth* and Coetzee himself, then we read in the emergent writer an increasing disaffection with deductive assumptions of an innate and self-contained structure – assumptions shared by structuralist approaches to narrative clearly rooted in Saussurean linguistics, and by approaches in other disciplines that apply the binary systems of computational logic. Thus the John of *Youth* comes to the realization that the 'threat of the toy [the computer] by which he earns his living, the threat that makes it more than just a toy, is that it will burn *either-or* paths in the brains of its users and thus lock them irreversibly into its binary logic' (Coetzee, *Youth* 160), and

> Finally he has no respect for any version of thinking that can be embodied in a computer's circuitry. The more he has to do with computing, the more it seems to him like chess: a tight little world defined by made-up rules, one that sucks in boys of a certain susceptible temperament and turns them half-crazy, as he is half-crazy, so that all the time they deludedly think they are playing the game, the game is in fact playing them. (Coetzee, *Youth* 149)

Ultimately, linguistically rooted structuralist approaches are not able to saturate Coetzee's own wide-ranging aesthetic enquiries, but these approaches, and others based on mathematical logic, evidently have a pivotal role to play in raising the questions that generate Coetzee's enquiry in the first place.

Structuralism and the theories in its wake have been censured for a notorious (if at least in some instances, arguable) lack of interest in historical or political concerns. And it is perhaps at least in part due to his structuralist leanings that this charge is sometimes levelled at Coetzee's fiction. But in many of Coetzee's explicit references to structuralism, it is interesting to note that the lessons learnt in these disciplines *give rise to* his own ethico-historical insights – and this informs his fiction in crucial ways. It is *thanks to* his immersion in generative linguistics and other forms of structuralism that Coetzee identifies his realization of the contingency of English as the most powerful imperial language. 'What structuralism did do for me [...] was to collapse dramatically the distance between high European culture and so-called primitive cultures,' says Coetzee. 'It became clear that fully as much *thinking* went into the productions of primitive cultures' (*Doubling the Point* 24), to the extent that 'the term *primitive* meant nothing' (*Doubling the Point* 52; see also 53). And although structuralism and related linguistic disciplines in themselves did not provide a key to the activity of writing fiction,[14] it is through his exposure to the grammars of other languages, including non-Indo-European languages (which Coetzee encountered in his forays into Chomskyan and other forms of structuralist linguistics), that the young writer would entertain thoughts more typically characterized as postcolonial.[15] His study of generative grammar 'at quite a technical level [...] gave the biggest jolt to a Western colonial whose imaginary identity had been sewn together (how thinly, and with how many rents!) from the tatters passed down to him by high modernist art' (*Doubling the Point* 24). Coetzee would go on to write an essay (as part of his doctorate at the University of Texas) on the morphology of languages that influenced one another in the early days of the Cape Colony – Nama, Malay and Dutch – and the scenes of colonial encounter that he would write into *Dusklands* had not only historical, but also linguistic specificity. The question of cultural contingency and its ethical implications (at the very least *signalled* in the confrontation of different languages), I take to be one of the leading concerns throughout Coetzee's fiction.

This brings me to the foundational argument of my book: throughout Coetzee's writing, in the critical essays as much as in the fiction, self-reflexive linguistic questions are at the core of his ethical enquiries, enquiries inflected by attentiveness to cultural and historical contingencies. By implication then, a sharper understanding of Coetzee's contributions to the fields of ethics and literary aesthetics in his fiction can be gained by tracking a path back to his studies in the linguistic sciences. In the course of the book I discuss the *links* between Coetzee's linguistic, aesthetic and ethical concerns through a series of questions. How does the grammar of 'I' or 'he' position the writing self – and in relation to what, or to whom (Chapter 1, 'Not I')? What are the linguistic constraints governing a meaningful encounter between 'you' and 'I' – or (differently put) how might one think of an ethics of address, especially when 'I' and 'you' are writer and reader (Chapter 2, 'You')? On what terms could one return to the idea of authorial consciousness, and what are the responsibilities of this authorial voice, especially with respect to the countervoices raised in literary writing (Chapter 3, 'Voice')? How does one write or speak to or *for* the other who has no voice, and what contribution can be made by literary, rather than strictly philosophical discourses (Chapter 4, 'Voiceless')? What do proper names tell us about the relations of power and the sites of authority of those who use these names, especially in colonial and postcolonial contexts (Chaper 5, 'Names')? What do the morphologies of words and the encounters between different languages reveal about cultural and historical contingency, and what are the ethical implications of running up against the limit of what can be said (Chapter 6, 'Etymologies')? Finally (in the conclusion, 'We'), what are the effects of playing these linguistic structures out in works of fiction – and more broadly, how might the languages of the arts transcend ordinary linguistic limits, perhaps recalibrating the conditions of possibility for the relation of one to the other? In what ways does this extend the range of ethical engagements of we, the readers?

From this brief listing of chapters, it will be evident that my presentational strategy throughout the book constitutes a departure from other book-length studies of Coetzee. In nearly all the extant monographs on Coetzee, two distinctive patterns emerge: a series of discussions of the novels in more or less chronological order,[16] and/or an undertaking to demonstrate the ways in which Coetzee's work embodies a given theoretical or philosophical position; Lacan and Levinas have provided the strongest critical lenses thus far.[17] The important and recent exception here is Stephen Mulhall's *The Wounded Animal: J.M. Coetzee and the Difficulty of Reality in Literature and Philosophy*. Mulhall's book focuses on *Elizabeth Costello*, and, as its title suggests, examines recent philosophical responses to Coetzee's writing, among them essays by philosophers Cora Diamond, Stanley Cavell and John McDowell, collected in the anthology, *Philosophy and Animal Life*. In their philosophical, rather than strictly literary or critical-theoretical impetus, *Philosophy and Animal Life* and *The Wounded Animal* constitute an important expansion to the field of Coetzee scholarship; I shall return to these texts in Chapter 4, 'Voiceless'.

Instead of dealing with themes in each novel considered as a discrete entitity (the characteristic approach in literary responses to Coetzee) my book offers a series of discussions on linguistico-ethical topics, each of which ranges across Coetzee's entire oeuvre. I have already given an indication of the subtle interweaving of Coetzee's activities as critic and artist, and, in taking heed of the difficult relation between these two roles, I do not discuss scenes and events within the fiction simply as a thematization or staging of a received philosophical or theoretical framework, but rather as part of Coetzee's experiments in narrative fiction, which gain an extra dimension when considered against the ground of his own participation in, and contribution to, contemporary literary-aesthetic debates. In other words, the emphasis throughout my book shifts from the more usual discussion of the *themes* of Coetzee's novels (whether we read those themes as theoretical or philosophical) to the aesthetic and ethical effects of the linguistic structures that the writer puts into play. As a consequence of this approach, my book is structured in terms of ideas and literary strategies which (as Elizabeth Costello does!) transgress the confines of each novel, and pose a challenge to the conventionally accepted limits of fictional, literary and academic discourses.

In the first two chapters, 'Not I' and 'You', I show how Coetzee's careful exploration of the grammar of person in Roman Jakobson and Emile Benveniste carries through to the fields of aesthetics and ethics, to become a discussion of what Coetzee calls the 'deep semantics of person'. Chapter 3, 'Voice', constitutes a hinge between discussion of the implications of Coetzee's experiments with structuralist conceptions of the 'death of the author' in the first half of my book, and a reinstating of some notion of authorial consciousness in the second half. Chapters 4, 5 and 6, 'Voiceless', 'Names' and 'Etymologies', carry the idea of authorial consciousness through, but in relation to its situatedness within ethical, cultural and historical contingencies. It is in Chapter 4 ('Voiceless') that I raise some of the questions that have also been of interest to contemporary analytic philosophers responding to Coetzee's work: what does literature have to offer in debates usually thought to be conducted best within the domain of philosophy? This question informs my discussions for the rest of the book, ending in a consideration of what is at stake, finally, in saying, 'we, the readers'.

1
Not I

I

The title of this chapter comes from Samuel Beckett's monologue-play of the same name. Throughout Beckett's *Not I*, the stage is empty and dark, except for a dimly lit and hooded Auditor who sits downstage on the left, intent on the words uttered by Mouth. A single light shines on Mouth, upstage and right, about eight feet above stage level. Apart from her mouth, the face and body of the actress who speaks the words are indiscernible in the deep shadows. For the entire duration of the play, the Auditor sits absolutely still, but makes four gestures of diminishing strength that punctuate Mouth's monologue at strategic moments. Mouth utters a severely fragmented and recursive discourse in the third person; it seems that the words constitute a desperate tension between the need to tell, and the refusal to adopt the position of 'I' in the recurrent thoughts and incidents that appear to be from Mouth's own life. At four pivotal moments, Mouth seems to be on the brink of saying 'I' – of acknowledging that the voice and thoughts are her own, of confessing that the confession is hers – and it is at these junctures that the Auditor moves.

Beckett explains these four movements in the Note at the end of the play:

Note

Movement: this consists in simple sideways raising of arms from sides and their falling back, in a gesture of helpless compassion. It lessens with each recurrence till scarcely perceptible at third.

19

There is just enough pause to contain it as MOUTH recovers from vehement refusal to relinquish third person. (Beckett, *Not I*)[1]

Here is Mouth's discourse at movement two and movement four. The ellipses are in the original:

all dead still but for the buzzing... when suddenly she realized... words were – ... what?... who?... no!... she!... (pause and movement 2)... realized... words were coming... imagine!... words were coming... a voice she did not recognize... at first... so long since it had sounded... then finally had to admit... could be none other... than her own... (Beckett, *Not I*)

The following passage occurs just after movement four, as the final curtain slowly begins to fall:

what?... who?... no!... she!... SHE!... (pause)... what she was trying... what to try... no matter... keep on... (curtain starts down)... hit on it in the end... then back... (Beckett, *Not I*)

At each of the four movements it is as if Mouth responds to an inner voice that the audience cannot hear, but at the same time, that voice seems to be the very one we have been listening to all along, except that in his complicated use of the third person, Beckett destabilizes any easy assumption that Mouth is the subject of her own discourse: the words are spoken, and the attribution of authorial or moral agency to the scenes that are voiced is by no means certain.

In his two most distinctly autobiographical works to date, *Boyhood* and *Youth*, Coetzee writes in the third person,[2] and elsewhere in his essays and even in interviews, he sometimes speaks with reference to himself in the third person, or an impersonal 'one' or 'you', or a passive syntactic construction – which avoids mention of agency altogether. In Coetzee, the question, 'on whose authority are these words spoken or written?' is just as complex as it is in Beckett. This chapter starts out with a discussion of the grammar of persons (this forms an important foundation for later chapters too) and moves on to explore the implications of Coetzee's use of the third person in his autobiographical fictions and in his interviews, especially where he speaks about himself as a writer. The chapter is preoccupied with Coetzee's persistent if subtle syntax of subjective displacement, but at the same time it confronts Coetzee's claims that seem to work in the opposite direction from the drive towards the displacement of the 'I': in the opening and closing interviews of *Doubling the Point* Coetzee says, 'in a larger sense all writing is autobiography: everything that you write, including criticism and fiction, writes you as you write it' and 'all writing is autobiography' (*Doubling the Point* 17 and 391). Reference to Coetzee's understanding of the verb 'to write' as an example of the classical 'middle voice' forms an important part of my argument.

Of specific concern in the discussion to follow in this chapter is the fact that Coetzee typically makes use of the third person in his essays and interviews when he is speaking about himself *as a writer*; his predilection for not saying 'I' (the use of the third person is not the only way of doing this) thus opens up onto Coetzee's sustained interrogation of the authority of the one who writes. This interrogation is very much part of Coetzee's project in fiction, but it also constitutes what one could perhaps consider to be the leading preoccupation in his critical writing. Questions relating to autobiography, confession, authorship and the authority of the writer are at the core of many of the critical pieces. Among these: 'A Note on Writing' (first published in 1984 and reprinted in *Doubling the Point*) – in which Coetzee discusses (if very briefly) 'to write' as an instance of the middle voice; 'Truth in Autobiography' (Coetzee's inaugural professorial address delivered at the University of Cape Town in October 1984); 'Confession and Double Thoughts: Tolstoy, Rousseau, Dostoevsky' (first published in 1985 and reprinted in *Doubling the Point*); and 'Erasmus: Madness and Rivalry' (first published in 1992 and reprinted in *Giving Offense*). The argument of the chapter is this: if linguistic exigency dictates that writing cannot *but* imply an 'I' who writes (a consideration of the 'middle voice' is crucial here) Coetzee, in his writing, and in a self-conscious way, engages linguistic and literary strategies to question the authority of that 'I' – strategies such as use of the third person, the deployment of fictional characters that articulate thoughts we are often tempted to identify as Coetzee's own, the self-questioning use of the genre of autobiography itself.

II

In this section I am primarily concerned with the grammar of person, as a way of gaining a clearer understanding of the literary impact of the distinction between the use of the first and the third person. Certainly, for Coetzee, the linguistic choice of the third person has a decisive impact. In one of his more recent interviews with Coetzee (conducted in July–August 2002), David Attwell, following Paul De Man, and referring to conversations in *Doubling the Point*, makes the observation that 'when one tries to put the historical self into writing, what emerges, inevitably, is a substitute for that self [...] all autobiography is, in fact, *autre*-biography'. Coetzee replies,

> Yes, all autobiography is *autre*-biography, but what is more important is where one goes from there. With regard to my own practice, I can only say that to rewrite *Boyhood* and *Youth* with *I* substituted for *he* throughout would leave you with two books only remotely related to their originals. This is an astonishing fact, yet any reader can confirm it within a few pages. (Coetzee and Attwell, 'All Autobiography is *Autre*-biography' 216)

In reading Coetzee, we may often get the sense that, as in the case of Beckett's Mouth in *Not I*, we are up against a 'vehement refusal to relinquish [the] third person' (Beckett, *Not I* 'Note'), especially in *Boyhood* and *Youth*. But we see also see the effect of the third person with unnerving clarity in the interviews when Coetzee speaks about his emergence as a writer. In the final interview in *Doubling the Point*, for instance, Coetzee refers to himself as a student:

> As a teenager, this person, this subject, the subject of this story, this I, though he more or less surreptitiously *writes*, decides to become, if at all possible, a scientist. (Coetzee, *Doubling the Point* 392–3)

and

> during his student years he, this person, this subject, my subject, steers clear of the right. (Coetzee, *Doubling the Point* 394)[3]

In Coetzee scholarship, nuanced attention has been paid to Coetzee's use of the third person, especially in the fictional auto-biographies. Of course, the use of the third person 'implicitly dissoci-ates the narrative voice from the narrated consciousness'; (Attridge, *J.M. Coetzee and the Ethics of Reading* 143); in Attwell's deft terms, the third person creates 'greater leverage' and a sense of 'self-detachment' (Coetzee and Attwell, 'All Autobiography is *Autre*-biography' 216); the use of the third person effects a 'distance' – which Jean Sévry calls 'this absence within a presence' (Sévry, 'Coetzee the Writer and the Writer of an Autobiography' 15).[4] However, Coetzee's use of the third person with reference to himself in *interviews* (not only in his fiction and his fictional autobiographies), makes us realize that the stakes are somewhat higher than we might at first have thought: the use of the third person in Coetzee is not only a straightforward matter of linguistic choice which has a distancing effect between narrating voice and narrated consciousness, neither is it reducible to the separation of the narrating self from an immature consciousness posited as a different person altogether (the sense we might get from *Boyhood* and *Youth*). Instead, at a more philosophical level, it has to do with questions of the relation between thought and language, of doubtful sites of consciousness within the self, and of the modes of effecting these sites in writing. I return to these questions in section III of this chapter.

For the moment, though, I am interested in the matter of the first and the third person as a linguistic choice that confronts the writer. The cue for this line of discussion comes from Coetzee's doctoral thesis, where he speaks about the consciousness of Beckett's character, Watt, as a third-person, past-tense rendering of Descartes' *Meditations*. 'The *Meditations* are written in the first person and the present tense', writes Coetzee in his thesis; 'if we rewrite them in the third person and the past tense we have something close to the phil-osophizing of Watt' (Coetzee, *The English Fiction of Samuel Beckett* 146). Coetzee then goes on to cite a passage from Descartes' *Meditation III*, rewritten in the past tense and the third person, which he juxta-poses with a passage from Beckett's *Watt*. Once again, we are privy to the laboratory operations of a linguistic experiment: What can the third person be made to do?[5] Significantly, too, in these observa-tions about Descartes and Beckett, we witness Coetzee responding to philosophical and literary texts from the perspective of the writer,

UNIVERSITY OF WINCHESTER
LIBRARY

where philosophers and novelists themselves are regarded as fellow-writers who face specific linguistic challenges. As we shall see, Coetzee is interested in the ways in which deeply philosophical questions (such as those of mind–body dualism, of the relation of thought to language, of the grounds of authority) can be raised, and in fact *generated* by linguistic choices on the part of the writer.

But first I would like to follow through on Coetzee's assertion that I quoted earlier, namely, that *Boyhood* and *Youth* would be only remotely related to their originals should they be written in the first person. Here is a passage from *Boyhood*:

> The secret and sacred word that binds him to the farm is *belong*. Out in the veld by himself he can breathe the word aloud: *I belong on the farm*. What he really believes, but does not utter, what he keeps to himself for fear that the spell will end, is a different form of the word: *I belong to the farm*. (Coetzee, *Boyhood* 95–6)

And here is the passage rewritten in the first person:[6]

> The secret and sacred word that binds me to the farm is *belong*. Out in the veld by myself I can breathe the word aloud: *I belong on the farm*. What I really believe, but do not utter, what I keep to myself for fear that the spell will end, is a different form of the word: *I belong to the farm*.

What is immediately striking in this experiment is the realization that grammatical person does not operate entirely independently of the verb. On the level of conjugation and concord of the verb, of course, this is obvious. But what interests me is this: even though the passage I have just cited from *Boyhood* is written in the present tense in both cases, the original, written in the third person, has the *feel* of being set in the past. There is good linguistic reason for this. 'I', 'you' and 'he', and other words such as 'here', 'now' and 'today' are what Roman Jakobson would call 'shifters' – 'I' can refer to a different person in each case, just as 'today' is not tied to only one particular date or day of the week. Where Jakobson refines earlier accounts of shifters (including those of Husserl), is to stress that 'Every shifter ... possesses its own general meaning. Thus *I* means the addresser (and *you*, the addressee) of the message to which it belongs', to the extent that 'shifters are distinguished from all other constitu-ents of the linguistic code solely by their compulsory reference to the given message (Jakobson, *On Language* 388–9). Emile Benveniste does further fine-tuning. In his discussion of subjectivity in lan-guage, Benveniste sets out with the definitions used by the Arab grammarians: 'the first person is *al-mutakallimu* "the one who speaks"; the second, *al-muḫāṭabu* "the one who is addressed"; but the third is *al-yā'ibu* "the one who is absent"' (Benveniste, *Problems in General Linguistics* 197). The first person, *by definition*, is the one who speaks; the third, *by definition*, the one who is absent. 'I' and 'you' are present to the site of the utterance, *at the time of the utter-ance*, in ways that 'he' need not be. Thus, in the case of 'I' and 'you', but not 'he', 'the instance of discourse that contains the verb *establishes the act at the same time that it sets up the subject*' (Benveniste, *Problems in General Linguistics* 229–30, my emphasis). Benveniste sees 'I' and 'you' as operating in a symmetrical way with respect to the time of the utterance:

> *I* signifies 'the person who is uttering the *present instance* of the discourse containing *I*'

And similarly,

> we obtain a symmetrical definition for *you* as the 'individual spo-ken to in the *present instance* of discourse containing the linguistic instance *you*'. (Benveniste, *Problems in General Linguistics* 218. My emphasis on 'present instance' in both these quotations)

Now while 'he' may refer to a different person each time, deter-mined by the context of the utterance, 'he' is not defined in terms of a speaker/addressee role with respect to the *present* utterance, as 'I' and 'you' are. Benveniste sets up a series of pairs of shifters, where the terms in the first column below have their reference determined by the space and time of the present utterance. The referents for the terms in the second column need not be present to the space and time of the utterance. In other words, the terms in the first column are self-referential with respect to the utterance: 'now' means the time *of the utterance*, 'I' refers to the speaker *of the utterance*, and 'I' and 'you' remain the speaker and the addressee *for the duration of the utterance*. This self-referentiality does not apply to the terms in the second column:

I	he
here	there
now	then
today	the very day
yesterday	the day before
tomorrow	the day after
next week	the following week
three days ago	three days before

(from Benveniste, Problems in
General Linguistics 219)

To replace 'I' with 'he' – or any of the other first-column terms with the correlating term in the second column, allows reference to a person or a thing outside of the time and space of the present utterance; in other words, the instance of discourse that contains the verb sets up 'he' at a time different to that of the utterance – even when that verb is written in the present tense. I return to the passages from *Boyhood*, taking seriously Coetzee's observation that, once one has recognized that all autobiography is *autre*-biography, 'what is more important is where one goes from there'. The original passage from *Boyhood*, written in the third person, sets the protagonist and his words apart from the time of narration, despite the fact that the passage is written in the present tense. The feelings expressed in this first passage are in keeping with the uninhibited intensity of a child's view. The second passage, rewritten in the first person, situates both narrating and narrated consciousness in the present of the utterance; in Benveniste's terms, it sets up the subject at the time of the utterance – and the effect of the passage from *Boyhood*, rewritten in the first person, is one of phoniness. The child (the narrated consciousness) in the first passage *preserves* his secret; it is revealed years later to us by a narrating consciousness. But in the second passage, where narrated and narrating consciousnesses are conflated in the 'I' which brings them to the present of the utterance, the secret is betrayed, to the extent that it is difficult to make sense of the passage. Even though Coetzee uses the present tense, the use of the third person enables him to effect two different time frames, separating the

narrated and narrating consciousnesses, but without the intervention of retrospective adult commentary we usually associate with a
first-person narrative written in the past tense.

Here is a passage from *Youth*:

> In the time he has been here he has changed a great deal; he is not
> sure it is for the better. During the winter just past there were
> times when he thought he would die of cold and misery and lone-
> liness. But he has pulled through, after a fashion. By the time the
> next winter arrives, cold and misery will have less purchase on
> him. Then he will be on his way to becoming a proper Londoner,
> hard as stone. Turning to stone was not one of his aims, but it may
> be what he will have to settle for. (Coetzee, *Youth* 113)

Again, the effect of the third person is to set the narrated consciousness in a time prior to that of the narration, to suggest that the
feelings held by the protagonist are no longer the narrator's own,
and further, that the narrator knows how things will turn out, especially in the sentence, 'By the time the next winter arrives, cold and
misery will have less purchase on him.' This goes somewhat against
a strong line of criticism which sees the use of the simultaneous present tense in Coetzee as denying the possibility of a retrospective
narrative view.[7] Certainly, both *Boyhood* and *Youth* are devoid of
explicit retrospective commentary or value judgements, but the use
of the third person enables the writer to disaggregate the narrated
consciousness from the time of the utterance, and hence from the
narrating consciousness, in a way that the first person does not – and
this is in the teeth of using the present tense. The third person in
Youth makes for a tone of ironic double perspective, which is surely
one of the sources of the humour in the book.[8] In the original passage from *Youth* quoted above, the young John's world view is just
slightly melodramatic – and funny; but what is the effect of the same
passage rewritten in the first person? With reference to the two col-
umns above, I have changed 'the next winter' to 'next winter':

> In the time I have been here I have changed a great deal; I am not
> sure it is for the better. During the winter just passed there were
> times when I thought I would die of cold and misery and loneli-
> ness. But I have pulled through, after a fashion. By the time next

winter arrives, cold and misery will have less purchase on me. Then I will be on my way to becoming a proper Londoner, hard as stone. Turning to stone was not one of my aims, but it may be what I will have to settle for.

In this second passage from *Youth* (rewritten in the first person) it is as if we are meant to take the protagonist's perspective at the face value of the narration itself, and the prose loses both depth and levity as a result.[9]

III

If at first the difference between the use of the first and the third person hardly seems philosophically promising, it is worth taking heed that Coetzee's experiment with the first and third persons in his doctoral thesis takes place within the context of a discussion of stylistic choices made by Beckett, as a riposte to Descartes, and to bear in mind that it is his essay on autobiography and confession that Coetzee, nearly ten years after writing the essay, would take to be pivotal in his own intellectual development; he took it to mark 'the beginning of a more broadly philosophical engagement with a situation in the world' (*Doubling the Point* 394).

Interestingly in this interview, Coetzee speaks about himself, and about the Confession essay, in a way that slips between first- and third-person pronouns, drawing attention to the vertiginous difficulty of attempting to locate sites of consciousness in language, or even in assuming that pronouns have the capacity to stake out those sites. Coetzee speaks about the 'situation in the world' as 'his situation and perhaps still mine' (*Doubling the Point* 394). At least part of the 'philosophical engagement' in the Confession essay that Coetzee refers to in the interview has to do with the relation between thought and language, and the possibility of rendering the truth about the self in language. Further, it has to do with a question of human rationality as it appropriates a world that it represents, or constructs for the self through language.

To return to Descartes and Beckett: discussions of Descartes in literary studies are characteristically focused through the problem of mind–body dualism, but what interests me for the purposes of the present discussion is Descartes' *conflation* of thought and language, which in turn asserts the superiority of human reason over the instinctive responses of other animals. In a letter of 5 February 1649 to Henry More, Descartes writes,

> speech is the only certain sign of thought hidden in a body. All men use it, however stupid and insane they may be, and though they may lack tongue and organs of voice; but no animals do. Consequently it can be taken as a real specific difference between men and dumb animals. (Descartes, *Philosophical Letters* 245)[10]

For Descartes, it is the freedom from instinct that enables the capacity for rational thought. Reason, and the language which tracks it, is not dependent on 'external stimuli or internal states, and is not restricted to any communicative function'. What this means, as Chomsky reads Descartes, is that language is

> free to serve as an instrument of free thought and self-expression. The limitless possibilities of thought and imagination are reflected in the creative aspect of language use. The language provides finite means but infinite possibilities of expression constrained only by rules of concept formation and sentence formation, these being in part particular and idiosyncratic but in part universal, a common human endowment. (Chomsky, *Cartesian Linguistics* 29)

It is worth pointing out here that Chomsky's *Cartesian Linguistics* is an important source of reference in Coetzee's doctoral thesis on Beckett. It is surely largely thanks to Chomsky's work that philosophical questions posed by Descartes, and then read by the Port-Royalists, are brought within the ambit of the linguistic preoccupations of transformational-generative grammar. Furthermore, the logic of generative grammar, namely, that 'language provides finite means but infinite possibilities of expression constrained only by rules of concept formation and sentence formation' seems to me to be crucial in an appreciation of Coetzee's writing as a series of experiments with the aesthetic and ethical effects that can be generated through linguistic and formal literary structures. The tension between finite means and infinite possibilities – and hence the creative use of language – is important for Chomsky in this sense: it means that language acquisition is not reducible to the idea that language is learnt through analogy. Thus Chomsky can assert that 'deep and surface structures need not be identical. The underlying organization of a sentence relevant to semantic interpretation is not necessarily revealed by the actual arrangement and phrasing of its given components' (Chomsky, *Cartesian Linguistics* 33). Let us bring this back to Coetzee's engagement with transformational-generative grammar: in Chomsky's distinction between deep and surface structures in language, and the transformations required between deep-level abstraction, and the everyday surface of linguistic utterances, Coetzee charts another distinction – a distinction between thought and syntax. But herein lies a difficulty: if there is a distinction to be drawn between the processes of thought and the patterns of language, how are we be able to tell which patterns in language are imitative of thought, and which are not, since 'our only approach to the preverbal mental activity that results in language is through that language itself' (Coetzee, *The English Fiction of Samuel Beckett* 87). It is along this fault line between thought and language, between narrated and narrating consciousnesses, that I would say the tracking of mental processes in Coetzee's fiction plays itself out.

Derek Attridge (perhaps with Coetzee's comment about the third person in *Boyhood* and *Youth* rather than Chomsky's *Cartesian Linguistics* in mind) demonstrates the tensions between narrated and narrating consciousness in his discussion of *Life & Times of Michael K*. He shows how Coetzee's repetition of phrases such as 'he thought' insistently reminds us – probably contrary to expectation – that we are *outside* Michael K's consciousness, which, of course, is in keeping with the effect of the third person (Attridge, *J.M. Coetzee and the Ethics of Reading* 50).

But what further complicates the narration in *Life & Times of Michael K* is the use of a version of *style indirect libre*. Reminiscent of Kafka's, the style of narration in *Life & Times of Michael K* is not straightforward first-person interior monologue, nor is it an external third-person perspective, nor is it a dominating authorial voice speaking on behalf of the characters. Instead, we have a voice that seems to vibrate *between* a narrating and narrated consciousness:

> He thought of the pumpkin leaves pushing through the earth. Tomorrow will be their last day, he thought: the day after that they will wilt, and the day after that they will die, while I am out

here in the mountains [...] There was a cord of tenderness that stretched from him to the patch of earth beside the dam and must be cut. It seemed to him that one could cut a cord like that only so many times before it would not grow again. (Coetzee, *Life & Times of Michael K* 90)

Typically, *style indirect libre* does not use phrases such as 'he wondered' and 'he thought', and it does not usually revert to the first person; instead *style indirect libre* makes use of the third person, while remaining focalized through the consciousness of a particular character. I would say that it is the perpetual shuttle from the third to the first person and back again (in a passage like the one I have just cited here) in parts one and three of *Michael K*, that creates a peculiar sensation about the relation between thought and language. Who is the agent of the thoughts, and who is in the subject-position with respect to the narrative? If there is a necessary connection between thought and language, then it becomes problematic to associate the thoughts purely with the protagonist, and the language purely with the narrator – the idea of protagonist and narrator as discrete entities is not something we can easily assume – despite the use of the third person. The narrative switch between the first and third persons draws attention to the precariously balanced tension between the literary consciousnesses at work in the novel, where each seems to place the other on hold, in the instant that its own existence is supervenient upon the other. 'We frequently encounter sentences that begin as statements about K's mental world', writes Attridge, 'but which carry on in language that hardly seems his' (Attridge, *J.M. Coetzee and the Ethics of Reading* 50). Attridge cites the following passage from the novel:

he wondered whether by now, with his filthy clothes and his air of gaunt exhaustion, he would not be passed over as a mere foot-loose vagrant from the depths of the country, too benighted to know that one needed papers to be on the road, too sunk in apathy to be of harm. (Coetzee, *Life & Times of Michael K* 54, cited in Attridge, *J.M. Coetzee and the Ethics of Reading* 50)

and then goes on to comment, 'Rewriting this in the first person – "I wonder whether by now, with my filthy clothes and my air of gaunt exhaustion..." – makes it instantly clear that this is not word-for-word representation of K's thought' (Attridge, *J.M. Coetzee and the Ethics of Reading* 50) – and this is despite the insistence on the part of the narrative voice that it *is* K's thought. I would argue that a characteristic feature of the narration in *Life & Times of Michael K* is this relentless switch in circuitry from the third to the first person, which gives a sense of flickering states of consciousness:

> There was a flutter of bats under the eaves. He lay on his bed listening to the noises on the night air, air denser than the air of day. Now I am here, he thought. Or at least I am somewhere. He went to sleep. (Coetzee, *Life & Times of Michael K* 71)

Passages like these, with their nervous oscillations between first and third persons, narrated and narrating consciousnesses, provoke further difficult questions about the nature of mental processes, and about the modes of representing them in a work of fiction. No longer can syntactic patterns be assumed to be the carefully plotted graph of rational and autonomous thought; I am reminded of a series of recurrent metaphors throughout Coetzee's reflections about this, perhaps most especially when he is writing about Beckett. In some of these metaphors, the line of controlled and ordered syntax reels in, as much as it is pulled off balance by, the turbulent depths of consciousness:

> But what I found, particularly in the Beckett of the late forties and early fifties [...] was an energy of quite a savage order, under the control of a syntax of the utmost lucidity. The thought was like a ravening dog; the prose was like a taut leash. (Coetzee, 'Homage' 6)

And

> the proliferation of anarchic life under the surface of the page. (Coetzee, *The English Fiction of Samuel Beckett* 4)

In other places, Beckett's narrative prose is presented as a symptom of involuntary synaptic connections:

> a central nervous flexion which causes the tics we see on the verbal surface. (Coetzee, *The English Fiction of Samuel Beckett* 78)

What is in question in all of these metaphors is a challenge to the assumption that syntax mirrors rational thought, that those 'thoughts' need be rational in the first place, and that the narrating and narrated consciousnesses that work towards the production of a narrative need have control over their thoughts-in-language. In *Life & Times of Michael K* questions such as these are addressed on a thematic level too: Michael K witnesses his thoughts taking on a life of their own in ways that make him question that they really are *his*:

> If these people really wanted to be rid of us, he thought (curiously he watched the thought begin to unfold itself in his head, like a plant growing), if they really wanted to forget us forever. (Coetzee, *Life & Times of Michael K* 129)

and

> It seemed more like Robert than like him, as he knew himself, to think like that. Would he have to say that the thought was Robert's and had merely found a home in him, or could he say that though the seed had come from Robert, the thought, having grown up inside him, was now his own? He did not know. (Coetzee, *Life & Times of Michael K* 130)

Coetzee's conclusion in his doctoral thesis about the patterns of thought and the patterns of syntax is that 'the relation between a thought and the syntax of the related (printed) sentence is associative rather than determinate' (*The English Fiction of Samuel Beckett* 157–8) – and in his thesis, he goes on to explore the effects of rhythm in this associative relation.[11]

To return, finally, to Descartes and Beckett: in Beckett's third-person variation on Descartes' philosophical theme, Coetzee reads a stylistic parody where language *breaks* with controlled reason, giving way to rhythm and sound:

> Parodying these traits [that is, the 'unwearying balancing of thesis and antithesis and its endless chains of If...But...If therefore...Or...For'...] Beckett also refines them, until finally his intricate syntactic structures develop a purely plastic content, losing, in the processes of their sound and rhythm, all meaning, even the most literal. (Coetzee, *The English Fiction of Samuel Beckett* 147)

IV

Yet if language breaks with an inner world, the break is never a clean one; at the very least, Coetzee's own reflections on thought and language, and on the use of the first and third persons, draw attention to a heightened sense of the difficult relation between narrating voice and narrated consciousness. As in Beckett, Coetzee's use of the third person chips away at one of the cornerstones of Western thinking, where rational thought is taken to be mirrored in language,[12] and the capacity for language, in turn, is taken to distinguish humans from other animals. Thus Benveniste:

> We can never get back to man separated from language and we shall never see him inventing it [...] It is a speaking man whom we find in the world, a man speaking to another man, and language provides the very definition of man'. (Benveniste, *Problems in General Linguistics* 224)

I shall revisit this question of human relations to other animals in Chapter 4, 'Voiceless', but for the moment, I would like to consider further the linguistic underpinnings of the relation between subjectivity and language. The question becomes particularly interesting when that subjectivity is the *self* in writing – which of course, comes back to Coetzee's fictional autobiographies, but also to a consideration of the way in which he presents himself as a writer in interviews. Coetzee is consistent in his understanding that all writing participates in the positing of this writing self, this 'I'. *All* writing is a kind of autobiography – and that includes the writing elicited in response to the interviewer's question.[13] In several of the interviews we see Coetzee speaking about himself in a variety of different subject positions, sometimes moving from one to the other within the same sentence: questions arise about the *sites* of consciousness, to which he, talking about himself as a writer, refers. In the final interview in *Doubling the Point*, for example, Coetzee resolutely speaks about himself in the third person up to the time that he went to the University of Texas, but then says,

> The discipline within which he (and *he* now begins to feel closer to *I*: *autre*biography shades back into autobiography) had trained

himself/myself to think brought illuminations that I can't imagine him or me reaching by any other route. (Coetzee, *Doubling the Point* 394)

and in the interview which David Attwell conducted after Coetzee's winning of the Nobel Prize for Literature in 2003, we get a further sense of a protean author travelling through a life-in-writing. Attwell initiates the shift to the third person: 'what does the future hold for the 2003 Nobel Laureate?' Coetzee answers in the third person ('already he is being peppered with invitations to travel far and wide'), shifts to an impersonal use of the second person ('you prove your competence as a writer and an inventor of stories, and then people clamour for you to make speeches and tell them what you think about the world'), after having said, in a first-person 'I' and in the conditional mode, that he 'would certainly feel uncomfortable in the role' of 'writer as sage'. And then further on in the interview, speaking about a lecture, now printed as an article, which he wrote some years earlier, Coetzee speaks in the passive voice, thus avoiding direct mention of himself as the author of that text, and even of the lecture: 'The article you refer to is a fairly hastily written piece, the text of a public lecture given in the days when I still did that kind of thing' (Coetzee and Attwell, 'An Exclusive Interview with J.M. Coetzee' 1). The person who wrote the article hastily, and gave the public lecture, seems only remotely connected to the 'I' now speaking in the interview.

If the use of the third person effects the distance that Attridge and Attwell have spoken about in relation to Coetzee's fictional characters, we begin to realize too (having started out with Samuel Beckett), that reference to one's own self in the third person is not an easy position to sustain; 'he' or 'she' is perhaps destined to cede ground to, or to falter in the presence of, an 'I' who speaks. The exigency is first of all a *linguistic* one, as we have already seen, thanks to Benveniste: 'in saying "I", I cannot *not* be speaking of myself. In the second person, "you" is necessarily designated by "I" and cannot be thought of outside a situation set up by starting with "I" ' (Benveniste, *Problems in General Linguistics* 197). Further on, Benveniste reiterates, '*I* refers to the act of individual discourse in which it is pronounced, and by this it designates the speaker' (Benveniste, *Problems in General Linguistics* 226). The corollary to this is that the one speaking (or writing) will automatically be in the subject position of 'I' – even when the word 'I' is not explicitly stated. For Benveniste this setting-up of subjectivity (with reference to 'I' and 'you') is fundamental to language, and 'Language is accordingly the possibility of subjectivity' (Benveniste, *Problems in General Linguistics* 227). The 'subjectivity' in question is the

> capacity of the speaker to posit himself as 'subject.' It is defined not by the feeling which everyone experiences of being himself (this feeling, to the degree that it can be taken note of, is only a reflection) but as the psychic unity that transcends the totality of the actual experiences it assembles and that makes the permanence of the consciousness. Now we hold that 'subjectivity,' [...] is only the emergence in the being of a fundamental property of language. 'Ego' is he who *says* 'ego.' That is where we see the foundation of 'subjectivity,' which is determined by the linguistic status of 'person'. (Benveniste, *Problems in General Linguistics* 224)

Further still (and still following Benveniste), the one in the position of speaker, the 'I' of the utterance, is in control of that utterance, to the extent that '[l]anguage is so organized that it permits each speaker to *appropriate to himself* an entire language by designating himself as *I*' (Benveniste, *Problems in General Linguistics* 226, Benveniste's emphasis) – that is to say, language is taken over by the speaking subject within the situation of address; authority is vested in the one who speaks, who takes up the position of 'I'. And the presumed authority of the writer is one that Coetzee plays into, but also challenges in his own fiction.[14] In response to a question where Tony Morphet speaks about *Foe* as a 'retreat from the South African situation', Coetzee responds, *'Foe* is a retreat from the South African situation, but only from that situation in a narrow temporal perspective. It is not a retreat from the subject of colonialism or from questions of power. What you call "the nature and processes of fiction" may also be called the question of *who writes*? Who takes up the position of power, pen in hand?' (Coetzee and Morphet, 'Two Interviews with J.M. Coetzee' 462).[15] Certainly, Susan Barton feels that her 'life is drearily suspended' until her story is written (*Foe* 63), and it is a decisive moment when she picks up Mr Foe's pen to assume the burden of her own story: 'your pen, your ink, I know, but somehow the pen becomes mine while I write with it, as though growing out of my hand' (*Foe* 66–7). Even so, it is Friday who is resistant to the position of power of the one who would write about him: 'Then there is the matter of Friday's tongue', Susan reflects,

> On the island I accepted that I should never learn how Friday lost his tongue [...] But what we can accept in life we cannot accept in history. To tell my story and be silent on Friday's tongue is no better than offering a book for sale with pages in it quietly left empty. (Coetzee, *Foe* 67)

And again, Susan insists that Friday's muteness paralyses her capacity to write, 'The story of Friday's tongue is a story unable to be told', but at the same time, 'The true story will not be heard till by art we have found a means of giving voice to Friday' (Coetzee, *Foe* 118).

Linguistic exigency dictates that the position of pre-eminence and control goes to the speaker, and this is in keeping with the long history of Western thinking that associates language with the expression of reason – and hence dominion – over other forms of consciousness. Yet as I have already suggested in this chapter, Coetzee, through the use of the third person, throws the balance of the speech utterance off-centre; where we would expect to find 'I' we now have 'he' – the one who is absent – in the phrasing of the Arab grammarians, but at the same time, the one who seems to hold authority in relation to the narrative recounted. What does this imply for the authority of the implied 'I' of the anonymous narrator, the 'I' of the writer? Thus the use of 'he' seems to proliferate the possible sites of occupation for 'I' – but the result is that the position of 'I', usually the position of authority with respect to the utterance is one that has been destabilized.

The matter becomes even more delicate in relation to Coetzee's use of the present tense in his fictional autobiographies. If, on the one hand, the use of the present tense places limits on what would ordinarily be possible through a strategy of narrative retrospection, the present tense, in an autobiography, reminds us that the person whose life is being recounted is also a writer. The time and situation of that writing are foregrounded in the use of the present tense – as, for instance, in the dramatic shift from the past to the present tense in the closing paragraphs of Charles Dickens' *David Copperfield* – but the *locus classicus* of the use of the present tense and the task *of the writer* in creating an autobiography is surely the opening passage of Rousseau's *Confessions*:

> Je forme une entreprise qui n'eut jamais d'exemple [...] Je veux montrer à mes semblables un homme dans toute la vérité de la nature; et cet homme, ce sera moi. (Rousseau, *Les Confessions* 5, cited in English translation in Coetzee, *Truth in Autobiography* 1)

> I am starting a project without precedent... I want to show my fellows a man in all the truth of nature; and this man, this will be me. (my translation)

The phrase 'cet homme, ce sera moi' is sometimes (and more gracefully) translated as 'that man being myself'. But what matters to me here is the use of the future 'sera'. Rousseau, as he sets out on his autobiographical confession, will be creating a self in writing – and he does not know what the end result will be. What is crucial is that the 'I' thus created will be as much a product of the writer's memories and *present* effort to comes to terms with his former self through writing, as it will be an account of a life lived. The image presented in an autobiography thus takes on a holographic quality, where the self written about intermittently fades out as the preoccupations of the writer come into focus. This is made clear in several passages in Rousseau's autobiographical writings: 'I will write what comes to me... I will give myself up simultaneously to the memory of the impression I received [in the past] and to [my] present feeling [about it], thus giving a twofold, two-level depiction of [*peindrai doublement*] the state of my soul' (Rousseau, 'Préambule du Manuscrit de Neufchâtel', cited in Coetzee, *Truth in Autobiography* 4).[16] This is one line of discussion that Coetzee initiates in his inaugural professorial address, *Truth in Autobiography* – where he cites both the above passages from Rousseau. Coetzee puts it in these terms:

> There is a sense in which, going over the history of his life from a specific point in time, the time of writing, an autobiographer can be said to be *making* the truth of his life [...] Telling the story of your life [...] is not only a matter of representing the past [...] but also a matter of representing the present in which you wrestle to explain

to yourself what it was that *really* happened that day, beneath the surface (so to speak), and write down an explanation which may be full of gaps and evasions but at least gives a representation of the motions of your mind as you try to understand yourself'. (Coetzee, *Truth in Autobiography* 3–4)

The confessional enterprise is as much 'one of *finding* the truth as of *telling* the truth', Coetzee insists (*Truth in Autobiography* 3) – which brings me to this: even though the use of the third person and the present tense in Coetzee's fictional autobiographies precludes a conventional retrospective narrative perspective, what this rather unusual grammatical combination does is to set up the sense of a dynamic dialogic interface between writing and written selves. 'I', 'you' and 'now' establish stable referents *for the duration of that discourse*. The writer of the autobiography is the implied 'I'; the reader, 'you'. But within that discourse, 'he' could refer to many different people at times other than that of the present utterance; 'he' is outside 'I-you', as Benveniste would put it. So to write about *yourself* as 'he', and in the present tense, is to transgress the more conventional pairing, third person: past tense. It is to pre-empt the possibility of seeing the events recounted from the past as unambiguously severed from the present, and the 'he' as unconnected to the 'I' who writes. It is to make possible the sensation of a *wrestling* (one of Coetzee's favourite words when it comes to talking about the difficulty of writing) between self and other, present and past, self and self – since the written site of that self is internally and dialogically split across self and other, present and past, writer and protagonist. Coetzee himself is most explicit about this: 'An autobiographer is not only a man who once upon a time lived a life in which he loved, fought, suffered, strove, was misunderstood, and of which he now tells the story; he is also a man engaged in writing a story. That story is written within the limits of a pact, the pact of autobiography, one of the many pacts negotiated over the years between writers and readers' (*Truth in Autobiography* 5).

Given that an autobiography is a narrative construct ('All autobiography is storytelling, all writing is autobiography' (*Doubling the Point* 391)), all written versions of the 'I' may well be 'fictions' – but given the further impossibility of *not* saying 'I', does writing 'yield *only* fictions' about the self? And even further still, Coetzee asks in the opening interview in *Doubling the Point*, 'How do I know when I have the truth about myself?' (Coetzee, *Doubling the Point* 17, my emphasis). These and related questions confront the young John of *Youth*, when the volatile Jacqueline (who has inflicted herself upon John as his flatmate) discovers his diary:

> The question of what should be permitted to go into his diary and what kept forever shrouded goes to the heart of all his writing. If he is to censor himself from expressing ignoble emotions – resentment at having his flat invaded, or shame at his own failures as a lover – how will those emotions ever be transfigured and turned into poetry? [...] Besides, who is to say the feelings he writes in his diary are his true feelings? Who is to say that at each moment while the pen moves he is truly himself? At one moment he might truly be himself, at another he might simply be making things up. How can he know for sure? Why should he even *want* to know for sure? (Coetzee, *Youth* 9–10)

'What is truth anyway?' he asks, 'If he is a mystery to himself, how can he be anything but a mystery to others?' (Coetzee, *Youth* 132). It is not only the narrated self who is 'he' to the writer, but the writer himself at the very moment of putting pen to paper. Again this problem can be traced back to preoccupations in transformational-generative grammar, and even further still (following Chomsky), to Antoine Arnauld's *Port-Royal Grammar* of 1660. The Port-Royal theory, as it is read by Chomsky, understands language as having a 'spiritual element' (a deep structure, in Chomsky's terms) and an outer, 'material element' – what Chomsky calls surface structure (Arnauld, *General and Rational Grammar: The Port-Royal Grammar* 65). In Chomsky's reading, the *Port-Royal Grammar* attempts to analyse the transformations that occur in relating deep structure to surface organization (see Chomsky, *Cartesian Linguistics* 38–9).[17] Thus while the deep structure is 'represented in the mind as the physical utterance is produced', actually to 'produce a sentence from the deep structure that conveys the thought that it expresses, it is necessary to apply rules of transformation that rearrange, replace, or delete items of the sentence' (Chomsky, *Cartesian Linguistics* 40). Taking these transformations into account, surface linguistic structures in speech (or writing) can be understood to trace inner mental processes, to be read as correlating signs for 'all of the diverse movements of our souls' (Arnauld, *General and Rational Grammar: The Port-Royal Grammar* 66, cited in Chomsky, *Cartesian Linguistics* 41). Leo Spitzer would go on to apply this idea of syntax as imitative of an inner world in his discussions of the novels of Marcel Proust. Proust's syntax, says Spitzer, represents 'in an almost onomatopoeic manner the movements of his soul' (cited in Coetzee, *The English Fiction of Samuel Beckett* 86), and this is where we see one of Coetzee's important departures from extreme versions of transformational-generative principles as they are applied to the domain of literature. Here is Coetzee's commentary in his doctoral thesis:

> Proust is dead. Even if he were alive it would be unlikely that he would be prepared to tell us what 'the movements of his soul' were when he composed his fiction. Even if he were prepared we would have no means of verifying his account, which would merely be another fiction. We would have no means of verifying it because, for the moment at least, our only approach to the preverbal mental activity that results in language is through that language itself. In this situation we can choose either to ignore thought and speak only of language, or to regard language as the graph of thought. But if we choose the latter course we cannot regard certain features or kinds of language as graphs of thought while others are not, for we have nothing but the words to base a distinction on. (Coetzee, *The English Fiction of Samuel Beckett* 87–8)

Thus the mystery of telling the truth in writing applies even in the case where the writer can be questioned in person, and even when the writer is writing about himself. The writer is not necessarily privy to a special kind of knowledge that the reader is not. A self is created in writing – it is not as if the self pre-exists the 'I' of writing, and is then retrospectively 'represented' in a way that can be subjected to verification.

Rimbaud's 'je est un autre' ('I is another') gains full force – if 'he' is the other of an 'I' who writes, this 'he' is not someone *else*, some discrete being who would affirm the present identity of an autonomous 'I'. Instead 'he' is relentlessly called up in 'I' (which includes instances where 'I' is not explicitly written onto the surface of the page), to the extent that the implied 'I' – or as it is written, 'he' – becomes a complex internal dialogue of selves. What I have been working towards in this chapter is the idea that the protean 'he' of *Boyhood*, *Youth* and several of the interviews, emerges as plural interlocutor in a dialogically refracted discourse of selves. If the implication of an 'I' is inevitable in any act of writing, Coetzee engages all strategies to question the presumed unitary authority of that 'I'. The creation of fictional characters, such as the eponymous Elizabeth Costello and JC in *Diary of a Bad Year*, who express opinions that we *may* be tempted to identify as Coetzee's own, is one such tactic. Whose ideas are they? What is the *distance* between a writer and his fictional characters – and a further difficult question emerges – where do we locate accountability for the views expressed?, especially when the writers themselves (Coetzee – but also Susan Barton, John, David Lurie, Elizabeth Costello, JC...) insistently raise unsettling questions about the possibility of finding or creating any truth at all about the self in writing. Further, how can you know? Is the ethical route then to state the not-knowing? This is where Lacan matters to Coetzee; notice, again, Coetzee's self-consciousness about the positioning of himself through personal pronouns:

> some of Lacan's most inspired remarks have been about speaking from a position of ignorance [...] When one is getting as close to the center of one's own endeavor as this question takes one – where am I when I write? – it may be best to be Lacanian and not to bother too much about what one means (can I interchange 'one' and 'I' in this context?); and that would entail not knowing too much about where one stands in relation to the advice – Lacan's – that one can afford to speak without 'thought'. (Coetzee, *Doubling the Point* 29–30)

Apart from the uneasiness about the occupation of a subject position, the passage is interesting because, once again, a question of pronouns is linked to a consideration of the relation between thought and language – and this leads me to what I take to be a crucial feature of Coetzee's philosophical appreciation of writing: that is to say, his understanding of the verb 'to write' as belonging to the classical middle voice, rather than to the active or the passive voice.

V

In his short essay, 'A Note on Writing' (reprinted in *Doubling the Point*), Coetzee reflects in some detail on aspects of Roland Barthes' essay, 'To Write: An Intransitive Verb?' Barthes, in turn, takes off from Benveniste's *Problems in General Linguistics*. Voice, or *diathesis*, writes Barthes, 'designates the way in which the subject of the verb is affected by the action' (Barthes, 'To Write: An Intransitive Verb?' 142). In the active voice, the subject is the agent of the action, in the passive, the subject suffers the action, but in the middle voice, the subject is both agent and patient (if I can put it this way) of the verb, as for example, in the verb 'to bathe' where this can be understood as 'to bathe oneself'. To consider the verb 'to write' as being of the middle voice, is to 'effect writing in being affected oneself' (Barthes, 'To Write: An Intransitive Verb?' 142) – it is to write, as much as it is to experience the effects of writing. The way this relates to a leading line of argument in this chapter is that it has to do with Coetzee's sustained interrogation of the authority of the one who writes, specifically in relation to a questioning of whether the writer has absolute and rational control over the meanings he or she produces in writing. Derrida nicely captures this experience of writing:

> What counted for me [...] is the act of writing or rather, since it is perhaps not altogether an act, the experience of writing: to leave a trace that dispenses with, that is even destined to dispense with the present of its originary inscription, of its 'author' as one might say in an insufficient way. (Derrida, 'A "Madness" Must Watch Over Thinking' 346)

As always in Derrida, this very brief excerpt is conceptually rich, and I take it to be part of the larger critical discussion in which Coetzee's 'A Note on Writing' also participates. First is the insistence on 'the experience of writing' rather than writing as an act in which the subject would be the unequivocal agent of the verb. This is the way 'to write' (and its correlates) is usually taken: as an active, transitive verb, without reflexivity. Coetzee lists everyday examples that are usually understood in this way – 'to use language', 'to write a book', 'to create characters', 'to express a thought'…But to think of these verbs simply as being active voice, transitive constructions, relies on an unspoken conception of the subject: 'a subject prior to, independent of, and untouched by the verb' (*Doubling the Point* 95. See also Barthes, 'To Write: An Intransitive Verb?' 143). What would it mean to think about the verb 'to write' as an example of the middle voice? In this scene, the subject does not have an *a priori* existence apart from the instant of discourse; the writing results in the emergence of a subject. It is this conception of the verb 'to write' as an instance of the middle voice, that surely underpins Coetzee's assertions about literary (and especially autobiographical) undertakings; I repeat – 'we can equally well see the confessional enterprise as one of *finding* the truth as of *telling* the truth' (*Truth in Autobiography* 3); 'There is a sense in which, going over the history of his life from a specific point in time, the time of writing, an autobiographer can be said to be *making* the truth of his life' (*Truth in Autobiography* 3–4).[18] Throughout his critical reflections, Coetzee is consistent in his assertions about not quite knowing what it is that he wanted to say in advance – meaning emerges in retrospect, once he has been through the experience of writing, sometimes independently of what might now only questionably be called his intentions with respect to what has been written:

> It is naive to think that writing is a simple two-stage process: first you decide what you want to say, then you say it. On the contrary, as all of us know, you write because you do not know what you want to say. Writing reveals to you what you wanted to say in the first place. In fact, it sometimes constructs what you want or wanted to say. What it reveals (or asserts) may be quite different from what you thought (or half-thought) you wanted to say in the first place. That is the sense in which one can say that writing writes us. (Coetzee, *Doubling the Point* 18)

Thus what one writes does not exist prior to the writing experience; the subject of writing (in both senses – the topic under discussion, and the 'I' who writes) comes into existence *in* the writing. In some of Coetzee's pronouncements I think it is fair to say that we detect a sympathetic resonance with much of what Derrida has to say about autobiography, where the experience of writing has a reflexive quality of 'writing-oneself':

> I just spoke of a 'pledge' [*gage*] or an 'engagement' of *oneself* in a strange autobiography; yes, but the self does not exist, it is not

present to itself before that which engages it in this way and which is not it. There is not a constituted subject that engages itself at a given moment in writing for some reason or another. It is *given* by writing, by the other [...] born by being given, delivered, offered and betrayed all at once. (Derrida, 'A "Madness" Must Watch Over Thinking' 347)

It is in this context that writing – and meaning – carry a more precarious relation to authorial intention than is often assumed to be the case, and we begin to get a clearer sense of Derrida's assertion (cited in the first excerpt above) that writing is 'destined to dispense with the present of its originary inscription, of its "author" as one might say in an insufficient way' (Derrida, 'A "Madness" Must Watch Over Thinking' 346). Thus while writing intractably implies a writer, the I who writes is not *simply* in control in advance of what gets written; the writer's intentions are not reducible to the meanings produced, just as the production of meaning is not reducible to authorial intention. This is brought clearly into focus in a more recent interview, in which Attwell asks Coetzee whether he still holds to the claim that he made ten years previously in *Doubling the Point*, namely, that 'all writing is autobiography'. Coetzee replies, 'I cannot believe that my thinking about autobiography has not been deepened to an extent by these reading and writing experiences [that is, the experience of reading, and also teaching, Wordsworth's *Prelude* and Roland Barthes' *Roland Barthes*, and the experience of writing *Boyhood* and *Youth*]. So perhaps we should distinguish: I cannot *intend* quite the same as I originally intended, though the two statements, then and now, may *mean* the same' (Coetzee and Attwell, 'All Autobiography is *Autre*-biography' 214).

VI

By this stage it should be clear that several statements that Coetzee makes about language and thought, about the self in writing, and about the practice of autobiography, can be traced back to a rigorous appreciation of the impact of linguistic mechanisms. At the same time, the features that Coetzee draws from the linguistics sciences may remain at the level of a somewhat technical analysis *in those disciplines* – but in Coetzee's fiction and critical writings, these linguistic exigencies are carried through to a philosophical level, and are shown to carry aesthetic and ethical weight. In this chapter I have begun to explore the literary import of grammatical technicalities of person, especially in relation to Coetzee's refraction of the self in writing through the use of a third-person 'he'. As with Beckett's Mouth in *Not I*, the characters in Coetzee's novels (especially the protagonists in the fictional autobiographies) seem to speak in voices that they do not recognize, but which they finally have to admit as being none other than their own. In later chapters I will be addressing the ethical and aesthetic consequences of linguistic features such as voice, agentless sentences, proper names and etymologies. What my discussions throughout the book hope to demonstrate is that the linguistic strategies that the author puts into play challenge, even while they assert, the putative authority of the writer.

2
You

This chapter explores the ethics and aesthetics of literary address – a field of enquiry that invites attention throughout Coetzee's oeuvre. Complex situations of address, and human encounters in a variety of forms, constitute a recurrent motif in the novels themselves. One thinks immediately of the playing-out of precarious and difficult 'I–you' relations within the fiction: the nuanced intensity of Magda's attempts to find a reciprocal language in *In the Heart of the Country*; the Medical Officer's fraught second-person address to Michael K in the middle section of *Life & Times of Michael K*; Mrs Curren's letter to her daughter, intended to be read after her own death, which comprises the entire text of *Age of Iron*. The striking portrayal of scenes of address in Coetzee's fiction, often cast in Coetzee scholarship as the relation of self to other – or a relation to 'alterity', in the sense that Continental philosopher, Emmanuel Levinas, uses the term – has attracted much critical attention in recent years.[1]

Of primary interest in the present chapter, however, is Coetzee's sustained philosophical engagement with questions about the logic of literary address as it appears in his critical writings. Part of my argument accounts for the attractions of what has rather loosely been called a 'Levinasian approach', but instead of reading scenes and incidents in the fiction as a 'staging'[2] of Levinasian ethics, I track Coetzee's own linguistic and philosophical touchstones in his critical essays, in an exploration of what Coetzee calls 'the deep semantics of person, as carried by the pronoun' (*Doubling the Point*

197). I begin with a discussion of Coetzee's essay, 'Achterberg's "Ballade van de Gasfitter": The Mystery of I and You' (first published in *PMLA* in 1977, and then reprinted in *Doubling the Point* in 1992) to follow a sequence of Coetzee's intellectual encounters with other writers. Questions of linguistics (Emile Benveniste and Roman Jakobson) gradually open onto the fields of ethics (with reference to the Jewish philosopher, Martin Buber) and literary aesthetics (the poetry and prose writings of Paul Celan). In reconstructing this conversation about the ethics and aesthetics of literary address, I move on from the Achterberg essay to discuss Coetzee's review in *Inner Workings*, 'Paul Celan and his Translators' (first published in the *New York Review of Books* in 2001). Levinas is in the wings of this conversation: he was strongly influenced by the ethical philosophy of Martin Buber, and, like Coetzee, has written about both Buber and Celan. As far as I know, Coetzee does not mention Levinas in his own essays or interviews. Of course, that a writer should fail to refer to a particular theorist or philosopher is not, *in itself*, reason enough to shy away from that theory or philosophy in one's own analysis of the work. Coetzee, in *Giving Offense*, comments on this in relation to his use of Foucault and Lacan in his response to Erasmus' *The Praise of Folly*: 'In its etymology, *theory* has to do with seeing. In reading Erasmus "in the light" of theories of our time, I aspire simply to make visible, to bring into sight, features of *The Praise of Folly* that may hitherto have been shadowed' (Coetzee, *Giving Offense* 85).

Nevertheless, an analysis of Coetzee's insistent attention to linguistic exigencies and their aesthetic and ethical consequences highlights the ways in which Coetzee forges his own linguistico-philosophical discourse, and thus participates in contemporary conversations in literary aesthetics. The positive contribution that Coetzee makes in *this* field of literary study seems to me to be rather neglected in the scholarship, yet, I would add, an attentiveness to it opens up different ways of engaging Coetzee's writing in contemporary interdisciplinary debates within the humanities.

Questions of translation arise in both of the Coetzee essays I will be discussing in this chapter (the Achterberg essay and 'Paul Celan and his Translators'), and this forms an important substrate of my argument throughout. The primary definition of translation is 'To bear, convey, or remove from one person, place or condition to another; to transfer, transport' (*OED*). I relate Coetzee's thoughts on translation to the ethics and aesthetics of literary address – that is to say, the idea of translation and address *as* a moment of transfer or movement from 'I' to 'you'. The chapter concludes by looking at Coetzee's references in *Giving Offense* to the Bakhtinian notion of internal dialogue, where 'you' becomes the hidden interlocutor, the countervoice, which the writer raises and responds to in a gesture that challenges assumptions about a supposed unitary authorial voice.

II

In an interview with David Attwell after his winning of the Nobel Prize in 2003, Coetzee responds to a question about *Elizabeth Costello*:

> I tend to resist invitations to interpret my own fiction. If there were a better, clearer, shorter way of saying what the fiction says, then why not scrap the fiction? (Coetzee and Attwell, 'An Exclusive Interview with J.M. Coetzee', 3)

If Coetzee's interviews and critical essays encompassed everything that the fiction attempted, in a better and clearer way; if the fiction did not offer anything *else*, why would we take the trouble to read it? But as a corollary to this question, one might ask: if Coetzee's fiction stages in a more colourful, entertaining and affectively powerful way what his literary-critical essays argue, then why not scrap the criticism? In a sense I am taking up the gauntlet thrown in a conversation between Attwell and Coetzee about *In the Heart of the Country* and the Achterberg essay. Attwell reads across these two works 'a curious tension between your respect for the linguistic-structural conditions of fiction, and the existential-historical dramas being played out within them' (*Doubling the Point* 59). 'You contrast the novel with the Achterberg essay in this respect', responds Coetzee, 'to the detriment of the essay', and he agrees with Attwell up to a point: 'there is something missing in the essay', he says, but,

> In its [i.e. the essay's] defense I would only say: you have to remember what is and what is not possible in discursive prose. In particular

you have to remember about passion, where a strange logic prevails. When a real passion of feeling is let loose in discursive prose, you feel that you are reading the utterances of a madman [...] The novel, on the other hand, allows the writer to *stage* his passion [...] But in the medium of prose commentary I can't be passionate without being mad. (Coetzee, *Doubling the Point* 60–1)

Now I think it is fair to say that Coetzee and Attwell are not in *absolute* agreement about what is missing from the Achterberg essay: for Coetzee it seems to be passion; for Attwell, historical situatedness. That aside, in the present chapter, instead of taking the preferred literary-critical route of discussing the 'ek' and 'jy' (I and you) of the Ravan edition of *In the Heart of the Country* – Magda's passionate longing for 'words of true exchange, wisselbare woorde' (although who could fail to be tempted by 'This is not going to be a dialogue, thank God' (*In the Heart of the Country* 101)) – my discussion takes seriously what *is* 'possible in discursive prose' and discusses the mystery of 'I' and 'You' in the Achterberg essay. Coetzee's most outspoken appeal for theoretically sophisticated literary criticism is perhaps to be found in the paper 'Die Skrywer en die Teorie' ('The Writer and Theory') that he presented at the 1980 SAVAL conference held in Bloemfontein – that is to say, the paper is presented three years after the publication of *In the Heart of the Country* and the Achterberg essay. In the paper Coetzee sketches out, and distances himself from, two related attitudes to literature and literary criticism. The first is the metaphor of criticism as parasite on the work of art[3] – the attitude that criticism, especially of a theoretically sophisticated kind, is ''n wesenlike steriele en verbeeldingslose bedrywigheid' ('in essence a sterile and unimaginative industry'), and further,

dat letterkundige werke in mindere or meerdere mate kritiese ontleding weerstaan, dat die grootste werke die taaiste weerstand bied, en dat dié in 'n werk wat ontleding totaal weerstaan die kern van die werk uitmaak. ('that literary works resist analysis to a greater or lesser extent, that the greatest works offer the toughest resistance, and that *that* within a work which absolutely resists analysis, constitutes its kernel.') (Coetzee, 'Die Skrywer en die Teorie' 155)

The second attitude to literature and theory that Coetzee challenges in his paper is the idea that any literary work written with conscious theoretical principles in mind will be stillborn, since literature, by its very nature, avoids or escapes theory (Coetzee, 'Die Skrywer en die Teorie' 155). The danger of the first attitude (that criticism is a derivative and uncreative, if potentially destructive, activity) is that it has the potential to encourage unreflective judgements, and an easy retreat into mystification on the part of the critic. Coetzee would prefer a different metaphor for the relation between literature and criticism, one in which

> letterkundige teks en kritiese teks parallel en mede-afhanklik sou bestaan, saam met ander tekste van die letterkunde, die filosofie ens. ('literary and critical texts would have a parallel and mutually-dependent existence, alongside other texts in literature and philosophy etc.') (Coetzee, 'Die Skrywer en die Teorie' 158)

A little later in the paper, Coetzee makes what must surely have been an outrageous assertion to his South African literary audience of 1980. I must confess, says Coetzee, that 'die beste kritiek vir my meer inhou as die letterkunde. Dit is miskien 'n skande, maar ek lees liewer Girard oor Sofokles of Barthes oor Balzac as romans' ('the best criticism holds more for me than literature does. It is perhaps scandalous, but I prefer reading Girard on Sophocles, or Barthes on Balzac, than novels') (Coetzee, 'Die Skrywer en die Teorie' 160). Taking this as a cue, then, in the present chapter I read Coetzee on Achterberg and Celan, rather than *In the Heart of the Country*.

Throughout his critical commentaries on his own work, and on the work of other writers, Coetzee explores, with meticulous intellectual rigour, questions about the linguistic, aesthetic and ethical challenges facing writers; he does not offer glib imperatives about the role of the artist, or solutions to dilemmas that his characters may face in his fiction *in terms of* a specified philosophy, delineated in advance. In the discussion to follow I am concerned to demonstrate Coetzee's level of theoretical engagement in debates in contemporary aesthetics, rather than to read scenes and events in his fiction as the staging of an imported and received theory or philosophy.[4] Certainly Coetzee's contribution to the literary world is not limited to the domain of his fiction. As I hope to show in this chapter, a

reading of the critical essays serves as a provocation to rethink existing disciplinary boundaries, and to explore the possibility of developing a new kind of literary-critical discourse.

In the course of this chapter I show precisely how matters of the
most poignant ethical concern in Coetzee can be traced back to his
interest in, and attentiveness to, linguistic exigencies. My discussion,
in giving a clearer sense of the extent to which Coetzee engages in
contemporary debates in aesthetics, takes on the quality of a palimpsest: in *Inner Workings*, Coetzee writes an essay on Paul Celan; Paul
Celan knew Martin Buber (he sought advice from Buber about con-
tinuing to write in German – (see Coetzee, *Inner Workings* 121)) and
in his own poetry explores with searing ethical urgency the distances
and proximities of 'I' and 'you'. In his prose writings, Celan writes
explicitly about the ethics and aesthetics of literary address. Derrida,
Blanchot, Levinas and Lacoue-Labarthe have all written important
pieces on Paul Celan. Coetzee (in *Inner Workings*) engages specifically
with Lacoue-Labarthe's *Poetry as Experience*, which in turn refers to
the works by Derrida, Blanchot and Levinas. Crucially for my purposes here (and bringing the discussion back full circle): Levinas has
written a great deal about, and was strongly influenced by, the ethical
thinking of Martin Buber – more so, I think, than Levinas himself
always admits.[5] And finally, it is Coetzee's juxtaposition of Buber
and Benveniste in the Achterberg essay that has launched my discussion of literary address in the first place.

Now in existing 'Levinasian' approaches to Coetzee, there is, to my
knowledge, no sustained reference to Coetzee's explicit engagements
with Buber, Celan and Lacoue-Labarthe, or to Coetzee's linguistico-
ethical understanding of what he calls 'the deep semantics of person'. Reading these works, not in isolation, but as being *in conversation*
with each other, provides a clearer rationale for bringing Levinas on
board in critical responses to Coetzee's work. But at the same time,
this conversational reading of the thinkers and writers mentioned
makes a case for a different kind of reference to Levinas in discussions of Coetzee than we have seen to date. I return to this question
in sections V and VI of this chapter.

III

The Achterberg essay provides the pivot for a tilting of thinking about
the *grammar* of person to thinking about the *'deep semantics* of person',

carried by the pronouns 'I' and 'you'. In his Achterberg essay, Coetzee refers to Emile Benveniste's seminal work, *Problems in General Linguistics*, with specific reference to the topic of pronouns. The pronouns 'I' and 'you' (and other deictics, such as 'here' and 'this'), Benveniste writes, following Roman Jakobson's account of linguistic shifters, 'do not refer to "reality" or to "objective" positions in space or time but to the utterance, unique each time, that contains them'. They are ' "empty" signs that are nonreferential with respect to "reality" '. Furthermore, '[t]hese signs are always available and become "full" as soon as a speaker introduces them into each instance of his discourse' (Benveniste, *Problems in General Linguistics* 219). In other words, referents for 'I' and 'you' are established *contingently*, in relation to the utterance in which they appear. The referents are different each time – they are not stable points of reference in the world, and are determined in a different way to those of nouns and proper names. It is surely in his reference to Benveniste in the Achterberg essay that we see Coetzee most clearly demonstrating the aesthetic and ethical ramifications of *linguistic* questions. Coetzee's reference to Benveniste, as an overwriting of the passage just cited, reads: 'As elements of a system of reference, *I* and *You* are empty. But the emptiness of the *I* can also be a freedom, a pure potentiality, a readiness for the embodying word' (*Doubling the Point* 72). Thus from origins of apparently seedless linguistic assiduity in Benveniste, Coetzee develops a discussion that now begins to take on a suggestive ethical resonance, and the argument gains force in Coetzee's linking of Benveniste's linguistic observations to the central ethical preoccupations of Martin Buber. In *I and Thou* Buber writes in profoundly moving ways about what he calls the 'I–You word pair'. 'When one says You', writes Buber (and Coetzee cites this sentence), 'the I of the word pair I–You is said, too' (Buber, *I and Thou* 54). Buber goes on to elaborate: 'I require a You to become; becoming I, I say You' (Buber, *I and Thou* 62). Yet, 'Whoever says You does not have something; he has nothing. *But he stands in relation*' (Buber, *I and Thou* 55, my emphasis). Buber's analysis does not have a linguistic base, just as Benveniste's project is not informed by ethical considerations. Nevertheless, a sentence such as the last one I have quoted from Buber here seems to echo Benveniste, but with a distinctively ethical inflection. Here is Benveniste:

Language is possible only because each speaker sets himself up as a *subject* by referring to himself as *I* in his discourse. Because of this, *I* posits another person, the one who, being, as he is, completely exterior to 'me,' becomes my echo to whom I say *you* and who says *you* to me. This polarity of persons is the fundamental condition in language, of which the process of communication, in which we share, is only a mere pragmatic consequence [...] neither of the terms can be conceived of without the other; they are complementary [...]

And so the old antimonies of 'I' and 'the other,' of the individual and society, fall. (Benveniste, *Problems in General Linguistics* 225)

In his essay on Achterberg, Coetzee's productive juxtaposition of Benveniste and Buber leads to what I take to be a crucial realization in any reading of Coetzee: if writing can be described in the starkest way as a matter of linguistic choice – the first person or the third? the present or the past tense? the active or the passive voice? – then those choices affect not only the style of the artwork as a whole (we have learnt this from Coetzee's thesis on Beckett),[6] but have implications for the ethical impact of the work. More specifically, linguistic choices on the part of the writer set up different conditions of possibility for the ways of relating I to you, both within the worlds of the fictional narratives themselves, and in terms of the 'I–you' relation between writer and reader. For example, what relation of power, or what conditions for a site of response are set up by the terms of address? What are the implications of speaking in one of the interlocutor's languages, at the expense of the other one? What are the implications for subjective agency and responsibility with regard to 'you' when the 'I' of the utterance is cast in the third person, rather than the first? A closer attentiveness to the linguistic constraints governing the relation will surely give a sharper sense of what is at stake in ethical terms, and provide a material grounding for the discussion too. What this means for critical responses to the work is that any exploration of language-related matters on Coetzee's part in his fiction is bound to have ethical implications (far be it the case that self-conscious reflection on language in Coetzee can be justly characterized in a pejorative way as insular postmodern game-playing). Conversely, a discussion of ethical themes in Coetzee's fiction that pays little heed to matters of linguistic concern is likely to have its shortcomings.[7]

But let us return to Martin Buber's ethical philosophy. Buber speaks of the 'I–You' relation as an 'encounter', as a 'relational event' that 'take[s] place and scatter[s]' (Buber, *I and Thou* 80). The difficult task is to maintain an open responsiveness that enables us to say 'You', without objectifying 'You' to an 'It':

> I do not find the human being to whom I say You in any Sometime and Somewhere. I can place him there and have to do this again and again, but immediately he becomes a He or a She, an It, and no longer remains my You. (Buber, *I and Thou* 59)

Further on, Buber elaborates: 'Only as things cease to be our You and become our It do they become subject to coordination. The You knows no system of coordinates' (Buber, *I and Thou* 81). Scenes of encounter as intricate 'relational event' are a recurrent feature in Coetzee's fiction. In conversation, Stephen Watson and Coetzee speak about *Dusklands* and *In the Heart of the Country* in explicitly Buberian terms. In response to Watson's observations about the psychology of power in the two novels, Coetzee elaborates:

> [Coetzee]: I think that the situation in both books is the situation you describe – of living among people without reciprocity, so that there's only an 'I' and the 'You' is not on the same basis, the 'You' is a debased 'You'.
> [Watson]: An 'It' in effect?
> [Coetzee]: Correct. And both of them feel, perhaps in different ways, that it's impossible to live that way, but lack the stature to transform that 'It' into a 'You', to, so to speak, create a society in which reciprocity exists; and therefore condemn themselves to desperate gestures towards establishing intimacy.[8]
> (Coetzee and Watson, 'Speaking: J.M. Coetzee' 23)

The conversation between Coetzee and Watson here takes place at the level of 'I–you/it' encounters as themes *internal* to the fictional worlds of the novels – the 'I' and 'you' of Magda and her servants, the violence of Jacobus Coetzee's exercising of colonial power. But I am interested in pursuing a line of discussion that analyses an 'I–you' relation instantiated by the material existence of the novel itself, before any analysis of its narrative themes. That is to say, I am interested in the fact of the novel as address between writer and reader, between the author of *Dusklands* and the person holding the book. It is at this level of discussion that I think that Levinas might come into his own in Coetzee scholarship – as we shall see in section VI. But on what basis does one effect the transition from one kind of discussion to the other? And how, precisely, does this relate to a key argument in this chapter, namely, that Coetzee's reflections on literary address make a positive contribution to debates in contemporary aesthetics? As a way of answering these questions I return to the Achterberg essay in the next section, taking heed of Coetzee's intricate and multivalent understanding of what is at stake in his own translation of Achterberg's sonnet sequence.

IV

In his essay on Achterberg's 'Ballade van de gasfitter', Coetzee sets out with a summary translation of the poems, and singles out as a problem for scholars the issue of finding stable referents for the personae, registered in the 'I' and the 'You' ('ik' and 'gij'/'ge'/'u') of the sonnet sequence. Coetzee's decision to capitalize the 'You' *as addressed by the gasfitter* in his English version, makes for a rather different poem to that of the Dutch original. In the English translation, the I–You relation is foregrounded, and (as the title of Coetzee's essay suggests) – it is foregrounded as a 'mystery'. Compare, for example, the following lines from the first sonnet of Achterberg's sequence,

> Daar wonen ene Jansen en de zijnen
> alsof ge mij in deze naam ontwijkt.
> (Achterberg in Coetzee, ed.,
> *Landscape with Rowers* 2)

and

> One Jansen lives there with his family –
> as if You could escape under that name.
> (Coetzee's translation,
> *Landscape with Rowers* 3)

The second-person pronoun in Achterberg's lines poses problems for the English translator. Although 'ge' in Dutch possibly has a closer cognate in the English 'thou', it has a more contemporary and colloquial resonance than 'thou' – or the Dutch 'gij', used elsewhere in the poem. An everyday 'you' in Dutch is 'jij' or more colloquially, 'je' – the form used in the direct speech of the supervisor in sonnet five and the imagined words accompanying the derisory gesture of the maid ('daghit') in sonnet eight. Neither 'thou' nor 'you' quite captures 'ge' in the lines just quoted from the first sonnet. Coetzee's choice of a capital 'y' is a considered response to the difficulty, yet inevitably, the 'You' of the English version introduces a new dynamic. In Coetzee's translation, rhythmic – and I would add, semantic – stress falls on the capitalized 'You' in the line 'as if You could escape under that name'; the metre of the Dutch 'alsof ge mij in deze naam ontwijkt' slides over 'ge', and does not explicitly draw attention to the I–you relation as a field of enquiry, as it does in the English version.[9]

Coetzee, of course, is deeply sensitive to the effects of translation, and to the authority of the translator, as he insistently reminds us throughout his work.[10] In this essay he goes so far as to raise the question whether his discussion is actually a study of the Dutch poem, or of his own English translation. But the 'question is a misleading one', Coetzee goes on to say, 'for my translation itself is part of the work of criticism' (*Doubling the Point* 88). Further, it is worth taking note that it is in *this* essay that Coetzee makes the comment, '[i]n a clear sense, all reading is translation, just as all translation is criticism' (*Doubling the Point* 90), and registers, 'I ask (and answer) questions that I have created for myself by my translation, that is, questions that come out of the structure of *my* created discourse, not out of Achterberg's' (*Doubling the Point* 71).

The term 'translation' operates on more than one level: it has to do not only with the translation of the poem from Dutch into English, but a translation that registers two different levels of 'I' and 'You': *within* the world of the poem, 'I' and 'You' are the personae in the sonnet sequence – the addressor and addressee, the first and second persons. But in the critic's discourse *about* the poem (that is to say, in the critic's interpretation, or translation of the poem), the 'I' and the 'You' of the poem become the topic of a conversation between the writer of the critical essay (an implied 'I'), and 'you' the reader of the essay on Achterberg's poem. In this axis of utterance the 'I' and the 'you' *within* the poem become the *object* of discussion, the 'it' – occupying the grammatical position of the third person – in the address from critic to reader. In paying attention to these different

tiers of address from I to you, the interest of Coetzee's Achterberg
essay moves beyond the identities and the physically written signifiers of 'I' and 'You' designating personae within the text of the
poem, to include a consideration of the implied 'I' and 'you' – of
writer and reader – instantiated by the very logic of literary address
itself. Thus Coetzee's essay explores the linguistico-philosophical
logic of the 'field of tension' between I and you (Coetzee, *Inner
Workings* 122), of an 'axis of utterance pass[ing] from *I*, the author,
through a phantom *you* who are my reader' (*Doubling the Point* 70).
The question that Coetzee explicitly sets himself, at least in part
through his translation of Achterberg's sonnet sequence in the double sense I have just mentioned, is 'not *what I* and *You* signify but *how*
they signify in the field of language and in the field of the poem'
(*Doubling the Point* 70).

To bring this back to Benveniste, and to pitch the discussion at the
level of I and you as writer and reader: recall that for Benveniste the
pronouns 'I' and 'you' 'do not refer to "reality" or to "objective" positions in space or time but to the utterance, unique each time, that
contains them'. They are ' "empty" signs that are nonreferential with
respect to "reality" '. Furthermore, '[t]hese signs are always available
and become "full" as soon as a speaker introduces them into each
instance of his discourse' (Benveniste, *Problems in General Linguistics*
219). If 'I' and 'you' are embodied in relation to a discourse, rather
than to an objective, static reality, then a literary text can be understood to be the site that *instantiates* an I–you relation, in each event
of its being read. Primordially, a literary text is for reading; it antici-
pates you, the reader, even while it may not be addressed to anyone
in particular.[11] Nevertheless, the text's calling forth of an always-
implied addressee, who in turn affirms the implied writing 'I', is
precarious and risky, never guaranteed in advance. And further, the
potential embodiment of you and I in relation to the discourse brings
about a peculiar understanding of the responsive engagements that
the writing initiates.

To write is to initiate the possibility of the words' being read. It is
to *invent* the possibility of a reader, of readers, of a shifting and incrementally more intricate network of paths from I to you, in a diachronous movement through time and space. The potential embodiment
of 'you' is necessitated by the logic of the utterance, but in their
grammatical capacity as shifters (in Roman Jakobson's sense), the

positions occupied by 'I' and 'you' are not tied down to geographic coordinates, to stable referents, to known and static identities. The pattern of lines tracing out the paths from I to you is kinetic, regenerated in each new instance of a text's-being-read through time, and unpredictable at the time of writing. Since the event of writing 'is each time singular, on the measure of the other's alterity', says Derrida, 'one must each time *invent*, not without a concept but each time exceeding the concept, without assurance or certainty' ('A "Madness" Must Watch Over Thinking' 360). Derrida speaks about the lines his writing throws out to potential readers as mapping out 'the most obscure, the most disconcerting, disrupted topology, the disruption of destination: of that which I thought it convenient to nickname *destinerrance* or *clandestination*' (Derrida, 'A "Madness" Must Watch Over Thinking' 350). Further, the readiness to engage you, the unknown reader, in ways that will not have been determined in advance, constitutes the freedom, but also the risk, of the literary encounter.

Poems are 'encounters', says Celan,

> paths from a voice to a listening You, natural paths, outlines for existence perhaps, for projecting ourselves into the search for ourselves... A kind of homecoming. (Celan, *Collected Prose* 53)

In his essay on Celan, Levinas cites this passage,[12] and adds the comment, 'Buber's categories!' (Levinas, 'Paul Celan: From Being to the Other' 42). In that the 'you' effected by the writing is 'a *pure potentiality*, a readiness for the embodying word' (Coetzee, *Doubling the Point* 72, my emphasis), we are in a better position to appreciate Coetzee's difficult responses to seemingly straightforward questions in interviews about his readers. 'I am hesitant to accept that my books are addressed to readers', says Coetzee in answer to a question, posed by Tony Morphet in 1983, about the putative South African reader of *Life & Times of Michael K*,

> Or at least I would argue that the concept of the reader in literature is a vastly more problematic one than one might at first think. Anyhow, it is important to me to assert that *Michael K* is not 'addressed' to anyone. (Coetzee and Morphet, 'Two Interviews with J.M. Coetzee' 456)

UNIVERSITY OF WINCHESTER LIBRARY

In the same interview Coetzee speaks about pursuing the logic of the story, not for the sake of a putative reader, or even for himself, but 'for its own sake. That is what it means to me to engage with a subject' (Coetzee and Morphet, 'Two Interviews with J.M. Coetzee' 458). But what that logic is may not be evident until it is written:

> The *feel* of writing fiction is one of freedom, of irresponsibility, or better, of responsibility toward something that has not yet emerged, that lies somewhere at the end of the road. (Coetzee, *Doubling the Point* 246)

I am reminded of the closing pages of *Waiting for the Barbarians*, where the magistrate meditates on his own (failed?) attempt to write 'the annals of an Imperial outpost': He writes something other than he intended, and casts himself as 'a man who lost his way long ago but presses on along a road that may lead nowhere' (Coetzee, *Waiting for the Barbarians* 168, 170). The *end* of literary address, in both senses of this word (purpose and destination), is one of subtle complexity.

The 'you' invoked by the written word is a 'pure potentiality' in Coetzee's terms, not reducible in such a way as to *answer* referentially directed questions like '"who?" [which] amounts to a "what?", to "what about him?"' (Levinas, *Otherwise than Being* 27). The 'you' is 'empty', and the site of the literary artwork is a non-site, a utopia. The poem 'searches for this place', says Celan, the space of this 'conversation' – and in discussing poems in this way, we 'dwell on the question of their where-from and where-to, an "open" question "without resolution", a question which points towards open, empty, free spaces' (Celan, *Collected Prose* 50), 'close to utopia' (52); in Levinas' terms,

> The movement thus described goes from place to the non-place, from here to utopia. That there is, in Celan's essay on the poem, an attempt to think transcendence, is obvious. *Poetry – conversion into the infinite of pure mortality and the dead letter.* (Levinas, 'Paul Celan: From Being to the Other' 42)

If we take seriously Coetzee's participation in these conversations about literary address, then we are in a position to appreciate his assertion that 'the concept of the reader in literature is a vastly more problematic one than one might at first think'. To fix a reader through a national identity (*the* South African reader), and to assume that the artwork is written *to* and *for* that identity, is to ignore the capacity for the invention and freedom of the artwork's transcendence in the pure potentiality of 'You'. The artwork is indifferent to the reader or the viewer's response, and perhaps it is in this sense that we can say that art is not *for* a specified reader. 'Art [...] posits man's physical and spiritual existence, but in none of its works is it concerned with his response', writes Walter Benjamin, 'No poem is intended for the reader, no picture for the beholder, no symphony for the listener' (Benjamin, 'The Task of the Translator' 72).[13] This is not to say that artworks are not to be read, or seen, or heard. But this is not what they are *for*. This is not where the artwork stops. Art offers intimations of transcendence. We need to see, or hear, or read the work in order to get some sense of that, but the purpose of art, perhaps (as David Lurie of *Disgrace* puts it), is to sound a 'single authentic note of immortal longing' (Coetzee, *Disgrace* 214). And this is why it is important to retain some sense of the 'pure potentiality' of you, my reader.

The 'you' as addressee of the literary work as a whole gains another dimension when a persona *within* the world of the novel or the poem is explicitly addressed as 'you': the reader then becomes a third party, a 'he' or 'she' in the grammatical position of the third person, *overhearing* the address from 'I' to 'you' *within* the world of the literary work, but at the same time, feeling the effects of being called upon as addressee of that utterance (the ability to respond to being called 'you', as we have learnt from Benveniste, presupposes a presence to the site of the discourse). But quite apart from this, the reader is the second-person addressee called to attention by the literary work as a whole (irrespective of any use of the word 'you' within the text itself). The use of a persona-addressee thus has the unnerving effect of placing the reader simultaneously in the grammatical position of the second and the third persons, at once present and absent with respect to a double-directedness and mutually exclusive trajectory of address. A reading of Celan's poetry, with its staging of anguished appeals to a 'you' within the poems themselves, has a vertiginous effect on the reader: am *I* the one appealed to, or called to account? Am *I* the survivor, or the beloved thus addressed? How should I respond with justice, and to whom? I would say that we experience something similar to this in a reading of *Age of Iron*. On the one hand we *become* the recipient of Mrs Curren's letter[14] (the letter comprises the entire text of the novel); we become the 'you' that the letter instantiates. 'To whom this writing then?' asks the Mrs Curren of *Age of Iron*. 'The answer: to you but not to you; to me; to you in me', and 'These words, as you read them, if you read them, enter you and draw breath again. They are, if you like, my way of living on' (*Age of Iron* 6, 131). It is difficult to distance *oneself* from these reflexive acts of embodiment in the very real and present instant of reading the words on the page. But on the other hand, we overhear a dying woman's deeply personal cry to her daughter in America, 'A daughter. Flesh of my flesh. You' (*Age of Iron* 11). It is uncertain whether the daughter will ever receive the letter, and if she does, it will be after her mother's death. How to do justice to an appeal which we have *over*heard, witnessed, how to become 'I', and say 'You' (in Buber's sense) to Mrs Curren, when we are power-less to change the direction of the axis of utterance and response, of writer and reader, of speaker and addressee?

These are some of the extraordinary relations between you and I, regenerated in each reading of *Age of Iron*. Coetzee writes about Celan: 'Celan's poems begin to address a Thou who may be more or less distant, more or less known. In the space between the speaking I and the Thou they find a new field of tension' (Coetzee, *Inner Workings* 122), but certainly this insight could equally well apply to much of Coetzee's own writing. In this 'field of tension', let us now turn to the role of the 'I'.

In the introduction I referred to Coetzee's engagement of structuralism – an important aspect of which is Coetzee's interest in Barthes' notion of the death of the author. But where the absence of the author in structuralist terms runs the risk of leading to pro-grammatic analyses of putatively self-enclosed texts, Celan's notion of art as a *distance* from the 'I' leads to a poignant ethical under-standing of the practice of literature – from the perspectives of both the writer and the reader. In the previous chapter, 'Not I', I dis-cussed the strategies of displacement of the first person that we find throughout Coetzee's work; what is important to me here is to locate Coetzee's reflections about the first person within the con-text of the immediate discussion about the ethics and aesthetics of literary address. 'The man whose eyes and mind are occupied with art', says Celan,

> forgets about himself. Art makes for the distance from the I. Art requires that we travel a certain space in a certain direction, on a certain road. (Celan, *Collected Prose* 44)

If the literary text instantiates an I–you encounter, and if the 'you' is empty, a pure potentiality, then the site and the nature of that encounter is not one that is *controlled* by the author – the lyric 'I' of art is uprooted from its historical source, to meet 'you', wherever you are embodying that sign of address. The projection of a self into the lyric 'I' of the work amounts to a *giving over* of 'I' to the unspecified time and place of the other. 'A seeking, dedicating itself to the other in the form of the poem', writes Levinas, 'A chant rises in the giving, the one-for-the-other' (Levinas, 'Paul Celan: From Being to the Other' 46). And Celan again:

> perhaps poetry, like art, moves with the oblivious self into the uncanny and strange to free itself. Though where? in which place? how? as what? This would mean art is the distance poetry must cover, no less and no more. (Celan, *Collected Prose* 44–5)

Though the writings of Levinas often come across as operating at a level of philosophical abstraction, a reading of Levinas' essay on Celan *in conversation* with the poet's creative and critical work in literary aesthetics enables us to understand better how Levinas' ideas might be relevant to a discussion of literature. Through the conversation which includes Celan, we are able to retrace a path back to Buber's ethical philosophy and to Benveniste's contributions in the linguistic sciences, especially on the topic of pronouns. The passages cited above (about the ethical relation art instantiates between you and I) seem less esoteric if we think of them as following through the ethical implications of linguistic insights, such as Benveniste's discussions about subjectivity in language. To be as specific as possible here – Levinas' phrase, 'one-for-the other' (which I have just cited) can be understood as articulating his radical ethical philosophy of involuntary self-sacrificing and self-substituting responsibility for the Other. Yet if this comes across as philosophical abstraction, I am nevertheless reminded of Benveniste's linguistically more technical account, '*I* posits another person, the one who, being, as he is, completely exterior to "me," becomes my echo to whom I say *you* and who says *you* to me' (Benveniste, *Problems in General Linguistics* 225).

As we have seen, Benveniste and Buber are important points of reference in Coetzee's own critical writing – all of which goes to suggests that recourse to Levinas (intimately acquainted with the work of Buber and Celan) in discussions of Coetzee's fiction may not be that fanciful after all. At the same time, when we read about Buber's I–thou relation, or about Celan's writing about the 'oblivious self', or about an encounter with the 'altogether other' of the artistic work, bearing in mind that Coetzee engages closely with *these* texts, then it seems worth the trouble to follow the trail from Benveniste, through to Buber and Celan, so clearly staked out in Coetzee's own explorations in linguistics, ethics and literary aesthetics, rather than applying Levinasian ethics, as if from outside of Coetzee's own critical engagements, in a reading of his fiction.

To return to Celan: any *response* to literature demands a 'becoming-I' on the part of the reader – and in that the artwork comes from a different time and place, the reader, too, is uprooted in that encounter:

> the poem speaks. It is mindful of its dates, but it speaks. True, it speaks only on its own, its very own behalf.
>
>   But I think [...] that the poem has always hoped, for this very reason, to speak also on behalf of the *strange* – no, I can no longer use this word here – *on behalf of the other*, who knows, perhaps of an *altogether other*. (Celan, *Collected Prose* 48)

V

An important question that arises in any reading of Celan's poetry has to do, at the most fundamental level, with the construction of meaning itself – which poses serious challenges to the critic or the translator. Ruptured syntax, neologistic words and metaphors...at the most basic level it is hard to make sense of the inner world of the poem, which seems to rely on intimately private allusions to historical events that are not directly mentioned. Celan's poetry has been labelled 'hermetic' – a label which he himself 'vehemently rejected' (see *Inner Workings* 116). But what is important here is that we have to ask: can we assume that the meaning of these poems operates *in terms of* a subsumptive message conveyed in language – or are there other ways of approaching Celan's work? In a letter which he wrote to Hans Bender in 1960, Celan makes the claim that 'craft [...] is the condition of all poetry' (Celan, *Collected Prose* 25). He goes on to elaborate:

> Craft means handiwork, a matter of hands. And these hands must belong to *one* person, i.e. a unique, mortal soul searching for its way with its voice and its dumbness. Only truthful hands write true poems. I cannot see any basic difference between a hand-shake and a poem. (Celan, *Collected Prose* 26)

'Poems are also gifts', Celan says; 'gifts to the attentive' (Celan, *Collected Prose* 26). These comments by Celan seem to demand a different kind of responsiveness to the literary work, one which recognizes the poem as an address to you, the reader, calling for – and coming into existence thanks to – your attention, prior to its conveying of a message open to comprehension and interpretation. The poem constitutes an *appeal* to you, before any subsumptive content can be appropriated as a familiar 'theme'. The poem is the *fact* of speaking to the other, Levinas writes in direct response to Celan's letter, a 'fact of speaking to the other [that] precedes all thematization' (Levinas, 'Paul Celan: From Being to the Other' 44). Further, poems are 'important by their interpellation rather than by their message; important by their attention!' (Levinas, 'Paul Celan: From Being to the Other' 43). The logic of address instantiates a site of response. In recognizing myself as the 'you' of this address, I may refuse to respond – but that will never be a simple non-response; it will be a refusal to respond.[15] In responding as addressee, the reader is responsible (following Buber now) for calling into being the 'I' of the I–You word pair. Ethical considerations (specifically about the relation of self to other) are thus brought into play, even before the message within the poem is read and understood.

Just how far can one go with this line of argument? At the very least, these are the questions that a reading of Celan's poetry presses us to ask: 'what is a poem whose "coding" is such that it foils in advance all attempts to decipher it?' asks Philippe Lacoue-Labarthe

(Lacoue-Labarthe, *Poetry as Experience* 14). And prompted by Hans-Georg Gadamer's defence of Celan against charges of obscurity, Coetzee poses these related questions: 'Does poetry offer a kind of knowledge different from that offered by history, and demand a different kind of receptivity? Is it possible to respond to poetry like Celan's, even to translate it, without fully understanding it?' (*Inner Workings* 117). For Levinas, the answer to Coetzee seems to be yes. In his piece on Celan (and elsewhere in later essays and interviews), Levinas insists on the performative, rather than the constative aspect of the literary work;[16] he casts the literary work (and Celan's poetry in particular) as an instance of what he would term the 'Saying', rather than the 'Said'. Language in general, for Levinas, should be considered in this dual aspect, where the saying takes precedence:

> Should language be thought uniquely as the communication of an idea or as information, and not also – *and perhaps above all* – as the fact of encountering the other as other, that is to say, already as response to him? (Levinas and Poirié, 'Interview with François Poirié' 47, my emphasis)

Further, 'Language is above all the fact of being addressed... which means the saying much more than the said' (Levinas et al., 'The Paradox of Morality' 170). Of course, this distinction between the saying and the said (which is most fully developed in *Otherwise than Being*) is closely tied to Levinas' understanding of ethics as a precognitive responsiveness to the other: 'Language as *saying* is an ethical openness to the other, as that which is *said* – reduced to a fixed or synchronized presence – it is an ontological closure to the other' (Levinas and Kearney, 'Dialogue with Emmanuel Levinas' 29).[17]

It is within this context that I think it is important to take heed of Celan's own response to one kind of critical approach to his work. 'Against pressure to recuperate him as a poet who had turned the Holocaust into something higher, namely poetry', writes Coetzee in *Inner Workings*,

> against the critical orthodoxy of the 1950s and early 1960s, with its view of the ideal poem as a self-enclosed aesthetic object, Celan insists that he practises an art of the real, an art that 'does not transfigure or render "poetical"; it names, it posits, it tries to

measure the area of the given and the possible.' (Coetzee, *Inner Workings* 120, citing Celan's reply to a questionnaire from the Flinker Bookstore in 1958. Celan, *Collected Prose* 16)

Coetzee stresses the material existence of the poetry as being significant in itself – even in the absence of our being able to read and understand it:

> Even if Celan's poems were totally incomprehensible [...] they would nevertheless stand in our way like a tomb, a tomb built by a 'Poet, Survivor, Jew' (the subtitle of Felstiner's study), insisting by its looming presence that we remember, even though the words inscribed on it may seem to belong to an undecipherable tongue. (*Inner Workings* 118, with reference to Felstiner, *Paul Celan: Poet, Survivor, Jew* 254)[18]

Certainly, throughout Coetzee's writing (both fiction and non-fiction) there is an appreciation of language as material substance – an appreciation that it is something that is seen and heard, as much as it is understood. Further, something recognized, or willed-to-be-recognized *as signifying, as wanting-to-say*, makes an ethical appeal, even in the absence of the reader's or the listener's comprehending it. Again this is a recurrent motif in Coetzee's fiction. I am thinking about the stone-writing at the end of *In the Heart of the Country*, of Friday's dancing and tuneless flute music in *Foe*, of the poplar slips that the Magistrate finds (in *Waiting for the Barbarians*), of JC's aged and poignantly illegible handwriting in *Diary of a Bad Year*. The sense of a signifying act *saying* through the fact of its perceptible materiality, rather than through an abstract semantics, is reiterated in Coetzee's thoughts on translation in the essay, 'Homage'. 'There is something physical in confronting the poem in the original', he writes, with reference to the Penguin collection of Rilke's poems,[19]

> something about the words themselves, in their own brute presence, in their own order, however obscurely you understand them, however obscurely you understand how they are combined, that cannot be provided by translation of any kind. The original words, the poet's words, are literally irreplaceable. (Coetzee, 'Homage' 5)

Nevertheless, I would not say that Coetzee goes as far as Levinas; Levinas places such ethical value on the performative aspect of language that any constative representation is seen to carry a negative ethical charge. This is made clear in his essay on aesthetics, 'Reality and its Shadow'. Characters represented in art[20] lead 'a lifeless life' (Levinas, 'Reality and its Shadow' 138); 'characters of a novel are beings that are shut up, prisoners', not because the artist 'represents being crushed by fate'; rather, 'beings enter their fate *because they are represented*' ('Reality and its Shadow' 139, my emphasis). This thought is carried through in Levinas' ethical philosophy: 'Thematization and conceptualization, which moreover are inseparable, are not peace with the other but suppression or possession of the other. For possession affirms the other, but within a negation of its independence'. In the next paragraph Levinas reiterates, 'Possession is preeminently the form in which the other becomes the same, by becoming mine' (Levinas, *Totality and Infinity* 46). To thematize, then, according to Levinas, carries a strongly negative charge in ethical terms. It is to reduce alterity to one's own conceptual scheme, to deny the otherness, the freedom of the other.

VI

Levinas' *Totality and Infinity* and *Otherwise than Being or Beyond Essence* together constitute a radical contribution to the field of ethics, where ethics is understood as a precognitive, self-sacrificing – even self-substituting – relation of responsibility towards the other. It is in his understanding of ethics that we see most clearly the influence of Levinas' thought in one strand of Coetzee criticism, but, given Levinas' response to art in 'Reality and its Shadow', I would be reticent to label this strand of Coetzee scholarship, especially the work of Derek Attridge, as a Levinasian *approach*. Attridge says as much in *The Singularity of Literature*: 'My appropriation of Levinas' thought is extremely selective', he writes, and 'his own discussions of literature and art do not go in the same direction as mine' (Attridge, *The Singularity of Literature* 141). For Attridge (and other prominent Coetzee scholars like Mike Marais), it is Levinas' ethical philosophy, rather than his work in aesthetics, that has provided the explicit impetus for discussions of Coetzee's fiction.

At the most obvious level, Levinas' preoccupation with the ethical relation to alterity is read as a recurrent theme in Coetzee's fiction. That is to say, there are numerous scenes in Coetzee's novels which have been read as staging a Levinasian relation to alterity – an encounter in which I cede the otherness of the other, without reducing the other to *my* conceptual frame of reference (in Levinas' terms, the 'same'). In the depth of my responsiveness (Levinas often uses the term 'passivity') to the challenge that the other poses to my conceptual range, I am *called into question* at such radical level that my subjective autonomy is at stake.[21] Characters such as Michael K, Friday in *Foe*, the unnamed barbarian girl in *Waiting for the Barbarians* and even Lucy in *Disgrace*, have been read as figures of alterity in that they make an ethical injunction to those who find themselves bound to respond to them. The medical officer, Susan Barton, the magistrate and David Lurie thus find themselves in an impossible ethical bind of having to respond with justice to that which eludes their cultural – and even their cognitive – grasp.[22] An interesting tension emerges here: to read these scenes as a themed staging of Levinas' *ethical* philosophy is to be up against the wall of what seems to be Levinas' *aesthetics*. In this context, it is hardly surprising that Levinas' two essays, 'Reality and its Shadow' and 'Paul Celan: From Being to the Other' (which deal directly with a question of literary aesthetics) have not featured in Attridge's responses to Coetzee.[23] While 'Reality and its Shadow' has little bearing on my discussion here,[24] the essay on Paul Celan (as I hope to have demonstrated in the previous section) seems to me to resonate with Coetzee's own interest in the question of literary address in an important way. In *The Singularity of Literature*, Attridge mentions Levinas' essay on Celan, but in a way that implies that it does not have much to offer towards a discussion of writers other than Celan, and hence towards the development of a literary aesthetic. Nevertheless, it seems to me that what Attridge *does* identify as his area of interest (with reference to work done by Robert Bernasconi and Simon Critchley) resonates strongly with the argument in Paul Celan's 'The Meridian' (which Celan first presented as a speech when he received the Georg Büchner Prize in Darmstadt in 1960), which is then taken up in Levinas' essay on Celan. Attridge expresses his predilection for 'a Levinasian hermeneutics which 'would perhaps be defined by its readiness for re-reading because it would have no interest in distilling the content of a text into a "said" '

(Attridge, *The Singularity of Literature* 141, citing Bernasconi and Critchley's introduction to *Re-reading Levinas* xi). Certainly, this is borne out in much of Attridge's elaboration of what he terms 'the singularity of literature': 'Reading a work of literature entails opening oneself to the unpredictable, the future, the other', says Attridge, 'and thereby accepting the responsibility laid upon one by the work's singularity and difference' (Attridge, *J.M. Coetzee and the Ethics of Reading* 111).

With yet another twist: I would say that a discussion of a theme in a novel, of a fictionalized 'staging' of ideas – even if those ideas have to do with the ethical responsiveness to alterity, or the self-reflexive exploration of the ethics of representation – surely operates at the level of a discussion of the novel's content, its 'said'. This is why I think that even the most nuanced and insightful analysis of themes and motifs in a novel could only superficially be called a 'Levinasian approach'. And this is the trouble: what *would* a literary aesthetics be (shall we say, a Levinasian *approach*) that did not take into account the themes, motifs, images – loosely, the content of the work? This brings us back full circle to the questions that Coetzee asks with such urgency in his essay on Celan (I repeat): 'Does poetry offer a kind of knowledge different from that offered by history, and demand a different kind of receptivity? Is it possible to respond to poetry like Celan's, even to translate it, without fully understanding it?' (*Inner Workings* 117). What Attridge develops in *The Singularity of Literature* and *J.M. Coetzee and the Ethics of Reading* is an argument for a related kind of receptivity, one which stresses the performativity of the work: 'The literary work is an *event* [...] for both its creator and its reader, and it is the reader [...] who brings the work into being, differently each time, in a singular performance of the work not so much as written as a writing' (Attridge, *J.M. Coetzee and the Ethics of Reading* 9). Although Attridge does not make a clear-cut distinction between the event of reading, and the staging of this event as a theme in the novel,[25] he makes a case for the literary texts as performances: they come into existence in the event of each singular reading. At this level of performative event, the literary text has the potential to interrupt familiar comfort zones, demanding that the reader respond to something other than the already known. But certainly in Attridge's own close readings of passages in Coetzee's novels,[26] the sense that the reader is deeply affected by the literary work on different levels (intellectual, affective, physical, as Attridge puts it) comes about *thanks to* an appreciation of this particular passage read within the context of thematic patterns discerned in the novel as an artistic whole, an appreciation of the effects of images, of Coetzee's choice of words, of his innovative use of syntactic structures and literary tropes... This kind of reading experience, in all its subtlety, seems to me to demand a sophisticated distillation of literary content. Certainly, I would be hard-pressed to concede, as Levinas seems to imply, that acts of conceptualization like these (on the part of both writer and reader), that give rise to the kind of literary experience Attridge talks about, are negative in *ethical* terms.

Coetzee's brief essay, 'Thematizing', which provides an account of the process of writing, makes a valuable contribution to these debates:

> As I reflect on the process of writing and ask myself how themes enter that process, it seems to me that a certain back-and-forth motion takes place. First you give yourself to (or throw yourself into) the writing, and go where it takes you. Then you step back and ask yourself where you are, whether you really want to be there. This interrogation entails conceptualizing, and specifically thematizing, what you have written (or what has been written out of you). (Coetzee, 'Thematizing' 289)

Thematizing, in Coetzee's account, is an ineluctable *part* of the practice of writing, which includes intervals of reading. Importantly Coetzee goes on to say:

> it is not the theme that counts, but thematizing. What themes emerge in the process are heuristic, provisional, and in that sense insignificant. The reasoning imagination thinks in themes because those are the only means it has; but the means are not the end. (Coetzee, 'Thematizing' 289)

Further, each reader may discover themes that the 'reasoning imagination' did not conceptualize at the time of writing – to the extent that the literary text 'works its way past the defenses of the hand writing it' (Coetzee, 'Thematizing' 289). The work of literature is not reducible to the discovery of its themes in each reading, including the rereading on the part of the writer at a later date, and perhaps this is indeed the different kind of receptivity and knowledge that literature, rather than history, demands. Thematizing may be an indispensable part of the process of writing and reading, but the production and bringing to light of themes is not the only thing that writing and reading are for, or where they end.

VII

'I think that the first language is the *response*', says Levinas in an interview (Levinas et al., 'The Paradox of Morality' 174, my emphasis); the context of this assertion is that of Levinas' understanding of the ethical relation – that is, the response to the authoritative demand made by the other, the ineluctable relation to alterity. In the same interview Levinas reminds his interlocutors about the close relation between the words, 'response' and 'responsibility' – *réponse* and *responsabilité* (Levinas et al., 'The Paradox of Morality' 169) – but as elsewhere in Levinas, the *impetus* of the discussion has to do with ethics, rather than linguistics. Now Coetzee is primarily a writer, rather than a philosopher in ethics, and for him the question arises this way round: what constraints and possibilities are brought to bear *by linguistic exigencies* on ethical relations – both within the fictional worlds of the novels themselves, and with reference to the relation between writers and readers? Further, how might a close analysis of those linguistic constraints assist us in our understanding of this ethical relation?

It is perhaps Mikhail Bakhtin who first comes to mind in considering what one might think of as a sociolinguistic philosophy of the response – and of course, Coetzee writes explicitly about Bakhtin in his own critical essays, most notably in the chapter on Breyten Breytenbach in *Giving Offense*, and in the essay on Dostoevsky in *Stranger Shores*.[27] '[A]ny speaker is himself a respondent to a greater or lesser degree', writes Bakhtin. 'He is not, after all the first speaker, the one who disturbs the eternal silence of the universe' (Bakhtin, 'The Problem of Speech Genres' 69). Each speech utterance, says Bakhtin, 'must be regarded primarily as a *response* to preceding utterances of the given sphere' ('The Problem of Speech Genres' 91). Thus instead of taking the grammatical sentence to be his unit of study, Bakhtin develops a theory of the utterance – which he defines in terms of the possibility it holds of eliciting a response; any utterance, then, is a response to previous utterances, and in turn, is inflected by its anticipation of future responses to it. The role of the listener, or reader – Bakhtin also uses the term, *other* – is thus an active one with respect to what is said.

Like Coetzee himself, Bakhtin provides the means for building a conceptual bridge between linguistic and ethical preoccupations in the working out of a typology of address and response. Differently put, Bakhtin goes some way towards refining our linguistico-ethical understanding of an I–you relation. The 'you' of the address, for Bakhtin, is an 'other person – "a stranger, a man you'll never know" – [who] fulfils his functions in dialogue outside the plot and outside his specificity in any plot, as a pure "man in man," a representative of "all others" for the "I"' (Bakhtin, *Problems of Dostoevsky's Poetics* 264) – we recall Coetzee's conception of 'you' as 'pure potentiality'.

Further, even though an utterance may have reference to something in the world, even though it may be directed towards some object, in its responsiveness to, and anticipation of *other utterances*, it is also always directed towards another person's speech, another discourse. The utterance never occurs in autonomous isolation from the discourse of the other; it is never free of other utterances, to the extent that '[o]ur practical everyday speech is full of other people's words' (Bakhtin, *Problems of Dostoevsky's Poetics* 195). It is in this context, with special reference to Dostoevsky, that Bakhtin speaks about the 'element of *address*' as being 'essential to every discourse'; every word is addressed to another word: 'there is only the word as address, the word dialogically contacting another word' (*Problems of Dostoevsky's Poetics* 237). And of course, this notion of utterance both as response to a previous utterance, and as anticipating a response to itself in turn, applies equally to literary utterances:

> Every literary discourse more or less sharply senses its own listener, reader, critic, and reflects in itself their anticipated objections, evaluations, points of view. In addition, literary discourse senses alongside itself another literary discourse, another style. (Bakhtin, *Problems of Dostoevsky's Poetics* 196)

Coetzee takes this further still, and what may have started out as a discussion about some aspect of language in Bakhtin, now takes on a deeply charged ethical resonance. '[I]n the process of responding to the writers one intuitively chooses to respond to', says Coetzee, 'one makes oneself into the person whom in the most intractable but also perhaps the most deeply ethical sense one wants to be' (Coetzee, 'Homage' 7). It is within this context that it is important to me to be attentive to Coetzee's own responses to, and intimate intellectual and creative engagements with other writers: in paying attention to the responsiveness at the core of Coetzee's life-in-writing, we are in a better position to appreciate the positive contribution he makes to contemporary literary-critical debates. In this chapter I have focused on one intervention in these debates, tracking Coetzee's engagement of the linguistic sciences, and continental ethics and aesthetics in his own reflections on literary address.

In sensing its own listener, each utterance carries the 'deep traces'[28] scored by the potential responsiveness of others – even before a speaking position is taken up by these others in an ordinary sense. The response, and the exact position of the listener may not be predictable (we have seen the implications of this via Buber and Celan), but a serious author, *attentive* to the mark of the other, taking on its impress, creates the sense of an internal dialogue *within* the writing. The assumption of an autonomous and omniscient authorial voice is thus radically open to question.

What this means, then, is that 'I' am no longer simply identified as sole speaker of a discrete and hermetically sealed-off discourse; 'you', my reader, are no longer the silent and passive auditor beyond the margins of this page. Instead, 'I' and 'you' activate each word on the page *dialogically*: to a certain extent I cede authorship to you. I am led to raise questions about the authority of the words I have just written, and if I, too, am the reader of these words, what then of my assumptions about a supposedly unitary writing self?[29] In the introduction, I cited Coetzee referring to a way of life that provides the means of interrogating our existence as one that is ethically responsible (Coetzee and Attwell, 'An Exclusive Interview with J.M. Coetzee' 3). If writing is part of Coetzee's way of life, and the act of writing necessarily instantiates you and I, then an exploration of what Coetzee terms 'the mystery of I and you' is an exploration, at a fundamental level, of an ethical relation.

3
Voice

I

'Homer deserves praise for many reasons', writes Aristotle in the *Poetics*,

> but above all because he alone among poets is not ignorant of what he should do in his own person. The poet in person should say as little as possible; that is not what makes him an imitator [...] after a brief preamble Homer introduces a man or woman or some other character – and none of them are characterless: they have character. (Aristotle, *Poetics* §60a)

The *Poetics* goes on to discuss the relative merits of the genres of tragedy and epic poetry. The dramatic form is superior, in Aristotle's view, since direct speech provides occasion for a more effective form of poetic imitation than third-person narrative does. Besides, drama has a 'vividness' – it is a source of 'intense pleasure'. 'Also, the end of imitation is attained in shorter length; what is more concentrated is more pleasant than what is watered down by being extended in time' (Aristotle, *Poetics* §62b).

In his praise for Homer, Aristotle is in accord with his teacher, Plato, who also thought Homer pre-eminent among the poets. But the passages from Aristotle that I have just quoted here could well be read as a subtle riposte to the conclusions reached in Book III of Plato's *Republic*, in which Socrates and his interlocutors discuss the different effects and implications of first-person direct speech, and

75

third-person narrative prose. Taking a line that Aristotle would later oppose, the Socrates of Plato's *Republic* argues that the poet ought to speak 'in his own person' as far as possible, (Plato, *The Republic* §394c) and in an admittedly pedestrian demonstration, he recasts Chryses' appeal to Agamemnon for the release of his daughter, and his invocation of the wrath of Apollo to descend upon the Achaeans, in third-person reported speech. Here is Chryses' prayer to Apollo in Homer's *Iliad*:

> Heare, thou god that bear'st the silver bow,
> That Chrysa guard'st, rulest Tenedos with strong hand, and the round
> Of Cilla most divine dost walke! O Smintheus, if crownd
> With thankfull offerings thy rich Phane I ever saw, or fir'd
> Fat thighs of oxen and of goates to thee, this grace desir'd
> Vouchsafe to me: paines for my teares let these rude Greekes repay,
> Forc'd with thy arrowes. (Homer, *The Iliad* Book I, lines 36–42)[1]

And here is Socrates' third-person rendition in what he calls 'simple narrative without representation':

> he prayed earnestly to Apollo, calling on him by all his titles and reminding him of the services he had rendered him in building temples and offering sacrifices; and he begged Apollo in his prayer that, in return, he would avenge his tears on the Achaeans with his arrows. (Plato, *The Republic* §394a–b)

'I understand', replies a less than enthusiastic Adeimantus to Socrates in Plato's dialogue. The trouble about first-person 'representation', for Socrates, it seems, is the *affective power* of the first person in relation to the audience – which would not be problematic if only good characters spoke in the first person, but the impersonation of, and the dangers of identification with, characters who are 'disgraceful' or 'madmen' or 'women' or 'slaves', or those who 'indulge in comic abuse and use foul language, drunk or sober', would be too dangerous an exposure for the Guardians of the envisioned ideal state (*The Republic* §395d–e; §396a). The underlying premise of the argument is not that the artist is master of a highly cultivated literary medium (this is a view we could more readily attribute to Aristotle), but that the poet who writes passages in the first person has a morally deficient predilection to deceive. Homer 'does his best to make us think that it is not [himself] but an aged priest who is talking' (§393a), the poet assimilates himself to another person and 'conceal[s] his own personality' (§393c), to the extent that the question arises whether the use of 'representation' in the form of first-person, direct speech, should be entirely forbidden in the literature of the ideal state (§394d).

Now what is interesting about this in relation to Coetzee? A common critical consensus about the use of the third person is that it distances the character from the narrating consciousness, perhaps even from the historical author.[2] But in Plato the emphasis tips the other way: the use of the third person in narrative prose *affirms* the identity of an authorial voice (what Aristotle, in his *Rhetoric*, would call *'ethos'*) as separate from the characters on the page, even though – or perhaps precisely because – the author does not *say* 'I'. In this chapter I shall be exploring the question of voice with specific reference to the playing-off of the countervoices raised by the creation of fictional characters in relation to each other, in relation to the voice of the narrator, and ultimately, in relation to the implied author that they affirm. In Chapter 1, 'Not I', I focused on Coetzee's use of the third person, Chapter 2, 'You', the second. The consideration of voice in the present chapter is as close as we shall get to discussing the first person. In the first two chapters I considered the implications of Coetzee's experiments with variations on the structuralist notion of the death of the author. This chapter asks what it might mean to reinstate some notion of authorial consciousness, now that the dust of Barthes and Foucault has settled, as JC might put it (Coetzee, *Diary of a Bad Year* 149–50).

My discussion in this chapter pivots on two of Coetzee's texts: *Diary of a Bad Year* and the essay 'Erasmus: Madness and Rivalry', which is reprinted in *Giving Offense*.[3] Coetzee's discussion in the Erasmus essay constitutes a rigorous response and contribution to a contemporary (if long-standing) literary-philosophical conversation, one that includes Descartes, Erasmus, Foucault, Derrida, Lacan and Shoshana Felman. The specific context of this discussion (especially as Coetzee enters into it in the Erasmus essay in *Giving Offense*) revolves around Foucault's attack on a post-Cartesian privileging of reason over madness – and in Felman the particular focus is on the relation between madness and literature: to what extent is it helpful to assume that literary writing is the product of rational authorial control, and what possibilities for the space of literature are opened should writer and reader relinquish that assumption? In my reflections on the operations of voice and countervoice raised in the literary text – a consideration of Coetzee's engagement with Bakhtin is crucial here – I have Aristotle's *Rhetoric* at the back of my mind:

> 2. But since rhetoric is concerned with making a judgment (people judge what is said in deliberation, and judicial proceedings are also a judgment), it is necessary not only to look to the argument, that it may be demonstrative and persuasive but also [for the speaker] to construct a view of himself as a certain kind of person and to prepare the judge; 3. for it makes much difference in regard to persuasion [...] *that the speaker seem to be a certain kind of person and that his hearers suppose him to be disposed toward them in a certain way and in addition if they, too, happen to be disposed in a certain way.* (Aristotle, *On Rhetoric* Book II, §1.2–3, my emphasis)

What is suggestive in this passage is the importance accorded, not only to the content of what is said, but to the speaker's construction of the place from which he or she speaks. The disposition of the speaker or writer towards the listeners or readers, and their disposition towards the speaker or writer in turn, makes for a particular angle of reception in the words spoken or written. It is this dialogic angle that preoccupies me in this chapter. My concern is to explore the question of attributing a position to the writer with reference to his writing; in other words, I am interested in the positions and dispositions of writer and reader which are effected by what is written, and the discussion demands an attentiveness to features of the writing other than the opinions or themes we might read as being reasonably expressed.

In section II I discuss a question of the strategic deployment of the author's name in relation to his fictional texts (with particular reference to *Diary of a Bad Year*) – which opens onto a reflection of Coetzee's extended use of putatively non-fictional critical discourses *within* his novels. In section III I extend a discussion (initiated in the previous chapter, 'You') of the verb 'to write' as an instance of the middle voice – by referring to Coetzee's engagement with Roland Barthes' essay, 'To Write: An Intransitive Verb', and Mikhail Bakhtin's work on Dostoevsky. In section IV I discuss Coetzee's interest in the question of writing and the positioning of subjectivity as it arises in his essay on Erasmus. This essay, in turn, follows closely Shoshana Felman's *Writing and Madness*. In section V, I bring together arguments from the previous two sections in a discussion of the theatrical strategies of *Diary of a Bad Year*, to conclude, in section VI, with a consideration of JC's final entry in the second diary of the novel – that is to say, JC's essay on Dostoevsky's realization of voice in *The Brothers Karamazov* – which brings me back to Coetzee's own essay on Dostoevsky in *Stranger Shores*.

Coetzee's formally varied strategies of raising the countervoices within his fiction amount to a sustained and rigorous questioning of what is at stake in holding a position of authority as writer. This chapter can be read as a continuation of the discussions about theme and form, and the tensions between the constative and performative effects of the literary text, that I raised in the previous chapter. Even in the instant of posing a radical challenge to the question of authorial control, this chapter argues, the singularity of a voice is affirmed. Further, the realization of that voice can be played out in ways other than the rationally controlled development of themes and ideas.

II

First, I would like to mention briefly the question of Coetzee's use of fictional characters who express views not unrelated to his own. In Chapter 1, 'Not I', I discussed the use of the third person in *Boyhood* and *Youth*, Coetzee's most distinctively autobiographical works to date. Yet in other novels, fictional characters – not only but especially Elizabeth Costello and JC (in *Diary of a Bad Year*) – embody aspects of their historical author's life. To mention one or two of these convergences between author and fictional character: JC, like Coetzee, was born in South Africa, lives in Australia, and is the author of *Waiting for the Barbarians* and a series of essays on censorship; Elizabeth Costello, a novelist, shares preoccupations over a range of topics – perhaps most importantly the question of human relations to other animals – that are difficult to distinguish from her author's own. As a doctoral student at the University of Texas, Coetzee developed literary ambitions, 'ambitions to speak one day, somehow, in his own voice' (*Doubling the Point* 53), yet throughout his oeuvre, the author's voice is refracted through reference to the self in the third person, and through the use of any number of fictional characters – Mrs Curren, the Dostoevsky of *The Master of Petersburg*, David Lurie, Paul Rayment, among others – whose lives bear some resemblance to Coetzee's. These strategies of authorial refraction on the one hand seem to run counter to the aspiration to speak in one's '*own* voice', but on the other hand, they enable Coetzee to present the idea of voice itself as a series of countervoices, interpellating in ways which challenge assumptions about a supposed unitary and transcendent 'I'. This, in turn, is consistent with what Coetzee considers to be the mark of a serious writer, and it is consistent also with his view that fiction, when it provides the means for interrogating an existence, has an ethical impetus. The matter does not rest here, however, as we shall see in the final section of this chapter; it is not as if the proliferation of fictional countervoices results in an anarchic cacophany that absolutely precludes the possibility of distilling the sounds of an author speaking 'in his own voice'.

In section IV I shall be expanding on the implications of the Lacanian reference in the passage I am about to quote,[4] but before coming to the Lacanian part of the discussion, the passage requires some comment here. First, the passage:

> There is a true sense in which writing is dialogic: a matter of awakening the countervoices in oneself and embarking upon speech with them. It is some measure of a writer's seriousness whether he does evoke/invoke those countervoices in himself, that is, step down from the position of what Lacan calls 'the subject supposed to know.' (*Doubling the Point* 65)

Of particular interest in this passage is that the countervoices are *in oneself*: the 'embarking upon speech with them' is not an ordinary dialogue between two discrete and autonomous beings. Instead, the self becomes a site of internal dialogic interaction – an 'internal polemic', as Bakhtin would say. It is through his allusive juxtaposition of Bakhtin and Lacan in his notion of 'countervoices', and his deployment of it in his fiction, that Coetzee provides the means for questioning the conventionally presumed unitary· authority of the writing self.

The context of the passage about countervoices that I have just cited here is a conversation with David Attwell about the strictures of the genre of the interview. The serious writer tries to raise counter-voices, but

> interviewers want speech, a flow of speech. That speech they record, take away, edit, censor, cutting away all its wayward-ness, till what is left conforms to a monologic ideal. (*Doubling the Point* 65)

The further implication is that, for the interviewer, the writer is the one supposed to know what his writing means – and further, *what* that writing means can be readily assimilated into a single authorial position. This is the danger of criticism too – reducing the author's work to a static monologic ideal. Of course, this is a risk of my present project too, not least because I place emphasis on Coetzee's interviews and critical essays. But in an attempt to be alert to count-ervoices, I hope to stress, throughout the book, Coetzee's engage-ments with the work of other writers. His fiction, but also the critical essays and interviews, can then be thought of as *responding*, intim-ately – to questions, to sources of literary inspiration, to philosoph-ical ideas – in ways that evoke a potential reader. In this sense, no writing stands in isolation. These sites of writing-in-response raise countervoices in each event of reading. This is why it matters to track references and allusions, to get a multilayered sense of the way in which the present text is 'full of other people's words' (Bakhtin, *Problems of Dostoevsky's Poetics* 195).

As a way of opening onto the discussion of *Diary of a Bad Year*, I would like to broach the question of the name of the author,[5] and of Coetzee's use of implied narrators and fictional characters who express views, or say words that are difficult not to think of as *his*. 'The author-narrator cannot of course be identified with the histor-ical Beckett' writes Coetzee in his doctoral thesis,

> But how sharply is it possible to draw a line between this author's sentences and those of his characters? Does each sentence in the text fall into one of these two classes, or are there also sentences of indeterminate origin or sentences which belong in both classes? In other words, can narrative point of view be treated as

a small-scale matter, a matter of sentences? (Coetzee, *The English Fiction of Samuel Beckett* 61)

What follows in the thesis is a detailed 15-page discussion of the computational logistics that might be brought to bear in the attempt to answer this question (asked of a novel of considerable length!), and a highly sophisticated – and technical – linguistic analysis of selected sentences, with a view to distinguishing different types of narrative point of view. The conclusion that Coetzee reaches, though, is that a better model for appreciating the variations in point of view is that of a continuum: 'Between autonomous characters telling their story (i.e. creating themselves) in an autonomous world and a man in a room writing 3,500 sentences there is a continuum of points. At any moment in the story the reader is being told what he knows of it by a voice speaking from one point or another along this continuum' (*The English Fiction of Samuel Beckett* 71–2). It is not as if each sentence can be plotted at a specific point on the continuum, since narrative point of view can shift, even within the same sentence.

These shifts attain a vertiginous subtlety in cases where the author's own name appears in the text, not least in Coetzee's oeuvre. I am thinking of the ancestral Coetzee in *Dusklands*, the autobiographical 'John' in *Boyhood* and *Youth*, the John of *Elizabeth Costello* – that is to say, the writer's son – and JC, the author of *Waiting for the Barbarians*, who happens to share the same initials, minus the middle M (the same *signature*? one is tempted to ask – in a sense the entire discussion to follow hinges on this) as the author of *Diary of a Bad Year*. It is certainly with a curious sensation that one comes to the end of *Diary of a Bad Year*: perhaps we have suspended disbelief in the character whom Anya calls Señor C, and whose first initial seems to be J – but once we have finished the novel, we turn over to a page with the author's acknowledgements, below which are the very last letters in the book: the initials, 'JMC' (*Diary of a Bad Year* 231). 'When a proper name is inscribed right on the text, within the text', writes Derrida,

obviously it is not a signature: it is a way of making the name into a work, of making work of the name, but without this inscription of the proper name having the value of any property rights so to speak. Whence the double relation to the name and to the loss of the name: by inscribing the name in the thing itself [...] from

one angle, I lose the signature, but, from another angle, I monu-
mentalize the name, I transform the name into a thing: like a
stone, like a monument. (Derrida, 'Counter-Signatures' 365–6)

The case of JC in *Diary of a Bad Year* is a little more subtle than
Derrida's discussion allows. To refer to *oneself* by name is usually to
position oneself in the third person, an 'it' as Buber might put it, or
more radically in Derrida's terms, 'to transform the name into a
thing'. But the theatrical structure of *Diary of a Bad Year* means that
the characters, JC and Anya, refer to *themselves* in the first person,
and the name of the author features in the novel, obliquely at best,
in the various ways that the characters call each other. *What* the protagonist's name really is is open to question: can it be Juan (as Alan
calls him), when he also seems to be the author of *Waiting for the
Barbarians*? And can we not see this slipperiness as an outrageous
intertextual reference to the very first words that Coetzee published
in a work of fiction – 'My name is Eugene Dawn. I cannot help that.
Here goes' (*Dusklands* 1)?

Diary of a Bad Year has an innovative physical presentation: there
are three bands of writing on each page, separated by horizontal
lines. In the top band we hear JC's academic voice. The top band
comprises a series of critical essays written for a German publication
(in the first section, 'Strong Opinions') and more colloquial reflections (in part two, 'Second Diary') on matters of topical concern. In
the middle band of text on each page we hear JC's first-person
account of his relationship (in the most nebulous possible sense of
this word) with a young woman, Anya, whom JC employs as his typ-
ist. In the third band at the bottom of the page (which starts a little
way into the novel), we hear Anya's first-person account of the incidents and conversations surrounding her work with JC, and her relationship and eventual break-up with her boyfriend, Alan. The text is
not constructed as conventional theatre, in which the utterances of
each character are in face-to-face dialogue with each other; in *Diary
of a Bad Year* each band of text runs alongside the others, but without
being in direct conversation. It is in Anya's band of text that JC is
called, but not exactly by name ('This young woman who declines to
call me by my name', mutters JC (60)) – in a variety of designations:
Señor C, Mister C, C, Senior Citizen and Juan – the term of address
that Alan uses and Anya reports in indirect discourse. JC,[6] in the top

two bands, remains the explicit 'I' of his own utterance – although, as we shall see, the top band (of critical essays) carries further subtleties still.

Through the use of the first person in *Diary of a Bad Year*, and the refractions of the historical author's proper name, the narrative point of view seems to shift, not only in the same sentence, but in the same phrase. In fact, a double narrative point of view seems to be contained in every word in the top band of text, transgressing the distinction that Roman Jakobson makes between the 'speech utterance' (the context of speaker and addressee – in this case, the historical author, J.M. Coetzee, and the readers of his novels) and the 'narrated utterance' (the topic of conversation within the speech utterance – the story of JC and Anya).[7] Thus, when one reads a sentence in which JC speaks about 'my novel', the default position would be to read this at the level of the narrated utterance – we can still attribute to this fictional character a fictional fiction; after all, Elizabeth Costello has gained literary fame for her fiction within fictions, *The House on Eccles Street*. But when JC says, 'my novel, *Waiting for the Barbarians*' (*Diary of a Bad Year* 171), it becomes impossible to dissociate fictional character and historical author – to the extent that we seem to have slipped inadvertently into a speech utterance: the historical author, J.M. Coetzee, relates an anecdote about his personal experience of being misquoted in an Australian newspaper. The name of the *novel* (*Waiting for the Barbarians*) inevitably summons up that of its author (or should that be authors?). 'J.M. Coetzee' has a ghostly presence in JC's authorship, and by extension, in everything that he writes.

The difficulty is compounded by JC's own self-conscious reflections about the difference between speaking 'in one's own person' and 'through one's art'. In the essay on Harold Pinter, JC speaks about Pinter's Nobel Prize acceptance speech in 2005, in which he attacked Tony Blair for his participation in the war in Iraq. 'When one speaks in one's own person', writes JC,

> that is, not through one's art – to denounce some politician or other, using the rhetoric of the agora, one embarks on a contest which one is likely to lose because it takes place on ground where one's opponent is far more practised and adept. (Coetzee, *Diary of a Bad Year* 127)

Is the historical author, J.M. Coetzee, speaking 'in his own person' here, or 'through his art'? At the very least, this is a question that the use of the first person, and the haunting presence of the author's name in *Diary of a Bad Year* leads us to ask.

The passage I have just quoted holds further depths. JC is the 'I' of the utterances in the top two bands of *Diary of a Bad Year*, but the way in which that I stands in relation to each band of discourse is very different. It is in the middle band that 'I' is explicitly stated, to the extent that 'I' is the controlling centre of the utterance:

> My first glimpse of her was in the laundry room. It was mid-morning on a quiet spring day and I was sitting, watching the washing go around, when this quite startling young woman walked in. (Coetzee, *Diary of a Bad Year* 3)

The stance of the 'I' in relation to the utterance – we get the sense that it exerts a centripetal force on the discourse around it – is completely different to the diction and syntax of subjective displacement that we typically find in the top band of JC's essays. The top band has been rather loosely taken to be the 'non-fictional' part of *Diary of a Bad Year* – but still, in JC's essays, we find the most elaborate and relentless syntactic constructions which *deflect* the attempt to attribute personal subjective agency, whether fictional *or* historical. Coetzee coins the phrase, 'a comic antigrammar of point of view', in his discussion of Beckett's *Murphy* (*Doubling the Point* 36); in the passage from *Diary of a Bad Year* (quoted above) about speaking in one's own voice as opposed to speaking through one's art, the relentless use of the impersonal 'one' comes across as a near parody of the tendency in academic (rather than fictional) discourse to abdicate the position of 'I', in a sidestepping of personal accountability for the views expressed.[8] The opening paragraphs of *Diary of a Bad Year* remind me of the opening sentences of Jane Austen's *Pride and Prejudice*:

> It is a truth universally acknowledged, that a single man in possession of a good fortune, must be in want of a wife.
> However little known the feelings or views of such a man may be on his first entering a neighbourhood, this truth is so well fixed in the minds of the surrounding families, that he is

considered as the rightful property of some one or other of their daughters. (Austen, *Pride and Prejudice* 11)

And here are the opening sentences of *Diary of a Bad Year*:

> Every account of the origins of the state starts from the premise that 'we' – not we the readers but some generic we so wide as to exclude no one – participate in its coming into being. But the fact is that the only 'we' we know – ourselves and the people close to us – are born into the state as far back as we can trace. The state is always there before we are. (Coetzee, *Diary of a Bad Year* 3)

A syntax which deflects personal agency is sustained throughout the top band of JC's academic essays in the section, 'Strong Opinions' – through the use of the impersonal 'one' or 'we' (already rendered anonymous in the first sentence of the novel), and other phrases and syntactic strategies (the use of the short passive, of the 'empty subject' in cases like 'there is...' or 'it is...') which make it difficult to establish the source of the point of view or opinion expressed. As in *Pride and Prejudice*, JC's world seems replete with 'truth[s] universally acknowledged'. The following examples are from the first page alone: 'every account of...'; 'the fact is that...'; 'the consensus is that'; 'if...we accept the premise that...then we must also accept its entailment', and again, 'the fact is that...'; 'they – we – are certainly powerless...'; 'in the myth of the founding of the state...'; 'it is hardly in our power...' (notice the empty subject in this last phrase) (*Diary of a Bad Year* 3).

Yet despite this syntactic drive towards agentlessness, the performatively reflexive effect of writing is to call out – or at least, to call for – the name of its writer. Before returning to my discussion of *Diary of a Bad Year* in section V, it is necessary to discuss the linguistico-philosophical underpinnings of Coetzee's use of the term 'counter-voice'. This is the ground of discussion in the next two sections, with specific reference to Coetzee's engagements with Bakhtin and Lacan.

III

In previous chapters (via Benveniste) we have come to an appreciation of the grammatical exigency of positing an 'I' and a 'you' in each instance of discourse. What this means is that any utterance has a double directedness: towards the referential object, the topic of the conversation, but also towards another discourse, another person's speech. Discourse has a 'twofold direction', writes Bakhtin (*Problems of Dostoevsky's Poetics* 185), and in taking heed of the second context (the directedness towards someone else's speech), any analysis of that discourse has to move beyond the usual ambit of linguistics or stylistics. It is this double-directedness that Susan Barton confronts when she writes her memoir of the island for Mr Foe, the author – who in turn (Susan hopes) will write and publish her story. 'More is at stake in the history you write, I will admit', she says in a letter to Mr Foe, 'for it must not only tell the truth about us but please its readers too' (Coetzee, *Foe* 63). At the same time, before her story is written, Susan's very existence is on the line. 'Will you not bear it in mind, however [she writes], that my life is drearily suspended till your writing is done?' (Coetzee, *Foe* 63). When she takes up Mr Foe's pen herself, the tension between telling the truth and pleasing the readers intensifies, and, with outrageous, if seemingly oblivious intertextual references to Daniel Defoe's *Robinson Crusoe*, Susan asks, 'Are these enough strange circumstances to make a story of? How long before I am driven to invent new and stranger circumstances: the salvage of tools and muskets from Cruso's ship; the building of a boat, or at least a skiff, and a venture to sail to the mainland; a landing by cannibals on the island, followed by a skirmish and many bloody deaths [...] Alas, will the day ever arrive when we can make a story without strange circumstances?' (Coetzee, *Foe* 67). Mr Foe never responds to Susan's letters, and entertaining the possibility of the death of her author, Susan drifts, despite herself, into what she calls 'one of the long, issueless colloquies' she conducts with Friday (Coetzee, *Foe* 78). Susan cites the colloquy in her ongoing letter to Mr Foe:

Or else I must assume the burden of our story. But what shall I write? You know how dull our life was, in truth. We faced no perils, no ravenous beasts, not even serpents. Food was plentiful, the sun was mild. No pirates landed on our shores, no freebooters, no cannibals save yourself, if you can be called a cannibal. (Coetzee, *Foe* 81)

Susan's meditation about the conditions of writing – her increasingly anguished concern about the disposition of the reader towards her text; the idea that her life is 'drearily suspended' until her story is written – leads us to appreciate the reflexive capacity of writing, or, slightly differently put, to think about the written text as creating a place in which the writer becomes the 'I' of the utterance. This is one of the central preoccupations of Coetzee's brief essay, 'A Note on Writing', where, as a response to Roland Barthes, Coetzee speaks about writing that leaves 'the writer [*scripteur*][9] inside the writing, not as a psychological subject [...] but as the agent of the action'. Barthes goes on to discuss the ways in which the 'field of the writer is nothing but writing itself, not as the pure "form" conceived by an aesthetic as art for art's sake, but, much more radically, as the only area [*espace*] for the one who writes' (Barthes, 'To Write: An Intransitive Verb?' 142 and 144 – cited in Coetzee, *Doubling the Point* 94). The writer (when we consider 'to write' as being in the middle voice) is not *anterior* to the text, but *interior* to it, as Barthes puts it. In Chapter 1, 'Not I', I spoke about the reflexive quality of the verb 'to write' when it is understood as an instance of the middle voice – writing is writing-oneself. To take this further: to write is to write-oneself into a position relative to you, the reader. In other words, we have a strange sense of 'I' (following Benveniste, the speaker or the writer of the utterance) *as a position*, as an instance of a relation to you in language, or an utterance that is oriented towards a reader's potential response. This position of 'I' is, in a complex sense, created by the perception on the part of the reader of the way in which the writer is disposed towards 'you' as the addressee: in each reading, *you* reinstantiate the place that 'I' marks in language, relative to yourself. This re-embodiment of 'I' in each reading of the text creates a voice to which the reader may respond, making possible (as Bakhtin would say) a dialogic interaction. Bakhtin takes insights from the linguistic sciences into a social atmosphere: his object of study is no longer an abstract *langue* as it is for Saussure, but 'language in its concrete living totality' (Bakhtin, *Problems of Dostoevsky's Poetics* 181). Further, the unit of the language in Bakhtin's study is not the linguistic sign (as it is in Saussure's semiology), or the proposition (as it is in an analytic philosophy of language) but the *utterance*, which Bakhtin describes as being delimited 'by a *change of speaking subjects*'. An utterance is preceded by the utterances of others, and in turn, is followed by other utterances still. The speaker 'ends his utterance in order to relinquish the floor to the other or to make room for the other's active responsive understanding' (Bakhtin, 'The Problem of Speech Genres' 71). The length of an utterance can range from a single-word rejoinder in everyday dialogue to a weighty novel or philosophical treatise, but the point about the utterance is that it has the capacity to evoke a response – 'one can agree or disagree with [an utterance], execute it, evaluate it, and so on (Bakhtin, 'The Problem of Speech Genres' 74). The idea of the potential embodiment of the shifters, 'I' and 'you' (which I raised in the second chapter, 'You') is crucial to Bakhtin's undertanding of utterances as a sequence of dialogic interactions:

> logical and semantically referential relationships, in order to become dialogic, must be embodied, that is, they must enter another sphere of existence: they must become *discourse*, that is, an utterance, and receive an *author*, that is, a creator of the given utterance whose position it expresses.
>
> Every utterance in this sense has its author, whom we hear in every utterance as its creator. Of the real author, as he exists outside the utterance, we can know absolutely nothing at all. And the forms of this real authorship can be very diverse [...] but in all cases we hear in it a unified creative will, a definite position, to which it is possible to react dialogically. A dialogic reaction personifies every utterance to which it responds. (Bakhtin, *Problems of Dostoevsky's Poetics* 184)

What is clear is that Bakhtin's discussions fall well beyond the ambit of the linguistic sciences – even while he engages those disciplines in a productive way. Bakhtin's ideas about the utterance can surely be read as an extended reflection on Aristotle's theory of civic discourse, especially in relation to the passage I cited at the beginning of this chapter from *The Rhetoric*, where the speaker creates a position – a voice – which disposes him towards the listener in a certain way, and which, in turn, disposes the listener in a certain way towards him. Writing, especially when it is thought of within the context of the middle voice, or as a Bakhtinian utterance, intractably seems to position the 'I' who emerges as writer; it seems inevitable that the reader should attribute to the writing a voice, and in so doing, the writing voice is placed into a dialogic relation with those who would respond to it.

IV

Shoshana Felman's *Writing and Madness*, an important reference text in Coetzee's own essay on Erasmus, constitutes a meditation on the relation between madness and literature.[10] In response to Foucault's *The History of Madness*, she writes,

> a book like Foucault's reminds us that throughout our cultural history, the madness that has been socially, politically, and philosophically repressed has nonetheless made itself heard, has survived as a speaking *subject* only in and through literary texts'. (Felman, *Writing and Madness* 15)

If madness has been repressed, excluded, placed outside the rational boundaries of the law, while literature cedes to madness the voice of the speaking subject, what then of the place of literature, and by implication, its authors? The question is of particular interest given that language itself banishes madness to a different site: 'the very status of language is that of a break with madness [...] With respect to "madness itself," language is always *somewhere else*' (Felman, *Writing and Madness* 44; cited in Coetzee, *Giving Offense* 87). This is important because it invites us to read a literary text in a different kind of way: if language embodies reason, and represses madness, and the literary text, constituted in language, nevertheless admits the voice of madness, then in order to perceive that voice, we should approach the language differently. For instance, we could consider not just what the language is reasonably *about* – but instead read past its subsumptive themes, and be more attentive to what it *does*. What the language of literature does may well operate on a level that is not available for discussion *within* a strictly rational linguistic field. To put this more clearly in relation to my previous section (with its emphasis on the directedness of an utterance towards a potential *response*, and not only towards its referential object): the discussion here may demand closer attention to the performative impact, rather than to the constative content of the work, in order to come to an appreciation of the realization of voice in literature. This is instead of an approach that would concentrate exclusively on the text in terms of its thematic content, or the ideas it expresses.

The invitation to a different emphasis in reading literature provokes further difficult questions about the relation between literary and philosophical discourses. To return to the nexus of conversation between Foucault, Derrida, Felman, Coetzee (and Lacan, as we shall see): the philosopher trying to enter madness *inside* of thought can only do this as part a fictional project, writes Coetzee (*Giving Offense* 87). But then the question arises, would that fictional project lie *inside* philosophy?[11] Felman has this to offer (I quote at some length so that the connections between seemingly disparate topics can be clearly seen):

> To state, as does Foucault, that the mad subject cannot situate himself within his fiction, that *inside* literature, he knows no longer *where* he is, is to imply indeed that fiction may not exactly be located '*inside of* thought,' that literature cannot be properly enclosed *within* philosophy, present, that is, to itself and at the same time present *to* philosophy: that the fiction is not always where we think, or where it thinks it is... All this can be summed up by saying that the role of fiction in philosophy is comparable to that of madness inside literature; and that the status, both of fiction in philosophy and of madness inside literature, is not *thematic*. Literature and madness by no means reside in theme, in the content of a statement. In the play of forces underlying the relationship between philosophy and fiction, literature and madness, the crucial problem is that of the subject's *place*, of his *position* with respect to the delusion. And the position of the subject is not defined by *what* he says, nor by what he talks *about*, but by the place – unknown to him – *from which* he speaks. (Felman, *Writing and Madness* 50; part of this passage is cited in Coetzee, *Giving Offense* 87)

It is within the context of discussions like these – especially when the focus sharpens on questions of the relation between the writer, what is written and what is known, that Coetzee refers to Lacan. First, here is the Lacan of *Écrits*, placing emphasis on the utterance as performative address, rather than as constative proposition:

> the function of language is not to inform but to evoke.
>
> What I seek in speech is the response of the other. What constitutes me as subject is my question. (Lacan, *Écrits* 86)

The paradox of the problem of writing and madness, as it is outlined by Felman above and then quoted by Coetzee ('Felman, whose
commentary I follow closely' writes Coetzee in *Giving Offense* 87) – is
this: how does one speak from the outside, a position of not knowing, madness, silence; but at the same time, evoke a just response,
through the very language provided by the inside – a language of
knowledge and reason. How could one accomplish this without
betraying[12] the outsider's position? In the dualism set up here, literature is placed on the outside, excluded from the discourse of reason
(which, of course, has its roots in Plato's *Republic*, where the poets are
banished from the just state because reason demands it[13]).

Lacan's response to the paradox of the inside and the outside, and
the position of the literary writer (in Coetzee's reading now) is

> to collaps[e] at least momentarily, the distance between the sub-
> ject speaking unheard from outside the inside and the subject
> speaking for him, Lacan or 'Lacan,' in his name, from inside – the
> distance, so to speak, between the silent madman and the archae-
> ologist of his silence. (Coetzee, *Giving Offense* 89)

Thus the writer speaks for (perhaps from?) a position that is silent,
mad, not-knowing – and in the process, the writing disrupts ready
assumptions about the distance between reason and madness,
language and silence, a knowing subject and knowledge. This
'knowledge' in literature now raises tricky questions about the
extent to which it has been generated by a reasoning subject. If for
Benveniste, the positing of a subject is inevitable once there is language, Lacan takes the idea to a radical limit: this subjectivity-
in-writing for Lacan is disaggregated from a more conventional
notion of a discrete, psychological, knowing agent anterior to the
writing. 'Writing's knowledge' (writes Shoshana Felman in her
commentary on Lacan)

> although usually 'presumed to be a subject' – believed to be an
> attribute of the (writing) subject – is nothing other in effect than
> the textual knowledge of what links the signifiers in the text (and
> not the signifieds) to one another: *knowledge that escapes* the sub-
> ject but through which the subject is precisely constituted as the
> one who *knows how to escape* – by means of signifiers – his own

self-presence. (Felman, *Writing and Madness* 132; part of this passage is quoted in Coetzee, *Giving Offense* 89)

In a chiasmatic reversal, as Felman suggests – and Coetzee elaborates – Lacan 'gives up the position of "the subject supposed to know" *[le sujet supposé savoir]* in the hope of finding himself in a position of knowledge, a knowledge supposed to be a subject *[le savoir supposé sujet]'* (Coetzee, *Giving Offense* 89). The knowledge supposed to be a subject, Lacan proposes as nothing less than *'a formula defining writing'* (Felman, *Madness and Writing* 132, citing Lacan's seminar of 9 April 1974, my emphasis). Lacan's and Bakhtin's theories of subjectivity and voice in language have a wide-ranging impact on Coetzee's practice as a writer: as a writer of fiction, a critic, a translator – and more broadly, as a scholar. But it is perhaps in *Boyhood* that we find the most graphic – and poignantly humorous – instances of this idea of 'knowledge supposed to be a subject'.

The child of *Boyhood* seems constantly harangued into taking sides, taking up a position in which one side mutually excludes the other: 'Who do you like, Smuts or Malan? Who do you like, Superman or Captain Marvel? Who do you like, the Russians or the Americans?' (Coetzee, *Boyhood* 27).[14] The instance of self-positioning in language that has the most disastrous consequences for the small John is when he replies to his teacher's impossible question that she springs on him at his new school in Worcester: 'What is your religion?'

He glances right and left. What is the right answer? What religions are there to choose from? Is it like Russians and Americans? His turn comes, 'What is your religion?' asks the teacher. He is sweating, he does not know what to say. 'Are you a Christian or a Roman Catholic or a Jew?' she demands impatiently. 'Roman Catholic,' he says. (Coetzee, *Boyhood* 18–19)

The upshot is that John is bullied by the Afrikaans boys – the Christians – who align him with the Jews, and take revenge on him 'for what the Jews did to Christ' (*Boyhood* 19); and John is treated as a liar by the Catholics, who quickly realize that he has not the slightest idea about the meanings of the words communion, catechism, confession or mass. John had chosen to say, 'Roman Catholic' 'because of Rome, because of Horatius and his two comrades, swords in their hands [...]

UNIVERSITY OF WINCHESTER
LIBRARY

defending the bridge over the Tiber against the Etruscan hordes' (*Boyhood* 20). It is only later that he begins to learn from the other Catholic boys what it is that he has committed himself to. Similarly with the Russians: 'he chose the Russians as he chose the Romans: because he likes the letter *r*, particularly the capital *R*, the strongest of all the letters' – and it is only *after* having chosen the Russians that 'he threw himself into reading about them'; *this* choice 'is a secret so dark that he can reveal it to no one' (*Boyhood* 27 and 26).

In Lacan we find an explicit and sustained inversion of Saussure's privileging of the signified (concept) over the signifier (the material substance of the sign), and throughout Coetzee's oeuvre, the fictional characters are often deeply attentive to the physicality of the signifiers of their writing – sometimes even at the expense of what the letters would normally be taken to signify.[15] The child of *Boyhood*, in choosing the Russians and the Romans because of the letter *r*, highlights the sense of disaggregation between signifier and signified, a tension between the physical impress of the letter, and its role in an abstract constellation of meaning. Yet the addressees of the boy's response, 'Roman Catholic', attribute to him as speaker a claim to knowing what the words mean – he is treated as being in the position of the subject supposed to know. But it is quite possible to write or to say words, the conventional meaning of which eludes the 'I' of the utterance. Knowledge in this sense escapes the subject, and at the same time, the subject is presented, but not present at the site of his utterance: the small boy is *not* a Roman Catholic.

If this is a graphic *example* (a Lacanian allegory, Teresa Dovey might call it) of the forces at work in the construction of subjectivity in language, the example also does important work in terms of the argument of this chapter. It is one of countless instances in Coetzee that sounds a cautionary note about attributing a position and knowing consciousness to the writing subject *purely* on the basis of what *we* take the words that he says to mean. It may not be possible to stake out a *non*position in writing (as Erasmus realized)[16] – and already we have some sense of this through an appreciation of the workings of the middle voice – the *writer* is not an autonomous subject anterior to the writing. To take a step further back, Benveniste considers the attribution of subjectivity to be the most basic of all operations in language: 'A language without the expression of person cannot be imagined', and 'The "personal pronouns" are never missing from among the signs of a language' (Benveniste, *Problems in General Linguistics* 225). So then, the writer, the speaker, is inside the utterance. *Nevertheless*, the relation between the writing and the engagement of the agent of that writing as one who knows, cannot simply be taken for granted. A scene such as the one I have cited from *Boyhood* thus prompts us to ask different kinds of questions of Coetzee's literary texts: questions on an entirely different footing from those seeking out the presumptive author's fully knowing and reasoned working-through of a literary or philosophical meaning or theme in advance of the writing itself. In what ways can the sense of authorial voice be realized in prose fiction in ways other than an attentiveness to the thematic staging of *ideas*, and in what ways does *Diary of a Bad Year* lead us to these kinds of questions?

V

In his final essay in the 'Second Diary' (in the top band of text), JC writes about rereading a chapter of Dostoevsky's *The Brothers Karamazov*, and finding himself deeply moved by it, despite having read the passage countless times before. The placing of this essay as the last one in *Diary of a Bad Year* gives it the affective power of the final chord in a fugue, especially since the middle and bottom bands of text are now taken up by *Anya's* voice. In other words, the essay on Dostoevsky brings JC's text to a close; for the last 40 pages or so, the middle band (which has been occupied by JC's first-person, journalistic narrative for most of the book), comprises the letter that Anya writes to JC from Brisbane. Anya is now a writer too; it is as if she has been released into the role. When she comes to greet JC for the last time (Anya is leaving Alan and moving out to spend time with her mother), JC embraces her:

> for a whole minute we stood clasped together, this shrunken old man and this earthly incarnation of heavenly beauty, and could have continued for a second minute, she would have permitted that, being generous of herself; but I thought, *Enough is enough*, and let her go. (Coetzee, *Diary of a Bad Year* 190)

JC's next essay (in the top band) is 'On the writing life' – and Anya's letter is carried through in the middle band to the end of the book.

Returning to JC's final essay on Dostoevsky: when he reads the passage where Ivan hands back his ticket of admission to the universe, JC finds himself 'sobbing uncontrollably' – why should he be so moved by the passage when, on his own admission, he holds an ethical view counter to that of Ivan? JC goes on to say,

> The answer has nothing to do with ethics or politics, everything to do with rhetoric. In his tirade against forgiveness Ivan shamelessly uses sentiment (martyred children) and caricature (cruel landowners) to advance his ends. Far more powerful than the substance of his argument, which is not strong, are the accents of anguish, the personal anguish of a soul unable to bear the horrors of this world. It is the voice of Ivan, as realized by Dostoevsky, not his reasoning, that sweeps me along. (Coetzee, *Diary of a Bad Year* 225)

This passage bears more than a faint echo of a comment Coetzee made in one of the interviews in *Doubling the Point*:

> (Let me add, *entirely* parenthetically, that I, as a person, as a personality, am overwhelmed, that my thinking is thrown into confusion and helplessness, by the fact of human suffering in the world, and not only human suffering. These fictional constructions of mine are paltry, ludicrous defenses against that being-overwhelmed, and, to me, transparently so.). (Coetzee, *Doubling the Point* 248)

It is Coetzee's realization of voice in *Diary of a Bad Year*, through narrative strategy, rather than through the development of the characters' arguments at the level of their content that interests me here. Still in the back of my mind is the excerpt from Aristotle's *Rhetoric* that I cited in the first section of this chapter, namely that it is necessary 'that the speaker seem to be a certain kind of person and that his hearers suppose him to be disposed toward them in a certain way, and in addition if they, too, happen to be disposed in a certain way' (Aristotle, *On Rhetoric* Book II, §1.3). As I trust much of my discussion throughout this book has demonstrated, the relative positions and dispositions of writers, personae and readers are at best precarious in relation to the utterance, even within the exigencies of the most carefully plotted rhetorical and narrative strategies. But the corollary seems to hold too: even when all rhetorical and narrative strategies are purposely deployed to disturb the attributing of positions and dispositions to speakers and listeners, to writers and readers, *still* the writing seems to effect the realization of an authorial voice.

The physical experience of reading *Diary of a Bad Year* has a great deal to do with the evocation of voice in the novel, even in the instant of its own refraction. On every page the reader confronts the choice of following one band of text through by turning the page, or by reading all three bands before turning the page. The first way of reading – reading only one band, rather than all three on the same page – seems to be actively encouraged when the last sentence of one band runs over onto the next page. The first time this occurs is in the bottom band – Anya's first-person account of events. To read in the same band here is to focus exclusively on Anya's account of JC's illegible handwriting, which signals JC's age, and (judging by Anya's level of engagement with his writing) further suggests that his opinions will have little currency among a younger generation of readers.

The experience of reading page by page at this point, rather than keeping within the band of Anya's text, is rather different. This reading dramatizes the generational gap, but it also dramatizes the experience of human existence itself as a site of turbulent interpellations – of (for instance) abstract thoughts, physical desires, public personae, private selves, the passage of time, self-centredness, and obligations and accountabilities that are at once personal, social and national. This is what it is like to read page by page, rather than following a single band through: Anya's comments on JC's physical decrepitude provide a disruptive undercurrent to his essay on national shame, which runs across the top of the page. 'He forms his letters clearly enough', writes Anya. The next part of her sentence (if we read strictly according to page) is interrupted by JC's ongoing disquisition on the ethics of international politics – or, if you like, it is JC who is distracted from his serious thinking about national shame by Anya's flirtatious physical presence and flagrant lack of interest in the content of what he writes. His essay begins, 'An article in a recent *New Yorker* makes it as plain as day that the US administration [...] not only sanctions the torture of prisoners taken in the so-called war on terror but is active in every way to subvert laws and conventions proscribing torture' (*Diary of a Bad Year* 39). 'He forms his letters clearly enough, m's and n's and u's and w's included [writes Anya *Diary of a Bad Year* 42], but when he has to write a whole passage he can't keep [page break, and switch to JC's essay at the top of page 43] Yet although it has been complicit in America's crimes, to say that Australia has fallen into the same anti-legality or extra-legality as America has would be stretching a point' (*Diary of a Bad Year* 43). The middle band across these pages comprises JC's report of a conversation in which Anya asks whether he thinks she should be a photographic model: 'She makes a moue, wriggles her hips. You know, she says. Wouldn't you like a picture of me? You could put it on your desk' (43), but then, reading down the page, we are back with Anya's report on JC's physical failings:

> the line straight, it dips like a plane nosediving into the sea or a baritone running out of breath. Never up always down.
>   Bad eyes, teeth even worse. If I was him I would have the lot pulled out and get a nice new pair of dentures fitted. No wife would put up with teeth like that ... (Coetzee, *Diary of a Bad Year* 43)

In the first place, the reader of *Diary of a Bad Year* has to *choose* which band of text to follow: which voice do we listen to? Each band of text is not in *direct* conversation with the other bands ('This is not going to be a dialogue, thank God', says the Magda of *In the Heart of the Country*, 'I can stretch my wings and fly where I will' (*In the Heart of the Country* 101)); the bands of text are simply juxtaposed on the same page. The different voices sometimes offer perspectives on the same theme or incident, although not necessarily at the same time; there is no 'voice-over' tying the different strands into a single narrative thread, but equally, one strand of text on its own sometimes lacks sense without recourse to one or both of the other strands. Nevertheless, certain topics of conversation become the sites of contesting voices: religious fundamentalists, the implications of reporting rape, questions of honour, old age and sexual desire, death ... The views of Alan (Anya's boyfriend) often enter these sites of contestation through speech of his that Anya reports.

Further, it is not as if each of the three strands of texts holds to a consistent position, or even a stable style of engagement with a topic.

As the novel progresses, we witness shifts within each strand, *thanks to* a responsiveness to perspectives articulated by the other voices. Anya volunteers her thoughts on JC's opinions:

> OK. This may sound brutal, but it isn't meant that way. There is a tone – I don't know the best word to describe it – a tone that really turns people off. A know-it-all tone. Everything is cut and dried: *I am the one with all the answers, here is how it is, don't argue, it won't get you anywhere.* (Coetzee, *Diary of a Bad Year* 70)

The high-handed 'here is how it is, don't argue' tone of JC's 'strong opinions' (as Anya reads them) gives way to the 'I' of the second diary – an 'I' of dreams, of the tenuous articulations of the self in what is presumed to be one's mother tongue, of reflections on ageing, of an imaginative entry into the lives of the birds in the park. The juxtaposition, without overarching evaluative narrative comment, of voices realized in writing that leaves different tracks, means that the writer does not occupy an authoritative position neutrally independent of each track. In Bakhtin's reflection about Dostoevsky,

> The object of authorial aspirations is certainly not this sum total of ideas in itself, as something neutral and identical with itself. No, the object is precisely *the passing of a theme through many and various voices*, its rigorous and, so to speak, irrevocable *multi-voicedness* and *vari-voicedness*. The very distribution of voices and their interaction is what matters to Dostoevsky. (Bakhtin, *Problems of Dostoevsky's Poetics* 265)

It is in this context, then, that the aspiration to 'speak in one's own voice' takes on the somewhat different connotation of raising the countervoices within oneself, of refracting utterances through them, rather than presuming to be in the anterior and transcendent position of what Lacan would call the 'subject supposed to know'. Bakhtin sees a juxtaposition of various voices as definitive of Dostoevsky's art: 'Dostoevsky's basic artistic effects are achieved by passing one and the same word through various voices all counterposed to one another' (Bakhtin, *Problems of Dostoevsky's Poetics* 256). Further, the *dialogic angle* of one word addressed to another word carries the pathos of signification that a monologic presentation of a theme would not:

> This transferral of words from one mouth to another, where the content remains the same although the tone and ultimate meaning are changed, is a fundamental device of Dostoevsky's. He forces heroes to recognize themselves, their idea, their own words, their orientation, their gesture in another person, in whom all these phenomena change their integrated and ultimate meaning and take on a different sound, the sound of parody or ridicule. (Bakhtin, *Problems of Dostoevsky's Poetics* 217)

Any attribution of an authorial position to the writer of *Diary of a Bad Year* would be one that is *incorporated* within these different voices, and the dialogic angle set up between them – it is not as if an autonomous authorial voice is outside and before the writing that we encounter as a multiplicity of voices. There is no author-narrator who prescribes a resolution to the collision of voices from a position of anonymous omniscience. Instead, the novel pitches a battle (to borrow JC's metaphor in his essay on Dostoevsky), and if the outcome of the battle is to be decided, it will be in the 'shaky moral imagination of the reader' (Wood, 'In a Cold Country' 7) rather than in any ethical prescriptions on the part of the author. What is demanded on the part of the writer, though, is a responsiveness to other voices, a willingness to be incorporated by them, to the extent that (in Celan's terms) the creation of art is the *distance* I must travel. A supposedly controlling 'I' is 'dismissed, is no longer privy' (Celan, *Collected Prose* 25), as the writing plays out the contrapuntal rhythms of different voices sounded in each reading. But paradoxically, through this process of radical refraction of an authorial self, the reader is intractably drawn into reconstituting that self – *as* integrally responsive.

The notion of rhythm is central in Coetzee's appreciation of literature; in his doctoral thesis on Beckett, Coetzee speaks about the author's 'rhythmic habits' and raises the question whether a 'rhythmical principle' may not even precede those of logic and syntax (*The English Fiction of Samuel Beckett* 91). In a footnote Coetzee goes so far as to assert that 'rhythms seem to be prior to words much of the time in *Watt*' (*The English Fiction of Samuel Beckett* 261). In his essay, 'Homage', Coetzee speaks about 'slowing

down the reading eye' – 'the principle, if not the body of techniques followed by Pound. That principle is broadly rhythmical'
('Homage' 6). The term, 'rhythmical principle', as Coetzee uses it,
has a wide reach: 'Rhythm is any simple pattern of sound, syntax,
or, on occasion, meaning, set up by local repetition in the text'
(*The English Fiction of Samuel Beckett* 91). The thesis includes
diagrams of the rhythmic structures of sentences in Beckett; and it
is an attention to the principle of rhythm (rather than a study of
'themes') that Coetzee hopes to discover 'how the Poundian magic
worked when it worked' ('Homage' 6). The 'deepest lessons one
learns from other writers are, I suspect, matters of rhythm', Coetzee
goes on to say ('Homage' 6–7).

I would argue that Coetzee's acute attentiveness to rhythmic pat-
terning in *Diary of a Bad Year* is fundamental to his realization of
different voices in each of the three bands of utterance. Where am
I headed with this? It seems to me that Coetzee's most recent 'experiment with prose' (*Youth* 61) demands a response that is not only
beyond the ambit of a stylistic discussion, but one that presses the
limit of conventional prose criticism. Taking the cue from the small
child, John, in *Boyhood*, I have been asking, not 'How do I evaluate
this novel on the abstract level of the ideas and themes the language
expresses as semantic content?' but 'What does this novel *look* like?
What does it *feel* like to read it? What does it *sound* like? And how
does the author use these extra-linguistic strategies in his realization of voice in the novel?' What I am working towards (and I return
to this in my concluding chapter) is that Coetzee's writing often
seems to play out tensions between what is understood, and what is
seen, or heard. His writing, then, is a material artwork in the world,
with physical affect, as much as it is an elucidation of abstract ideas
and themes. The scene of the novel becomes a physical *site* of engagement between writer and reader. I return to the question of
rhythm.

Anya's sentences are characteristically single, monosyllabic rhythmic units – a unit of rhythm is coterminous with the end of the
sentence:

> Alan comes into the room while I am typing. So what are you up
> to now? he says. Typing for the old man, I say. What is it about? he
> says. Samurai, I say. He comes and reads over my shoulder. Birth

certificates for animals, he says – is he crazy? (Coetzee, *Diary of a Bad Year* 36)

Anya's rhythm offsets that of JC, with its insistent periodic sentences of rhetorical persuasion. Typically, especially in the top band, JC's sentences have a complex hierarchically tiered syntax of subordination, and hence a large range in pace, vocal pitch and modulation:

> Liberals, in Australia as in South Africa, feel that it should be left to the market to decide who shall rise and who shall not. The role of government should be self-limited: to create conditions in which individuals can bring their aspirations, their drive, their training, and whatever other forms of intangible capital they have, to the market, which will then (here comes the moment when economic philosophy turns to religious faith) reward them more or less in proportion to their contribution (their 'input'). (Coetzee, *Diary of a Bad Year* 117)

Clearly, an appreciation of the way in which voice is realized in *Diary of a Bad Year* demands a reading that is not reducible to an assessment of the arguments and ideas put forward by the characters. 'Ideas are certainly important – who would deny that?' writes Coetzee,

> but the fact is, the ideas that operate in novels and poems, once they are unpicked from their context and laid out on the laboratory table, usually turn out to be uncomplicated, even banal. Whereas a style, an attitude to the world, as it soaks in, becomes part of the personality, part of the self, ultimately indistinguishable from the self. ('Homage' 7)

The pace of reading is affected by these switches in rhythm from one band to the next in *Diary of a Bad Year*, and regardless of what the characters are speaking about, their embodiment in the respective rhythms of their language already makes for different interactions on the part of the reader, perhaps influencing one's decision whether to turn the page, or to change the pace by interacting with a different voice on the same page. One of Coetzee's strongest objections in his doctoral thesis to the methods of stylostatistics is that it rests on the assumption that the experience of work of literature is 'a linear experience composed of a series of smaller experiences succeeding each other in time'. He writes, 'I would identify the crippling weakness of stylostatistics as its domination by this metaphor of linearity' (Coetzee, *The English Fiction of Samuel Beckett* 161–2). *Diary of a Bad Year* is surely a performative corroboration of that view.

VI

I return now, finally, to JC's closing essay in *Diary of a Bad Year*. If style is 'an attitude to the world...part of the personality, part of the self, ultimately indistinguishable from the self', then a response to another writer in which one appreciates, intimately, that writer's style, is also a response which incorporates that writer's voice, or *ethos*, to use Aristotle's term. Thus, when Coetzee says that the 'deepest lessons' he learns from other writers are 'lessons of rhythm' – we realize that this is a comment that carries ethical weight. Far be it an imitation of a superficial practice – it is an expression of what Coetzee would call an 'ethic of writing' ('Homage' 7). This is the import of the closing sentences of JC's text:

> By their example [i.e. Tolstoy's and Dostoevsky's] one becomes a better artist; and by better I do not mean more skilful but ethically better. They annihilate one's impurer pretensions; they clear one's eyesight; they fortify one's arm. (Coetzee, *Diary of a Bad Year* 227)

Again, JC echoes one of Coetzee's own critical essays (I have referred to this passage in Chapter 2, 'You'): 'To put it another way: in the process of responding to the writers one intuitively chooses to respond to, one makes oneself into the person whom in the most intractable but also perhaps the most deeply ethical sense one wants to be' (Coetzee, 'Homage' 7).

This ethic of responsiveness to the writing of the other, which becomes *part of* 'one's own voice' thus has the effect of refracting the authority of the 'I' across a multiplicity of countervoices, and it is through an attentiveness to these countervoices that one has a more nuanced sense of what an interviewer might term 'the position' or 'the role' of the writer. What is 'the position' of the writer

J.M. Coetzee? Any attempt to answer that question needs to take into account the countervoices raised in the writing – so that 'the position' of the writer, even in interviews and critical essays, emerges as a site of *responding*, in the most engaged way, to the writers who have mattered to him most. This I-as-responding is then the site of an internal dialogue – a 'microdialogue', as Bakhtin would say, and further still, *within* a 'single dismantled conscious-ness' (Bakhtin, *Problems of Dostoevsky's Poetics* 221). The 'I' of the utterance no longer holds a unified and anterior stance with respect to what is written; the writing activates voice as internally dialogic – and this applies to Coetzee's critical writing as much as it does to his fiction. Coetzee speaks explicitly about this in the final interview of *Doubling the Point*, where he refers to his own essay on Rousseau, Tolstoy and Dostoevsky as 'a submerged dialogue between two per-sons' (*Doubling the Point* 392); it is not as if there is an independent consciousness that precedes and controls puppet-like speech in a dialogue between other characters.

The 'position' of the writer, then, is radically multiple – refracted through countervoices that transgress a supposed presence in time and space. This is what I have tried to stress in recourse to Coetzee's interviews and critical essays too: it is not as if what Coetzee says at these writing-sites provides privileged access to dilemmas raised in the fiction. Instead, the author's writing, whether fiction *or* non-fiction, carries within it residual encounters with innumerable other writers. In this chapter I have highlighted just a few of Coetzee's responsive intellectual encounters that I take to have some outlet in *Diary of a Bad Year* – encounters in which (in one sequence) Coetzee writes about Erasmus in the specific context of Shoshana Felman writing about Foucault and Derrida (who write about Descartes), and Lacan; and in another sequence, Coetzee writing about Bakhtin writing about Dostoevsky, who, in turn, prompts Coetzee to write about JC writing about Dostoevsky – and *this* writing ultimately causes the literary critic to write about *Diary of a Bad Year*. But by now it should be clear that to 'write about *Diary of a Bad Year*' is to thread a few interweaving strands of a conversation of untold intricacy – and we begin to get a better sense of the import of asking (often too glibly) about 'the position' of the author. If writing intractably tempts us to attribute it to a 'subject supposed to know', Coetzee pulls out all the literary stops to switch the terms of the conversation, so that we think instead of the implications of approaching a text supposed to be a subject. In so doing, Coetzee plays up the countervoices that collide in the writing – but it is that very writing that provides the place for the one who writes. And this is where I think that Coetzee departs from Bakhtin: 'what Bakhtin leaves out', says Coetzee (I have referred to this conversation in the introduction) is 'that to the degree that Dostoevskian dialogism grows out of Dostoevsky's *own* moral character, out of his ideals, and out of his being as a writer, it is only distantly imitable' (Coetzee, *Stranger Shores* 145–6, my emphasis). In the teeth of the notion of 'countervoice' then, Coetzee makes an appeal for the singularity of an authorial voice. Dostoevsky's dialogic style, for Coetzee, is not simply reducible to 'ideological position', or 'novelistic technique' (as Bakhtin may sometimes be taken to imply); instead, Dostoevsky's dialogism is a matter 'of the most radical intellectual and even spiritual courage' (*Stranger Shores* 145) in that, with integrity, he submits his *own* convictions to the same tests as he does those of others who take an opposing view. Thus even in the moment of exposing the contingency of cultural or personal beliefs (or, differently put, *because* of the responsiveness to countervoices), the singularity of an authorial voice is affirmed.

In the next chapter I will be considering *Disgrace* as a text responding to the fiction of Thomas Hardy and Franz Kafka, specifically in relation to the question of human relations to other animals: what does fiction have to contribute to a discussion we would normally consider to fall within the domain of philosophical ethics? This is a leading question in *The Lives of Animals*.

4
Voiceless

I

The title of this chapter is the name of an animal rights organization in Australia; Coetzee is their patron. The question of 'voice', as we have seen in previous chapters, falls within the ambit of linguistics (the active, passive and middle voices), broader cultural and sociolinguistic practices (Bakhtin's double-voiced and dialogic voices)[1] and Coetzee's aesthetics and ethics of writing (his notion of counter-voice). The concept of 'voice' begins to take on ethical ramifications in relation to questions of subjective agency, and of the authority vested in the one who speaks or writes. The present chapter discusses a recurrent theme in Coetzee's fiction – the question of voice and voicelessness within an ethical context of human relations to animals: on what basis can one relate to animals other than human, when they are voiceless in human terms? What are the implications for one's sense of self as a rational speaking agent when one's interlocutor does not respond, or offers no reciprocal engagement in the language available to the speaker? How does one act with justice on this other's behalf? Questions such as these open onto preoccupations in recent philosophical engagements with Coetzee's work, which are perhaps best understood to be sparked by the first publication of Coetzee's 1997 Tanner Lectures, *The Lives of Animals*. The first edition of *The Lives of Animals* is edited and introduced by Amy Gutmann, founding director of Princeton's University Centre for Human Values, and the publication includes responses by other philosophers, critics and psychologists – perhaps most notable among them the animal ethics philosopher, Peter Singer. *The Lives of Animals* features prominently in a recent publication, *Philosophy and Animal Life* (2008), with contributions by philosophers Stanley Cavell, Cora Diamond, John McDowell, Ian Hacking and Cary Wolfe. At the core of this volume is a question of the 'relations among language, thinking, and our relations to nonhuman animals' (Hacking, *Philosophy and Animal Life* 10). Stephen Mulhall's *The Wounded Animal* (2009) takes Cora Diamond's 'The Difficulty of Reality and the Difficulty of Philosophy' (in *Philosophy and Animal Life*) as its main impetus, and, in a rigorous engagement with Coetzee's *Elizabeth Costello*, explores the different capacities of philosophy and literature to represent reality, and our ethical responses to it, as resistant to thinking. In this chapter I am interested in related questions, but with specific reference to *Disgrace*. Set in post-apartheid South Africa, the novel invites a consideration of the impact of cultural and historical contingencies in any discussion of ethics.

On 22 February 2007, Voiceless (the animal rights group in Australia) opened an art exhibition at the Sherman Gallery in Sydney, entitled 'Voiceless: I feel therefore I am'. For the exhibition opening, Coetzee wrote an address[2] which bears distinctive echoes of Elizabeth Costello's Gates Lecture in *The Lives of Animals*. My chapter starts out by broaching a question of the role that the arts (as opposed to strictly philosophical discourses) might have to play in serious human thinking about our relation to other animals. The chapter then moves on to a consideration of David Lurie's relation to the dogs in *Disgrace*, with specific reference to what I take to be two important literary intertexts in the novel: Thomas Hardy's *Jude the Obscure* (read within the context of Hardy's ethical reading of Darwin) and – to a lesser extent – Franz Kafka's short story, 'Investigations of a Dog'.

II

In *Giving Offense*, Coetzee imagines a male writer-pornographer who creates a self-reflexive account of power and desire, 'not in the discursive terms of "theory," but in the form of a representation, an enactment, perhaps in the medium of film' (Coetzee, *Giving Offense* 72). What would save the film from suffering the fate of pornography – that is to say, delegitimization – 'except perhaps its *seriousness* (if that were recognized) as a philosophical project?' (Coetzee, *Giving Offense* 73).

In this question that the imagined writer might pose to feminist Catherine MacKinnon, the *'philosophical* project' is placed squarely on the side of the law; should the project not be recognized as philosophical, the representation/enactment/film would be outlawed. The imagined exchange here reminds me of another famous dialogue, Plato's *Republic*, in which Socrates delineates the 'ancient antagonism' (§607b) between the philosophers and the poets in high-spirited terms.[3] Socrates, Glaucon, Adeimantus and others are trying to work out their vision of a just state, and they reach the conclusion that poetry and the dramatic arts ought to be banished from it. Once you admit 'the sweet lyric or epic muse', says Socrates, 'pleasure and pain become your rulers instead of law and the rational principles commonly accepted as best' (Plato, *The Republic* §607a); the poet

> wakens and encourages and strengthens the lower elements in the mind to the detriment of reason, which is like giving power and political control to the worst elements in the state and ruining the better elements. The dramatic poet produces a similarly bad state of affairs in the mind of the individual, by encouraging the unreasoning part of it. (Plato, *The Republic* §605b–c)

In short, Socrates concludes that the 'gravest charge against poetry still remains. It has a terrible power to corrupt even the best characters, with very few exceptions' (Plato, *The Republic* §605c). But if, since its earliest inception, philosophy identifies itself as being on the side of reason, and poetry and the arts generally as being on the side of 'feelings' (§605d), of 'instinctive desires' (§606a), of the 'comic instinct' (§606c) and of 'desires and feelings of pleasure and pain' (§606d), then the implication (perhaps even the defining assumption) is that the arts have nothing to contribute to questions usually thought to fall within the domain of philosophy, and more specifically still, questions (such as those of ethics), require a working-through grounded in reason, rather than in aesthetic affect.

Of course, it is a view such as this one that the Elizabeth Costello of *Lives of Animals* sets out to question. 'And that, you see, is my dilemma this afternoon', she says,

> Both reason and seven decades of life experience tell me that reason is neither the being of the universe nor the being of God. On

the contrary, reason looks to me suspiciously like the being of human thought; worse than that, like the being of one tendency in human thought. Reason is the being of a certain spectrum of human thinking. And if this is so, if that is what I believe, then why should I bow to reason this afternoon and content myself with embroidering on the discourse of the old philosophers? (Coetzee, *The Lives of Animals* 23)

Now at a level of strategic literary-philosophical *presentation* of *The Lives of Animals*, even prior to the emergence of the work's explicit thematic concerns, or of the individual delineation of the characters, Coetzee himself raises questions about the presumed priority accorded to philosophical reason in 'human thinking'. In 1997, Coetzee was invited to present the Tanner Lectures on Human Values at Princeton University. He responded by reading two fictional short stories in these lectures, under the title *The Lives of Animals*. The protagonist, Elizabeth Costello (on the strength of her reputation as a novelist), has been invited to present the annual Gates Lecture at Appleton College. Instead of speaking 'about herself and her fiction, as her sponsors would no doubt like', Costello decides to speak about what her son, John, calls 'a hobbyhorse of hers' – that is to say, the question of human relations to animals (Coetzee, *The Lives of Animals* 16). As Stephen Mulhall and Amy Gutmann both point out, the Tanner lectures usually take the form of a philosophical discussion; Coetzee's decision to present a *fictional* discourse (even before we understand what that fiction is about) at the very least prompts us to revisit the longstanding controversy between the philosophers and the poets,[4] and I would go so far as to suggest that questions of the relation between criticism and fiction, reason and affect, philosophy and the creative arts, are never far from the surface of Coetzee's writing.

The passage from *Giving Offense* that I cited at the beginning of this section distinctly links the idea of 'seriousness' to a project that is recognized as 'philosophical', but the very next sentence in *Giving Offense* reads: 'Seriousness is, for a certain kind of artist, *an imperative uniting the aesthetic and the ethical*' (Coetzee, *Giving Offense* 73, my emphasis).[5] It is this linking of the aesthetic and the ethical that matters for the discussion to follow: are there other modes of human thinking, apart from philosophical reasoning, that might make a positive contribution to a field such as ethics? Keeping this question in mind leads me to revisit Coetzee's relation to Russian Formalism and other offshoots of the Prague School. Coetzee engages the work of the likes of Viktor Shklovsky, Roman Jakobson and Mikhail Bakhtin (among others) in ways that *yoke* aesthetic and ethical concerns; a question of form is never easily contained within, nor reducible to, an insular discussion of art for art's sake in ways that we might superficially think of as a Formalist approach. One of the entries in the 'Strong Opinions' section of *Diary of a Bad Year* provides an explicit cue for the linking of a Formalist aesthetic to ethical concerns. In his essay, 'On the slaughter of animals', JC points out that we are so used to seeing cooking programmes on television, that the process of transforming raw food into cooked 'looks perfectly normal'; we have become habituated to this daily practice to the extent that it appears natural. 'But', JC continues,

> to someone unused to eating meat, the spectacle must be highly unnatural. For among the fruit and vegetables and oils and herbs and spices lie chunks of flesh hacked mere days ago from the body of some creature killed purposely and with violence. (Coetzee, *Diary of a Bad Year* 63)

The argument here follows Viktor Shklovsky's seminal essay, 'Art as Technique', first published in 1917. As 'perception becomes habitual, it becomes automatic', writes Shklovsky ('Art as Technique' 11), and the 'economy of mental effort' (Shklovsky, 'Art as Technique' 5) means that daily practices go on without any thoughtful engagement:

> And so life is reckoned as nothing. Habitualization devours works, clothes, furniture, one's wife, and the fear of war. 'If the whole complex lives of many people go on unconsciously, then such lives are as if they had never been'.[6] (Shklovsky, 'Art as Technique' 12)

Returning to the kitchen: 'It is important', writes JC, 'that not everyone should lose this way of seeing the kitchen – seeing it with what Viktor Shklovsky would call an estranged eye, as a place where, after the murders, the bodies of the dead are brought to be done up (disguised) before they are devoured' (*Diary of a Bad Year* 63). In Shklovsky, it is explicitly the function of *art*, rather than of analytic philosophy, to develop the ability to see with an 'estranged eye':

> And art exists that one may recover the sensation of life; it exists to make one feel things, to make the stone *stony*. The purpose of art is to impart the sensation of things as they are perceived and not as they are known. The technique of art is to make objects 'unfamiliar,' to make forms difficult, to increase the difficulty and length of perception because the process of aesthetic perception is an aesthetic end in itself and must be prolonged. (Shklovsky, 'Art as Technique' 12)

The process of perception may be an aesthetic end in itself, but in turn, this aesthetic end has the potential to form the basis of ethical practice in the sense that Coetzee understands ethical practice – that is to say, as a way of life that provides the means for *interrogating* our existence. To look at the world with an 'estranged eye' is to see things from a different perspective, which is perhaps one way of initiating that interrogation. Through Shklovsky's aesthetic of defamiliarization, and Coetzee's references to it, we begin to understand the ways in which Coetzee's Tanner Lectures, taking the form of a literary artwork, rather than a purely philosophical disquisition about animal rights, provoke a different kind of 'human thinking', in their *mode of saying*. It is in this context that it is important to take Coetzee's allusions and references to other works of literature just as seriously as his references to explicitly philosophical and/or theoretical material, even, perhaps *especially* when those literary works are dealing with questions conventionally recognized as 'philosophical'.[7] Further, this demands a different kind of receptiveness on the part of the reader. We get a sense of this in Thomas Hardy's preface to the first edition of *Jude the Obscure*, published in August 1895. Hardy's novel is a pivotal point of reference in *Disgrace* – not least in its profoundly ethical preoccupation with the question of human relations to other animals. And yet, despite its philosophical concerns, for Hardy, the construction of a rational, consistent and sustained argument is of secondary importance. As he writes in the preface,

> *Jude the Obscure* is simply an endeavour to give shape and coherence to a series of seemings, or personal impressions, the

questions of their consistency or their discordance, of their permanence or their transitoriness, being regarded as not of the first moment. (Hardy, *Jude the Obscure* 39–40)

In the following section I track Coetzee's references to *Jude the Obscure* in *Disgrace*, specifically within the context of Hardy's own conception of the ethical implications of Darwin's theory of evolution. As we shall see, Hardy and Coetzee, after Darwin, have different grounds upon which they base an appeal for human ethical relations to other animals. Nevertheless, the question as it emerges in both Hardy and Coetzee is given a *literary*, rather than a purely philosophical treatment. In Coetzee's approach to the matter at least part of the challenge is the question: how best to convey *through one's writing* the obligations and difficulties of human responses to animals?

III

The quotation in *Disgrace*, 'because we are too menny', comes from Hardy's novel, *Jude the Obscure*. It is the suicide note left by Jude's child, little Father Time, when he hangs himself and his two infant siblings. What else, apart from this quotation, one might ask, does Coetzee carry over from Hardy? The immediately attractive answer is to argue (as Michiel Heyns does), that Coetzee, like Hardy, metes out a malign destiny to his characters. In *Disgrace*, Heyns suggests, the 'predetermined pessimism' is a function of ' "perversity" as plot principle'; in other words, 'the predetermined negative consequences of any supposedly free act on the part of the protagonist' (Heyns, ' "Call no man happy": Perversity as Narrative Principle in *Disgrace*' 58). Certainly, Coetzee himself has written about Hardy within the context of the latter's attraction for Schopenhauer's pessimism. Whether Hardy had the philosopher specifically in mind or not, Coetzee observes with grim satisfaction, 'Schopenhauer's brand of pessimistic determinism was clearly congenial to him' (Coetzee, *Stranger Shores* 152). Yet despite the critical attention accorded to Schopenhauer's influence on Hardy, Hardy himself rarely mentions the philosopher,[8] and in one of these references, he asserts that his own 'pages show harmony of view with Darwin, Huxley, Spencer, Comte, Hume, Mill, and others, all of whom [he] used to read more than Schopenhauer' (Hardy, *The Literary Notebooks of Thomas Hardy*, vol. 1 335). It is Hardy's assertion of 'harmony of view' with Darwin, rather than with Schopenhauer, that is pertinent for the discussion to follow.

Of specific interest is Hardy's perception of the ethical implications of Darwin's *The Origin of Species*: on the basis of the new claim that the entire animal kingdom shares a common ancestor, Hardy asserts, our ethical obligations should be directed not only towards humans, but towards non-human animals as well. Hardy's notion of ethics thus departs from a Christian, anthropocentric position. Further still, Hardy's understanding of ethics is not tied to any institutional form of theology. Tess of the d'Urbervilles (to mention just one example), remonstrates with Alec because he has 'mixed in his dull brain two matters, theology and morals, which in the primitive days of mankind had been quite distinct' (Hardy, *Tess of the d'Urbervilles* 289). Concomitant with this non-anthropocentric ethic is Hardy's questioning of Western conceptions concerning human identity, and it is this questioning that Coetzee takes up in *Disgrace*. Coetzee extends Hardy's exploration of the subject's relatedness to other sentient beings within the context of a natural world indifferent to the individual's plight or to contingent ethico-cultural values – but with this difference. For Hardy biological kinship in itself grounds ethics, but Coetzee constructs a searing imaginative enquiry into the validity and dangerous consequences of conflating biology and ethics, even in the instant that his fiction constitutes an appeal against cruelty to fellow-creatures.

The quotation from Hardy's novel in *Disgrace* 'implicitly links the killing of dogs and the killing of children', as Michiel Heyns points out (Heyns, ' "Call no man happy": Perversity as Narrative Principle in *Disgrace*' 61). What interests me here is that the linking of human and animal deaths in terms of our ethical responses to both is something that we already find in *Hardy* – thanks to the latter's reading of and admiration for Darwin: 'In the present state of affairs', wrote Hardy to his friend, Edward Clodd,

> there would appear to be no logical reason why the smaller children, say, of overcrowded families, should not be used for sporting purposes. Darwin has revealed that there would be no difference in principle; moreover, these children would often escape lives

intrinsically less happy than those of wild birds and other animals. (Hardy, *The Life of Thomas Hardy* 321–2)

In the most provocative way, Hardy is making an appeal for an ethical response to *all* living creatures – an appeal which he considered crucial to his literary endeavour. 'What are my books', Hardy asked, 'but one long plea against "man's inhumanity to man" – to woman – and to the lower animals?' (Jacobus, 'Sue the Obscure' 308). Hardy identifies his project as a 'plea' and not as a formal philosophical argument; yet it was in Darwin – a natural scientist rather than a philosopher himself – that Hardy would find an elaborate a justification for his views on ethics. In the conclusion of *The Origin of Species*, Darwin obliquely draws attention to the ethical implications of his own findings. He repeatedly stresses the significance of the interconnectedness of all creatures through the process of natural selection, to the extent that even seemingly discrete species are linked to other life forms as 'varieties', in that they share a history of communal descent. At the same time, Darwin draws attention to the contingency of a human taxonomy marking the boundaries between questionably discrete species:

> On the view that species are only strongly marked and permanent varieties, and that each species first existed as a variety, we can see why it is that no line of demarcation can be drawn between species, commonly supposed to have been produced by special acts of creation, and varieties which are acknowledged to have been produced by secondary laws. (Darwin, *The Origin of Species* 354)

The naming of individual species is nothing less than a *genealogy* – in the most literal and physical sense possible, as Darwin himself points out: 'Our classifications will come to be, as far as they can be so made, genealogies; and will then truly give what may be called the plan of creation' (Darwin, *The Origin of Species* 366). Further, we begin to trace the genealogical pattern in the physical contiguities of supposedly very different life forms:

> The real affinities of all organic beings are due to inheritance or community of descent. The Natural System is a genealogical arrangement, in which we have to discover the lines of descent by

the most permanent characters, however slight their vital importance may be.

The framework of bones being the same in the hand of a man,
wing of a bat, fin of the porpoise, and leg of the horse, the same
number of vertebrae forming the neck of the giraffe and of the
elephant, and innumerable other such facts, at once explain themselves on the theory of descent with slow and slight successive
modifications. (Darwin, *The Origin of Species* 360–1)

For Darwin the question of the interconnectedness of life forms is
decidedly one of biological fact, and any ethical consequences are
implied, rather than overtly stated, but for Hardy, the theory of community of descent has implications for the scope of our ethical
practices. In fact, Hardy considered the awareness of an ethical obligation towards fellow-beings (whether human or not) to be the most
important consequence of Darwin's work. In a letter to the
Humanitarian League, dated 10 April 1910, Hardy wrote,

Few people seem to perceive fully as yet that the most far-reaching
consequence of the establishment of the common origin of all
species is ethical; that it logically involved a readjustment of altruistic morals by enlarging as a *necessity of rightness* the application
of what has been called 'The Golden Rule' beyond the area of
mere mankind to that of the whole animal kingdom. Possibly
Darwin himself did not wholly perceive it, though he alluded to
it. (Hardy, *The Life of Thomas Hardy* 349)

In another letter, Hardy insists that the discovery that 'all organic
creatures are of one family' extends ethical obligations beyond
humanity to 'the whole conscious world collectively' (*The Life of
Thomas Hardy* 346).

Of seminal importance is that man and non-human animals *alike*
are part of Darwin's 'Natural System', where the 'genealogical arrangement' is to be understood in a literal, rather than a metaphorical
way. Yet at a more radical level – even before subtle affinities between
different life forms come to light – birth, procreation and death are
physical aspects of biological existence, which (as Bev Shaw in
Disgrace would be quick to point out) humans share with animals.
Jude Fawley, in Hardy's novel, has momentary flashes of this insight,

an idea of himself *in relation* to other living creatures: their hunger, their impulse to procreate and their mortality are things that he recognizes in his own existence. Thus, for example (at the peril of a beating, a sacking and the wrath of Aunt Drusilla), Jude decides to let the rooks feast on Farmer Troutham's newly planted seeds:

> They stayed and ate, inky spots on the nut-brown soil, and Jude enjoyed their appetite. A magic thread of fellow-feeling united his own life with theirs. Puny and sorry as those lives were, they much resembled his own. (Hardy, *Jude the Obscure* 54)[9]

David Lurie, Coetzee's fictional character in *Disgrace*, shares sentiments comparable to those of Hardy's Jude Fawley. The plight of the slaughter-sheep in *Disgrace* becomes insufferable and Lurie tugs them over to the abundant grass at the damside (Coetzee, *Disgrace* 123). The parallel with Jude is taken further, not least because Coetzee, like Hardy, makes use of syntactic structures where the attribution of subjective agency becomes complicated:

> A bond seems to have come into existence between himself and the two Persians, he does not know how [...] suddenly and without reason, their lot has become important to him.
> He stands before them, under the sun, waiting for the buzz in his mind to settle, waiting for a sign. (Coetzee, *Disgrace* 126)

Of particular interest are these three parallel sentences:

1. A magic thread of fellow-feeling united his own life with theirs (Hardy);
2. A bond seems to have come into existence between himself and the two Persians (Coetzee);[10]
3. their lot has become important to him (Coetzee),

specifically in relation to the question of agency. In his essay, 'The Rhetoric of the Passive in English', Coetzee sets up a linguistic question (again, asked from the perspective of the writer):

> my concern here will be with the rhetorical potential of the passive [...] I start with the question: In the hands of writers who use

the passive in a complex and systematic way, what can it be made to do? (Coetzee, *Doubling the Point* 159)

It is a question like this one that I think should be more frequently asked of Coetzee; in a sense this is what I have done in the previous three chapters – asking what person and voice can be made to do. In the discussion to follow I pay particular attention to the active/passive constructions of the verb in relation to the question of agency. The use of the active or passive voice has an impact on the syntactic sequencing of the sentence, and hence on the position of the subject of the sentence. Since the syntactic subject is not that easily disaggregated from the idea of a semantic subject, the use of the active or passive voice has repercussions for our understanding of the importance we attach to subjective agency in the sentence. My question here is this: in the hands of the writer who uses the agentless sentence in a complex and systematic way, what can it be made to do? More specifically still, I am interested in the way in which Coetzee uses agentless sentences when his human characters experience some kind of ethical tie to other creatures. Characters such as David Lurie and Elizabeth Costello often find themselves overwhelmed by their exposure to animal suffering – to the extent that they are not able to grasp, or address in any rational way, what it is that confronts them. They are thrown off the supposed control centre of reasoning human agency. After helping Bev Shaw to euthanize dogs at the animal clinic, Lurie, driving home in Lucy's kombi one Sunday afternoon,

> actually has to stop at the roadside to recover himself. Tears flow down his face that he cannot stop; his hands shake.
> He does not understand what is happening to him [...]
> His whole being is gripped by what happens in the theatre. (Coetzee, *Disgrace* 143)[11]

This sense of 'being gripped', of 'being overwhelmed' (*Doubling the Point* 248), of being unable to understand or control with logical thought the tide of feeling for the suffering of a fellow-mortal is underscored by both Hardy and Coetzee in the syntactic structures of their sentences – such as the ones I have numbered and cited above. The usual syntactic structure of sentences in English is Subject,

Verb, Object. This is the structure of sentence 1 from *Jude the Obscure* ('A magic thread of fellow-feeling united his own life with theirs') – but what makes the sentence such a dizzying one is this: the usual S-V-O structure, as Coetzee points out in his essay on Newton, 'has come to be associated with a certain meaning: it is iconic both of time order and of causal order' (Coetzee, *Doubling the Point* 190), and further still, '[t]hough it is possible to produce purely syntactic, non-semantic definitions of subjecthood (case marking in Latin, position to the left of the verb phrase in underlying structure in English), the link between syntactic subjecthood and semantic agency is not easily broken' (Coetzee, *Doubling the Point* 189). In 1, the subject of the sentence is 'a magic thread of fellow-feeling', but (on a level of semantics now) thoughts and feelings are usually the *object* of a conscious, subjective agent – that is to say, the agent of the feeling is the subject who 'has' the feelings. But Hardy's sentence is agentless in this respect; Jude's life is united to that of the rooks *by the fellow-feeling*. As Raj Mesthrie explained in conversation,[12] the reflexive 'his own' and the reciprocal 'his ... with theirs' have the effect of blurring agentivity even further, which, in turn, insists on the realization that 'fellow-feeling' is a non-subject (it is certainly not an agent). Thus even while the sentence follows a syntactic S-V-O structure (making it easy to assume that it is written in the active voice), in its blurring of subjective agency, the *feel* of the sentence is more that of the middle voice – of experiencing things – rather than of a subjective agent acting on a patient.

In sentence 2 ('A bond seems to have come into existence between himself and the two Persians'), the word 'seems' creates what linguists would say is an 'empty subject' or 'dummy subject'[13]: 'the man seems sick' can be analysed as '— seems (that) the man is sick'. In other words, there is no subject in the main clause, but English creates an empty or 'dummy' subject, like 'it' or 'there', as in 'it is raining' or (to take some examples from *Disgrace*) 'There is a moment of utter stillness' and 'There may be things to learn' (*Disgrace*, 218).[14] Again, 2 is not a straightforward S-V-O sentence in the active voice; the assumption of subjective agency is not guaranteed, and it also has the feel of the middle voice. Verbs like 'to become', and 'to be' are copular or linking verbs. In sentence 3 ('their lot has become important to him'), there is again no agent, making for a semantics very similar to that of 1 and 2. The 'to him' is in the dative case (it is an indirect object), which is to say, it is written neither in the active voice (he deemed their lot important) nor in the passive voice (their lot affected him). This syntactic ambiguity underwrites the semantic context in which the sentences occur. In the narrative comments about the sensation Lurie undergoes ('he does not know how' and 'suddenly and without reason'), Coetzee provides further challenges to the more usually presumed priority of conscious agency and rational thinking in the working through and adopting of an ethical response to other animals.

The cumulative effect of syntactic structures in sentences such as the ones I have been discussing here is to emphasize both Jude Fawley's and David Lurie's inability to account, in a ratiocinative way, for their altruistic responses to their fellow-creatures, which, in turn, reminds me of Michael K's question, 'Is that how morals come, unbidden, in the course of events, when you least expect them?' (Coetzee, *Life & Times of Michael K* 249). Lurie tries to make sense of his mourning the deaths of creatures who themselves are oblivious to the concept of mourning, but '[l]ooking into his heart, he can find only a vague sadness' (Coetzee, *Disgrace* 127). As he casts a jaundiced eye over the mutton chops swimming in the gravy on his plate, he resolves to ask forgiveness (131). Similarly, when Jude finds himself in the position of having to slaughter Arabella's pig, he feels

> dissatisfied with himself as a man at what he had done, though aware of his lack of common-sense, and that the deed would have amounted to the same thing if carried out by deputy. The white snow, stained with the blood of his fellow-mortal, wore an illogical look to him as a lover of justice, not to say a Christian; but he could not see how the matter was to be mended. No doubt he was, as his wife had called him, a tender-hearted fool. (Hardy, *Jude the Obscure* 111–12)

Both Jude and Lurie recognize that their responses to animals will not be valued in societal terms, and that their individual sentiments are not enough to change generally accepted human interactions with animals. Jude quite concedes that he is regarded a 'tender-hearted fool' and acknowledges that his attitude to this one creature will do nothing to alleviate his overwhelming sense of the human degradation that takes place every day in the treatment of animals. As JC of *Diary of a Bad Year* observes,

> It is too much to expect that a single fifteen-minute television programme should have a lasting effect on the conduct of the cattle trade. It would be ludicrous to expect hardened Egyptian abattoir workers to single out cattle from Australia for special, gentler treatment during their last hour on earth. And indeed common sense is on the workers' side. If an animal is going to have its throat cut, does it really matter that it has its leg tendons cut too? (Coetzee, *Diary of a Bad Year* 65)

With similar sentiments to those of Jude in Hardy's novel, David Lurie of *Disgrace* considers buying the sheep from Petrus so that they need not be slaughtered – but to what end? 'When did a sheep last die of old age?' Lurie asks (123). Further, Lurie's saving the honour of dog corpses, in worldly terms, is by his own admission 'stupid, daft, wrongheaded' (*Disgrace* 146).

Nevertheless, in both Hardy and Coetzee we get a strong sense that the inability to rationalize a response to fellow-creatures in terms set by social consensus, or even reasoned argument, does not *in itself* necessitate the view that that response should be dismissed. 'Common sense' may well be on the side of the abattoir workers in Egypt, but that does not vindicate, in ethical terms, the hacking of an animal's tendons to make it easier to control on its way to the slaughterhouse. Lurie recognizes that other species do not have morals or an appreciation of ethics in the way that humans do; he takes care of the dead dogs for no other reason than for 'his idea of the world, a world in which men do not use shovels to beat corpses into a more convenient shape for processing' (Coetzee, *Disgrace* 146). Jude's and Lurie's responses to other animals expose a limit – and perhaps the limitations – of rational thinking when it comes to responding with justice to the suffering of the other. In both Hardy and Coetzee, the syntax and other verbal constructions related to the passive voice challenge the priority usually accorded to rational human thought in the working-through of an ethical response to other animals.

IV

Jude's and Lurie's responses to non-human animals are out of joint
with the societal practices of their respective times, but both novels
suggest that it is the protagonist who stands the higher moral ground.
It is within the context of Jude's regard for his fellow-mortals, for
instance, that his exclusion from the University of Christminster, on
the basis of his working-class background, strikes the reader as
unutterably bigoted, especially when Jude writes, *with his stone-
mason's chalk*, a verse from the book of Job on the wall of the college
from which he is barred entry:

> 'I have understanding as well as you; I am not inferior to you: yea,
> who knoweth not such things as these' Job xii. 3. (Hardy, *Jude the
> Obscure* 169)

Likewise, Lurie's experiences on the farm, and his disinterested
care for the dead dogs at Bev Shaw's clinic, render his own social
circle vacuous and small-minded. I am thinking, for example, of
Rosalind's tirade when she meets Lurie in a Claremont coffee shop:

> And now look at you. You have thrown away your life, and for
> what? [...] You have lost your job, your name is mud, your friends
> avoid you, you hide out in Torrance Road like a tortoise afraid to
> stick its neck out of its shell. People who aren't good enough to tie
> your shoelaces make jokes about you. Your shirt isn't ironed, God
> know[s] who gave you that haircut. (Coetzee, *Disgrace* 189)

It is perhaps at this point that we are most attracted to the version of
responsibility carried out (rather than articulated) by Bev Shaw, and
that we begin to make sense of Lucy's handing over of the title deeds
to Petrus. There is something to be said for turning one's back on
the 'scenes from Western life' as they are portrayed in the novel and
for getting 'closer to the ground' (Coetzee, *Disgrace* 210). This is the
phrase that Bev Shaw uses to describe Lucy, and indeed, Lucy seems
to embody a response divested of cultural baggage. She recognizes,
for example, the disjunction between Western notions of land
ownership, and her very physical interaction with the soil: 'Stop
calling it *the farm*, David', she says, 'This is not a farm, it's just a

piece of land where I grow things' (Coetzee, *Disgrace* 200). Lucy's attitude to 'possession' of the land here reminds us of that of Michael K as he sets up his shelter on the Visagies' farm, fully cognizant of his individual transience against the illimitable reaches of geological time and space of the Karoo landscape:

> The worst mistake, he told himself, would be to try to found a new house, a rival line, on his small beginnings out at the dam. Even his tools should be of wood and leather and gut, materials the insects would eat when one day he no longer needed them. (Coetzee, *Life & Times of Michael K* 142–3)

From Lucy's point of view, handing over the title deeds to Petrus is just another exercise in 'abstraction' (Coetzee, *Disgrace* 112) – it will not change what she does with water, earth and living things. Lurie is at first appalled at the prospect of his daughter becoming a peasant, a *bywoner*, a tenant on Petrus' land, but there is an overriding sense in Coetzee that an ownership of the land itself is at best a kind of tenancy in a larger scheme of things. I have in mind specific references to the farm in *Boyhood*:

> in his secret heart he knows what the farm in its way knows too: that Voëlfontein belongs to no one. The farm is greater than any of them. The farm exists from eternity to eternity. When they are all dead, when even the farmhouse has fallen into ruin like the kraals on the hillside, the farm will still be here. (Coetzee, *Boyhood* 96)

Michael K, like Coetzee, reflects upon his transitory passing through the landscape:

> He thought of himself not as something heavy that left tracks behind it, but if anything as a speck upon the surface of an earth too deeply asleep to notice the scratch of ant-feet, the rasp of butterfly teeth, the tumbling of dust. (Coetzee, *Life & Times of Michael K* 133)

It is within the context of 'passing through' that Lurie's arrival on Lucy's farm *as a visitor* at the novel's close is significant.[15] Lucy offers

Lurie tea 'as if he were a visitor. Good. Visitorship, visitation: a new footing, a new start' (Coetzee, *Disgrace* 218). This visit is implicitly linked to the movements of migratory birds across the landscape, and in its iteration of the word 'speck' the following passage from *Disgrace* recalls the extract I have just cited from *Michael K*:

> From the last hillcrest the farm opens out before him [...] the old dam on which he can make out specks that must be the ducks and larger specks that must be the wild geese, Lucy's visitors from afar. (Coetzee, *Disgrace* 216)

If, on the one hand, human social life seems far removed from the rest of the sentient world, Coetzee's novels also offer a sustained vision of humanity's shared – and parallel – existence with other animals. David Attwell argues for a recovery of 'value' at *this* 'horizon of consciousness' – that of the 'simply ontological', of 'being', of 'ontology shorn of system' (Attwell, 'Race in *Disgrace*' 339–40). It is through the composition of his opera that Lurie hopes to resonate a sound that cuts across all cultural divides, that expresses something common to all forms of animal existence, both human and other animals. On the one hand it 'would have been nice to be returned triumphant to society as the author of an eccentric little chamber opera', but at best Lurie hopes 'that somewhere from amidst the welter of sound there will dart up, like a bird, a single authentic note of immortal longing' (Coetzee, *Disgrace* 214). Teresa, in Lurie's opera, may, in this sense, be 'the last one left who can save him'. It is she who 'has immortal longings, and sings her longings. She will not be dead' (*Disgrace* 209). This note of immortal longing is visceral in its effect, resonating a commonality of being in its sheer physicality: 'A woman in love, wallowing in love; a cat on a roof, howling; complex proteins swirling in the blood, distending the sexual organs, making the palms sweat and voice thicken as the soul hurls its longings to the skies' (*Disgrace* 185). The single note, for a fleeting moment, seems on the brink of tapping into a unity of all physical existence:

> When he strums the strings, the dog sits up, cocks its head, listens. When he hums Teresa's line, and the humming begins to swell with feeling (it is as though his larynx thickens: he can feel the hammer of blood in his throat), the dog smacks its lips

and seems on the point of singing too, or howling. (Coetzee, *Disgrace* 215)

In the physical cry of her longing, Teresa is 'past honour' (209), and dogs, too, know nothing of 'honour and dishonour' (146). Clearly Attwell's argument for the recovery of value at the level of 'the fact of a biological existence' (Attwell, 'Race in *Disgrace*' 339) has its attractions. It is in this that Attwell finds what he calls 'Coetzee's ethical turn' – 'a consciousness of what it means to be alive, sharing the precariousness of creation's biological energy' (Attwell, 'Race in *Disgrace*' 339). Attwell reads this emphasis on 'being', 'ontology', as being 'inimical to philosophy' (Attwell, 'Race in *Disgrace*' 340). This seems to me a continuation of Hardy's reading of an ethics that he takes to be intrinsic to Darwin's theory, namely, that the idea of a shared biological existence *itself* prescribes an ethical relation to fellow-creatures. But what I would like to suggest now is that the role of culture or 'system' or 'philosophy', cannot be dismissed quite as easily as Attwell implies, even in the instant that we may feel inclined to accept his insights about Coetzee's ethics. The vexed question of the relation between a physical 'biological energy' and a culturally mediated philosophical ethics requires further discussion.

For Thomas Hardy, a biological kinship with other creatures seems ground enough for human ethical obligations towards them. Yet, like Coetzee in his doctoral thesis on Beckett, we might ask (when presented with the percentage number indicating the genetic proximity of humans to other species, for example): 'What do the figures tell us?, and specifically, What do the measures measure?' (*The English Fiction of Samuel Beckett* 159).[16] In Jonathan Marks' terms, 'The extent to which our DNA resembles an ape's predicts nothing about our general similarity to apes, much less about any moral or political consequences arising from it' and 'Sameness/otherness is a philosophical paradox that is resolved by argument, not by data' (Marks, *What It Means to Be 98% Chimpanzee* 5 and 22).

The recognition and appreciation of the ethical implications of one's biological connectedness to other existents, is dependent upon a sophisticated, if contingent, cultural code. This is what the philosopher, O'Hearne, points out to Elizabeth Costello in *The Lives of Animals*: 'The notion that we have an obligation to animals themselves to treat them compassionately [...] is very recent, very Western, and even very Anglo-Saxon' (Coetzee, *The Lives of Animals* 60). A related idea comes through in Coetzee's address read at the opening of the Voiceless art exhibition; in the closing paragraphs, he highlights the paradox of distance and proximity to other creatures by stressing the *humanity* of animal rights groups like Voiceless, and the necessity of a philosophical approach and a cultural practice that is true to the exercising of that humanity with regard to other species:

> This enterprise is a curious one in one respect: that the fellow beings on whose behalf we are acting are unaware of what we are up to and, if we succeed, are unlikely to thank us. There is even a sense in which they do not know what is wrong. They do certainly not know what is wrong in the same way that we know what is wrong [...] So, even though we may feel very close to our fellow creatures as we act for them, this remains a human enterprise from beginning to end. (Coetzee, *Voiceless: I Feel Therefore I Am* 2)

Humans have an advantage over other creatures in their capacity for abstract thought, Coetzee goes on to say. While this capacity may distance us from other animals, it is also our obligation to *use* these 'intellectual energies' in disciplines such as ethics, philosophy of mind and jurisprudence, in conjunction with the 'practical energies' of organizations like Voiceless, in the hope of effecting change in the way we treat animals.

In the same moment that he mentions his 'single authentic note of immortal longing', that might connect him to all sentient beings, Lurie questions whether he will be able to recognize or even hear that single note himself. He decides to 'leave that to the scholars of the future, if there are still scholars by then' (Coetzee, *Disgrace* 214). The process of recognizing and *attributing value* to any phenomenon, even of the most physical kind, is culturally bound, and cultures themselves are ephemeral.

This is something that Kafka reiterates, not least in his short story, 'Investigations of a Dog' (told by a first-person canine narrator), which I take to be an important intertext in *Disgrace*. In *Disgrace*, dogs' urine (a biological fact of canine existence) is given a complex range of meanings, one of which has negative connotations, linked as it is in Lurie's mind to Lucy's rape. By contrast, in Kafka's short story, dogs' urine, far from having negative connotations, or from being presented as a neutral biological fact, is granted the most elaborate and *positive* ethical resonances. 'Water the ground as much as you can', the young narrator's mother tells him as she sends him out into the world,

> the earth needs our water to nourish it and only at that price provides us with our food, the emergence of which, however, and this should not be forgotten, can also be hastened by certain spells, songs and ritual movements. (Kafka, 'Investigations of a Dog' 95)

Although he does not mention this short story, Attwell is surely right when he speaks of Kafka's 'dignifying presence' (Attwell, 'Race in *Disgrace*' 340) – and a further question in Kafka arises: who are 'we' to presume that other species have social agreements any less subtle and intricate than our own? But the point is this: biological facts *in themselves* are meaningless. They may gain a certain ethical resonance if we accord a value to them, and the accordance of these values is dependent upon a contingent philosophical and cultural system.

V

It is the *contingency* of value systems that Coetzee emphasizes throughout his fiction – but with this difficult twist: the contingency of one's set of beliefs or cultural practices in itself is not reason enough to dismiss it. The unrelenting playing-out of this idea in *Disgrace* surely has much to do with the heightened sense of unease one experiences in reading the novel.

First, let us return to the scene where, for a fleeting moment, it seems possible that some sort of universal communion could be effected through the opera Lurie is composing, as he plinks the theme tunes out on a toy banjo, and the dog responds to the sounds. Coetzee's choice of a *banjo* as David Lurie's musical instrument gives me pause, not least when I think of Rudyard Kipling's poem of 1894, 'The Song of the Banjo', with its lines,

> I'm the Prophet of the Utterly Absurd,
> Of the Patently Impossible and Vain –
> [...]
> I – the war-drum of the White Man round the world!

Perhaps Kipling's 'The Song of the Banjo' is the source of inspiration for the title of Coetzee's collection of essays, *Stranger Shores*. Kipling's poem:

> In desire of many marvels over sea,
> Where the new-raised tropic city sweats and roars,
> I have sailed with Young Ulysses from the quay
> Till the anchor rumbled down on stranger shores.
> (Kipling, 'The Song of the Banjo' lines 37–40)

In Bev Shaw's backyard one morning, playing the banjo, and composing and singing snatches from the lines he will give to Teresa Guiccioli in his opera, Lurie glances up to see three little boys staring at him over the wall. When Lurie stands up,

> the boys drop down and scamper off whooping with excitement. What a tale to tell back home: a mad old man who sits among the dogs singing to himself!
> Mad indeed. How can he ever explain, to them, to their parents, to D Village, what Teresa and her lover have done to deserve being brought back to this world? (Coetzee, *Disgrace* 212)

Further, one might ask, what colonial history does Lurie, with his European Romanticism and his banjo, inevitably call up as he tinkles away in the region that was once the Eastern frontier of the Cape Colony? The five-string banjo was first played by African-American slaves, and was popularized in the 1830s in American minstrel shows, most notably by the white minstrel singer, Joel Walker Sweeney. Thus, for Jack Chernos, 'no instrument has a history as tied to racism and prejudice as the banjo' (Chernos, 'The Five-String Banjo: A Most Controversial of Instruments'). In South Africa the banjo calls up associations of 'Tweede Nuwe Jaar', the annual Minstrel Carnival which takes place on the second of January in Cape Town and commemorates the emancipation of slaves in the Cape Colony. This socio-historical aside may well be extraneous to what is explicit in the text of *Disgrace*, but I am mindful of Coetzee's discussion about the translation of his fiction. 'Are my books easy or hard to translate?' he asks,

> Sentence by sentence, my prose is generally lucid, in the sense that the syntactic relations among words, and the logical force of

constructions, are as clear as I can make them. On the other hand, I sometimes use words with the full freight of their history behind them, and that freight is not easily carried across to another language. My English does not happen to be embedded in any particular sociolinguistic landscape, which relieves the translator of one vexatious burden; on the other hand, I do tend to be allusive, and not always to signal the presence of allusion. (Coetzee, 'Roads to Translation' 143)

The 'song of the banjo' is surely the countervoice that Coetzee raises here, posed as the means of attaining the single, ideal transcendent note that Lurie hopes for. Recent philosophical engagements with Coetzee's work, in their focus on the nexus of the limits of thought, literary and philosophical representation, and human relations to other animals, pay almost exclusive attention to *Elizabeth Costello*, with an even more specific interest in the two chapters that constitute *The Lives of Animals*. But these philosophical concerns (presented in universal terms) gain a peculiar urgency in *Disgrace*, where questions of conceptual systems, of modes of representation, of the characters' ethical obligations, are inextricably meshed within a specific historical time and place. This is reiterated throughout the novel (as we shall see in subsequent chapters) – to the extent that even the question of relations to other animals cannot be neatly sealed off from South Africa's human socio-political preoccupations. 'There is no funding any longer', says Lucy about Bev Shaw's animal clinic, 'On the list of the nation's priorities, animals come nowhere' (*Disgrace* 73).

It is precisely the contingency of his Western cultural values that Lurie has to confront – and question, on his daughter's smallholding in the Eastern Cape. At the outset of the novel he is presented as a veritable repository of European Romanticism. He teaches Romantic poetry at the Cape Technical University; he interprets his relationship with Soraya as a Baudelairean experience of *'luxe et volupté'* (the reference is to Baudelaire's poem, 'L'Invitation au Voyage' – an invitation to travel to the Netherlands (*Disgrace* 1));[17] and Lurie is composing an opera: *Byron in Italy*. His arrival on Lucy's farm, and his fraught relations to the Xhosa-speaking Petrus, on the one hand seem to be a playing out of a colonial history 'come full circle' (*Disgrace* 175).

Nevertheless, the contingency and ephemerality of Lurie's values – and the further fact that his ethical paradigm is supervenient upon a vexed colonial history – does not in itself necessitate the view that this paradigm is absolutely without worth, or that it should be relinquished. Lurie's cultural values are under threat; he is called upon to question them *because* they are relative. If these values were absolute, everyone would naturally subscribe to them, without question or contestation, but Lurie's experiences on his daughter's smallholding lead him to interrogate his existence. The means he has to do this is *with reference to* the very culture that he is led to question. In his last visit to Lucy, Lurie contemplates his future role as grandparent. He acknowledges that he is inescapably part of a transtemporal 'line of existences', irrespective of his cultural and intellectual affiliations. It is a line in which his share, his gift, will become gradually less and less 'till it may as well be forgotten' (*Disgrace* 217). As Breyten Breytenbach points out in *Dog Heart*: 'We are painted in the colours of disappearance here... We are only visiting... It must die away' (Breytenbach, *Dog Heart: A Memoir* 145, cited in Coetzee, *Stranger Shores* 313). Nevertheless, in full recognition of the evanescence and contingency of his cultural moment, Lurie turns to Victor Hugo, the French Romantic 'poet of grandfatherhood' in the expectation that '[t]here may be things to learn' (*Disgrace* 218). Hugo wrote a series of poems collected under the title, *L'Art d'être Grandpère* (*The Art of Being a Grandfather*), but the poem I refer to here appears in *Les Feuilles D'Automne* (*Autumn Leaves*).[18] In Hugo's poem, 'Lorsque l'Enfant Paraît', the physical presence of a young child in the family (Hugo stresses the child's innocence and joy) disarms, and dissolves into smiles, all grave adult talk of politics, of God, and even of poets (I am mindful here of Coetzee's comment in his Voiceless exhibition address: 'children provide the brightest hope. Children have tender hearts, that is to say, children have hearts that have not yet been hardened by years of cruel and unnatural battering' (Coetzee, *Voiceless: I Feel Therefore I Am* 2)). Perhaps it is the following verse from Hugo's poem that resonates through David Lurie's reflections,

> Quelquefois nous parlons, en remuant la flamme,
> De patrie et de Dieu, des poëtes, de l'âme
> Qui s'élève en priant;

L'enfant paraît, adieu le ciel et la patrie
Et les poëtes saints! La grave causerie
    S'arrête en souriant.

(Sometimes we speak, while stoking the fire,
Of homeland and of God, of poets, of the soul
    Which rises, praying;
The child appears, farewell heaven and homeland
And saintly poets! Solemn talk
    Stops, smiling.)

(my translation)

Lurie, via Hugo, and also through the music he is composing on a toy banjo, reconsiders his own identity in relation to the transtemporal links he bears to his fellow-mortals. His moral imagination undergoes an expansion[19] through his recourse to a European culture that is, at the same time, complicit in a violent history of colonialism.

VI

I return, finally, to Hardy's ethical reading of Darwin. Darwin attributes value to the insight that the affinities of life forms can be traced through links which cut across time. He calls it a 'grand fact' which has an edifying effect on man's altered view of his place in a vast and complex scheme of things. The recognition that each individual carries traces of an ancient history, for Darwin, alters one's response to that individual. 'When I view all beings not as special creations', writes Darwin, 'but as the lineal descendants of some few beings which lived long before the first bed of the Silurian system was deposited, they seem to me to become ennobled' (Darwin, *The Origin of Species* 368). Each individual, in Darwin's eyes, is present as a trace of the past – there is a curious sense of the transtemporality of the individual life as a carrier of something larger than a conventional Western notion of a self-contained rational human identity allows. A response which acknowledges the individual life (whether human or animal) as an instant in a larger sequence of existence, and accords a value to that acknowledgement, demands at once an ethical understanding of the individual as intrinsically *relational* both temporally and spatially. David Lurie's reflections lead to the thought that to respond to the other, and even to oneself, is to respond to much more than just one supposedly autonomous living entity. The corollary to this is that Lurie's own death will not bring with it the termination of his gift to a long line of existences (as he sees it), and hence his own death is not as absolute, perhaps not as 'tragic' as it might be in a more conventional sense.

The ending of *Disgrace* is, at the very least, ambivalent. It is clear that Lucy's child will be cared for and loved; and Lurie's relationship to his daughter and to his future grandchild seems to represent 'a new footing, a new start' (*Disgrace* 218) for something which extends far beyond the immediate family. Nevertheless, the new footing comes about only after a series of unforgettably violent physical acts.

It is not always clear in Darwin whether the evolutionary process by means of natural selection is purely random, or whether it has a teleological orientation towards 'improvement' and ultimately 'perfection'. In several instances, it seems that Darwin's argument rests on the latter understanding, where 'perfection' is not specified as being relative to the surrounding conditions. Thus, for example, in the penultimate paragraph of *The Origin of Species*, Darwin writes, 'as natural selection works solely by and for the good of each being, all corporeal and mental endowments will tend to progress towards perfection' (*The Origin of Species* 368). Hardy, however, is consistently aware of the fact that any notion of 'perfection' is relative, in that it is determined by adaptability to the environment. In his literary notebook, he copied the following passage from Theodore Watts:

> *Science tells us that*, in the struggle for life, the surviving organism is not necessarily that which is absolutely the best in an ideal sense, though it must be that which is most in harmony with surrounding conditions. (Hardy, *The Literary Notebooks of Thomas Hardy*, vol. 1 40)

On this view of the evolutionary process, change is not teleological; neither is it synonymous with progress. The survival of one individual, or group, or species often comes about at the expense of another, and competition for limited resources is more aggressive in a discriminatory society where certain members have nothing to lose. This is the scene played out in *Disgrace*, not only in terms of

UNIVERSITY OF WINCHESTER
LIBRARY

human relations to the dogs ('The trouble is, there are just too many of them [...] Too many by our standards, not by theirs. (*Disgrace* 85)), but also in terms of human relations to each other: 'When I am added in', says Lurie to Bev Shaw about the difficulty he has relating to Lucy and Petrus 'we become too many. Too many in too small a space. Like spiders in a bottle' (*Disgrace* 209). Competition for limited resources leads to a confrontation of conflicting cultural value systems, but conflict arises because at the most basic level, vested interests are the *same*: that is to say, the interest in survival (hence the importance of territory), and the instinct to ensure the continuance of one's line. Evolutionary change, whether purely biological or social, proceeds beyond the reach of sentiment, heedless of any cultural perception of ethical responsibility. 'Too many people, too few things', Lurie observes wryly, and in the ensuing struggle, any finer sentiments of 'pity and terror are irrelevant' (*Disgrace* 98). Lucy survives, despite the physical violation of her sophisticated, culturally based conception of self. But in a novel which questions the ability to step meaningfully outside of culture (even in the recognition of the contingency of that culture, and a violent history not easily dissociated from it), then perhaps at best we can say that Lucy survives. In Bev Shaw's word, she is 'adaptable' (*Disgrace* 210).

5
Names

When death cuts all other links, there remains still the name.

(*The Master of Petersburg*)

I

In an interview with J.M. Coetzee in 1983, Tony Morphet comments on the setting of *Life & Times of Michael K*: 'The location of the story is very highly specified. Cape Town – Stellenbosch – Prince Albert – somewhere between 1985–1990' (Coetzee and Morphet, 'Two Interviews with J.M. Coetzee 455). A similar observation might be made of later novels such as *Age of Iron* and *Disgrace*, where Coetzee's literary landscapes are evoked with equally striking particularity. The migrations of the fictional characters are meticulously tracked in the recognizable co-ordinates of named towns, roads, and landmarks of South Africa's Cape regions: Salem, Grahamstown, Port Elizabeth, Donkin Square, Guguletu, Buitenkant Street, Schoonder Street, Rondebosch Common, Signal Hill, Touws River, the Outeniqua Mountains... Tony Morphet, in his interview with Coetzee, suggests that the use of familiar place-names brings *Michael K* 'very close to us' (by 'us' he means a South African readership), and Morphet asks whether Coetzee is 'looking for a more direct and immediate conversation with South African readers' (Coetzee and Morphet 455). It is tempting to assume immediate reference to – and direct conversation about – the real world when a writer makes use of recognizable names,[1] and yet Coetzee's novels – arguably this includes *Boyhood*

133

and *Youth* – are works of fiction. In this chapter fiction clashes with history in the name, and, in conjunction with the following chapter, 'Etymologies', my discussion extends one of the lines of enquiry intimated in the previous chapter, that is to say, an exploration of the topographic and socio-historical specificity of much of Coetzee's oeuvre.

For the protagonist of *Youth*, South African place-names have an almost talismanic quality: sitting in the British Museum, the young John is deeply affected by thoughts of the country of his birth when he reads the South African place-names in the early travel writings of the likes of Barrow and Burchell:

> It gives him an eerie feeling to sit in London reading about streets – Waalstraat, Buitengracht, Buitencingel – along which he alone, of all the people around him with their heads buried in their books, has walked. But even more than by accounts of old Cape Town is he captivated by stories of ventures into the interior [...] Zwartberg, Leeuwrivier, Dwyka: it is his country, the country of his heart, that he is reading about. (Coetzee, *Youth* 137)

But in the 1983 interview with Tony Morphet, Coetzee does not accede to the suggestion of direct and immediate address to his readers in his own use of familiar place names in *Life & Times of Michael K*:

> The geography is, I fear, less trustworthy than you imagine – not because I deliberately set about altering the reality of Sea Point or Prince Albert but because I don't have much interest in, or can't seriously engage myself with, the kind of realism that takes pride in copying the 'real' world. (Coetzee and Morphet, 'Two Interviews with J.M. Coetzee' 455)

Coetzee's response thus raises a difficult literary-philosophical question: can we readily assume an 'everyday' mode of reference in *fiction's* use of names, especially in its use of recognizable place-names? Michael Green confronts the issue with particular reference to the 'Marianhill' (with one 'n') of *Elizabeth Costello:* to what extent does it refer to the extratextual 'Mariannhill' (with a double 'n') in KwaZulu-Natal? Is it a spelling mistake, or a self-conscious fictional gesture? And what are we to make of the entirely different features of Coetzee's Marianhill ('in rural Zululand' with a 'dirt road winding up into the barren hills' (*Elizabeth Costello* 116, 141)) and the contemporary referent of the Mariannhill that Green describes ('the tarred, busy, multi-laned M1, which can scarcely be described as "winding" as it cuts its brutal way between the industrial parks which have sprung up around Mariannhill and the predominantly black residential areas formed as locations for labour during the apartheid years' (Green, 'Deplorations' 136)). What Green finds outrageous, however, is not so much the differences in detail between these two Marian(n)hills,[2] but the 'scandalizing effect' of Sister Bridget's gesture as she waves her hand towards the window and says, 'This is reality: the reality of Zululand, the reality of Africa. It is the reality now and the reality of the future as far as we can see it' (*Elizabeth Costello* 141). Green's concern is to test the effects of the elision of a material history, in Coetzee's fictional text, on readers who are familiar with that history. At least 'one small, highly circumscribed group of readers is disqualified from participating in the text's negotiations with its referents,' he concludes (Green, 'Deplorations' 154).

David Attwell shares related concerns in his discussion of Mrs Curren's attempt to reach Mr Thabane by phone in *Age of Iron*. The word, 'Thabanchu' occurs to Mrs Curren, who, at the time, is in terrible pain, and suffering from the side-effects of her sedative medication as she slips in and out of consciousness. Thaba 'Nchu is the name of a Wesleyan mission station in the Free State Province of South Africa, but to Mrs Curren, who is about to phone Mr Thabane, the word, 'Thabanchu' appears as a confusing linguistic puzzle: 'Nine letters, anagram for what?' (*Age of Iron* 173). Understandably, the history of the mission station does not explicitly surface in Mrs Curren's utterance of 'Thabanchu' at this moment, yet Attwell goes so far as to suggest that 'so well known and so *literary* is the name in South African letters[3] that it seems reasonable to suggest that it [the history of Thaba 'Nchu] is being *disavowed*' (Attwell, 'J.M. Coetzee and the Idea of Africa', forthcoming paper, my emphasis). However, I would argue that it is precisely Coetzee's mention of the names of the mission stations in his novels in the first place that *offers occasion* for those histories to be told; both Attwell and Green go on to tell these histories – it matters intensely to them that they should.

I am reminded here about Coetzee's discussion of an exchange with his Chinese translator. The magistrate of *Waiting for the Barbarians* refers to the 'Summer Palace' and 'the globe surmounted by the tiger rampant that symbolized eternal domination' (*Waiting for the Barbarians* 146). 'It would be highly appreciated', wrote Coetzee's Chinese translator, 'if you could help clarify what Summer Palace and globe surmounted by the tiger rampant … refer to. I wonder if [they] refer to the Old Summer Palace in Beijing that was destroyed by British and French allied force in 1848' (cited in Coetzee, 'Roads to Translation' 144). Coetzee's response is characteristically attuned to the complexities of the question:

> The question may seem simple, but it holds surprising depths. It may mean: Are the words 'Summer Palace…' *intended* to refer to the historical Summer Palace? It may also mean: Do the words refer to the historical Summer Palace? (Coetzee, 'Roads to Translation' 144, Coetzee's emphasis)

Coetzee himself is able to answer the first question – he 'did not consciously intend to refer to the palace in Beijing, and certainly did not intend to evoke the historical sack of that palace, with its attendant national humiliations', even if some associations with imperial China were consciously evoked in his novel. But in relation to the second question:

> As for whether the words in question do refer to the palace in Beijing, as author I am powerless to say. *The words are written*; I cannot control the associations they awaken. But my translator is not so powerless: a nudge here, a nuance there, and the reader may be either directed towards or headed off from the Beijing of 1848. (Coetzee, 'Roads to Translation' 145, my emphasis)

Both Attwell and Green are concerned with the effect on the *reader* who knows a history that is called up in a name, even when that history is not explicitly narrated; the implication is that Coetzee gives his reader short shrift. My focus and interests in names are different: I consider the challenges facing the *writer* in using familiar names that may or may not evoke associations for the reader. The precise range of associations and histories that can be evoked by a name often exceeds the conscious intention of the writer, let alone that of the implied narrator, or the characters in the novel. This entails a certain risk on the part of the writer.

In the present chapter, then, the argument is this: a question about the 'whereabouts' of the characters in Coetzee's fiction (a 'whereabouts' often registered in recognizable place-names) oscillates relentlessly between discourses of the topographic and the typographic, to the extent that writing about place becomes an interrogation about the place of writing. In Coetzee this interrogation is never simply an inward-looking 'art for art's sake'. From *Dusklands* onwards the calling into question of the place of writing has intimately to do with the positioning of a colonial subject, with the testing of the authority of the one who writes, with representations of landscape that attempt to mark sites of human significance. In Coetzee the question of names has less to do with the *geography* of the place than it has to do with the *history* of its namers. I take my conceptual bearings from Coetzee's non-fiction, and conclude with a discussion of landscape in the films of contemporary South African artist and film-maker, William Kentridge – whose work also features in Coetzee's essays. The chapter reads J.M. Coetzee's use of names in his fiction as a response to Samuel Beckett's *The Unnamable* – that is to say, as a postcolonial countersignature to a modernist text.

II

Here are the opening sentences of Samuel Beckett's *The Unnamable*: 'Where now? Who now? When now? Unquestioning. I, say I.' (267). This narrative gesture constitutes at once a challenge to the reader to anchor reference in the world (in a 'where', 'who' and 'when'), and an outrageous thwarting of any attempt to do just that, as the deictics, 'now' and 'I' mercilessly reel the reader in to the time and place of the discourse itself.[4] This aporetic tension between reference (which is questioned, rather than asserted) and deixis (which, as we shall see, is also deflected), means that the text is never set into narrative motion. The novel enacts what Coetzee identifies as the 'inability to attain the separation of creator and creature, namer and named, with which the act of creating, naming, begins' (Coetzee, *Doubling the Point* 37). Coetzee's juxtaposition, almost a conflation, of naming and creating, reminds me of Heidegger: 'Building and plastic creation

[...] always happen already, and happen only, in the open region of saying and naming' (Heidegger, 'The Origin of the Work of Art' 199). But in Beckett, the protagonist-narrator is in a state of suspension before an act of naming-creating; the 'subject of an incapacity to affirm and an inability to be silent' (Coetzee, *Doubling the Point* 43–4), who suffers from 'the madness of having to speak and not being able to' (Beckett, *The Unnamable* 297). Even in the deictic 'I' the Unnamable has no foothold in the narrative, no sure linguistic site from which to speak. The Unnamable is forced to speak 'of things that don't concern me [...] that they have crammed me full of to prevent me from saying who I am, where I am' (297). Attempts to assume the subject speaking position of 'I' – to pivot the narrative on a narrating 'I' – are endlessly deferred: 'I seem to speak, it is not I, about me, it is not about me' (267).

It is in the context of Beckett's *The Unnamable* that the opening sentences of J.M. Coetzee's first work of fiction, *Dusklands*, have such extraordinary narrative force: 'My name is Eugene Dawn. I cannot help that. Here goes' (Coetzee, *Dusklands* 1). As the inaugural narrative declaration of Coetzee's entire fictional oeuvre, Dawn's announcement is an extravagant affirmation of the naming-creating that will have brought him, and all that follows his assertion, into existence. It is as if Coetzee experiments with the flip-side of Beckett's narrative coin: what happens when the protagonist and his world are *inexorably* named? In one of his essays on Beckett, Coetzee draws attention to the conjuring[5] power of nominal declarations: 'make a single sure affirmation, and from it the whole contingent world of bicycles and greatcoats can, with a little patience, a little diligence, be deduced' (Coetzee, *Doubling the Point* 43). This is how the Unnamable baits the reader: 'Equate me, without pity or scruple, with him who exists, somehow, no matter how, no finicking, with him whose story this story had the brief ambition to be. Better, ascribe to me a body. Better still, arrogate to me a mind. Speak of a world of my own, sometimes referred to as the inner, without choking' (Beckett, *The Unnamable* 359). I cannot help reading this instruction as an outrageous subtext to the opening sentence of *Disgrace*, where, with declarative and ostensive particularity, the narrative voice presents to us a protagonist with body, mind, and an idiosyncratic psychological state: 'For a man of his age, fifty-two, divorced, he has, to his mind, solved the problem of sex rather well' (Coetzee, *Disgrace* 1).

Yet if the affirmation is sure, it is also surely fictional. An inaugural narrative gesture ostentatiously stakes fictional ground in the instant that the possibility of contemplating a self arises. Here is the Unnamable:

> Did I wait somewhere for this place to be ready to receive me? Or did it wait for me to come and people it? By far the better of these hypotheses, from the point of view of usefulness, is the former, and I shall often have occasion to fall back on it. But both are distasteful. I shall say therefore that our beginnings coincide, that this place was made for me, and I for it, at the same instant. And the sounds I do not yet know have not yet made themselves heard. (Beckett, *The Unnamable* 271–2)

The coincidence of fictional self and narrative place is unremitting in Beckett: 'what I say, what I shall say, if I can, relates to the place where I am [...] What I say, what I may say, on this subject, the subject of me and my abode, has already been said since, having always been here, I am here still. At last a piece of reasoning that pleases me, and worthy of my situation' (276).

In his essay, 'The First Sentence of Yvonne Burgess' *The Strike*', Coetzee identifies Burgess' opening sentence as being of the type, 'There was once ...' The first sentence of *The Strike* reads, 'Finlay closed the book and considered the title appreciatively.' Coetzee comments:

> If we want a gloss on the meaning of 'There was once' we can go to the Majorcan storyteller's formula 'Era e non era,' which signals that all succeeding assertions [...] are made in the split was-and-was-not mode of fiction. 'Finlay' and 'the,' pseudo-definitional though they are, are not thereby nonreferential, but their reference is oblique. *They refer not to a man and a book but to the body of discourse that follows*: all assertions succeeding 'Finlay closed the book' are signaled to be in the as-if mode. (Coetzee, *Doubling the Point* 91–2, my emphasis)

Coetzee's narratives draw attention to vacillations between presumed reference to a recognizable world, and reference to their own fictional discourse. This is striking in *In the Heart of the Country*, where the 'as-if' mode is foregrounded to the extent that (as in Beckett) the 'was not' threatens to erode any putative 'was'. Magda speaks of 'the ribbon of [her] meditations, black on white, floating like a mist five feet above the ground' (Coetzee, *In the Heart of the Country* 64). She reflects:

> Am I, I wonder, a thing among things, a body propelled along a track by sinews and bony levers, or am I a monologue moving through time, approximately five feet above the ground, if the ground does not turn out to be just another word, in which case I am indeed lost? Whatever the case, I am plainly not myself in as clear a way as I might wish. (Coetzee, *In the Heart of the Country* 62)

If the contingency of the fictional world rests on a 'single sure affirmation', that affirmation itself is not exempt from the very contingencies it instantiates. The narrating 'I' on whom the fiction turns is just as much a consequence of the 'bicycles and greatcoats' as it is the cause. It is thus that the Unnamable can say, whimsically, 'the best is to think about myself as fixed and at the centre of this place, whatever its shape and extent may be' (Beckett, *The Unnamable* 271). Magda, too, is the arbitrary pivot on whom a fiction turns, even as she herself creates it; little wonder that she should feel that she is not straightforwardly herself. Further, even in order to question her own ontological status, Magda disrupts complacent assumptions on the part of the reader about an either/or structure in the pair, real world/fictional world: the 'I' of her utterance seems to straddle both.

The presumed sequential logic of reference (that is to say, first the thing, then the name) is inverted in *The Unnamable* – 'I have an ocean to drink, so there is an ocean then' (Beckett, *The Unnamable* 288) – and is taken further in the black humour of *In the Heart of the Country*: 'Why is it left to me to give life not only to myself, minute after surly minute, but to everyone else on the farm, and to the farm itself, every stick and stone of it?' and 'I make it all up in order that it shall make me up. I cannot stop now' (Coetzee, *In the Heart of the Country* 72 and 73). Magda's reflections are certainly an extension of The Unnamable's parting words, 'you must go on, I can't go on, I'll go on' (Beckett, *The Unnamable* 382), and in Coetzee's own terms again,

> It is naive to think that writing is a simple two-stage process: first you decide what you want to say, then you say it. On the contrary [...] you write because you do not know what you want to say [...] In fact, it sometimes constructs what you want or wanted to say [...] That is the sense in which one can say that writing writes us. (Coetzee, *Doubling the Point* 18)

III

The 'problem of names', especially as it arises for the writer, is explicitly addressed in *Dusklands*: 'More significant to me than the marital problem' (says Eugene Dawn) 'is the problem of names.' He claims to be a 'specialist in relations rather than names' and adds:

> It would be a healthy corrective to learn the names of the song-birds, and also the names of a good selection of plants and insects [...]
>   There is no doubt that contact with reality can be invigorating. I hope that firm and prolonged intercourse with reality, if I can manage it, will have a good effect on my character as well as my health, and perhaps even improve my writing. (Coetzee, *Dusklands* 36)

The act of creative writing is relentlessly bound up in a question of names –

> I would appreciate a firm grasp of cicadas, Dutch elm blight, and orioles, to mention three names, and the capacity to spin them into long, dense paragraphs which would give the reader a clear sense of the complex natural reality in whose midst I now indubitably am. (Coetzee, *Dusklands* 36–7)

This passage is significant in an important respect: it is a turning point in recognizing that in Coetzee, self-reflexive questions about names and modes of reference in fiction are *part* of a sustained interrogation throughout Coetzee's oeuvre of the supposed sovereignty of a rational self, and of the apartheid legacy of colonialism. Names, for Coetzee, assert a division between namer and named, creator and creature – between 'consciousness and the objects of consciousness' (Coetzee, *Doubling the Point* 37). The success of the name cedes authority to the one who names; but in complex ways it is an authority that is at once necessary, sought after and contested by Coetzee, the author.

To return to the passage just cited: if 'cicadas', 'orioles' and 'Dutch elm blight' give a clear sense of a 'complex natural reality', the syntactic structures undermine the controlling distance that these names effect: the use of the conditional tense holds Dawn's knowledge of names in suspension, and the deictic 'now' diverts attention away from the world named to the scene of naming. The 'indubitably' is thus rendered ironic, to the extent that 'whose' of 'in whose midst' almost runs the risk of referring to the reader, and 'now' is difficult to dissociate from the moment of the writing's-being-read. The place of writing becomes the focus of attention, and ousts the 'complex natural reality' that the names are meant to call into being in the first place. The passage continues: 'I spend many analytic hours puzzling out the tricks which their authors perform to give to their monologues [...] the air of a real world through the looking-glass. A lexicon of common nouns seems to be a prerequisite. Perhaps I was not born to be a writer' (Coetzee, *Dusklands* 37).

In one of the interviews in *Doubling the Point*, David Attwell and Coetzee speak about the intricate relations between modernism, postmodernism and postcolonialism, where the suggestion arises that the self-reflexiveness of modernism is politically irresponsible. Coetzee responds in an interesting way:

> the general position Lukács takes on what he calls realism as against modernist decadence carries a great deal of power, political and moral, in South Africa today [i.e. 1989–1991]: one's first duty as a writer is to represent social and historical processes; drawing the procedures of representation into question is time-wasting; and so forth. (Coetzee, *Doubling the Point* 202)

One detects a note of impatience in Coetzee's response here; the 'and so forth' puts into question the validity of the assertions that precede it. It is easy to assume that a self-reflexive fictional enterprise and a world of socio-political engagement are mutually exclusive. Yet Coetzee is cognizant of the subtle connections between these two worlds. If the 'problem of names', as Eugene Dawn would have it, calls into question the procedures of representation, it also calls into question the relation between namer and named, the authority of the namer, the responsive range that the call of a name instantiates.

The notion of contingency has already arisen in this chapter within the context of the status of a narrative hinged on an initial assertion announcing the 'as-if' mode of fiction. Now the contingency of names gains urgency in relation to questions of culture and history. It is in this context that the calling into question of the procedures of representation is part of an ethical concern with 'social and historical processes'. Cultures within which nominal systems arise are themselves shown to be contingent by the very names that bespeak them.

We see this clearly in *Dusklands*: 'The criteria for a new discovery employed by the gentlemen from Europe were surely parochial. They required that every specimen fill a hole in their European taxonomies' (Coetzee, *Dusklands* 116). The name of the grass called *Aristida brevifolia* in Europe, called *Twaa* by the Bushman, and *boesmansgras* by the frontiersman, gives a sense of culturally dependent and therefore relative nominal systems, in which one system does not *naturally* take precedence over another: 'And if we accept such concepts as a Bushman taxonomy and a Bushman discovery, must we not accept the concepts of a frontiersman taxonomy and a frontiersman discovery?' (*Dusklands* 116). Once again, the conceptual conjunction of naming and creating is asserted, but this time, within the context of a moment of colonial 'discovery':

'I do not know this, my people do not know it, but at the same time I know what it is like, it is like *rooigras*, it is a kind of *rooigras*, I will call it *boesmansgras*' – that is the type of the inward moment of discovery. In this way Coetzee rode like a god through a world only partly named, differentiating and bringing it into existence. (Coetzee, *Dusklands* 116)

The act of naming is one of *conjuration* – with all the multivalency of that word in force. It is 'a magic spell' an 'incantation' or 'charm' (*OED*) – it brings the world into existence as if by magic,[6] or by a primal act of creation. Yet 'conjuration' also means 'a swearing together; a making of a league by a common oath; a conspiracy...a solemn charging or calling upon by appeal to something sacred or binding' (*OED*). *All* these meanings have pertinence in the passages cited from *Dusklands*: if the act of naming calls a world into being, it does so in so far as there is a taxonomic pact *among those who speak the language*. Even *Twaa* finds place, perhaps, in 'an unspoken botanical order' among the Bushmen (Coetzee, *Dusklands* 116), but at the same time, *Twaa* is not 'binding', makes no solemn charge or appeal to those not versed in this 'unspoken botanical order'. Similarly, *Aristida brevifolia* does not have the impact of the 'in common' beyond the cognitive field of a European taxonomy. Thus the conjunctive word-pair, naming-creating, is not one of extravagant or easy optimism about the triumph of a universal language. In the instant of its affirmation, it speaks too of a cultural contingency.

By now at least this much should be clear: names may be arbitrarily related to their referents, but they are not arbitrarily related to other *names*, slotting as they do, into sophisticated linguistic and taxonomic systems.[7] These taxonomic systems are supervenient upon the cultural context in which they arise, so that the names tell us as much about the *namers*, as they do about their putative referents. That one name should hold, that another should fall into disuse, that a name for a particular referent should change in time: all of these nominative drifts track narratives of the contingency and ephemerality of the society of namers, rather than of the referents so named. Names speak of the shifting literary landscapes in which those who hold the authority to name are also revealed.

'When Europeans first arrived in southern Africa,' (writes Coetzee in *Giving Offense*),

> they called themselves *Christians* and indigenous people *wild* or *heathen*. The dyad *Christian/heathen* later mutated, taking a succession of forms, among them *civilized/primitive, European/native, white/nonwhite*. But in each case, no matter what the nominally opposed terms, there was a constant feature: it was always the Christian (or white or European or civilized person) in whose power it lay to apply the names – the name for himself, the name for the other. (Coetzee, *Giving Offense* 1)

To view names in this way is to look beyond a simple relation of referent/name, or even a Saussurean signified/signifier. The discussion opens onto questions about the sites of cultural domination, about the parameters of response drawn up for the one named, and about the field of responsibility that each act of naming instantiates. An intricate ethics is thus brought to bear in any event of naming, not least of which is the way in which names draw the limit to the ground of response for the one called. Names calibrate the social settings and the balance of power between namer and named. Coetzee speaks of the 'impotence of which being-named is the sign', of the realization that 'naming includes control over deictic distance: it can put the one named at a measured arm's length quite as readily as it can draw the one named affectionately nearer' (Coetzee, *Giving Offense* 2). But, as Coetzee himself suggests, it is whether or not you have the power to apply the names (regardless of whether you are the namer or the one named) that most dramatically affects positionality on the slide-rules of distance and proximity, authority and subjection. Names speak of the *relation* between namer and named, rather than simply of the referent itself. This is why David Lurie is so appalled when he learns the name of the boy who is one of his daughter's rapists: the name is not *other* enough to effect the boy's distance from a Western civilization in which Lurie finds himself so at home: 'His name is Pollux' says Lucy, to which Lurie replies:

> 'Not Mncedisi? Not Nqabayakhe? Nothing unpronounceable, just Pollux?'
> 'P-O-L-L-U-X. And David, can we have some relief from that terrible irony of yours?' (Coetzee, *Disgrace* 200)

The name 'Pollux', evoking as it does a Greek myth with its associated European cultural heritage, does not effect the 'measured arm's length' that Lurie would have liked in the distance he would have had through a name he found unpronounceable. In an extreme case, the refusal to name, or to be named in turn, is an attempt to place the other outside of a perceived responsive range.[8] When Lurie sees Pollux spying on Lucy through the bathroom it is *Lurie* – that bastion of European civilized Romanticism – who falls into an 'elemental rage', who strikes Pollux and shouts, *'You swine! [...] You filthy swine!'* He thinks, 'So this is what it is like [...] This is what it is like to be a savage!' (206). It is perhaps the realization that a balance of power has shifted,[9] and that 'swine' has no purchase on the young man who is possibly the father of his grandson, that leads Lurie to comment, finally, 'Pollux! What a name!' (207). The namer's relation to the other is implicated in the name that he or she is obliged to use, and in this case, Lurie is powerless to *choose* that name.

Being in the position of the one who chooses the names is to be in the position of power; but since names speak of the relation between namer and named, the name for the other is also a way of positioning the self. This throwback effect of names reminds me again of the logic of the middle voice, and of Coetzee's linguistico-philosophical understanding of the term, writing: 'in a larger sense', says Coetzee, 'all writing is autobiography: everything that you write, including criticism and fiction, writes you as you write it' (Coetzee, *Doubling the Point* 17). We use names to refer to something, or to call someone at a place in language, but equally, the names we use give an indication of the place from which we call. That *name-place* is at a complex intersection of social, cultural and historical routes.

Coetzee speaks of writing that entails 'an awareness, as you put pen to paper, that you are setting in train a certain play of signifiers with their own ghostly history of past interplay' (*Doubling the Point* 63). How does the writer negotiate the effects of this ghostly history? And what part, precisely, do names have to play in this? Perhaps this is the postcolonial response to modernism when it comes to names – whereas a modernist text may question the capacity of names, universally, to refer meaningfully at all, a postcolonial text is likely to chart the particular socio-historic configurations that are brought to bear in each naming event. Differently put: where a modernist writer questions the efficacy of his or her medium in universal terms, the postcolonial writer is interested in that medium's specific historical effects.

IV

To name a landscape is to mark sites of human significance on indifferent ground. In an inversion of the expected sequence – first the landscape, then the name – we can say that a landscape becomes literary (which is to say, it is given written form) precisely *because* it is named. This is the logic of Heidegger's 'The Origin of the Work of

Art' – it is the building of the temple that announces the precinct as holy, the ground as native, rather than the other way round (Heidegger, 'The Origin of the Work of Art' 167–8). But given the 'ghostly history' of language, any attempt *to signify* the landscape by name[10] is to signal a human relation to that place at a particular moment in time. Time itself recedes, and the landscape, too, changes, but incrementally, the name carries with it the traces of the human histories that have made that place significant. 'When death cuts all other links,' says the Dostoevsky of *The Master of Petersburg*, 'there remains still the name' (Coetzee, *The Master of Petersburg* 5). It is when the *name* changes that certain histories are elided, and that the place is marked in a different way for future recollection: the name of a place gives an indication of whose past is deemed worthy of recalling as history.[11] This in-built historiography of place-names is not entirely obliterated, even when those names are taken up within a fictional frame.

For artist and film-maker William Kentridge, it is the historiography of names that is lost in visual representations of place – in picturesque painting, for example – and in the sites themselves. Here is William Kentridge on the name, 'Sharpeville':

> the *word Sharpeville* conjures up, both locally, and I would imagine internationally, a whole series of things, the centre of which is the infamous massacre of sixty-nine people outside a police station in the township outside Vereeniging [...] But at the site itself, there is almost no trace of what happened there. This is natural. It is an area that is still used, an area in which people live and go to work. It is not a museum. There are no bloodstains. The ghosts of the people do not walk the streets. Scenes of battles, great and small, disappear, are absorbed by the terrain, except in those few places where memorials are specifically erected, monuments established, as outposts, as defences against this process of disremembering and absorption. (Kentridge, 'Felix in Exile: Geography of Memory' 127, my emphasis)

The name itself functions as an outpost against a process of disremembering and absorption, and Kentridge, in his own work, explores, as much as he practises in his techniques, the tensions between memory and forgetting, between monuments and fences on the one hand, and the landscape's process of absorption on the other. Thus Kentridge is interested in depicting 'a landscape that is articulated or *given a meaning by incidents across it*, pieces of civil engineering, the lines of pipes, culverts, fences,' what he calls 'the variety of the ephemera of human intervention on the landscape' (Kentridge, 'Landscape in a State of Siege' 110, my emphasis). The technique that Kentridge uses in his animated films is one of 'imperfect erasure' (Kentridge and Cameron, 'An Interview with William Kentridge' 67) – a charcoal image is drawn, photographed, rubbed out and slightly altered, photographed again, and so on. But the erasures are never absolute, so that traces of the previous image are still visible in the present one. Time passing is projected onto a spatial, visible plane as palimpsest; the history of the place is refracted through an increasingly complex network of lines: the procession of layered drawing and gradated fading away gives to the passing of time a visible spatial depth. When this comes to the depiction of human subjects: we *see* a 'multiplicity of the self passing through time, which would end up as a single self if the moment was frozen in a photograph, in a fixed drawing' (Kentridge and Cameron, 'An Interview with William Kentridge' 67). One thinks of the dance film that David Lurie shows to Melanie Isaacs in his flat in Cape Town:

> Two dancers on a bare stage move through their steps. Recorded by a stroboscopic camera, their images, ghosts of their movements, fan out behind them like wingbeats [...] the instant of the present and the past of that instant, evanescent, caught in the same space. (Coetzee, *Disgrace* 14–15)

In visual terms, this is the way in which William Kentridge plays up the 'ghostly history' of the signifier, doing justice to his sense there can be no 'simple response to a place whose appearance is so different from its history' (Kentridge, 'Landscape in a State of Siege' 110). Kentridge's project, writes Coetzee, is about the 'unburying' of the past of the South African landscape (Coetzee, *'History of the Main Complaint'* 84). Perceptions of landscape and the resources of memory are interrelated, and projected onto the synchronicity of a single visual field.

Now, to return to the novels: it seems to me that Coetzee is also preoccupied with a stroboscopic vision of landscape: temporally different, yet spatially coincident images of the past and of the present are superimposed, throwing the landscape into historical relief. In the writer's literary landscapes, the planes of present appearance and historical past converge *in the name*. Human ephemera are poignantly recorded in the remains of the name – for future readers.

At one of their halts, (August 18) the expedition left behind: the ashes of the night fire, combustion complete, a feature of dry climates; faeces dotted in mounds over a broad area, herbivore in the open, carnivore behind rocks; urine stains with minute traces of copper salts; tea leaves; the leg-bones of a springbok; five inches of braided oxhide rope; tobacco ash; and a musket ball. The faeces dried in the course of the day. Ropes and bones were eaten by a hyena on August 22. A storm on November 2 scattered all else. The musket ball was not there on August 18, 1933. (Coetzee, *Dusklands* 118–19)

There seems to be no end to the literary *list*, even in the instant that it records a disappearance:

From scalp and beard, dead hair and scales. From the ears, crumbs of wax. From the nose, mucus and blood [...] From the eyes, tears and a rheumy paste. From the mouth, blood, rotten teeth, calculus, phlegm, vomit. From the skin, pus, blood, scabs, weeping plasma [...] sweat, sebum, scales, hair. Nail fragments, interdigital decay. Urine and the minuter kidneystones [...] Smegma [...] Faecal matter, blood, pus [...] Semen [...] These relicts, deposited over Southern Africa in two swathes, soon disappeared under sun, wind, rain and the attentions of the insect kingdom, though their atomic constituents are still of course among us. *Scripta manent.* (Coetzee, *Dusklands* 119)

What these elaborate lists enact is that *the name itself* is the 'relict', the 'surviving trace', that which is 'left by death' (*OED*). The writing remains: *scripta manent,* which reminds me again of Beckett, and of the indelible trace of reference in any use of language: 'If I could speak and yet say nothing, really nothing? [...] But it seems impossible to speak and yet say nothing, you think you have succeeded, but you always overlook something, a little yes, a little no, enough to exterminate a regiment of dragoons' (Beckett, *The Unnamable* 277). Molloy can say, 'What I'd like now is to speak of the things that are left' (Beckett, *Molloy* 9), but the writing itself is the thing that is left, and through it, a historical past breaks in on the surface 'now' of each utterance. The literary landscape of *Disgrace* constitutes a striking instance of the palimpsestic interplay between what Thomas Hardy would call 'the transitory in Earth's long order' (Hardy, 'At Castle Boterel' line 23), and the relicts of the name. Immediately evident in the novel is the legacy, but also the evanescence of a colonial social geography in a new post-apartheid Cape. There are several examples of this: David Lurie's reference to the Eastern Cape as 'Old Kaffraria,' for instance (*Disgrace* 122), or his reflections on his daughter, Lucy, who farms in the Eastern Cape on what used to be the frontier between colonial settlers and the indigenous Xhosa people. 'A frontier farmer of the new breed. In the old days cattle and maize. Today, dogs and daffodils' (*Disgrace* 62). The following comment of Lurie's on the shifting urban landscape of Cape Town leads me back to the passages I cited earlier from *Giving Offense*:

> He has been away less than three months, yet in that time the shanty settlements have crossed the highway and spread east of the airport. The stream of cars has to slow down while a child with a stick herds a stray cow off the road. Inexorably, he thinks, the country is coming to the city. Soon there will be cattle again on Rondebosch Common; soon history will have come full circle. (Coetzee, *Disgrace* 175)

Lurie's choice of the term 'shanty settlement' is what interests me here. He does not say 'squatter camp' or 'informal settlement' – both of which would have been in common use at the time of writing *Disgrace:* both terms insist on the transitoriness of these settlements. But neither are the shanty towns referred to by name, and the terms 'settler' and 'settlement' in South Africa constitute a chiasmatic intersection of seemingly contradictory associations: if on the one hand, a settler is presumably here to stay, a settler is also a newcomer, a colonizer, an outsider, one whose home is elsewhere, and therefore, one who is expected to leave again. It is the term 'settler' that provides the context for the discussion of names in *Giving Offense*. 'Settlers, in the idiom of white South Africa,' writes Coetzee,

> are those Britishers who took up land grants in Kenya and the Rhodesias, people who refused to put down roots in Africa, who sent their children abroad to be educated, and spoke of England as 'Home.' When the Mau Mau got going, the settlers fled. To South Africans, white as well as black, *a settler is a transient, no matter what the dictionary says*. (Coetzee, *Giving Offense* 1, my emphasis)

Lurie refers to Lucy as 'this sturdy young settler' (*Disgrace* 61), but from Petrus' perspective (according to Lurie), 'Lucy is merely a transient' (117). In *Disgrace* the legacy of those settlers is inevitably called up in the names – Grahamstown, Salem, Port Elizabeth, New Brighton Station, the Kenton Road – even as human communities coalesce and dissipate across the terrain.

V

I return to the interview with Tony Morphet where I set out: the physical geography of Coetzee's novels may well be less 'reliable' than we are tempted to assume; the place of writing itself becomes an active site in the signifying landscape. The novel, for Coetzee, 'becomes less a *thing* than a *place* where one goes every day for several hours a day for years on end. What happens in that place has less and less discernible relation to the daily life one lives or the lives people are living around one' (*Doubling the Point* 205, Coetzee's emphasis). But if the question of a physical geography, in a certain sense, is irrelevant to a literary landscape, the 'ghostly history' of the names, and hence of the namers who signify this landscape, are not. It is thanks to the imperfect erasure of these histories, even in a work of fiction, that names have any hold at all. The names that a writer uses are outposts in a landscape that in itself is oblivious to human memories of that place. Names trigger sites of individual memory as the reader traces patterns of significance in the language of literature. It is in this sense that a question of names has less to do with the geography of the place than it has to do with the history of those who have chosen, who use and who recognize the names. At the same time, these names are a poignant reminder of the forgetting, the transience, or the fears they are created as bastions against.

6
Etymologies

In his essay, 'A Sedimentation of the Mind: Earth Projects' (1968), the artist, Robert Smithson, writes:

> Words and rocks contain a language that follows a syntax of splits and ruptures. Look at any *word* long enough and you will see it open up into a series of faults, into a terrain of particles each containing its own void. This discomforting language of fragmentation offers no easy gestalt solution; the certainties of didactic discourse are hurled into the erosion of the poetic principle. (Smithson, 'A Sedimentation of the Mind' 107)

Several of Coetzee's characters (for the most part intellectuals, writers, academics) find themselves staring at words, exploring the possibility of a necessary – perhaps even a primal – link between a name and its referent. Characters like Mrs Curren, the Magistrate, David Lurie, Elizabeth Costello and Paul Rayment pick out isolated words, reconfigure them in declension, compare related words in different languages, trace etymological roots. A question of language – English in particular – and its capacity to articulate the truth, is pivotal in the worlds of Coetzee's fictions: one immediately thinks of David Lurie's conviction that 'English is an unfit medium for the truth of South Africa' (*Disgrace* 117) and his yearning to sound, at the very least, 'a single authentic note' in the opera he is composing (*Disgrace* 214). Ever since Plato's *Cratylus*, the earliest existing philosophical text on names, we have come to recognize that linguistic – and especially etymological – enquiries never end in affirmative consolidations of a 'correctness' of names by nature.[1] Differently put, in Smithson's terms, etymological forays do not hit reassuring bedrock. Yet (and this is the first argument of the chapter), despite the fact that linguistic foundations are demonstrably friable, that cultural beliefs (which depend on that language) are contingent constructs, Coetzee, through his fiction, reiterates the value of creating a space for voices to be heard – even in the instant of exposing the underlying faultline of splits and ruptures. This part of my discussion develops in the interfold of the topographic and the textual – I begin with Coetzee's early consideration of the implications of writing about the African continent in English. The argument hinges on the etymology of the word 'care', especially as it arises in *Age of Iron* and *Slow Man*, and leads to questions about the ways in which language, rather than landscape, draws the limit between notions of 'native' and 'foreign'.

Thus the first part of the chapter discusses the limit of a *particular* language – English – within a specific socio-historic configuration. It is through a second etymology in Coetzee, namely that of the word 'torture', that my discussion opens onto a consideration of the implications for literary representation of the limits of language *in general*. A leading preoccupation in much of Coetzee's writing is this: how does one write about something *else*, but within the constraints of recognizable language in which the words one chooses have been said before, thus dictating in advance what can be said? How does one write the other, the singular, the as-yet-untold, in language that inexorably follows tracks of the known, the familiar, the already-said?[2] Coetzee alerts us to this dilemma in his essay, 'Isaac Newton and the Ideal of a Transparent Scientific Language' (in *Doubling the Point*), where he refers to Newton's attempts to explain, not only in the language of pure mathematics, but also in Latin and English, the force of gravitational attraction. Instead of assuming that Newton found a Whorfian 'seamless continuity [...] between syntax and logic and world view' (*Doubling the Point* 184), Coetzee speaks of Newton's 'real struggle', of signs of Newton's 'wrestling to make the thought fit into the language, to make the language express the thought, signs perhaps even of an incapacity of language to express certain thoughts, or of thought unable to think itself out because of the limitations of its medium' (*Doubling the Point* 194 and 184).

The second part of this chapter explores the ways in which Coetzee himself confronts the difficulty of bringing meaningfully into linguistic range that which is not immediately recognizable or sayable in any *given* language. The discussion extends a line of argument that I initiated in the previous chapter: Coetzee's seemingly opposite preoccupations with history and with postcolonial themes on the one hand, and with self-reflexive postmodern strategies on the other, are inextricably connected. The moment of attempting to reach out beyond the limits of a given conceptual or representational scheme, and hence beyond what has been sayable in the language before, is also a linguistic breaking-point, and in this moment, Coetzee's characters self-reflexively expose, as much as they attempt to shift, their discursive limits. As a way of opening onto the preoccupation with aesthetics in the conclusion of the book, this chapter ends with a reflection about the space of the literary artwork itself: on what terms can it become a *site* of engagement between writer and reader, and in what ways does the artwork have the potential to erode the limits that the language of its own construction sets?

II

Smithson's provocative linking of 'words and rocks' through a 'syntax of splits and ruptures' is relevant to Coetzee in complex ways. In *White Writing* (1988), Coetzee speaks of the 'quest for an authentic language' to depict the African landscape. He carefully formulates the question: 'Is there a language in which people of European identity, or if not of European identity then of a highly problematical South African-colonial identity, can speak to Africa and be spoken to by Africa?' (*White Writing* 7–8). The quest for this authentic language thus takes place 'within a framework in which language, consciousness, and landscape are interrelated' (*White Writing* 7). Further, the writer whose native tongue is English bears the 'burden of finding a home in Africa for a consciousness formed in and by a language whose history lies on another continent' (*White Writing* 173). The 'burden' is one that Coetzee recognizes in the writings of the nineteenth-century English botanist and explorer, William Burchell (see *White Writing* 36–44), and in *Youth*, Coetzee cites Burchell as a source of his own literary inspiration:

> The challenge [Coetzee] faces is a purely literary one: to write a book whose horizon of knowledge will be that of Burchell's time, the 1820s, yet whose response to the world around it will be alive in a way that Burchell, despite his energy and intelligence and curiosity and sang-froid, could not be because he was an Englishman in a foreign country, his mind half occupied with Pembrokeshire and the sisters he had left behind. (Coetzee, *Youth* 138)

The writer using a European language and literary tradition is faced with a predicament: on the one hand, Africa can be named in negative relation to Europe, as in Burchell's opening comment on a sunrise viewed from the top of Table Mountain:

> I perceived in it nothing remarkable. I observed none of those streams of light which, in England, may often be seen radiating from the sun, just before it appears above the horizon, and which are so trite a feature in pictures of sunrise. (Burchell, *Travels in the Interior of Southern Africa* vol. 1 40)

As Coetzee points out (in a different context), it is a 'self-defeating process' to 'nam[e] Africa by defining it as non-Europe – self-defeating because in each particular in which Africa is identified to be non-European, it remains Europe, not Africa, that is named' (*White Writing* 164). On the other hand, to name Africa without reference to Europe or to a European aesthetic of landscape presents tough challenges of its own. Thus Olive Schreiner (as Ralph Iron) writes in the 1883 preface *to The Story of an African Farm:* 'Sadly [the writer] must squeeze the colour from his brush, and dip it into the grey pigments around him. He must paint what lies before him' (Schreiner, 'Preface' to *The Story of an African Farm* 30). What room does this leave for the aesthetic imagination? For Schreiner, '[t]hose brilliant phases and shapes which the imagination sees in far-off lands are not for him to portray' (Schreiner, 'Preface' 30); for Coetzee, writing a hundred years later, the imaginary landscape of *Waiting for the Barbarians* 'represented a challenge to my power of *envisioning,*

while the Karoo threatened only the tedium of reproduction, reproduction of a phraseology in which the Karoo has been done to death
in a century of writing and overwriting (drab bushes, stunted trees,
heat-stunned flats, shrilling of cicadas, and so forth)' (Coetzee,
Doubling the Point 142).

III

Within the fictional worlds of Coetzee's novels, characters express
misgivings that European languages and cultures offer any legitimate medium of response to South Africa at all. Insistently in
Disgrace, the socio-political aftermath of colonialism is indexed in
the anachronistic disjuncture between a European language and
intellectual literary heritage on the one hand, and the Africa it
attempts to address, or represent on the other. Lurie's near-
obsessive interest in being articulate himself results in his unearth-
ing of a number of European resonances in each English word he
so carefully turns over. Here are just three examples:

A man of patience, energy, resilience. A peasant, a *paysan*, a man
of the country. (Coetzee, *Disgrace* 117)

She loves the land and the old, *ländliche* way of life. (Coetzee,
Disgrace 113)

Modern English *friend* from Old English *freond*, from *freon*, to love.
(Coetzee, *Disgrace* 102)

A curious tension arises in these examples. On a semantic level the
words raise associations of chthonic rootedness ('paysan', 'ländliche'), of home and community ('neighbour', 'friend', 'benefactor').
But the trans-lingual and etymological enquiries themselves, regardless of what the words *mean*, recall a distant culture and a time past.[3]
To invoke the histories and etymological connections of these words,
while saying them *in South Africa* is to place the speaker in a double
bind. On the one hand the testing of language is generated by a sincere desire to speak the truth, to find the right word. On the other
hand, the etymological forays, which expose European roots, are a
conscious reminder of an imperial elsewhere, which draws attention
to the amphibology of the individual words, and hence to the precariousness of supposed univocal meanings. This is something that

Coetzee deliberately exploits in his writing. '[W]hat I like about English', Coetzee says in an interview with Jean Sévry,

> and what I certainly don't find in Afrikaans, what does not exist in Afrikaans, is a historical layer in the language that enables you to work with historical contrasts and oppositions in prose [...] there is a genetic diversity about the language, which after all is not only a Germanic language with very heavy romance overlays, but is also a language which is very receptive to imported neologisms so that macaronic effects are possible – you can work with contrasts in the etymological basis of words. (Coetzee and Sévry, 'An Interview with J.M. Coetzee' 2)

Coetzee's attention to the effects of the historical traces of his artistic medium reminds me of Jacques Derrida's 'Force and Signification' – an early essay which offers a detailed and provocative reading of Jean Rousset's structuralist work, *Forme et Signification: Essais sur les structures littéraires de Corneille à Claudel*.[4] In what amounts to a sustained *critique* of a structuralist approach, especially as it is evinced by Rousset, Derrida makes the point that structuralism practises a certain literary geometry; it 'grants an absolute privilege to spatial models, mathematical functions, lines, and forms [...] in fact, time itself is always reduced. To a *dimension* in the best of cases' (Derrida, 'Force and Signification' 16). Rousset, in Derrida's reading, is preoccupied with the lines that trace out the internal thematic structures and patterns of the work, but to delineate the thematic patterns in this way is to presuppose a static structural and temporal boundary of that literary work in advance. It is to consider the work as self-contained *representation*, rather than as a complex, historically inflected *appeal*; it is to disregard the implications of the heritage of its medium, as much as it is to ignore the impact of the address sent out to potential future readers. This is the sense in which we can understand Derrida's interesting claim that 'there is no *space* of the work, if by space we mean *presence* and *synopsis*' (Derrida, 'Force and Signification' 14). In its lapse in the attention given to forces of meaning over time, a structuralist reading is conducted in *purely* spatial terms, running the risk of overlooking a

> history, more difficult to conceive: the history of the meaning of the work itself, of its *operation*. This history of the meaning of

the work is not only its *past*, the eve or the sleep in which it precedes itself in an author's intentions, but is also the impossibility of its ever being *present*, of its ever being summarized by some absolute simultaneity or instantaneousness. (Derrida, 'Force and Signification' 14)

Spelling out etymologies, testing the valency of English spoken in Africa, mentioning place-names no longer in use – these are just some of the ways in which Coetzee *invites* attention to the effects of historical forces operative in his fiction, at the level of the constitutive medium of the work. In leading the reader to ask unsettling questions about the assumed ahistoric presence of a work of fiction – through self-conscious reflection on the temporal contingency of an explicitly historically situated language that, at the same time, generates the fictional narrative – Coetzee's writing brings about a convergence of postcolonial and postmodern concerns.[5]

IV

It is the fissile propensity of language (rather than a stabilized grounding in a unitary essence) that is reiterated in each elaborate etymology provided by Coetzee's characters. English words in Africa are diachronous in their evocation of another era and another continent – what concerns me now are the *ethical* implications of internal semantic splits exposed in etymological quests. In Plato's *Cratylus*, Socrates provokes Hermogenes into agreeing that a 'professor of the science of language should be able to give a very lucid explanation of first names, or let him be assured he will only talk nonsense about the rest' (Plato, *Cratylus* §426a–b). In Coetzee, however, the recognition of a 'foundational fiction' (*Giving Offense* 14) and 'false etymologies' (*Age of Iron* 22) does not necessarily invalidate the structures built on those foundations – even when it comes to matters of ethics. My example (from *Age of Iron* and *Slow Man*) is the phrase 'take care of'.[6]

Elizabeth Curren, a professor of classics who has terminal cancer, gives a little lecture to Vercueil, the homeless man she has taken into her house:

the spirit of charity has perished in this country [...] those who accept charity despise it, while those who give with a despairing heart. What is the point of charity if it does not go from heart to heart? What do you think charity is? Soup? Money? *Charity*: from the Latin word for the heart. (Coetzee, *Age of Iron* 22)

In the first place, the value system and the language Mrs Curren invokes have no leverage in the totalitarian, apartheid South Africa of the 1980s. Hers is the 'authority of the dying and the authority of the classics', as Coetzee puts it in an interview with David Attwell (*Doubling the Point* 250), both of which 'are denied and even derided in her world: the first because hers is a private death, the second because it speaks from long ago and far away' (*Doubling the Point* 250). Yet for Coetzee, what matters is that a voice such as Mrs Curren's is heard, so that 'even in an age of iron, pity is not silenced'; this despite the fact that Mrs Curren speaks 'from a totally untenable historical position' (*Doubling the Point* 250). Thus Coetzee creates a space for the 'private,' the 'long ago' and the 'far away' in the here and now. Coetzee himself does not offer programmatic ethical imperatives in the way that his characters often do (think of Elizabeth Costello, or of Mrs Curren – 'How shall I be saved? By doing what I do not want to do. That is the first step: that I know. I must love, first of all, the unlovable' (*Age of Iron* 136)).[7] But even though Mrs Curren's position may be historically untenable, Coetzee's staging of it in a 'contest' does not amount to its dismissal; the actual outcome of the contest is, in fact, irrelevant. What matters is that a countervoice is heard. More specifically (as I have discussed in several places throughout the book) it is precisely the extent to which an author plays up the 'dialogic' propensity of writing that Coetzee takes to be a 'measure of a writer's seriousness' (Coetzee, *Doubling the Point* 65). From the perspective of the writer it is 'a matter of awakening the countervoices in oneself and embarking upon speech with them' (*Doubling the Point* 65). In *Slow Man* Paul Rayment has a childhood memory of mixing all his coloured plasticine bricks together until he has one huge ball of *'leaden purple'*. The bright colours 'will never return because of entropy, which is irreversible and irrevocable and rules the universe' (*Slow Man* 119). To let Mrs Curren have her say is to preserve one small chink of colour in the purple ball.

Almost immediately after Elizabeth Curren's pronouncement that caritas is 'from the Latin word for the heart', she adds, 'A lie: charity, *caritas*, has nothing to do with the heart. *But what does it matter if my sermons rest on false etymologies?* [...] Care: the true root of charity' (*Age of Iron* 22, my emphasis, except for *caritas*). Mrs Curren's comment leads us to revisit, in a more nuanced way, Plato's *Cratylus*, and Coetzee's thoughts about linguistic reference (specifically in *White Writing*). The interlocutors in the *Cratylus* set out from the assumption that 'the correct name indicates the nature of the thing' (§428e), whereas Coetzee (whose views are subtly distinct from those of David Lurie) holds to a primal rift between signifier and signified: in *no* language do we find a case where 'things are their names' by nature. (Coetzee, *White Writing* 9).[8] But, as we learn from the *Cratylus*, whether one can provide 'a lucid explanation of first names' or not does not prove one's theory of reference either way (§426a–b). Further (I borrow Robert Smithson's phrasing again), *the fact that* Mrs Curren's ethical view draws on a 'poetic principle' (the fictive association of caritas and 'heart') rather than on 'the certainties of didactic discourse' (Smithson, 'A Sedimentation of the Mind' 107), does not, *in itself,* make her view any less valid.

To extend the implications that arise from Smithson, and to bring us back to Coetzee – that one's ethical system is based on contingent social constructs, rather than on universal 'essences', is, in practice, irrelevant. The exposure of a constructed, rather than a 'natural' base, is certainly not reason enough to scrap the system.[9] Coetzee provides a graphic example of this in *Giving Offense*. The states of dignity and innocence, he points out, are elaborate social constructs – we are not born with dignity or innocence; we do not possess them 'inherently'. Thus,

> [a]ffronts to the innocence of our children or to the dignity of our persons are attacks not upon our essential being but upon constructs – constructs by which we live, but constructs nevertheless. This is not to say that affronts to innocence or dignity are not real affronts [...] The infringements are real; what is infringed, however, is not our essence, but a foundational fiction to which we more or less wholeheartedly subscribe, *a fiction that may well be indispensable for a just society,* namely, that human beings have a dignity that sets them apart from animals and consequently protects them from being treated like animals. (*Giving Offense* 14, my emphasis)

UNIVERSITY OF WINCHESTER
LIBRARY

It is in this context that the title of Smithson's essay is interesting: 'A *Sedimentation* of the Mind' creates an image of the mind silted up with words which have become naturalized. This is the way in which words assume their power over us: the foundational fiction itself seems natural. With an added ironic twist (and following on from the previous chapter), it is precisely the recognition of the *contingency* of one's cultural belief, rather than an unswerving conviction that it represents the ultimate truth, that can provide the basis for an ethical response. It is worth remembering that things might have been different.[10]

Foundational fictions are one thing – but often the linguistic scrutiny of a word or phrase unearths contradictory meanings that threaten to undermine the entire edifice – Robert Smithson again: 'Look at any *word* long enough, and you will see it open up into a series of faults, into a terrain of particles each containing its own void' (Smithson, 'A Sedimentation of the Mind' 107). It is this 'series of faults', this 'void' that confronts Paul Rayment as he stares at the words 'take care of'. Marijana Jokić (the Croatian nurse employed to look after him following his cycling accident which results in his leg being amputated), asks an innocent enough question: 'who is going to take care of you?' (*Slow Man* 43). But the question provokes mental crisis in Rayment. Echoes of *Age of Iron*, *Disgrace* and *Elizabeth Costello* remind us yet again that questions of ethics, as is so often the case in Coetzee, are intricately bound up in questions of language.[11] In the first place Marijana's question is not univocal: 'presumably there is a more charitable way of interpreting the question – as *Who is going to be your stay and support?*, for instance' (*Slow Man* 43). While the spoken exchange that ensues has to do with his biographic circumstances, Rayment's internal monologue rages:

> her question echoes in his mind. Who is going to take care of you? The more he stares at the words *take care of,* the more inscrutable they seem. He remembers a dog they had when he was a child in Lourdes, lying in its basket in the last stages of canine distemper [...] '*Bon, je m'en occupe,*' his father said at a certain point [...] Five minutes later, from the woods, he heard the flat report of a shotgun, and that was that, he never saw the dog again. *Je m'en occupe*: I'll take charge of it; I'll take care of it; I'll do what has to be done.

That kind of caring, with a shotgun, was certainly not what Marijana had in mind. Nevertheless, it lay englobed in the phrase, waiting to leak out. (Coetzee, *Slow Man* 43–4)

Instead of consoling him that Marijana's 'care' is more than 'just nursing' (33), Rayment's attempts to get to the bottom of the phrase call up chilling childhood memories and erode any certainties he may have had about meaningful communication with the one person in the world who seems to care about him now. Far from offering reassurance, the phrase brings to the linguistic surface of the dialogue a few bleak particulars: Rayment is a foreigner in Australia; he has no family in Adelaide; he has lost contact with his relatives in Europe. Further, 'what of his reply: *I'll take care of myself?* What did his words mean, objectively?' As if despite the intentions of its speakers, meanings proliferate, and the phrase provokes Rayment's (extravagantly detailed) thoughts of suicide:

Did the taking care, the caretaking he spoke of extend to donning his best suit and swallowing down his cache of pills, two at a time, with a glass of hot milk, and lying down in his bed with his hands folded across his breast? (Coetzee, *Slow Man* 44)[12]

But if 'taking care', at a psychological level, harbours contradictory and potentially destructive meanings, it is worth recalling Coetzee's own comments on Freudian psychoanalysis. Psychoanalysis, says Coetzee, 'has scientific ambitions, and science has no ethical content'. He goes on to elaborate:

What psychoanalysis has to say about ethical impulses may be illuminating (I give as an instance the link Freud points to between pity and destructiveness) but is ultimately of no ethical weight. That is to say, whatever one thinks the psychological origins of love or charity may be, one must still act with love and charity. The outrage felt by many of Freud's first readers – that he was subverting their moral world – was therefore misplaced. (Coetzee, *Doubling the Point* 244)

Besides, the semantic waywardness of language is precisely what makes literary writing dialogic.

'Care' is the 'true root of charity', Mrs Curren asserts, and these are her concerns: 'the spirit of charity has perished in this country' (Coetzee, *Age of Iron* 22); she is

> trying to keep a soul alive in times not hospitable to the soul.
> Easy to give alms to the orphaned, the destitute, the hungry. Harder to give alms to the bitter-hearted [...] But the alms I give to Vercueil are hardest of all. What I give he does not forgive me for giving. No charity in him, no forgiveness. (*Charity?* Says Vercueil. *Forgiveness?*) Without his forgiveness I give without charity, serve without love. (Coetzee, *Age of Iron* 130–1)

It is not always easy to know what to make of Mrs Curren's meditations, especially given her own frequent retractions, qualifiers and reformulations (as in 'I may seem to understand what I say, but, believe me, I do not' (*Age of Iron* 131)). Yet, at the very least, this much is clear: her personal engagements are played out within a specific socio-political landscape, and her dilemmas arise in an aporetic ethical space – a space at once personal and political, inalienable and foreign:

> Now that child is buried and we walk upon him. Let me tell you, when I walk upon this land, this South Africa, I have a gathering feeling of walking upon black faces. They are dead but their spirit has not left them. They lie there heavy and obdurate, waiting for my feet to pass, waiting for me to go, waiting to be raised up again. (Coetzee, *Age of Iron* 125–6)

Despite her abhorrence of the police violence that has led to Bheki's death, despite her own efforts to save the boy's life, Mrs Curren, in a passage such as the one above, gives intimations that she is implicated in the horrors of apartheid.

V

Without making crude pronouncements about realism, it is possible to link Mrs Curren's life events and preoccupations (also those of the characters in *Disgrace*) to historic and geographic co-ordinates: calendars and maps are points of reference that, within the fictive worlds

of these novels, determine the socio-historical moment, and that distinguish the native from the foreign. Yet even in his most 'realistic'
writing, Coetzee warns against taking these reference points at face
value, as I argued in the previous chapter. In an essay on one of
William Kentridge's films, *History of the Main Complaint*, Coetzee
comments again on the different logic at work when it comes to reference in a work of fiction. Of William Kentridge's film he writes,
'the streets belong to a bygone, more provincial age, the 1940s or
1950s. But it would be a mistake to conclude, from this and from
Soho's office decor, that Kentridge's films are about a past era'
(Coetzee, *'History of the Main Complaint'* 87). Thus even when the
physical geography of the place, and historical moments in time are
ostensively legible in the text, the references to space and time within
an artwork operate differently, reminding me again of Smithson's
'abstract geology' (Smithson, 'A Sedimentation of the Mind' 100).
Reflections about objective time and space thus cede ground to
reflections about literary representation, to reflections about
Coetzee's deployment of the logical operations of language within
the worlds of his fiction. In *Slow Man*, questions arise not so much
about the relation between language and topographic space, but
about the relation between a language and its speakers. My focal
point is still that of English, and even more specifically, the word
'care'. It is the characters' relation to the English language, rather
than to a physical geographic location, that dictates the boundary
between the native and the foreign, the chthonic and what Elizabeth
Costello calls the 'butterfly' (*Slow Man* 198).

Paul Rayment imagines writing a letter to Marijana, apologizing
for his indiscretion, thanking her for the care she has given him, and
pleading her to accept his offer to pay for her son's education. In the
letter, he will write:

> You have taken care of me; now I want to give something back, if
> you will let me. I offer to take care of you [...] I offer to do so because
> in my heart, in my core, I care for you. (Coetzee, *Slow Man* 165)[13]

But Rayment does not write this letter. *'Care'*, he thinks,

> he can set the word down on paper, but he would be too diffident
> to mouth it, make it his own speech. Too much an English word,

an insider's word. Perhaps Marijana of the Balkans, giver of care, compelled even more than he to conduct her life in a foreign tongue, will share his diffidence. (Coetzee, *Slow Man* 165)

It is the English language, not Australia, that casts Rayment and Marijana as foreigners. In the English-speaking world, Rayment continues (the passage recalls *Age of Iron*) 'caring should not be assumed to have anything to do with the heart'. He contemplates adding a final comment in the imagined letter: *'Excuse the language lesson [...] I too am on foreign soil' (Slow Man* 165). Language, landscape and consciousness are thus more closely interrelated than before in Coetzee, to the extent that *language itself* appears to be the only ground. Elizabeth Costello, a character in *Slow Man* who seems to be the author of the very fiction we are reading, also thinks about English in this way. Rayment tells her:

English has never been mine in the way it is yours. Nothing to do with fluency [...] But English came to me too late. It did not come with my mother's milk. In fact it did not come at all. (Coetzee, *Slow Man* 197)

To this, Costello responds: 'You know, there are those whom I call the chthonic, the ones who stand with their feet planted in their native earth; and then there are the butterflies [...] temporary residents, alighting here, alighting there. You claim to be a butterfly' (*Slow Man* 198). The 'burden', perhaps, facing the likes of Rayment and Marijana – to reformulate the sentence from *White Writing* that I cited near the outset of this chapter – is not to find a home in Australia, but to find one in the English language. Rayment, speaking English, feels like a 'ventriloquist's dummy' (*Slow Man* 198), and Elizabeth offers to teach him to speak like a true native. 'How does a native speak?' Rayment asks, to which Costello replies, 'From the heart' (*Slow Man* 231).

If the novel warns us about the dangers of entropy, of subsuming differences into a totality, it is perhaps even more insistent in its appeal to reinstantiate Mrs Curren's 'false etymology' – that is to say, to realign care, charity, *caritas*, and heart. Paul Rayment, since his accident, has been subjected to a ruthless 'regimen of care' (32); to indifferent 'motions of caring' (15); to the patronizing care of the welfare system (22); to an absence of 'loving care' (261) and to the 'care' of his leg, which amounts to its having been amputated without his informed consent (10). Elizabeth Costello seems to have been given the task of writing a book about Paul Rayment – she too looks upon him 'with a sinking heart, with everything but love'. Rayment would like to say to her, *'Have a little charity* [...] *Then perhaps you may find it in you to write'* (*Slow Man* 162). Is charity the space of art's response? In what way can it bring about an ethical engagement on the part of the viewer or reader? I shall return to this question in my conclusion.

Up to this point in the chapter, I have focused on individual words within a *particular* language, and within a specific socio-historic configuration. It is through the etymology of the word 'torture' that my discussion now opens onto a consideration of the implications for literary representation of the limits of language *in general*.

VI

I begin by considering in some detail excerpts from *Disgrace* and *Waiting for the Barbarians* in relation to the writings of Holocaust writer, Jean Améry.[14] Coetzee surely had Améry in mind, strikingly so, while writing certain passages for *Waiting for the Barbarians*. In this part of the chapter I explore the consequences of the author's attempt to translate into writing something that is essentially extra-linguistic. If the intensity of physical events is betrayed by the familiar and figurative patterns of prose, are there ways in which Coetzee hints (as he says Kafka does) 'that it is possible, for snatches, however brief, to think outside one's own language' (*Doubling the Point* 198) and to convey that in writing? What, then, are the ethical implications of *linguistic* commentary in moments of traumatic human confrontation, or of physical suffering, or of pain, in Coetzee's work? The point of departure in this section is the series of events and responses surrounding Lucy's rape in *Disgrace*; the discussion then moves on (with particular reference to *Waiting for the Barbarians*) to consider the implications, for literary writing, of Jean Améry's account of the time he spent in Nazi concentration camps. I am not suggesting that the events Coetzee portrays in *Disgrace* are comparable to those of which Jean Améry writes. Nevertheless, it seems clear to me that Coetzee is acquainted with Améry's *At the Mind's Limits*, and shares the latter's concern about the difficulty – perhaps even the impossibility – of conveying extreme physical and psychological suffering in literary language.

David Lurie regains consciousness to find himself locked in the lavatory while his daughter, Lucy, is being gang-raped in the bedroom on a smallholding outside Salem in the Eastern Cape. In this incident we see the most complicated clash of events at once political, personal and brutally physical – a clash that resists sanguine assimilation in prose. If at first the *languages* of Italian and French – that Lurie suddenly thinks about – are laughably outlandish, the horror of Lucy and Lurie's experience soon exceeds measure in any language, and it is the *experience* that simultaneously falls beyond structured linguistic reach, even while it encroaches upon, and disrupts, that linguistic terrain. The ability to articulate these events with a strong conviction that the truth is being told, is rendered questionable.

Lurie will shortly be doused in methylated spirits and set alight. He mordantly reflects on his uselessness and helplessness:

> He speaks Italian, he speaks French, but Italian and French will not save him here in darkest Africa. He is helpless, an Aunt Sally, a figure from a cartoon, a missionary in cassock and topi waiting with clasped hands and upcast eyes while the savages jaw away in their own lingo preparatory to plunging him into their boiling cauldron. Mission work: what has it left behind, that huge enterprise of upliftment? Nothing that he can see. (Coetzee, *Disgrace* 95)

Lurie's parodic and ludicrous image here, at a moment when his continued existence (and that of his daughter) is by no means assured, reminds me of Jean Améry's observation about the effects of what he calls 'the problem of the confrontation of intellect and horror' (Améry, *At the Mind's Limits* 6). The experience of time spent in Auschwitz and Bergen-Belsen, writes Améry, did not make him 'wiser' or 'deeper' or 'better, more human, more humane, and more mature ethically' – instead he gained the certain insight that

> for the greatest part the intellect is a *ludus* and that we are nothing more – or, better said, before we entered the camp we were nothing

more – than *homines ludentes*. With that we lost a good deal of
arrogance, of metaphysical conceit, but also quite a bit of our
naïve joy in the intellect that we falsely imagined was the sense of
life. (Améry, *At the Mind's Limits* 20)

Perhaps it is something of this 'naïve joy in the intellect' that Lucy
recognizes in Lurie, and from which she distances herself. She balks
at reporting her rape to the police, and further, it would be self-
defeating to try to explain why to her father. From Lucy's perspective, Lurie, in his relentless entreaties for an explanation from her,
puts her on 'trial', demands that she 'justify [her]self' (*Disgrace* 133),
and in the process, he perpetuates a violation of her right *not to be
called to account*. Lurie himself, however, almost immediately seeks a
rationale for the incident and constructs theories about the day of
horror on the farm – he purposely 'hold[s] to the theory and the
comforts of the theory' (98); he analyses the incident, and Lucy's
response to it, in terms of narrative 'abstractions' (112),[15] he comes up
with 'reading[s]' (118). 'It was history speaking through them', he
says to Lucy. 'A history of wrong. Think of it that way, if it helps'
(156). But for Lucy, 'That doesn't make it easier' – all the words in the
world have no bearing on the 'shock [that] simply doesn't go away'
(156); for Lucy, Lurie's readings inevitably constitute 'misreading[s]'
(112), and his incessant interrogations culminate in Lucy's response:

> 'I can't talk any more, David, I just can't,' she says, speaking softly,
> rapidly, as though afraid the words will dry up. 'I know I am not being
> clear. I wish I could explain but I can't.' (Coetzee, *Disgrace* 155)

Yet Lurie himself senses the paradox of translating the exorbitant
trauma of that day into ordinary language. On the way home from
the hospital, Bill Shaw comments to Lurie: 'A shocking business [...]
Atrocious [...] It's like being in a war all over again' (102). Lurie's
thoughts are telling: 'He does not bother to reply. The day is not dead
yet but living. *War, atrocity*: every word with which one tries to wrap
up this day, the day swallows down its black throat' (102). That night,
and the next morning, the words and ditty of a familiar nursery
rhyme torment Lurie's thoughts – *Oh dear, what can the matter be? /
Two old ladies locked in the lavatory / They were there from Monday to
Saturday / Nobody knew they were there.* 'A chant from his childhood',

Lurie reflects, 'come back to point a jeering finger' (109): the traumatic events of the day surface in Lurie's consciousness in the language of sing-song cultural clichés; the intellect, in language ruts like these, loses its capacity to transcend (see Améry, *At the Mind's Limits* 7). It is in this context that I think one can empathize with Lucy's *resistance* to telling, explaining, and – by implication – superficially ordering her terrible experience into a coherent narrative open to public reading. This brings me back to Jean Améry. 'To reach out beyond concrete reality with words', he writes,

> became before our very eyes a game that was not only worthless and an impermissible luxury but also mocking and evil. Hourly, the physical world delivered proof that its insufferableness could be coped with only through means inherent in that world. In other words: nowhere else in the world did reality have as much effective power as in the camp, nowhere else was reality so real. In no other place did the attempt to transcend it prove so hopeless and so shoddy. (Améry, *At the Mind's Limits* 19)

Jean Améry was born in Vienna in 1912, as Hans Mayer. He worked for the resistance in Belgium, survived arrest and torture by the Gestapo in the vault of Fort Breendonk, and spent time in Auschwitz and Bergen-Belsen. It would be 20 years before Améry spoke publicly about his experiences. 'I cannot say that during the time I was silent I had forgotten or "repressed" the twelve years of German fate, or of my own', writes Améry in 1966, in the preface to the first edition (written in German) of *At the Mind's Limits*. 'For two decades I had been in search of the time that was impossible to lose, but it had been difficult to talk about it' (Améry, *At the Mind's Limits* xiii).

In his essay on Améry, Sebald cites this passage, and comments on it in ways that link it to central preoccupations of this chapter. Sebald writes that

> [t]he paradox of searching for a time which, to the author's own distress, cannot in the last resort be forgotten entails the quest for a form of language in which experiences paralysing the power of articulation could be expressed. (Sebald, *On the Natural History of Destruction* 154)

If the enormity of an event paralyses the power of articulation, rendering the language that is inherited and shared 'shoddy' and 'hopeless' (to recall Améry's terms), then any attempt at just expression *demands* a break with what has been deemed sayable in the language before. Yet if articulation itself is paralysed by what remains unsaid, then, at the very least, a linguistic breaking-point can be registered, giving intimations of the attempt to shift a discursive limit, of the attempt to alter the field of linguistic response. In Coetzee (as in Améry), it is in the *unprecedented* instance[16] of confrontation, or of suffering or of an attempt at communication, that the discourse self-reflexively turns in on the linguistic mechanism placed under the strain of its own enquiry. I am thinking (I mention just a few examples here) of the colonial encounters in *Dusklands*,[17] of the scene of the magistrate's torture in *Waiting for the Barbarians* (128–33) of Mrs Curren's attempts to reach Florence, who lives in Guguletu, by phone (*Age of Iron* 147–9; 173–4), and of David Lurie's sustained interest in exploring extralinguistic ways of communicating with other sentient beings.

The focus of my discussion now is a sequence of events from *Waiting for the Barbarians*, where extremes of physical experience erupt into enquiries about the limit of language. The enquiry presses into isolated words, cleaving them in ways that expose semantic faultlines and intensify scepticism about what can meaningfully be said. To be more precise: the appreciation of meaning in language depends on the recognition of past usage, of what has been said before. What happens, then, in the attempt to articulate what could not be anticipated, when an event has made such an extreme and unprecedented physical demand that the worn paths of language offer no *meaningful* ground for discursive abstraction? (see Améry, *At the Mind's Limits* 25–6). The magistrate of *Waiting for the Barbarians* faces Mandel, his torturer:

> I look into his clear blue eyes, as clear as if there were crystal lenses slipped over his eyeballs. He looks back at me. I have no idea what he sees. Thinking of him, I have said the words *torture ... torturer* to myself, but they are strange words, and the more I repeat them the more strange they grow, till they lie like stones on my tongue.
> (Coetzee, *Waiting for the Barbarians* 129)

The image of staring at words, the analogy of words and stones (a recurrent and important motif in Coetzee from *Dusklands* onwards), reminds me again of Robert Smithson's essay, which I quoted at the outset of this chapter: 'Look at any *word* long enough and you will see it open up into a series of faults, into a terrain of particles each containing its own void. This discomforting language of fragmentation offers no easy gestalt solution; the certainties of didactic discourse are hurled into the erosion of the poetic principle' (Smithson, 'A Sedimentation of the Mind' 107). In Coetzee and in Améry it is the fragmentation of the language itself that has to become the focus of discussion, as the inconceivable reality of the event resists containment in the didactic and predictable ruts of the words that would speak about it. Both writers, in the realizaton of the enormity of the event, bear witness to the *language* as it becomes fragmented, as words become void. I quote at some length, and juxtapose two passages – the first from *Waiting for the Barbarians*:

> If I can hold my arms stiff, if I am acrobat enough to swing a foot up and hook it around the rope, I will be able to hang upside down and not be hurt: that is my last thought before they begin to hoist me. But I am as weak as a baby, my arms come up behind my back, and as my feet leave the ground I feel a terrible tearing in my shoulders as though whole sheets of muscle are giving way. (Coetzee, *Waiting for the Barbarians* 132)

The second passage is from Améry's *At the Mind's Limits*:

> In the bunker there hung from the vaulted ceiling a chain that above ran into a roll. At its bottom end it bore a heavy, broadly curved iron hook. I was led to the instrument. The hook gripped into the shackle that held my hands together behind my back. Then I was raised with the chain until I hung about a metre above the floor. In such a position, or rather, when hanging this way, with your hands behind your back...when you are already expending your utmost strength, when sweat has already appeared on your forehead and lips, and you are breathing in gasps, you will not answer any questions. Accomplices? Addresses? Meeting places? You hardly hear it. All your life is gathered in a single limited area of the body, the shoulder joints, and it does not

react...And now there was a crackling and splintering in my shoulders that my body has not forgotten until this hour. The balls sprang from their sockets. My own body weight caused luxation; I fell into a void and now hung by my dislocated arms which had been torn high from behind and were now twisted over my head. Torture, from Latin *toquere*, to twist. What visual instruction in etymology! (Améry, *At the Mind's Limits* 32–3; also cited in Sebald, *On the Natural History of Destruction* 156)

Sebald comments on this passage from Améry: 'The phrase with which this curiously objective passage concludes, provocatively deviating almost into the ridiculous, shows that the composure, the *impassibilité* allowing Améry to recapitulate such extreme experiences has here reached breaking point [...] He knows that he is operating on the borders of what language can convey' (Sebald, *On the Natural History of Destruction* 156). At the same time, the attempt at a just recollection of the event in discursive prose *demands* the arrest of language – because any words used to describe the extreme, of which one cannot make sense, will, at best, be euphemistically figurative. 'It would be totally senseless to try and describe here the pain that was inflicted on me', writes Améry,

One comparison would only stand for the other, and in the end we would be hoaxed by turn on the hopeless merry-go-round of figurative speech. The pain was what it was. Beyond that there is nothing to say. Qualities of feeling [...] mark the limit of the capacity of language to communicate. If someone wanted to impart his physical pain, he would be forced to inflict it and thereby become a torturer himself. (Améry, *At the Mind's Limits* 33)

By now at least this much should be clear: the attempt to articulate the extreme precipitates writer and reader to the periphery of what can be said. If the language used is reciprocally recognized and shared, then whatever falls beyond that given language will not be expressed. But the attempt to voice that which is without precedent breaks in on the smooth historical sequence of linguistic utterances. The irruption caused by the not-yet-said has radical consequences: it disturbs the assumption that a meaningful language, recognized and shared by addressor and addressee, is being spoken at all.

I return to the scene of the magistrate's torture from *Waiting for the Barbarians*:

> From my throat comes the first mournful dry bellow, like the pouring of gravel [...] I bellow again and again, there is nothing I can do to stop it, the noise comes out of a body that knows itself damaged perhaps beyond repair and roars its fright [...] Someone gives me a push and I begin to float back and forth in an arc a foot above the ground like a great old moth with its wings pinched together, roaring, shouting. 'He is calling his barbarian friends,' someone observes, 'That is barbarian language you hear.' There is laughter. (Coetzee, *Waiting for the Barbarians*, 132–3)

The damaged body, without premeditation, roars its truth in a way that cannot be recapitulated with integrity in the organizing patterns and structures of language. But this extralinguistic truth is aggressively suppressed by the Empire, through the act of supposedly ceding it a sense in the language of the derided other. Much later, the magistrate finds himself trapped in the ethically fraught negotiation between the potential reach and the limit of what he writes. Despite his intention to write 'the annals of an imperial outpost', he writes instead: 'No one who paid a visit to this oasis ... failed to be struck by the charm of life here ... This was paradise on earth.' The magistrate is appalled:

> For a long while I stare at the plea I have written. It would be disappointing to know that the poplar slips I have spent so much time on contain a message as devious, as equivocal, as reprehensible as this.
> 'Perhaps by the end of winter,' I think [...] 'I will abandon the locutions of a civil servant with literary ambitions and begin to tell the truth.' (Coetzee, *Waiting for the Barbarians* 168–9)

If, following the Wittgenstein of the *Tractatus* now, '*The limits of my language* mean the limits of my world (Wittgenstein, *Tractatus* §5.6 – '*Die Grenzen meiner Sprache* bedeuten die Grenzen meiner Welt'), it is not that there is nothing at all beyond the limit of language; instead, it is only that of which we can make linguistic sense that can be brought within its ambit. As Bernhard Weiss pointed out to me in an e-mail conversation, 'the contentious term here is "bedeuten", which is usually translated as "means" or "denotes". Obviously nothing stands outside the limits of my world, but something does stand outside the limits of my language, namely, nonsense'. Wittgenstein spells this out in the preface to the *Tractatus*: the limit can 'only be drawn in language and what lies on the other side of the limit will be simply nonsense' (Wittgenstein, *Tractatus* 27). We can make sense of the 'charm of life' as the magistrate puts it – it is much more amenable to being played out in patterns across the surface of narrative prose.[18]

VII

Thoughts of etymologies in Coetzee often seem to be occasioned by an enquiry into the capacity of language to tell the truth. Repeatedly, though, the etymological quest registers a linguistic breaking-point, where language seems inadequate to the demands made of it. In this chapter (extending the discussion of names in Chapter 5) I have shown how Coetzee, in foregrounding his characters' experiments with etymological sequences, and other morphological variations, invites attention to the effects of the contingency of cultural knowledge, social context and history *at work*, not only in the themes of his fiction, but also in the medium of its own construction. Section VI of this chapter has addressed the implications, for literary representation, of the limits of language in general, and, in keeping with the central argument of my book as a whole, I have shown how self-reflexive linguistic questions can be at the very core of ethical enquiry. In the concluding chapter to follow, I link the linguistic and ethical questions I have raised more explicitly to the domain of literary aesthetics.

7
Conclusion: We

I

In a striking incident in *Slow Man*, Paul Rayment shows Marijana's teenage son, Drago, his collection of Fauchery photographs – photographs of Australia's goldrush in the 1850s. On his death, Rayment will donate his photographs to a national archive. 'It will become public property. Part of our historical record' (*Slow Man* 177). Without warning, Rayment finds himself close to tears:

> Why? Because he dares to mention his own death to this boy, this forerunner of the generation that will take over his world and trample on it? Perhaps. But more likely it is because of *our. Our record, yours and mine.* Because just possibly this image before them, this distribution of particles of silver that records the way the sunlight fell, one day in 1855, on the faces of two long-dead Irishwomen, an image in whose making he, the little boy from Lourdes, had no part and in which Drago, son of Dubrovnik, has had no part either, may, like a mystical charm – *I was here, I lived, I suffered* – have the power to draw them together. (Coetzee, *Slow Man* 177)

The passage provides several points for discussion in this concluding chapter: what 'drawing together' of its viewers or readers does an image or a literary work have the potential to effect? What 'mystical charm' dictates that such extraordinary affective power can be generated through the seemingly neutral material of a work (the

176

'distribution of particles of silver')? And, from the perspective of the artist, how are these effects to be generated through the physical medium of the work; if the authority of art is generated purely through 'tricks of rhetoric', writes the JC of *Diary of a Bad Year*, 'then Plato was surely justified in expelling poets from his ideal republic' (*Diary of a Bad Year* 151). Finally, what testament to – and of – humanity do we find in works of art?

II

In Coetzee's writing, the process of 'drawing together' (signalled in 'we') often comes with negative connotations of exclusion, or of coercion, a loss of individual freedoms, the subjection of self to an unsavoury institutional or national apparatus. 'We' is not a simple plurality, as the linguist, Benveniste observes – it is 'not a multiplication of identical objects but a *junction* between "I" and the "non-I"' (Benveniste, *Problems in General Linguistics* 202). That 'non-I' can be 'you', or 'they', making for different possible equations: 'we' equals 'I plus you', or 'I plus them', or 'I plus you plus them' – or in more pointedly exclusive forms – 'I plus you minus them' and 'I plus them minus you'. Coetzee often draws attention to these different configurations of 'we'. Emmanuel Egudu, the African novelist in *Elizabeth Costello*, bombastically holds forth on the Western convention of reading in private: 'we are not like that in Africa. We do not like to cut ourselves off from other people [...] reading a book by yourself is not sharing [...] It is not our way' (*Elizabeth Costello* 40). '*We, we, we*', Elizabeth Costello mordantly comments, '*We Africans. It is not our* way. She has never liked *we* in its exclusive form' (*Elizabeth Costello* 40–1). David Lurie's 'we' is also one of flagrant exclusion: he is appalled at Petrus' announcement of his intention to marry Lucy (David's daughter), especially since David suspects Petrus of being somehow implicated in Lucy's rape. 'This is not how we do things', David lashes out. '*We*: he is on the point of saying, *We Westerners*' (*Disgrace* 202). What is evident is that the identification of a 'we' depends on its exclusions, bringing with it a measure of violence against those not included within its range. But, since it is never a simple plurality of identical subjects of equal standing, 'we' can also exercise violence against those coerced within its would-be totality.[1] It is only 'I' who is in the subject-position of speaker of the utterance. As we have already learnt from Benveniste, 'you' are the addressee, 'he' is the 'one who is absent' (Benveniste, *Problems in General Linguistics* 197).

What this means is that in any use of 'we', 'I' speaks on behalf of those who are logically excluded from the speaking subject position of the utterance – either as addressees, or, even more dangerously, by virtue of their absence. The use of 'we' has a performative effect: the 'non-I' component of 'we' is brought within its circumference by *saying* 'we', and it is only after the utterance that any resistance to inclusion within the 'we' can be articulated. In Coetzee (again, in both his fiction and his critical writings) we often find resistance to this gesture of coercion that comes with the act of saying 'we'. 'The notion of personal identity has dramatically narrowed in our times', writes Coetzee in an essay on Salman Rushdie's *The Moor's Last Sigh*, 'Identity has become in the first place a matter of group identification: of claiming membership of a group, or being claimed by a group' (Coetzee, *Stranger Shores* 200), and it is against this membership in both senses that Coetzee's protagonists frequently revolt – 'I am not the *we* of anyone', says the Paul Rayment of *Slow Man* (193).

Diary of a Bad Year opens with a reflection on the implications of the pervasive – and performative – message that 'we' brings into existence an actively complicit and totalitarian national identity: 'Every account of the origins of the state starts from the premise that "we" – not we the readers but some generic we so wide as to exclude no one – participate in its coming into being' (*Diary of a Bad Year* 3). What hope, then, for the writer who wishes to voice resistance to the state, to operate beyond the compass of the national 'we' in which he seems not only to be included, but actively complicit. This is the question that arises in Coetzee's essay on Erasmus (in *Giving Offense*), and also in the piece, 'Into the Dark Chamber' (in *Doubling the Point*), where Coetzee refers specifically to the difficulty of writing the torture scenes in *Waiting for the Barbarians*:

> For the writer the deeper problem is *not* to allow himself to be impaled on the dilemma proposed by the state, namely, either to ignore its obscenities or else to produce representations of them. The true challenge is: how not to play the game by the rules of the state, how to establish one's own authority, how to imagine torture and death on one's own terms. (Coetzee, *Doubling the Point* 364)

It is in this sense that the writer entertains the possibility of not being co-opted into a 'we': being part of a 'we' carries with it the threat of enforced compliance and subjection, and the reader begins to appreciate what is at stake in some of Coetzee's pronouncements, such as 'I am not a herald of community or anything else, as you correctly recognize' (*Doubling the Point* 341). I am reminded here of Derrida's response to an interviewer's question about the notion of 'community': 'If by community one implies, as is often the case, a harmonious group, consensus, and fundamental agreement beneath the phenomena of discord or war, then I don't believe in it very much and I sense it as much a threat as a promise' (Derrida, 'A "Madness" Must Watch Over Thinking' 355).

Throughout my discussions I have stressed Coetzee's insistence on the ethical value of providing the means of interrogating one's exist-ence. Raising the countervoice, and being responsive to it, is one such strategy open to the writer of fiction. Here it is important to register Coetzee's recognition of the inevitability of political compli-city, but also of its importance to the serious writer. 'I would regard it as morally questionable to write something like the second part of *Dusklands* – a *fiction*, note – from a position that is not historically complicit' (*Doubling the Point* 343), he remarks as a valuable after-thought in his interview with David Attwell about South African writers. In the closing parts of this interview, the discussion turns to a reflection about the designation, 'Afrikaner'. It will be a long time before the 'brandmark' can be withdrawn with any 'moral author-ity', and Coetzee himself does not consider it within his power to 'withdraw from the gang' either; yet neither is it his 'heart's desire to be counted apart' (*Doubling the Point* 343) – perhaps not least for the ethical reason voiced in his afterthought. The danger of one's histor-ical situatedness is that it can be used to occult anything considered beyond range of a self-designated 'we' – where that 'we' may be defined on the basis of language, cultural heritage, political persua-sion. This is what the Susan Barton of *Foe* recognizes: 'We deplore the barbarism of whoever maimed [Friday]', she says, 'yet have we, his later masters, not reason to be secretly grateful? For as long as he is dumb we can tell ourselves his desires are dark to us, and continue to use him as we wish' (Coetzee, *Foe* 148).

But let us return to the image of the Fauchery photograph with which I opened this chapter. *Despite* all the difficulties attendant upon saying 'we' which I have outlined here, the incident in *Slow Man*, in which Paul Rayment and Drago Jokić are drawn together by looking at a nineteenth-century photograph, is a poignantly positive one. It is important to register, though, that the *'our'* does not override their difference, or even the distance between the two characters. The *'our'* still retains the double reference of *'yours and mine'* (*Slow Man* 177), and if anything, the narrative voice plays up, rather than elides, the generation gap between Rayment and Drago, and stresses their further differences in national origin, culture and value systems. Emphasized, too, is their distance in history from the moment that the photograph was taken. *And yet*, the image has a 'mystical charm' that may 'just possibly' (at least, from Rayment's perspective) bring them together. The 'we' that is perhaps possible begins to emerge as a transcendent position of intersubjectivity, where the point of connection is all the more powerful because the distinctiveness of each party is insisted upon, rather than suppressed. At the same time, the *'our'* is transcendent in its potential arcing over distances in historical time and space – not only between Drago and Rayment, but between the unknown photographer and the Irishwomen in the image. In the recognition of the *'I was here, I lived, I suffered'* spoken by the distribution of silver particles on a piece of paper, the *'our'* transcends historical distance between the two Irishwomen in the nineteenth century and Drago and Rayment in the twenty-first.

At this point I am drawn to a brief consideration of another important preoccupation in Coetzee: the question of translation, specifically within the context of characters' reflections about their relation to their mother tongue. This will bring me back to further thoughts about the self in writing in section IV, and to my final conclusions in section V.

III

On the one hand the idea of translation seems to dramatize the negative implications of saying 'we' in the name of a group identification: translation depends on the drive to subsume the foreign within the boundaries of the familiar; it delimits a 'we' by excluding what is posited as being beyond translatable range. Yet in his seminal paper, 'The Task of the Translator', Walter Benjamin develops a theory of translation not unlike the kind of drawing together that we witness in the photograph incident in *Slow Man*. In the discussion to follow I bring these ideas back to Coetzee's notion of 'countervoice'. First, though, I would like to stress that the *theory* of translation is a different discipline altogether from the *practice* of translation. When Coetzee himself writes specifically about translation (importantly in 'Roads to Translation' and in several of the reviews published in *Inner Workings*), his interests, from the perspective of a writer, have more to do with the practice of translation, rather than with any theory about it. In his essay, 'Roads to Translation' Coetzee goes so far as to say that a theory of translation may not have anything to offer to the practising translator: 'I doubt very much that there is or can be such a thing as a theory of translation – not one, at any rate, from which practitioners of translation will have much to learn' ('Roads to Translation' 151). But here I am drawing on Benjamin's theory of translation within the context of a theory of literature, what Coetzee himself terms 'a legitimate branch of aesthetics' ('Roads to Translation' 151), to further the discussion about Coetzee's ethics and aesthetics of *writing*.

Walter Benjamin, in 'The Task of the Translator', cites Pannwitz:

> The basic error of the translator is that he preserves the state in which his own language happens to be instead of allowing his language to be powerfully affected by the foreign tongue [...] He must expand and deepen his language by means of the foreign language. (cited in Benjamin, 'The Task of the Translator' 79)

For Benjamin it is 'the task of the translator to release in his own language that pure language which is under the spell of another, to liberate the language imprisoned in a work in his re-creation of that work. For the sake of pure language he breaks through decayed barriers of his own language' (Benjamin, 'The Task of the Translator' 78). In tracking the path of the 'life of the word in its transfer' (Bakhtin, *Problems of Dostoevsky's Poetics* 202), so that traces of *both* languages are retained (as countervoices, let us say), the act of translation has the capacity to give intimations of a language transcending both source and target text. A translation will not articulate this transcendent language in any direct way, but will set up a relation between languages as a series of interpellations, hence challenging the limits of the target language in its receptiveness to, and even alteration by, the source language. The translation comes across as an internal dialogue between different languages – which brings the whole question of translation into the domain of ethics in at least one specific sense that Coetzee gives to it, that is to say, as a means of questioning the presumed unitary authority of the one who has language at his disposal.

This logic of translation takes on a broader, if metaphoric application: it has to do with the question of translating thoughts into language, of translating the self into writing. 'Do I have a mother tongue?' asks the JC of *Diary of a Bad Year*. '[A]t times, as I listen to the words of English that emerge from my mouth', he writes, 'I have a disquieting sense that the one I hear is not the one I call *myself*: Rather, it is as though some other person (but who?) were being imitated, followed, even mimicked. *Larvatus prodeo*'[2] (*Diary of a Bad Year* 195) – and English, supposedly his mother tongue, leads him to the thought that perhaps all languages are foreign languages, 'alien to our animal being'. Yet in English, specifically, JC has 'the uneasy feeling that there is something false going on' (Coetzee, *Diary of a Bad Year* 197), as if his words, and the self that he presents in language, are forever haunted by the thought that he speaks in translation. Yet what is this 'other language' of which his writing seems but a residual trace?[3] Even though the process of writing (rather than speaking) seems less disquieting for JC, the relation between himself, and what he has written, is open to question:

> Are these words, printed out on paper, truly what I wanted to say? Is it ever good enough, as a phenomenological account, to say that deep inside I knew what I wanted to say, after which I searched out the appropriate verbal tokens and moved them around until I had succeeded in saying what I wanted to say? Would it not be more accurate to say that I fiddle with a sentence until the words on the page 'sound' or 'are' right, and then stop fiddling and say to myself, 'That must have been what you wanted to say'? If so, who is it who judges what sounds or is right? Is it necessarily I ('I')? (Coetzee, *Diary of a Bad Year* 196)

Part of the difficulty in dealing with a passage like this one in *Diary of a Bad Year* is that it follows very closely views that Coetzee himself ('himself'!) has put out in his critical essays and interviews. But *at the same time* (we see this in the passage from *Doubling the Point* just below), Coetzee insists that the problem of relating the writing to the intentions and ideas of the one who writes, applies to *all kinds of writing*. It is not as if fiction raises peculiar questions about authorial intention that other kinds of writing do not. Here is the passage from the first interview in *Doubling the Point* that JC echoes in his essay on the mother tongue:

> As you write – *I am speaking about any kind of writing* – you have a feel of whether you are getting closer to 'it' or not. You have a sensing mechanism, a feedback loop of some kind; without that mechanism you could not write. It is naive to think that writing is a simple two-stage process: first you decide what you wanted to say, then you say it'. (Coetzee, *Doubling the Point* 18, my emphasis)

This is a view that Coetzee articulates throughout his writing. Here is just one further instance, this time from an early interview with Tony Morphet:

> Morphet: [in the lead-up to his question Morphet refers to *Dusklands, In the Heart of the Country, Waiting for the Barbarians* and *Life & Times of Michael K*] your total project appears to record the drama of the ruling South African consciousness. Would you accept this description?
> Coetzee: I don't know. It sounds very grand, the way you put it. There never was a master plan, though obviously certain subjects get written out and one has to move on. But then, meaning is so often something one half-discovers, half-creates in retrospect. So maybe there is a plan, now. (Coetzee and Morphet, 'Two Interviews with J.M. Coetzee' 460)

It is within this rich context, and with a sensitivity to the verb 'to write' as an instance of the middle voice, that Coetzee asserts that 'writing writes us' (*Doubling the Point* 18), that 'languages [speak] people' (*Doubling the Point* 53), that 'all writing is autobiography' (*Doubling the Point* 391) – in the teeth of challenging complacent assumptions about authorial intention. This places the literary critic of Coetzee's work in a delicate position. On the one hand, as a scholar of literature with a particular interest in fiction, one is resistant to a method that would use Coetzee's critical work as a shortcut to interpreting the themes in the novels. But on the other hand, Coetzee has produced no less than five volumes of critical essays – and numerous other short pieces besides. At what cost does one set the critical writing aside, not least because Coetzee's ('Coetzee's') aesthetic and ethical views – especially, but not only – since the publication of *Elizabeth Costello*, become part of the fiction in such a flagrant way? At best, perhaps, one can take careful heed of Mrs Curren's adjuration to her daughter:

> It would be easier for you, I know, if the story came from someone else, if it were a stranger's voice sounding in your ear. But the fact is, there is no one else. I am the only one. I am the one writing: I, I. So I ask you: attend to the writing, not to me. (Coetzee, *Age of Iron* 103–4)

Yet to attend to the writing – particularly if we take the verb 'to write' as an instance of the middle voice (and, like Coetzee, 'I am speaking about any kind of writing' (*Doubling the Point* 18)) – is inescapably to attend to the position and disposition of the writer that the writing makes possible.

Throughout the book I have been attentive to Coetzee's critical writings not simply as a hermeneutic lens through which to read the fiction. Instead, the critical essays and the fiction work in tandem; Coetzee's oeuvre constitutes a life-in-writing which develops a literary-critical discourse that systematically presses at the limits of received conceptions about fiction and literary criticism. In the process Coetzee makes a contribution to serious thinking within the fields of ethics and aesthetics, and this contribution, in turn, is an affirmation of the value of literary discourses within contemporary philosophical debates.

IV

In using the phrase 'a life-in-writing' I think of writing as a sediment of the self. '[I]t may well seem strange', writes French phenomenologist, Maurice Merleau-Ponty, 'that the spontaneous acts through which man has patterned his life should be deposited, like some sediment, outside himself and lead an anonymous existence as things' (Merleau-Ponty, *Phenomenology of Perception* 348). Writing is one such anonymous thing, but, Merleau-Ponty continues,

> In the cultural object, I feel the close presence of others beneath a veil of anonymity. *Someone* uses the pipe for smoking, the spoon for eating, the bell for summoning, and it is through the perception of a human act and another person that the perception of a cultural world could be verified. (Merleau-Ponty, *Phenomenology of Perception* 348)

It is this tension, between the anonymity of the material object, and the perception of a human act, that writing, as a site of engagement between writer and reader, has the capacity to enact with such extraordinary affective power. In the entry, 'My father' in *Diary of a Bad Year*, JC tells of a package that arrives from South Africa – among which is a small cardboard box of things – pencil sketches, photographs, badges and ribbons, a diary started but broken off after a few weeks – which were given to JC when his father died 30 years previously. 'At the bottom of the box, some scattered papers from his last years, including words scrawled on a torn-off scrap of newspaper: 'can something be done Im dying' (*Diary of a Bad Year* 165). JC reflects,

> here he is reduced to this pitiful little box of keepsakes; and here am I, their ageing guardian. Who will save them once I am gone? What will become of them? The thought wrings my heart'. (Coetzee, *Diary of a Bad Year* 166)

Throughout his work, Coetzee is attentive to writing as material presence in the world. In hospital, after his bicycle accident, Paul Rayment regains consciousness one noisy letter of the alphabet at a time, through the physical action of his typewriter keyboard:

> He is being rocked from side to side, transported. From afar voices reach him, a hubbub rising and falling to a rhythm of his own. What is going on? [...] Something is coming to him. A letter at a time, *clack clack clack*, a message is being typed on a rose-pink

screen that trembles like water each time he blinks and is therefore quite likely his own inner eyelid. E-R-T-Y, say the letters, then
F-R-I-V-O-L, then a trembling, then E, then Q-W-E-R-T-Y, on and
on. (Coetzee, *Slow Man* 3)

In several other places in Coetzee's oeuvre, language, or rather, a
presumed meaning, is manifest in physical, if sometimes inscrutable
or enigmatic signs (the marks on the barbarian girl's body; the little
wooden slips painted with an archaic script (*Waiting for the Barbarians*);
Friday's strange drawings of eyes and feet (*Foe*)). The cumulative
effect of these images of meaning as graphic inscription is a challenge to thinking about a signifying system purely in terms of an
abstract Saussurean *langue* – a system of universal and abstract rules.
Throughout Coetzee's work, meaning emerges through a physical
and historically situated medium, and writing, even if it is illegible,
obscure, incomprehensible, is the material object – sometimes the
artwork – that survives its writers, and its meaning: '*Scripta manent*'
(*Dusklands* 119). Thus the magistrate of *Waiting for the Barbarians*
never fathoms the script on the 256 poplar slips – is it writing at all?
he wonders, or perhaps 'elements of a picture whose outline would
leap at me if I struck on the right arrangement: a map of the land of
the barbarians in olden times, or a representation of a lost pantheon'
(*Waiting for the Barbarians* 17) – but it is the poplar slips that remain,
and that are testament to human acts on the part of the barbarians,
and the human act on the part of the magistrate in the respectful
care he takes to preserve the slips:

> I think: 'When one day people come scratching around in the
> ruins, they will be more interested in the relics from the desert
> than in anything I may leave behind. And rightly so.' (Thus I
> spend an evening coating the slips one by one in linseed oil and
> wrapping them in an oilcloth. When the wind lets up, I promise
> myself, I will go out and bury them where I found them). (Coetzee,
> *Waiting for the Barbarians* 169)

It is this notion of survival, of a physical remainder in time,
rather than any abstract and culturally contingent property, or idea
of canonicity, that Coetzee takes as definitive of 'the classic' in art.

'Whatever popular opinion may say, whatever the classics them-selves may claim', he writes,

> the classic does not belong to an ideal order, nor is it attained by
> adhering to one set of ideas or another. On the contrary, the clas-
> sic is the human; or, at least, it is what survives of the human.
> (Coetzee, *Giving Offense* 162)

In his insistence on art as an enduring testament to humanity,
Coetzee is once again very much part of a continental discussion
in literary aesthetics, a discussion that is perhaps best understood
as responding to Adorno's notorious pronouncement that 'to write
poetry after Auschwitz is barbaric' (Adorno, *Prisms* 34, cited in
Inner Workings 120). Celan evinces what seems to be an entirely
different approach to that of Adorno. In an address delivered in
1958 Celan says:

> There remained in the midst of the losses this one thing:
> language.
>   It, the language, remained, not lost, yes in spite of everything.
> But it had to pass through frightful muting, pass through the
> thousand darknesses of deathbringing speech. It passed through
> and gave back no words for what had happened; yet it passed
> through this happening. Passed through and could come to light
> again, 'enriched' by all this. (Celan, *Selected Poems and Prose of
> Paul Celan*, trans. John Felstiner 395, cited in *Inner Workings* 121)[4]

Lacoue-Labarthe, responding to the difficulty of understanding
Celan's poetry at the most basic level, writes: 'What should we think
of poetry (or what of thought is left in poetry) that must refuse,
sometimes with great stubbornness, to signify?' (Lacoue-Labarthe,
Poetry as Experience 14). And of Celan's poem, 'Tübingen, January',
Lacoue-Labarthe asks,

> what saves this poem from wreckage in, and the wreckage of,
> poetry? How does it happen that in poetry, out of poetry, all is
> not lost, that a possibility of articulating something still
> remains, if only in stuttering, if only in an incomprehensible

and incommunicable language, an idiolect or idiom. (Lacoue-Labarthe, *Poetry as Experience* 23)

It is at this point that we need to revisit Adorno's assertion about poetry after Auschwitz more carefully than if it were an isolated aphorism – even though Adorno did retract his statement in 1966 (see *Inner Workings* 120). In his essay, 'Cultural Criticism and Society', Adorno asks what an effective 'cultural criticism' might entail. 'The more total society becomes, the greater the reification of the mind and the more paradoxical its effort to escape reification on its own', writes Adorno, in ways that remind me of the excerpts from Jean Améry's *At the Mind's Limits* that I cited in the previous chapter. Adorno continues:

> Even the most extreme consciousness of doom threatens to degenerate into idle chatter. Cultural criticism finds itself faced with the final stage of the dialectic of culture and barbarism. To write poetry after Auschwitz is barbaric. (Adorno, *Prisms* 34)

When one reads the last sentence just cited here within the context of the larger discussion which insists that 'traditional culture has become worthless today' in that it is '[n]eutralized and ready-made', then we begin to appreciate that a 'barbaric' poetry would be one that attempts to give voice to something not reducible to the idle chatter of culture *in its own terms*. Adorno's assertion is thus more nuanced than is often given out. Nevertheless, Lacoue-Labarthe and Coetzee take a more evidently positive approach than Adorno does: the poem survives the event it voices. The *poem* is what is left, the poem is possible as *'singbarer Rest*, the singable remainder' the 'singable residue' as Lacoue-Labarthe puts it, following Celan (Lacoue-Labarthe, *Poetry as Experience* 21, 23), and Coetzee extends the thought. An implicit claim of Celan's poem 'Death Fugue',[5] says Coetzee, is that 'language can measure up to any subject whatsoever: however unspeakable the Holocaust might be there is a poetry that can speak it' (Coetzee, *Inner Workings* 120).

What remains in a reading of the artwork, even if the words do not strictly follow a reasoned narrative or philosophical argument, is the recognition on the part of the reader of the poet's human attempt to voice an appeal against the unspeakable.

V

I return now to the context of the discussion in which Coetzee says, 'I am not a herald of community' (*Doubling the Point* 341). In the interview about South African writers, David Attwell refers to the essay, 'Into the Dark Chamber' in which Coetzee focuses on the morality of representing torture in literature. But Attwell raises the stakes of the conversation in an interesting and important way: 'behind this question [i.e. the morality of representing torture] is a larger one, about the authority in South Africa of ethical judgement itself'. Contemporary white South African literature, Attwell goes on to suggest, 'has been better at subverting colonial traditions than at replacing them with the imaginative possibility of a moral community' (*Doubling the Point* 339). Coetzee responds in a subtle way: if the imagining of such a community is perceived as the socially instituted duty of the writer, this is something that Coetzee would have misgivings about. Nevertheless, what he does speak about with a sense of urgency in this interview is an understanding of the 'duty' of the writer as an articulation of 'conscience' that is 'something constitutional to the writer': a 'transcendental imperative' (*Doubling the Point* 340). Again Attwell deepens the terms of the conversation in his recognition that Coetzee, while 'declining the role of herald to a reconstructed social order', is engaged in a life of writing that 'also seems to project, at a much deeper level, a certain faith in the idea, or the possibility of an ethical community' (340). It is Attwell's use of the word 'herald' that interests Coetzee, and picking up on the term 'transcendental imperative' his response alludes, quite specifically, to Plato and Kant. In *The Republic*, Socrates and his friends, in their attempt to answer the question 'What is justice?', envisage in elaborate detail the possible workings of an ideal state. Coetzee, in his response to Attwell, suggests that 'community has its basis in an awareness and acceptance of a common justice'; that is to say, an 'awareness of an idea of justice, somewhere, that transcends laws and lawmaking' (*Doubling the Point* 340). The reference to Plato is sustained in Coetzee's image of the cave (see Book VII of Plato's *Republic*): the writer's intimation of a community grounded in an awareness of justice is 'flickering or dimmed – the kind of awareness you would have if you were a prisoner in a cave, say, watching the shadows of ideas flickering on the walls. To be a herald you would have to have slipped your chains for a while and wandered about in the real world' (*Doubling the Point* 340–1). And this is surely what constitutes the *pathos* of Coetzee's fiction: the characters (in many instances writers or artists themselves) write from inside the cave, from a position of historical situatedness, and their intimations of freedom or justice seem remote from the society in which they live. Yet even in the recognition that they speak for ideals that may be untenable in their time and place, the transcendent imperative (for the characters themselves, and for Coetzee) is to give voice to those intimations. 'Why does one choose the side of justice when it is not in one's material interest to do so?' Coetzee asks within the context of a discussion about *Waiting for the Barbarians* in the final interview in *Doubling the Point*,

> The Magistrate gives the rather Platonic answer: because we are born with the idea of justice. The essay ['Confession and Double Thoughts'], if only implicitly, asks the question: Why should I be interested in the truth about myself when the truth may not be in my interest? To which, I suppose, I continue to give a Platonic answer: because we are born with the idea of the truth.' (Coetzee, *Doubling the Point* 394–5)

The voices that Coetzee realizes in his fiction – voices of characters (let me say, writers) like Susan Barton, Mrs Curren, the magistrate, David Lurie, Elizabeth Costello and JC, all speak from the limited and fallible perspective of prisoners in the cave. And yet, or perhaps precisely *because* they are not the shining heralds of a new social order, their human attempts to articulate a different grounding for the societies in which they live carry extraordinary affective power. This is what Coetzee speaks about in relation to Gordimer's novel, *Burger's Daughter*, in his essay, 'Into the Dark Chamber':

> What Rosa suffers and waits for is a time when humanity will be restored across the face of society, and therefore when all human acts, including the flogging of an animal, will be returned to the ambit of moral judgement. In such a society it will once again be *meaningful* for the gaze of the author, the gaze of authority and authoritative judgement, to be turned upon scenes of torture'. (Coetzee, *Doubling the Point* 368)

The hopelessly divided epistemologies that typically underwrite the fictional worlds inhabited by Coetzee's characters are often counterposed by Coetzee's realization of a single voice appealing to some utopian idea of a community based in a shared sense of justice and freedom 'that transcends laws and lawmaking' (*Doubling the Point* 340). For Kant,

> we can explain nothing but that which we can reduce to laws, the object of which can be given in some possible experience. But freedom is a mere Idea, the objective reality of which can in no wise be shown according to laws of nature, and consequently not in any possible experience; and for this reason it can never be comprehended or understood, because we cannot support it by any sort of example or analogy [...] Now where determination according to laws of nature ceases, there all *explanation* ceases also, and nothing remains but *defence, i.e.* the removal of the objections of those who pretend to have seen deeper into the nature of things and thereupon boldly declare freedom impossible. (Kant, *Fundamental Principles of the Metaphysics of Morals* §4.459)

The ideals of freedom or justice cannot be explained with reference to a set of laws, but that in itself is not reason enough to denounce their possibility – indeed, for Kant this denunciation would constitute an unethical response. Coetzee writes,

> I am someone who has intimations of freedom (as every chained prisoner has) and constructs representations – which are shadows themselves – of people slipping their chains and turning their faces to the light. I do not imagine freedom, freedom *an sich*; I do not represent it. Freedom is another name for the unimaginable, says Kant, and he is right. (Coetzee, *Doubling the Point* 341)

Several characters in Coetzee seem to act in the name of a possible shadow-community slipping its chains: Elizabeth Costello delivers two deeply unsettling lectures to an academic audience on the injustice of the treatment of animals in the human food industry. Her own son, John, does not wish his mother's views to impinge upon his daily life ('In a few days, blessedly, she will be on her way to her next destination, and he will be able to get back to his work'), even while he acknowledges her right to, and the sincerity of, her convictions (*The Lives of Animals* 17). 'It's been such a short visit,' he says to Elizabeth Costello when she leaves, 'I haven't had time to make sense of why you have become so intense about the animal business.' Elizabeth knows she is pressing the limit of what is socially acceptable in her outrageous plea against the human treatment of other animals ('it rivals anything that the Third Reich was capable of, indeed dwarfs it' (*The Lives of Animals* 21)), at the same time that she is led to question her own sanity:

> It's that I no longer know where I am. I seem to move around perfectly easily among people, to have perfectly normal relations with them. Is it possible, I ask myself, that all of them are participants in a crime of stupefying proportions? Am I fantasizing it all? I must be mad! Yet every day I see the evidences. The very people I suspect produce the evidence, exhibit it, offer it to me. Corpses. Fragments of corpses that they have bought for money. (Coetzee, *The Lives of Animals* 69)

David Lurie, too, speaks for this shadow-community when he intervenes in the beating of the corpses of the dogs entering the incinerator. There is no practical virtue in his doing so; it is a utopian gesture, purely for his idea of a more humane world. Mrs Curren also seems to respond to a personal transcendent imperative. She realizes the risks of her 'wager on trust' in asking the desultory Vercueil to post her letter to her daughter after her death, but, 'If there is the slightest breath of trust, obligation, piety left behind when I am gone he will surely take it' she says,

> Because I cannot trust Vercueil I must trust him.
> I am trying to keep a soul alive in times not hospitable to the soul. (Coetzee, *Age of Iron* 130)

The *fact* of Mrs Curren's letter, together with her intention about its delivery (rather than the thematic content of what her letter says), is a written testament to an idea of a better world. And this testament is reasserted each time the letter – and hence Coetzee's novel – is read: 'Now I put my life in his hands instead. This is my life, these words, these tracings of the movements of crabbed digits over the page. These words, as you read them, if you read them, enter you and draw breath again' (*Age of Iron* 131). It seems to me that this is an important part of what Coetzee's novels are for. Through his writing, Coetzee raises a series of countervoices and embarks upon speech with them; the writing is what remains of one person's awareness and elaboration of an idea of justice that could possibly form the basis of a lasting community.

I return, finally, to the scene with which I opened this chapter, where Paul Rayment and the teenager, Drago Jokić, examine the nineteenth-century Fauchery photograph. The two dimensional paper card with its distribution of silver particles has an objective materiality in time and space – but the space of the image is not reducible to static spatio-temporal co-ordinates. The photograph of the 'long-dead Irishwomen' provokes an empathetic response across centuries, and will continue to reach out to an illimitable future; far-off continents are reeled in to a small scrap of paper as Rayment, the 'boy from Lourdes' and Drago, 'son of Dubrovnik' meet, with understanding, the gaze of two Irishwomen in Australia. Geography and time are refracted through silver particles and effect what artist and film-maker, William Kentridge, would call a 'distant connectedness' (Kentridge and Cameron, 'An Interview with William Kentridge' 72). The artwork, in the moment of its reception, thus reconfigures ordinary conceptions of time and space.

And yet, as we have seen throughout Coetzee's writing, it is surely when the medium of the artwork is at the breaking-point of what it can convey, when the artist is forced to articulate that there is perhaps 'too much truth for art to hold' (Coetzee, *Doubling the Point* 99), that the work exposes and plays a creative part in shifting the limit of what can be said, and what can be imagined. That act of saying and imagining rests on the responsiveness – or shall we say the charity – of we, the readers: the ageing guardians of what is written.

UNIVERSITY OF WINCHESTER
LIBRARY

Notes

Introduction

1. I have two points of reference in the back of my mind. The first is Wittgenstein: *'Essence* is expressed in grammar' ('Das *Wesen* ist in der Grammatik ausgesprochen') and 'Grammar tells what kind of object anything is' ('Welche Art von Gegenstand etwas ist, sagt die Grammatik') (Wittgenstein, *Philosophical Investigations* §371 and §373). In *Philosophical Investigations* Wittgenstein goes on to ask: '[D]oes it depend wholly on our grammar what will be called (logically) possible and what not, – i.e. what that grammar permits?' ('Also hängt es ganz von unserer Grammatik ab, was (logisch) möglich genannt wird, und was nicht – nämlich eben was sie zuläßt?' (Wittgenstein, *Philosophical Investigations* §520). My second reference point is Richard Ohmann's account of literary style. Ohmann is an important critical resource for Coetzee in his doctoral thesis, *The English Fiction of Samuel Beckett* (see especially 157–9). In Ohmann's analysis of literary style, I read echoes of a Wittgensteinian conception of grammar: 'So far I have been outlining a theory of style which describes choices that I have called epistemic. These choices are important, for they are the critic's key to a writer's mode of experience. They show what sort of place the world is for him, what parts of it are significant or trivial. They show how he thinks, how he comes to know, how he imposes order on the ephemeral pandemonium of experience' (Ohmann, 'Prolegomena to the Analysis of Prose Style' 408). It is perhaps worth mentioning that for Wittgenstein 'Arithmetic is the grammar of numbers. Kinds of number can only be distinguished by the arithmetical rules relating to them' (Wittgenstein, *Philosophical Remarks* §108). For a deft account of Wittgenstein's use of the term, 'grammar', see H.L. Finch's *Wittgenstein*, especially Chapter 4, 'Grammar as Deep Culture'.
2. Nevertheless, Brian Macaskill's article, 'Charting J.M. Coetzee's Middle Voice', constitutes an important step in this direction. In one of his footnotes, Macaskill cites Dick Penner, Stephen Watson and Susan VanZanten Gallagher as recognizing the importance of an attentiveness to matters of linguistic concern in a discussion of Coetzee's broader ethical preoccupations, even if they do not follow this through in any length themselves (Macaskill, 'Charting J.M. Coetzee's Middle Voice' 445–6). The works of Rita Barnard, Zoë Wicomb, Mark Sanders, Jean Sévry and Derek Attridge also demonstrate fine attentiveness to the implications of linguistic nuance – but I would not say that this constitutes the main impetus of their enquiries.
3. See especially Chapter 6 of the thesis, pp. 159–62.

4. It is important to realize that there are several quite distinct branches of linguistics with which Coetzee engages: transformational-generative grammar, structural linguistics, and analytic language philosophy with its roots in formal logic, to name some of them. Stylistics – the focus of enquiry in Coetzee's doctoral thesis – constitutes another diverse discipline, some variants of which have a strong linguistic base. Coetzee clarifies the differences between 'structural and generative-transformational approaches to style': 'In the former the analyst typically describes the structure of a work of literature in terms of the interrelations of parts [...] In the latter the analyst typically constructs a generative grammar which would produce the sentences of the work under analysis, making the grammar as nearly isomorphic as possible with the grammar of the language in which the work is written' (Coetzee, *The English Fiction of Samuel Beckett* 238–9).

5. Coetzee's brief but thought-provoking essay, 'A Note on Writing' (in *Doubling the Point* 94–5), engages with Barthes' essay 'To Write: An Intransitive Verb?'

6. Coetzee cites part of this passage within the context of a discussion about Breyten Breytenbach's prison writings and South African censorship (*Giving Offense* 223–7).

7. The essay is reprinted in *Doubling the Point*; Coetzee comments on the essay in the final retrospective interview (see *Doubling the Point* 391–4).

8. Bakhtin, in *Problems of Dostoevsky's Poetics*, voices a similar concern about stylistics: 'On the whole it is impossible, while remaining within the limits of linguistic stylistics, to tackle the proper artistic problem of style. No single formal linguistic definition of a word can cover all its artistic functions in the work. The authentic style-generating factors remain outside the field of vision available to linguistic stylistics (Bakhtin, *Problems of Dostoevsky's Poetics* 225). Coetzee refers to Bakhtin in his essay, 'Confession and Double Thoughts: Tolstoy, Rousseau, Dostoevsky', written in 1982–83 (see Coetzee, *Doubling the Point* 392) and first published in 1985. Bakhtin's *Problems of Dostoevsky's Poetics* was translated into English in 1984. In the version of the 'Confession and Double Thoughts' essay published in *Doubling the Point*, Coetzee cites this English translation; in his original essay (published in *Comparative Literature* in 1985), he refers to the French translation of *Problems of Dostoevsky's Poetics* which was published in 1970.

9. Roland Barthes, in 'The Death of the Author', writes: 'For him [i.e. Mallarmé], for us too, it is language which speaks, not the author; to write is, through a prerequisite impersonality (not at all to be confused with the castrating objectivity of the realist novelist), to reach that point where only language acts, "performs", and not "me" ' (Barthes, 'The Death of the Author' 1467).

10. Another one of Coetzee's computer poems, 'Hero and Bad Mother in Epic, a poem', was published in *Staffrider* in 1978. *Staffrider* was the pre-eminent literary journal during the apartheid years, famous as a

platform for protest writing. To have published a computer-generated poem in *Staffrider* in 1978, just two years after the Soweto uprising, is to have operated well beyond the literary-critical expectations and orthodoxies of the time.

11. 'It makes a great deal of sense [says Coetzee in an interview with David Attwell] to assimilate Chomskyan linguistics to structuralism [...] if only because of the similar weight the two enterprises give to innate structures' (*Doubling the Point* 24).

12. In his recent book, *The Philosophy of Philosophy*, Timothy Williamson, a contemporary analytic philosopher, speaks about the 'mundane but vital role' that the imagination plays in philosophical thought experiments (179). He goes on to say, 'There is a debate as to whether thought experiments in science reduce to arguments [...] or contain an irreducible imaginative element [...] The present account of thought experiments in philosophy goes some way towards reconciling the two sides: thought experiments do constitute arguments, but the imagination plays an irreducible role in warranting the premises' (Williamson, *The Philosophy of Philosophy* fn 7, 187–8). Stephen Mulhall's discussion of thought experiments in relation to *Elizabeth Costello* has a different focus (see Mulhall, *The Wounded Animal* 23–7). '[T]hought experiments in ethics presuppose that we can get clearer about what we think concerning a single, specific moral issue by abstracting it from the complex web of interrelated matters of fact and of valuation within which we usually encounter and respond to it. But what if the issue means what it does to us, has the moral significance has for us, precisely because of its place in that complex web? If so, to abstract it from that context is to ask us to think about something else altogether – something other than the issue that interested us in the first place; it is, in effect, to change the subject' (Mulhall, *The Wounded Animal* 27).

13. The term 'singularity' has gained literary currency in recent Coetzee scholarship, especially since the publication of Derek Attridge's two books of 2004: *J.M. Coetzee and the Ethics of Reading: Literature in the Event* and *The Singularity of Literature*. I enter into conversation with Attridge's work in Chapter 2, 'You'.

14. Coetzee writes, 'the actual productions of structuralist analysis [...] though meant to show the creative mind at work, never provided me or any other writer, I believe, with a model or even a suggestion of how to write. In that sense structuralism remained a firmly academic movement' (*Doubling the Point* 24). Coetzee goes on to add, 'Nothing one picks up from generative linguistics or from other forms of structuralism helps one to put together a novel' (*Doubling the Point* 25).

15. It is his reading of Noam Chomsky, Jerrold Katz and the universal grammarians that leads Coetzee to ask, 'If a latter-day ark were ever commissioned to take the best that mankind has to offer and make a fresh start on the farther planets [...] might we not leave Shakespeare's plays and Beethoven's quartets behind to make room for the last speaker of Dyirbal,

even though that last speaker might be a fat old woman who scratched herself and smelled bad?' (*Doubling the Point* 52–3).

16. Prominent among these: Dominic Head's *J.M. Coetzee*, David Attwell's *J.M. Coetzee: South Africa and the Politics of Writing* and Dick Penner's *Countries of the Mind*.

17. The very first monograph published on Coetzee (in 1984) is Teresa Dovey's *The Novels of J.M. Coetzee: Lacanian Allegories*. Derek Attridge's *J.M. Coetzee and the Ethics of Reading: Literature in the Event* and Stefan Helgesson's *Writing in Crisis: Ethics and History in Gordimer, Ndebele and Coetzee* offer readings of Coetzee with extensive reference to Levinasian ethics, as does Mike Marais in a number of articles. See especially his ' "Little Enough, Less than Little: Nothing": Ethics, Engagement, and Change in the Fiction of J.M. Coetzee', 'Disarming Silence: Ethical Resistance in J.M. Coetzee's *Foe*' and 'Literature and the Labour of Negation: J.M. Coetzee's *Life & Times of Michael K*'. Marais' essay, ' "After the Death of a Certain God": a Case for Levinasian Ethics', constitutes a response to Lucy Graham's ' "Yes, I am giving him up": Sacrificial Responsibility and Likeness with Dogs in J.M. Coetzee's Recent Fiction'.

1 Not I

1. There are no page numbers on the play script. The note appears after the text of Mouth's monologue.

2. At my time of writing this, the third of Coetzee's 'autobiographical' works, *Summertime*, has not yet been published. Presumably, like *Boyhood* and *Youth*, it is written in the third person. Nevertheless, I cannot help entertaining the thought that there may be further experiments with the use of the first and the third person. The narrative strategy in *Diary of a Bad Year* (where JC has a first-person command over parts of the text) and a comment in the final interview in *Doubling the Point*, make me wonder about this. In this interview Coetzee speaks about his youth in the third person – but makes a self-conscious return to the first person (*Doubling the Point* 394).

3. I take Jean Sévry's essay, 'Coetzee the Writer and the Writer of an Autobiography', and the interview that he conducted with Coetzee in 1986, to be among the most valuable contributions to Coetzee scholarship. Sévry follows an interesting line of discussion in which he stresses the *continuity* between the interviews in *Doubling the Point* and the fictional autobiography of *Boyhood*. In his essay, Sévry cites parts of both the passages I have quoted here – but with a slight misquotation in the first passage. In Sévry's essay the cited part reads, 'As a teenager, this person, this subject, the subject of this I' (Sévry, 'Coetzee the Writer and the Writer of an Autobiography' 15).

4. For illuminating accounts of Coetzee's use of the third person see Jean Sévry's essay, 'Coetzee the Writer and the Writer of an Autobiography', and Chapter 6 of Derek Attridge's *J.M. Coetzee and the*

Ethics of Reading – 'Confessing in the Third Person: *Boyhood* and *Youth*'. Sévry discusses the interviews in *Doubling the Point* within the context of the genre of confession. Coetzee found in the interviews with Attwell, Sévry suggests, 'another possibility for the writer to tell more about himself' (Sévry, 'Coetzee the Writer and the Writer of an Autobiography' 15). Sévry and Attridge both discuss Coetzee's essay, 'Confession and Double Thoughts' and the final, retrospective interview in *Doubling the Point* in relation to Coetzee's fictional autobiographies.

5. I am echoing a question that Coetzee asks, 'In the hands of writers who use the passive in a complex and systematic way, what can it be made to do?' (Coetzee, *Doubling the Point* 159).

6. In *J.M. Coetzee and the Ethics of Reading*, Derek Attridge takes a passage from *Life & Times of Michael K* and points out that it would be very different if it were written in the first person. I shall be returning to Attridge's discussion of this a little later in the chapter.

7. See especially Chapters 3 and 4 of Kjetil Enstad's doctoral thesis, and also Derek Attridge: 'the use of the present tense both heightens the immediacy of the narrated events and denies the text any retrospection, any place from which the writer can reflect on and express regret about (or approval of) the acts and attitudes described' (Attridge, *J.M. Coetzee and the Ethics of Reading* 143).

8. See Hermione Lee's 'Uneasy Guest': '*Youth* is the ultimately alienated and alienating autobiography: not an inward exploration, or an ethical indictment of the author/subject, but a self-parody' (Lee, 'Uneasy Guest' 15).

9. I cannot resist thinking of this passage in *Youth* as a parodic take on Michael K's version of existentialism. Here is K: 'He is like a stone, a pebble that, having lain around quietly minding its own business since the dawn of time, is now suddenly picked up and tossed randomly from hand to hand. A hard little stone, barely aware of its surroundings, enveloped in itself and its interior life' and 'He might help people, he might not help them, he did not know beforehand, anything was possible. He did not seem to have a belief, or did not seem to have a belief regarding help. Perhaps I am the stony ground, he thought' (Coetzee, *Life & Times of Michael K* 185 and 65).

10. Chomsky cites a different translation in *Cartesian Linguistics*: 'the word is the sole sign and the only certain mark of the presence of thought hidden and wrapped up in the body; now all men, the most stupid and the most foolish, those even who are deprived of the organs of speech, make use of signs, whereas the brutes never do anything of the kind; which may be taken for the true distinction between man and brute' (Descartes' letter of 5 February 1649 to Henry More, cited in Chomsky, *Cartesian Linguistics* 6).

11. I shall return to the question of rhythm in Chapter 3, 'Voice'.

12. In *Cartesian Linguistics* Chomsky cites Leibniz and Schlegel. Leibniz: 'les langues sont le meilleur miroir de l'esprit humain', and Schlegel: 'so unzertrennlich ist Geist und Sprache, so wesentlich Eins Gedanke und

Wort, dass wir, so gewiss wir den Gedanken als das eigentümliche Vorrecht des Menschen betrachten, auch das Wort, nach seiner innern Bedeutung und Würde als das ursprüngliche Wesen des Menschen nennen können (cited in Chomsky, *Cartesian Linguistics* 29–30).

13. 'If we accept, for the moment, that all writing is autobiography, then the statement that all writing is autobiography is itself autobiography, a moment in the autobiographical enterprise. Which is a roundabout way of saying that the remarks you refer to, published in *Doubling the Point*, do not exist outside of time and outside of my life story' (Coetzee and Attwell, 'All Autobiography Is *Autre*-biography' 214).

14. Coetzee writes of *Foe*: 'My novel, *Foe*, if it is about any single subject, is about authorship: about what it means to be an author in the professional sense (the profession of author was just beginning to mean something in Daniel Defoe's day) but also in a sense that verges, if not on the divine, then at least on the demiurgic: sole author, sole creator', and 'The notion that one can be an author as one can be a baker is fairly fundamental to my conception of *Foe*' (Coetzee, 'Roads to Translation' 145).

15. I return to the difficult nexus of questions about colonialism, writing and power in Chapter 5, 'Names'.

16. 'j'aurai toujours celui qui me viendra, j'en changerai selon mon humeur sans scrupule, je dirai chaque chose comme je la sens, comme je la vois, sans recherche, sans gêne, sans m'embarrasser de la bigarrure. En me livrant à la fois au souvenir de l'impression reçue et au sentiment présent je peindrai doublement l'état de mon âme' (Rousseau, 'Préambule du Manuscrit de Neufchâtel').

17. Chomsky claims contemporary transformational generative grammar to be 'a modern and more explicit version of the Port-Royal theory' (*Cartesian Linguistics* 38–9).

18. In one of the interviews in *Doubling the Point* Coetzee says that he found himself reading Chomsky and the new universal grammarians 'to discover himself suspecting that languages spoke people or at the very least spoke through them' (*Doubling the Point* 53).

2 You

1. See endnote number 17 of the introduction.

2. Coetzee himself uses the verb 'stage', within the context of the possibilities opened up by fiction, but foreclosed by academic prose (See *Doubling the Point* 60–1). I discuss this passage a little later in the chapter. 'Staging' is a key term in Derek Attridge's readings of Coetzee.

3. Hillis Miller's groundbreaking 'The Critic as Host' was first presented at the MLA conference in December 1976, in response to M.H. Abrams' paper, 'The Deconstructive Angel'. It seems to me helpful to think of Coetzee's 'Die Skrywer en die Teorie' within the context of this debate.

4. While stressing the importance of contemporary European philosophy in Coetzee's own writing, my critical approach is thus rather different

from one kind of reading which *applies* a philosophical framework in a reading of the novel. See, for example, Monson's essay on *Life & Times of Michael K*.

5. In an interview with François Poirié, Levinas acknowledges his debt to Buber: 'The relation to the other man is irreducible to the knowledge of an object. This is certainly a terrain of reflection where Buber has been before me [...] the interpersonal relation is distinguished from the object relation in a very convincing and brilliant way, and with much finesse' (Levinas and Poirié, 72).

6. Recall that Coetzee defines literary style as 'linguistic choice within the economy of the work of art as a formal whole' in the abstract of his doctoral thesis.

7. While much critical attention has been devoted to Coetzee's engagements with ethics, his preoccupation with linguistics has attracted relatively little discussion. The *link* between linguistics and ethics has not been the focus of any book-length study. Here are some noteworthy articles that discuss related issues: Zoë Wicomb's 'Translations in the Yard of Africa' examines David Lurie's preoccupation with the grammatical aspect of the perfective, and discusses *Disgrace* as a text that 'struggles with translation as concept-metaphor for the postapartheid condition' (Wicomb, 'Translations in the Yard of Africa' 209). Mark Sanders analyses verbal tense and aspect in *Disgrace*, and argues that 'the novel's syntax reinforces the critical reflection it provokes about the Truth and Reconciliation Commission's attempts to come to terms with the historical legacy of apartheid' (Sanders, 'Disgrace' 363). I have found Rita Barnard's broader discussions of language and translation in Coetzee particularly interesting. See especially 'J.M. Coetzee's *Disgrace* and the South African Pastoral' and 'J.M. Coetzee in/and Afrikaans'. Perhaps the most extensive consideration of the broader political ramifications of a linguistic feature is Brian Macaskill's 'Charting J.M. Coetzee's Middle Voice'.

8. Buber's I–thou relation reverberates throughout Levinas, but in Levinas it is the notion of asymmetry, rather than reciprocity, that underwrites his understanding of the ethical relation: 'To recognize the Other is to give. But it is to give to the master, to the lord, to him whom one approaches as 'You' in a dimension of height' (Levinas, *Totality and Infinity* 75).

9. Thanks to Marguerite van Beeck Calkoen for assistance here. Throughout Coetzee's translation as it is published in *Landscape with Rowers*, the 'You' is capitalized in relation to the 'I' assumed by the gasfitter-speaker, but is not capitalized when the 'you' is shared as the addressee of the apple hawker's call, in the line, 'The apple hawker lures you with his call' (sonnet one). Nevertheless, I wonder how much should be made of this; in *PMLA* (where Coetzee's Achterberg essay first appeared in 1977) and in *Doubling the Point*, the 'You' is capitalized in the line I have just quoted.

10. I am thinking specifically of 'Roads to Translation' and the return in several essays in *Inner Workings* to the question of translation.

11. I had a thought-provoking conversation about this with novelist Zoë Wicomb and playwright and political philosopher, Drucilla Cornell (14 January 2009). Writing is to be read, but it is not an address, says Wicomb; her books are not *for* anyone; it's just that a story demands to be told. Cornell poses the question, Do we not always write *for* our daughters?

12. Levinas' reading is closely tied to the French translation of Celan that he was using. The passage from Celan that Levinas cites here in French is translated into English by Michael Smith as follows: the poem 'becomes dialogue, is often an impassioned dialogue... meetings, paths of a voice toward a vigilant Thou' (Levinas, 'Paul Celan: From Being to the Other' 42).

13. The title of Coetzee's essay, 'Roads to Translation', is perhaps a tacit allusion to Benjamin's 'The Task of the Translator'. Benjamin cites Mallarmé – 'The imperfection of languages consists in their plurality, the supreme one is lacking [...] the immortal word still remains silent' (cited and translated in endnote *i* of Benjamin, 'The Task of the Translator' 80) – and Benjamin then goes on to comment: 'If the task of the translator is viewed in this light, the roads toward a solution seem to be all the more obscure and impenetrable' (Benjamin, 'The Task of the Translator' 77).

14. Just as in *Foe*, *I* read the story Susan Barton sends to the author, Mr Foe, and whom she addresses as 'you'.

15. See Derrida's 'Passions' in *On the Name* for an enquiry about the invitation, and the conditions of response.

16. J.L. Austin famously distinguished between constative and performative uses of language in the William James lectures which he delivered at Harvard University in 1955. See his *How to Do Things with Words*.

17. These ideas go some way towards informing Derek Attridge's distinction between 'allegory' and 'literature' and his understanding of the literary experience as a singular event that makes an ethical demand on the reader. 'Allegory, one might say, deals with the *already known*, whereas literature opens a space for the other. Allegory announces a moral code, literature invites an ethical response' (Attridge, *J.M. Coetzee and the Ethics of Reading* 64).

18. Felstiner writes: 'A stifled voice still voices its predicament. What concerned Celan was not his poetry's but the world's obscurity and the language which that called for' (Felstiner, *Paul Celan: Poet, Survivor, Jew* 254).

19. Coetzee offers this explanation: 'Patrick Bridgewater's Penguin collection, in which the German text (in regular-size print) was accompanied by a plain English crib in smaller print, following as far as possible the original word order, still seems to me the best format for a reader who knows a little of the source language, and who is looking not for a substitute poem, in his own language, but for markers that will allow him to explore the wondrous alien territory in his own way, unhampered, with as little direction as possible, even at the risk of misreading the lay of the land' (Coetzee, 'Homage' 5).

20. Levinas is speaking specifically about statues here, but as part of the discussion he refers to Gogol, Dickens, Chekhov, Molière, Cervantes and Shakespeare.

21. 'A calling into question of the same – which cannot occur within the egoist spontaneity of the same – is brought about by the other. We name this calling into question of my spontaneity by the presence of the Other ethics. The strangeness of the Other, his irreducibility to the I, to my thoughts and my possessions, is precisely accomplished as a calling into question of my spontaneity, as ethics' (Levinas, *Totality and Infinity* 43).

22. See especially (for example), Chapter 3 of Attridge's *J.M. Coetzee and the Ethics of Reading*: 'Mrs. Curren's response to the other in the form of Vercueil can be read as a kind of heightened staging of the very issue of otherness, a story that is continuous with the attempts by such "philosophical" writers as Levinas, Blanchot, and Derrida to find ways of engaging this issue' (Attridge, *J.M. Coetzee and the Ethics of Reading* 103).

23. Attridge mentions both of these essays, but he does not engage with them in any detail (See Attridge, *The Singularity of Literature* 141).

24. 'Reality and its Shadow', first published in *Les Temps Modernes* in 1948, speaks about the artwork as an arrest of time: time is 'immobilized' (139) 'suspended' (138), 'congealed' (138). The artist effects 'fixity' (139), 'petrification' (140), 'death' (138). In places the claims about art in this essay come across as an extreme, even a parodic, version of those made in Plato's *Republic*: 'Art does not know a particular type of reality; it contrasts with knowledge. It is the very event of obscuring, a descent of the night, an invasion of shadow. To put it in theological terms [...] art does not belong to the order of revelation. Nor does it belong to that of creation, which moves in just the opposite direction' (Levinas, 'Reality and its Shadow' 132). For further discussion of Levinas' two different approaches to literary aesthetics, see my article, 'Embodying "You": Levinas and a Question of the Second Person'.

25. I do think that the distinction is an important one, and to conflate them runs the risk of leading to philosophical confusions.

26. I am thinking, for example, of the discussion of a passage from *Waiting for the Barbarians* in *J.M. Coetzee and the Ethics of Reading*, pp. 43–6.

27. Coetzee does not speak much about Bakhtin in interviews, which may seem surprising – but this is surely simply because his interviewers do not raise the question (See Coetzee's own misgivings about interviews in *Doubling the Point* 64–6).

28. See Bakhtin, *Problems of Dostoevsky's Poetics* 197. I have quoted the surrounding passage in the introduction, and Coetzee cites it in *Giving Offense* 223.

29. This sense of dialogue internal to writing (both fiction and non-fiction) is a recurrent topic of conversation in Coetzee. In the concluding, retrospective interview in *Doubling the Point*, Coetzee refers to his essay on Tolstoy, Rousseau and Dostoevsky; in retrospect, Coetzee says that he perceives 'a submerged dialogue between two persons. One is a person

I desired to be and was feeling my way toward. The other is more shadowy: let us call him the person I then was, though he may be the person I still am' (*Doubling the Point* 392).

3 Voice

1. I have used Chapman's Homer here. Chapman's translation is both famous and notorious for its poetic license, but it attempts to capture what Allardyce Nicoll calls the 'resounding vigour' of the work (*Chapman's Homer* xiii). This is Andrew Lang's prose translation of the passage cited: 'Hearken to me, god of the silver bow that standest over Chryse and holy Killa, and rulest Tenedos with might; even as erst thou heardest my prayer, and didst me honour, and mightily afflictedst the people of the Achaians, even so now fulfil me this my desire; remove thou from the Danaans forthwith the loathly pestilence' (Homer, *The Iliad of Homer*, trans. Andrew Lang 24).
2. We have seen this in Chapter 1, 'Not I', with specific reference to Coetzee's fictional autobiographies.
3. In the essay, 'Erasmus: Madness and Rivalry', Coetzee offers a philosophical reflection on the 'possibility of a position for the critic of the scene of political rivalry, a position not simply impartial between the rivals, but also, by self-definition, off the stage of rivalry altogether, a *non*position' (Coetzee, *Giving Offense* 84). See Macaskill's 'Charting J.M. Coetzee's Middle Voice' for an innovative reading of this aspect of the essay in relation to Coetzee's own interest with the operations of the middle voice.
4. I have spoken briefly about this passage in the introduction, with reference to the title of my book.
5. For a rather different discussion of the author's name, see the footnote on pages 94–5 of Derek Attridge's *J.M. Coetzee and the Ethics of Reading*.
6. There is certainly at least a question about what the reader should call this character.
7. See Roman Jakobson's *On Language*, p. 390.
8. Of course, we can have fictions about academic discourses. In the essay on Harold Pinter, JC, at the same time that he himself uses a grammar of subjective displacement, admits that 'it takes some gumption to speak as Pinter has spoken [that is, 'in his own person' ...]. What he has done may be foolhardy but it is not cowardly' (*Diary of a Bad Year* 127).
9. Barthes is insistent in his use of the word, *scripteur*, rather than *écrivain*. *Écrivain* is the word most commonly used for the English, 'author' – it carries abstract associations much more readily than *scripteur*, with its connotation of the physical impress of printing.
10. This is not the place to delineate the subtle contours of a conversation that includes Derrida's and Felman's vertiginously acute responses to Foucault's reading of the first of Descartes' *Meditations*.
11. Recall the conversation between Attwell and Coetzee that I cited in the previous chapter: what may be a 'real passion of feeling' in fiction would

appear as the 'utterances of a madman' in discursive prose (*Doubling the Point* 60).

12. Inescapably, I am using the word 'betray' in a double sense here: to make the position known, and consequently, not to be true to it.

13. More of which in the following chapter, 'Voiceless'. In Benjamin Jowett's translation, Socrates banishes the poets from the just state 'for reason constrained us' §607b; in Desmond Lee's version, the 'character [of poetry] was such as to give us good grounds for so doing and [...] our argument required it'. The word used in the original is *logos*. (See Coetzee's footnote #7 on p. 247 of *Giving Offense*).

14. Rita Barnard, in her essay, 'Coetzee in/and Afrikaans' speaks about this passage within the context of another binary the small John has to confront: English or Afrikaans.

15. The child of *Boyhood* again: 'His mother's name is Vera: Vera, with its icy capital *V*, an arrow plunging downwards' (*Boyhood* 27). Susan Barton: 'there is never a lack of things to write of. It is as though animalcules of words lie dissolved in your ink-well, ready to be dipped up and flow from the pen and take form on the paper' (*Foe* 93).

16. Coetzee reads Erasmus: 'What is it *to take a position?* Is there a position which is not a position, a position of *ek-stasis* in which one knows without knowing, sees without seeing? *The Praise of Folly* marks out such a "position"' (*Giving Offense* 99–100).

4   Voiceless

1. For Coetzee's discussion of Breyten Breytenbach's use of a Bakhtinian dialogic and 'double-voiced' discourse (which are distinct concepts), see *Giving Offense* 223–7).

2. Coetzee wrote the address, but did not present it himself. Voiceless ambassador, Hugo Weaving, read the address at the exhibition opening.

3. I have written about Plato's *Republic* in some detail in a review essay, 'Ancient Antagonisms'. See Stephen Mulhall's introduction to his recent book, *The Wounded Animal: J.M. Coetzee and the Difficulty of Reality in Literature and Philosophy*. Mulhall's introduction, 'The Ancient Quarrel', opens with a discussion of the *Republic*, and situates the 'quarrel' between the philosophers and the poets within a contemporary debate: Onora O'Neill's review essay of Stephen Clark's *The Moral Status of Animals*, and Cora Diamond's critique of O'Neill's review. Unless otherwise stated, I am using Desmond Lee's translation of *The Republic*.

4. With reference to the Clark–O'Neill–Diamond debate, Mulhall demonstrates in rigorous detail that 'Coetzee's intervention is [...] not in any sense an attempt to revive a philosophically moribund debate; it is rather a contribution to an utterly contemporary controversy' (Mulhall, *The Wounded Animal* 18).

5. I am reminded of Wittgenstein's 'Ethics and aesthetics are one' ('Ethik und Aesthetik sind Eins') (Wittgenstein, *Tractatus Logico-Philosophicus* §6.421).

6. Shklovsky is quoting from Tolstoy's *Diary*; the entry is dated 29 February 1897. In a footnote Shklovsky points out that the date has been transcribed incorrectly. It should read 1 March 1897.

7. See Chapter 3 of Coetzee's doctoral thesis in which he discusses Beckett's short story, 'Dante and the Lobster'. 'In the structure of ideas the lobster stands for a living thing on which man practices an unthinking god-like cruelty, and so could theoretically be replaced by, say, a Strasbourg goose' (Coetzee, *The English Fiction of Samuel Beckett* 37).

8. There is only one reference to Schopenhauer in *The Life of Thomas Hardy*, (accepted to be largely autobiographical), where Hardy mentions Schopenhauer together with Hartmann and Haeckel – 'persons called pessimists' (315).

9. Bertie Stephens was Hardy's gardener between 1926 and 1937. He wrote about his own professional predicaments occasioned by Hardy's regard for his fellow creatures: 'The garden was often visited by a hare which somehow managed to get over the wall which surrounded it. It would eat the carrot tops and do a great deal of damage to other growing plants [...] Mr Hardy, when I told him of its visits and the destruction it caused, said: "I do not mind it in the garden. They are animals, let them carry on." He was very fond of animals and birds, and would never allow me to trap or shoot them however destructive they were to the fruit or vegetables. He insisted that I allow all birds to do as they liked in the garden. This attitude did not always please me, especially when some carefully cultivated fruit was destroyed. We netted the raspberries and strawberries to protect them against birds, but after Mr Hardy's death Mrs Hardy employed a builder to erect a permanent fruit cage for the purpose. This was a great improvement and a big saving of time for me' (Gibson, ed., *Thomas Hardy: Interviews and Recollections* 226–7).

10. I am reminded of a parallel passage in *Life & Times of Michael K*: 'There was a cord of tenderness that stretched from him to the patch of earth beside the dam and must be cut. It seemed to him that one could cut a cord like that only so many times before it would not grow again' (Coetzee, *Life & Times of Michael K* 90).

11. I am reminded of Coetzee's important aside in one of the interviews in *Doubling the Point*: '(Let me add, *entirely* parenthetically, that I, as a person, as a personality, am overwhelmed, that my thinking is thrown into confusion and helplessness, by the fact of suffering in the world, and not only human suffering. These fictional constructions of mine are paltry, ludicrous defences against that being-overwhelmed, and, to me, transparently so.)' (Coetzee, *Doubling the Point* 248).

12. Sincere thanks to Raj Mesthrie for his assistance with the linguistic analysis here; my discussion follows very closely an e-mail exchange of 5 February 2009.

13. I am still tracking my conversation with Raj Mesthrie.

14. See volume 9, 'Passives and Impersonals', of *The Encyclopedia of Language and Linguistics*, ed. Keith Brown. In the example, 'there was celebrating in the street', we find an instance of the 'promotion of non-obvious

("dummy") objects' to induce the 'demotion' of the subject (*The Encyclopedia of Language and Linguistics* 237).

15. Marais discusses the visit within the context of Levinasian ethics (Marais, '"Little enough, less than little: nothing" Ethics, Engagement, and Change in the Fiction of J.M. Coetzee' 176–7).

16. My favourite example of genetic proximity: humans share 40 per cent of their genes with bananas (Tattersall, *Becoming Human* 109). At first I was not going to include this information, and my rather corny discussion about it in the article that forms the basis of this chapter (the reference for the article is in the acknowledgements at the front of the book). But when by chance I found Erik Grayson's comment about my essay on the Internet, I could not resist including part of my discussion, embedded in Grayson's journal entry: 'in a completely unrelated note, Clarkson pens what may be the single greatest bit of prose I have ever seen in a piece of literary criticism, especially when taken out of context: "Humankind shares 40 per cent of its genes with the banana. This may surprise you, but I would hazard a guess that the staggering ontological fact *in itself* does little to appease your general sense of miserable alienation, let alone your more profound European Angst (to which the young John of Coetzee's *Youth* so ardently aspires (Coetzee, *Youth* 48–9))"' (Clarkson cited in Grayson, entry for *Sobriquet Magazine*, 27 June 2008). Grayson's Internet journal about the secondary reading he is doing for his dissertation is an invaluable resource for Coetzee scholars.

17. The phrase, repeated three times in Baudelaire's 'L'Invitation au Voyage', reads, 'Luxe, calme et volupté'. The word 'calme' then, is elided in the description of Lurie's weekly encounters with Soraya.

18. Thanks to Elizabeth Snyman for pointing me in this direction.

19. I am echoing Stephen Mulhall's discussion of Cora Diamond's work on the relations between philosophy, literature and ethics: 'Diamond repeatedly emphasizes the capacity of literature, and so of literary examples, to enlarge our moral imagination, to educate the heart towards enlarged and deepened moral sympathies' (Mulhall, *The Wounded Animal* 13).

5 Names

1. In this chapter I use the word 'name' in the broadest sense – the proper and common nouns that name a landscape and the selves and others who people it. My discussion begins and ends with a consideration of Coetzee's use of place-names.

2. I cannot resist reminding you of the Marianna of *Slow Man*. Unlike Marijana Jokić's name, Elizabeth Costello insists: 'Her name is Marianna, as I said, with two *n*s' (Coetzee, *Slow Man* 98). 'Marianna', says Paul Rayment, 'testing the name on his tongue, tasting the two *n*s: I know that is your name, but is that what people call you?' (*Slow Man* 109). Recall the opening sentences of Nabokov's *Lolita:* 'LOLITA, light of my life, fire of my loins. My sin, my soul. Lo-lee-ta: the tip of the tongue

taking a trip of three steps down the palate to tap, at three, on the teeth. Lo. Lee. Ta' (Nabokov, *Lolita* 9).

3. The reference here is to Thaba 'Nchu as it features in Sol Plaatje's novel, *Mhudi*.

4. Of course, I am taking the cue from Emile Benveniste: '*I* refers to the act of individual discourse in which it is pronounced, and by this it designates the speaker' (Benveniste, *Problems in General Linguistics* 226) and 'there is no other criterion [...] by which to indicate "the time at which one *is*" except to take it as "the time at which one *is speaking*." This is the eternally "present" moment [...] Linguistic time is *self-referential*' (Benveniste, *Problems in General Linguistics* 227).

5. I use the word in two senses – 'effecting by magic' and 'swearing together'. More of this later.

6. Dostoevsky's utterance of the deceased Pavel's name in *The Master of Petersburg* has connotations of a charm or a spell: 'Silently he forms his lips over his son's name, three times, four times. He is trying to cast a spell' (Coetzee, *The Master of Petersburg* 5). '*Pavel!* he whispers over and over, using the word as a charm' (60). Another meaning in the OED is pertinent here: 'The effecting of something supernatural by a spell or by the invocation of a sacred name'. In *The Master of Petersburg* the incantation of Pavel's name is explicitly linked to the myth of Orpheus (*The Master of Petersburg* 5).

7. This holds true of proper names of persons – where surnames, especially, but also given names – hold place within a genealogy and/or other taxonomic patterns. To call someone by name is to call that person at a place in language. A nickname, an alias, a *nom de plume* – all of these, in different ways, bring about shifts in the linguistic site of response, in the responsive field, of the one named. See Chapter 4 of my doctoral thesis, *Naming and Personal Identity in the Novels of Charles Dickens*.

8. Charles Dickens was aware of this, as we see in his outrageous article of 1853, 'The Noble Savage': 'I have not the least belief in the Noble Savage. I consider him a prodigious nuisance, and an enormous superstition. His calling rum fire-water, and me a paleface, wholly fail to reconcile me to him. *I don't care what he calls me.* I call him a savage, and I call a savage something highly desirable to be civilised off the face of the earth' (Dickens 337, my emphasis). See my doctoral thesis (169–73). For an extended discussion about the distinction between notions of the 'irresponsible' and the 'non-responsible' (which arises in relation to Dickens) see my paper, 'The Time of Address,' *Law and the Politics of Reconciliation*, pp. 229–40.

9. 'The subject of names in Coetzee's work is worth an essay in itself', writes Derek Attridge in a footnote in *J.M. Coetzee and the Ethics of Reading* (fn. 3, 94). Attridge suggests starting with a discussion of Coetzee's own withholding of his first names. Further, an essay on names in Coetzee would 'point out the repeated undermining of their supposed simple referentiality, and the making evident of the power relations within which

they function' (94. See also footnote 20, 106). On questions about the reference of names in fiction, see my article, 'Dickens and the *Cratylus*' in the *British Journal of Aesthetics*. For an extended discussion of naming and power relations, see Chapter 2 of my doctoral thesis.

10. I use 'signify' in both senses: to refer to the landscape by name, but also, to invest the landscape with significance by naming it.

11. Place-name changes in South Africa, especially since the first democratic elections in 1994, constitute a striking case. The most infamous example is surely Sophiatown, renamed Triomf in 1955, at the time of the forced removal of residents classified as non-white, to make way for poor white Afrikaners. Triomf was renamed Sophiatown in 2005. See Beavon's *Johannesburg: The Making and Shaping of the City*, 2004.

6 Etymologies

1. I have discussed Plato's *Cratylus* elsewhere in more detail, with specific reference to proper names in fiction (See my article 'Dickens and the *Cratylus*', in the *British Journal of Aesthetics*). As he launches into his extravagant etymological explanations, Socrates warns that his 'notions of original names are truly wild and ridiculous' (§426b) and that his 'ignorance of these names involves an ignorance of secondary words' since he is 'reduced to explaining these from elements of which he knows nothing' (§426a).

2. See Philippe Lacoue-Labarthe's *The Poetry of Experience*, which offers philosophically revelatory discussions of the poetry of Paul Celan: 'What is a work of poetry that, forswearing the repetition of the disastrous, deadly, already-said, makes itself absolutely singular?' (Lacoue-Labarthe, *The Poetry of Experience* 14) and further, 'My question asks not just about the "text," but about the singular *experience* coming into writing; it asks if, being singular, experience can be written, or if from the moment of writing its very singularity is not forever lost and borne away in one way or another, at origin or en route to destination, by the very fact of language' (Lacoue-Labarthe, *The Poetry of Experience* 15). Coetzee engages with Lacoue-Labarthe's text in his own essay on Paul Celan in *Inner Workings*.

3. Rita Barnard makes a related point about the many foreign words in the novel. She singles out the word, *'eingewurzelt'* (rooted in): '[t]he word, redolent with notions of organic community and peasant tradition, is intended to affirm the man's [Ettinger's] tenacity. But the very fact that it is a German word effectively undermines its dictionary definition: Ettinger's origins [...] may be too European for him to survive without a brood of sons on the post-apartheid platteland' (Barnard, 'J.M. Coetzee's *Disgrace* and the South African Pastoral' 206–7).

4. I have written in detail about 'Force and Signification' in an essay, 'Drawing the Line: Justice and the Art of Reconciliation', in which I ask what a post-apartheid aesthetic might entail.

5. See Coetzee's remark (made in a different context) at the end of his interview with Jean Sévry: 'aesthetic exploration and [...] revolutionary literature [...] are not incompatible and people who say they are incompatible are simply mistaken' (Coetzee and Sévry, 'An Interview with J.M. Coetzee' 7).

6. Arthur Rose questions the possibility and the limits of an 'ethics of gratitude' in a care-relation. To what extent is there an onus on the donor to allow the recipient to express gratitude? See Rose's MA dissertation, *The Poetics of Reciprocity in Selected Fictions by J.M. Coetzee*.

7. See Coetzee's entire response to David Attwell, and especially this part: 'There is no ethical imperative that I claim access to. Elizabeth is the one who believes in *should*, who believes in *believes in*' (Coetzee, *Doubling the Point* 250). Mike Marais offers a different perspective, in which he reads Coetzee as issuing ethical imperatives to his characters: 'Coetzee tasks his protagonist [i.e. David Lurie] with the ethical obligation of developing a sympathetic imagination' ('J.M. Coetzee's *Disgrace* and the Task of the Imagination' 76). Marais aligns the imperatives Mrs Curren sets for herself, and 'the task of the imagination' that (in Marais' argument) Coetzee assigns to Lurie: 'In order to sympathize with Lucy, Lurie must sympathize with Pollux. Like Mrs Curren, in *Age of Iron*, who realizes that, to love her daughter, she must love the "unlovable" John [...] Lurie must sympathize despite himself. He must sympathize with Pollux precisely because he cannot find it in himself to do so' (Marais, 'J.M. Coetzee's *Disgrace* and the Task of the Imagination' 82).

8. Here Coetzee seems to conflate 'signified' and referent (*White Writing* 8–9), which, in turn, has implications for critics trying to respond to Coetzee's use of isolated signifiers, such as 'Africa'.

9. Incidently, this is what Cratylus, in Plato's dialogue, maintains: 'I cannot be satisfied that a name which is incorrectly given is a name at all' (Plato, 'Cratylus' §433c).

10. This paragraph is closely based on a conversation I had with Stephen Clarkson.

11. Elizabeth Costello tries out words for her sexual encounter with the old, bedridden Mr Phillips: 'Not *eros*, certainly – too grotesque for that. *Agape*? Again, perhaps not. Does that mean the Greeks would have no word for it? Would one have to wait for the Christians to come along with the right word: *caritas*?' (*Elizabeth Costello* 154).

12. The disruptive counter-meaning of 'taking care' draws attention to the rift in communication between Lucy and her father, David Lurie, in *Disgrace*:

> 'I don't understand. I thought you took care of it [Lucy's unborn child], you and your GP.'
>
> 'No.'
>
> 'What do you mean, no? You mean you didn't take care of it?'
>
> 'I have taken care. I have taken every reasonable care short of what you are hinting at. But I am not having an abortion'. (Coetzee, *Disgrace* 197–8)

13. Coetzee makes extensive use of italics in *Slow Man*, which often reflect Paul Rayment's words in imagined dialogues with others.
14. Thanks to Stephen Clarkson for alerting me to W.G. Sebald's *On the Natural History of Destruction*, which includes an essay on Jean Améry.
15. Améry again: 'even in direct experience everyday reality is nothing but codified abstraction. Only in rare moments of life do we truly stand face to face with the event and, with it, reality' (Améry, *At the Mind's Limits* 26).
16. My own language here pulls against what I want to say: 'unprecedented' is precisely 'of an unexampled kind' (*OED*) – but an 'instance' implies an 'illustrative example' of a general assertion, or argument or truth (*OED*). The phrase, 'unprecedented instance', thus paradoxically enacts the problem under discussion.
17. For example, the discussion of European, Bushman and frontiersman taxonomies (Coetzee, *Dusklands* 115–16); the fanciful etymology of 'the appellation *Hottentot*' (*Dusklands* 113); the section, 'Sojourn in the land of the Great Namaqua': 'I spoke slowly, as befitted the opening of negotiations with possibly unfriendly powers [...] I was unsure whether my Hottentot, picked up at my nurse's knee and overburdened with imperative constructions, was compatible with theirs: might I not, for example, precipitate hostilities with one of those innocent toneshift puns [!nop⁴] "stone" for [!nop²] "peace", for which my countrymen were so mocked?' (*Dusklands* 66). A discussion of these encounters requires an essay of its own.
18. I am echoing an image (used in a slightly different context) in *Youth*: 'Prose is like a flat, tranquil sheet of water on which one can tack about at one's leisure, making patterns on the surface' (Coetzee, *Youth* 61).

7 Conclusion: We

1. In my article, 'Who Are "We"? Don't Make Me Laugh' (in *Law and Critique*), I explore uses of the word 'we' in post-apartheid South African fiction with reference to African Communitarian philosophies, and to Jean-Luc Nancy's conception of the 'inoperative community' ('la communauté desoeuvrée'). The three novels I discuss in the article are Phaswane Mpe's *Welcome To Our Hillbrow*, Ivan Vladislavić's *The Restless Supermarket* and Marlene van Niekerk's *Triomf.*
2. Derrida's *Monolingualism of the Other* can be considered as an extended thinking-through of the imagined statement, in good French, by a subject of French culture: 'I only have one language; it is not mine' (Derrida, *Monolingualism of the Other* 2).
3. Again, this reminds me of a passage in which Derrida speaks about the act of writing itself: 'There is always for me, and I believe there *must be more than one* language, mine and the other [...] and I must try to write in such a way that the language of the other does not suffer in mine, suffers me to come without suffering from it, receives the hospitality of

mine without getting lost or integrated there. And reciprocally [...] we have no neutral measure here, no *common measure* given by a third party. This has to be invented at every moment, with every sentence, without assurance, without absolute guardrails. Which is as much as to say that madness, a certain "madness" *must* keep a lookout over every step, and finally watch over thinking, as reason does also' (Derrida, 'A "Madness" Must Watch Over Thinking' 363).

4. Compare Rosmarie Waldrop's translation: 'Only one thing remained reachable, close and secure amid all losses: language. Yes, language. In spite of everything, it remained secure against loss. But it had to go through its own loss of answers, through terrifying silence, through the thousand darknesses of murderous speech. It went through. It gave me no words for what was happening, but went through it. Went through and could resurface, "enriched" by it all' (Celan, *Paul Celan: Collected Prose* 34).

5. Coetzee takes Celan's poem 'Death Fugue' to be 'one of the landmark poems of the twentieth century', and suggests that Adorno's retraction of his claim that to 'write poetry after Auschwitz is barbaric' is perhaps a concession to Celan's poem (*Inner Workings* 119, 120).

Bibliography

Abrams, M.H. 'The Deconstructive Angel', *Critical Enquiry*, 3 (1977): 425–32.

Adorno, T. *Prisms*, trans. Samuel and Shierry Weber (Cambridge, Massachusetts: MIT Press, 1981).

Aristotle. *On Rhetoric: A Theory of Civic Discourse*, trans. George A. Kennedy (New York and Oxford: Oxford University Press, 1991).

——. *Poetics*, trans. Malcolm Heath (London: Penguin, 1996).

Arnauld, A. and Lancelot, C. *General and Rational Grammar: The Port-Royal Grammar*, eds and trans. J. Rieux and B. Rollin (The Hague and Paris: Mouton, 1975).

Attridge, D. *J.M. Coetzee and the Ethics of Reading: (Literature in the Event)* (Scottsville: University of KwaZulu-Natal Press; Chicago and London: University of Chicago Press, 2005).

——. *The Singularity of Literature* (London and New York: Routledge, 2004).

Attwell, D. 'J.M. Coetzee and the Idea of Africa', *Journal of Literary Studies* (forthcoming).

——. *J.M. Coetzee: South Africa and the Politics of Writing* (Berkeley: University of California Press, and Cape Town: David Philip, 1993).

——. 'Race in Disgrace', *Interventions*, 4.3 (2002): 331–41.

Austen, J. *Pride and Prejudice* (Bristol: Purnell, 1977).

Austin, J.L. *How to Do Things with Words*, The William James Lectures delivered at Harvard University in 1955 (Oxford: Clarendon Press, 1965).

Bakhtin, M.M. *Problems of Dostoevsky's Poetics*, ed. and trans. Caryl Emerson (Minneapolis: University of Minnesota Press, 1984).

——. *Speech Genres and Other Late Essays*, trans. Vern M. McGee, eds C. Emerson and M. Holquist (Austin: University of Texas Press, 1986).

Barnard, R. 'J.M. Coetzee's *Disgrace* and the South African Pastoral', *Contemporary Literature*, 44.2 (Summer 2003): 199–224.

——. 'Coetzee in/and Afrikaans' *Journal of Literary Studies* (forthcoming).

Barthes, R. 'The Death of the Author', trans. Stephen Heath, *The Norton Anthology of Theory and Criticism*, general ed. V. Leitch (New York and London: W.W. Norton & Company, 2001), pp. 1466–70.

——. 'Introduction to the Structural Analysis of Narratives', trans. Stephen Heath, *Barthes: Selected Writings*, ed. S. Sontag (Oxford: Fontana/Collins, 1983), pp. 251–95.

——. 'To Write: An Intransitive Verb?', *The Structuralist Controversy: The Language of Criticism and the Sciences of Man*, trans. Ricard Macksey and Eugenio Donato (Baltimore and London: Johns Hopkins University Press, 1972), pp. 134–56.

Baudelaire, C. *Les Fleurs du Mal* (Paris: Éditions Garnier, 1961).

Beavon, K. *Johannesburg: The Making and Shaping of the City* (Pretoria: University of South Africa Press, 2004).

Beckett, S. *The Beckett Trilogy: Molloy, Malone Dies, The Unnamable* (London: Picador, 1979).

——. *Not I* (London: Faber and Faber, 1973).

Benjamin, W. 'The Task of the Translator', trans. Harry Zohn, *Modern Criticism and Theory: A Reader*, 3rd edition, eds D. Lodge and N. Wood (Harlow, England: Pearson Longman, 2008), pp. 72–80.

Benveniste, E. *Problems in General Linguistics*, trans. Mary Elizabeth Meek (Coral Gables, Florida: University of Miami Press, 1971).

Breytenbach, B. *Dog Heart: A Memoir* (New York: Harcourt Brace, 1999).

Brown, K., ed. *Encyclopedia of Language and Linguistics*, 2nd edition. Volume 9: *Passives and Impersonals* (Oxford: Elsevier, 2006).

Buber, M. *I and Thou*, trans. Walter Kaufmann (Edinburgh: T. & T. Clark, 1970).

Burchell, W. *Travels in the Interior of Southern Africa*, 2 volumes (Cape Town: Struik, 1967).

Cavell, S., Diamond, C., McDowell, J., Hacking, I. and Wolfe, C. *Philosophy and Animal Life* (New York: Columbia University Press, 2008).

Celan, P. *Collected Prose*, trans. Rosmarie Waldrop (Manchester: Carcanet Press, 1986).

Chernos, J. 'The Five-String Banjo: A Most Controversial of Instruments' (www.department-of-justice.org, accessed 27 May 2009).

Chomsky, N. *Cartesian Linguistics: A Chapter in the History of Rationalist Thought* (New York and London: Harper & Row, 1966).

Clarkson, C. 'Ancient Antagonisms', *English Academy Review*, 25.2 (October 2008): 101–10.

——. 'Derek Attridge in the Event', *Journal of Literary Studies*, 21.3/4 (December 2005): 379–86.

——. 'Dickens and the *Cratylus*', *British Journal of Aesthetics*, 39.1 (January 1999) 53–61.

——. ' "Done because we are too menny": Ethics and Identity in J.M. Coetzee's *Disgrace*', *Current Writing*, 15.2 (October 2003): 77–90.

——. 'Drawing the Line: Justice and the Art of Reconciliation', *Justice and Reconciliation in Post-Apartheid South Africa*, eds F. Du Bois and A. Du Bois-Pedain (Cambridge: Cambridge University Press, 2008), pp. 267–88.

——. 'Embodying "You": Levinas and a Question of the Second Person', *Journal of Literary Semantics*, 34 (2005): 95–105.

——. *Naming and Personal Identity in the Novels of Charles Dickens: A Philosophical Approach* (Doctoral Thesis, University of York, November 1999).

——. 'Remains of the Name', *Literary Landscapes from Modernism to Postcolonialism*, eds A. de Lange, G. Fincham, J. Lothe and J. Hawthorn (Houndmills: Palgrave, 2008), pp. 125–42.

——. 'The Time of Address', *Law and the Politics of Reconciliation*, ed. S. Veitch (Edinburgh: Ashgate, 2007), pp. 229–40.

——. 'Who Are "We"? Don't Make Me Laugh', *Law and Critique*, 18 (2007): 361–74.

Coetzee, J.M. 'Achterberg's "Ballade van de Gasfitter": The Mystery of I and You', *PMLA*, 92.2 (1977): 285–96.

——. *Age of Iron* (New York and London: Penguin, 1990).

——. *Boyhood: Scenes from Provincial Life* (London: Secker & Warburg, 1997).

——. 'Computer Poem', *The Lion and the Impala*, 2.1 (March–April 1963): 12–13.

——. 'Confession and Double Thoughts: Tolstoy, Rousseau, Dostoevsky', *Comparative Literature*, 37.3 (Summer 1985): 193–232.

——. *Diary of a Bad Year* (London: Harvill Secker 2007).

——. *Disgrace* (London: Secker and Warburg, 1999).

——. *Doubling the Point: Essays and Interviews*, ed. D. Attwell (Cambridge, Massachusetts and London: Harvard University Press, 1992).

——. *Dusklands* (London: Vintage, 1998).

——. *Elizabeth Costello* (London: Secker & Warburg, 1999).

——. *The English Fiction of Samuel Beckett: An Essay in Stylistic Analysis* (Doctoral Thesis, University of Texas at Austin, January 1969).

——. *Foe* (London: Penguin, 1987).

——. *Giving Offense: Essays on Censorship* (Chicago and London: University of Chicago Press, 1996).

——, 'He and His Man': *The Nobel Lecture in Literature 2003* (London: Penguin, 2004).

——. 'Hero and Bad Mother in Epic, a poem', *Staffrider*, 1.1 (March 1978): 36.

——. 'History of the Main Complaint', *William Kentridge* (New York: Phaidon, 1999), pp. 82–93.

——. 'Homage', *The Threepenny Review*, 53 (Spring 1993): 5–7.

——. *Inner Workings: Essays 2000–2005* (London: Harvill Secker, 2007).

——. *In the Heart of the Country* (Johannesburg: Ravan Press, 1979).

——, ed. and trans. *Landscape with Rowers: Poetry from the Netherlands* (Princeton and Oxford: Princeton University Press, 2004).

——. *Life & Times of Michael K* (Harmondsworth: Penguin, 1983).

——. 'Linguistics at the Millennium', opening address at the *Linguistics at the Millennium* conference held at the University of Cape Town, January 2000 (Photocopy UCT African Studies Library).

——. *The Lives of Animals*, ed. A. Gutmann (Princeton: Princeton University Press, 1999).

——. *The Master of Petersburg* (London: Vintage, 2004).

——. 'The Novel Today' *Upstream*, 6.1 (1988): 2–5.

——. 'Roads to Translation', *Meanjin*, Special Issue on Translation: *Tongues: Translation: Only Connect*, 64.4 (2005): 141–51.

——. 'Die Skrywer en die Teorie', SAVAL Conference Proceedings (Bloemfontein 1980): 155–61.

——. *Slow Man* (London: Secker & Warburg 2005).

——. *Stranger Shores: Essays 1986–1999* (London: Secker & Warburg, 2001).

——. 'Thematizing', *The Return of Thematic Criticism*, ed. W. Sollors (Cambridge, Massachusetts and London: Harvard University Press, 1993), p. 289.

——. *Truth in Autobiography* (Inaugural Lecture, University of Cape Town, 3 October 1984. University of Cape Town Printing Department, New Series No. 94).

——. *Voiceless: I Feel Therefore I Am* (Address written by Coetzee and read by Hugh Weaving at the exhibition opening held at the Sherman Galleries, 22 February 2007, www.voiceless.org.au, accessed 8 December 2008).

——. *Waiting for the Barbarians* (London: Vintage, 2004).

——. *White Writing: On the Culture of Letters in South Africa* (New Haven and London: Radix, in association with Yale University Press, 1988).

——. *The Works of Ford Madox Ford with Particular Reference to the Novels* (MA Dissertation, University of Cape Town, November 1963).

——. *Youth* (London: Secker & Warburg, 2002).

Coetzee, J.M. and Attwell, D. ' "All Autobiography Is *Autre*-biography": J.M. Coetzee interviewed by David Attwell', *Selves in Question: Interviews on Southern African Auto/biography*, eds J. Lütge Coullie, S. Meyer, T. Ngwenya and T. Olver (Honolulu: University of Hawai'i Press, 2006), pp. 213–18.

——. 'An Exclusive Interview with J.M. Coetzee', *DN.se* (8 December 2003, www.dn.se, accessed 4 December 2008).

Coetzee, J.M. and Morphet, T. 'Two Interviews with J.M. Coetzee, 1983 and 1987', *Tri-Quarterly* Special Issue: *From South Africa*, 69 (Spring/Summer 1987): 454–64.

Coetzee, J.M. and Sévry, J. 'An Interview with J.M. Coetzee', *Commonwealth*, 9 (Autumn 1986): 1–7.

Coetzee, J.M. and Watson, S. 'Speaking: J.M. Coetzee', *Speak*, 1.3 (May/June 1978): 21–4.

Crystal, D. *The Cambridge Encyclopedia of Language* (Cambridge: Cambridge University Press, 1987).

Darwin, C. *The Origin of Species*, 1st edition (Ware: Wordsworth, 1998).

Defoe, D. *The Life & Strange Surprizing Adventures of Robinson Crusoe of York, Mariner* (New York: Peter Pauper Press, no date).

Derrida, J. 'Cogito and the History of Madness', *Writing and Difference*, trans. Alan Bass (Chicago: University of Chicago Press, 1978), pp. 31–63.

——. 'Counter-Signatures', *Points…Interviews, 1974–1994*, ed. E. Weber, trans. Peggy Kamuf and others (Stanford: Stanford University Press, 1992), pp. 365–71.

——. 'Force and Signification', *Writing and Difference*, trans. Alan Bass (Chicago: University of Chicago Press, 1978), pp. 3–30.

——. 'A "Madness" Must Watch Over Thinking', *Points…Interviews, 1974–1994*, ed. E. Weber, trans. Peggy Kamuf et al, (Stanford: Stanford University Press, 1992), pp. 339–64.

——. *Monolingualism of the Other; or, The Prosthesis of Origin*, trans. Patrick Mensah (Stanford: Stanford University Press, 1998).

——. 'Passions', *On the Name* (Stanford: Stanford University Press, 1995), pp. 3–31.

Descartes, R. *The Meditations and Selections from the Principles of René Descartes*, trans. John Veitch (La Salle, Illinois: Open Court Publishing Company, 1950).
——. *Philosophical Letters*, ed. and trans. Anthony Kenny (Oxford: Basil Blackwell, 1970).
Dickens, C. *David Copperfield* (Harmondsworth: Penguin, 1966).
——. 'The Noble Savage', *Household Words*, 168 (Saturday, 11 June 1853) 337–9.
Dostoevsky, F. *The Brothers Karamazov*, trans. Constance Garnett (New York: International Collectors Library, no date).
Dovey, T. *The Novels of J.M. Coetzee: Lacanian Allegories* (Craighall: A.D. Donker, 1984).
Enstad, K. *'The voice that strains to soar away from the ludicrous instrument': Language and Narration in the Novels of J.M. Coetzee* (Doctoral thesis, University of Oslo, 2008).
Felman, S. *Writing and Madness*, trans. Martha Evans and Shoshana Felman with Brian Massumi (Ithaca, New York: Cornell University Press, 1985).
Felstiner, J. *Paul Celan: Poet, Survivor, Jew* (New Haven and London: Yale University Press, 1995).
Finch, H.L. *Wittgenstein* (Rockport, Massachusetts: Element Books, 1995).
Foucault, M. *The History of Madness*, trans. Jonathan Murphy and Jean Khalfa (London and New York: Routledge, 2006).
Gibson, J. ed. *Thomas Hardy: Interviews and Recollections* (Houndmills and London: Macmillan, 1999).
Graham, L. ' "Yes, I am giving him up": Sacrificial Responsibility and Likeness with Dogs in J.M. Coetzee's Recent Fiction', *Scrutiny2*, 7.1 (2002): 4–15.
Grayson, E. Untitled entry for *Sobriquet Magazine* 43.28 (Friday 27 June 2008, www.sobriquetmagazine.com, accessed 28 May 2009).
Green, C. 'We Are All Animal Now', text for the exhibition, *Voiceless: I Feel Therefore I Am* (22 February 2007, www.shermangalleries.com.au, accessed 2 January 2009).
Green, M. 'Deplorations', *English in Africa*, 33.2 (October 2006): 135–58.
Hardy, F. *The Life of Thomas Hardy 1840–1928* (London: Macmillan, 1962).
Hardy, T. 'At Castle Boterel', *The New Wessex Selection of Thomas Hardy's Poetry*, eds J. Wain and E. Wain (London: Macmillan, 1978), p. 117.
——. *Jude the Obscure* (Harmondsworth: Penguin, 1985).
——. *The Literary Notebooks of Thomas Hardy*. 2 vols. ed. A. Lennart Björk (London and Basingstoke: Macmillan, 1985).
——. *Tess of the d'Urbervilles* (Ware: Wordsworth, 1993).
Head, D. *J.M. Coetzee* (Cambridge: Cambridge University Press, 1997).
——. *The Cambridge Introduction to J.M. Coetzee* (Cambridge: Cambridge University Press, 2009).
Heidegger, M. 'The Origin of the Work of Art', trans. Albert Hofstadter, *Martin Heidegger: Basic Writings*, ed. D.F. Krell (New York: HarperCollins, 1977), pp. 139–212.
Helgesson, S. *Writing in Crisis: Ethics and History in Gordimer, Ndebele and Coetzee* (Scottsville: University of KwaZulu-Natal Press, 2004).

Heyns, M. '"Call no man happy": Perversity as Narrative Principle in *Disgrace', English Studies in Africa*, 45.1 (2002): 57–65.

Homer, *Chapman's Homer: The Iliad, The Odyssey and The Lesser Homerica*, ed. A. Nicoll (London: Routledge and Kegan Paul, 1957).

——, *The Iliad of Homer*, trans. Andrew Lang, Walter Leaf and Ernest Myers (New York: Airmont, 1966).

Jacobus, M. 'Sue the Obscure', *Essays in Criticism*, 25.3 (July 1975): 304–28.

Jakobson, R. *On Language*, eds L. Waugh and M. Monville-Burston (Cambridge, Massachusetts: Harvard University Press, 1990).

Jennings, K. *Women and Words: J.M. Coetzee's Female Characters and their Relationship to Language and Silence* (MA dissertation, University of Cape Town: September 2007).

Kafka, F. 'Investigations of a Dog', *Metamorphosis and Other Stories*, trans. Willa and Edwin Muir (London: Penguin, 1961), pp. 83–126.

Kant, I. *Fundamental Principles of the Metaphysics of Morals*, trans. Thomas K. Abbott, *Basic Writings of Kant* (New York: The Modern Library, 2001), pp. 143–221.

Katz, J. *The Philosophy of Language* (New York and London: Harper & Row, 1966).

Kentridge, W. 'Felix in Exile: Geography of Memory', *William Kentridge* (New York: Phaidon, 1999), pp. 122–7.

——. 'Landscape in a State of Siege', *William Kentridge* (New York: Phaidon, 1999), pp. 108–11.

Kentridge W. and Cameron, D. 'An Interview with William Kentridge', *William Kentridge* (Chicago: New Museum of Contemporary Art in association with Harry N. Abrams, 2001), pp. 67–74.

Kipling, R. 'The Song of the Banjo' (www.poemhunter.com, accessed 27 November 2008).

Lacan, J. *Écrits: A Selection*, trans. Alan Sheridan (London: Tavistock Publications, 1977).

Lacoue-Labarthe, P. *Poetry as Experience*, trans. Andrea Tarnowski (Stanford: Stanford University Press, 1999).

Lee, H. 'Uneasy Guest', *London Review of Books*, 24.13 (11 July 2002): 14–15.

Levinas, E. *Otherwise than Being or Beyond Essence*, trans. A. Lingis (The Hague: Martinus Nijhoff, 1981).

——. 'Paul Celan: From Being to the Other', *Proper Names*, trans. Michael Smith (Stanford: Stanford University Press 1996), pp. 40–6.

——. 'Reality and its Shadow', *The Levinas Reader*, ed. S. Hand, trans. A. Lingis (Oxford: Basil Blackwell, 1989), pp. 130–59.

——. *Totality and Infinity*, trans. Alphonso Lingis (Dordrecht: Kluwer, 1991).

Levinas, E. and Kearney, R. 'Dialogue with Emmanuel Levinas', trans. Richard Kearney, *Face to Face with Levinas*, ed. R. Cohen (Albany: State University of New York, 1986), pp. 13–40.

Levinas, E. and Poirié, F. 'Interview with François Poirié', trans. Jill Robbins and Marcus Coelen with Thomas Loebel, *Is it Righteous to Be? Interviews with Emmanuel Levinas*, ed. J. Robbins (Stanford: Stanford University Press, 2001), pp. 23–83.

Levinas, E., Wright, T., Hughes, P. and Ainley, A. 'The Paradox of Morality: An Interview with Emmanuel Levinas', trans. Andrew Benjamin and Tamra Wright, *The Provocation of Levinas*, eds R. Bernasconi and D. Wood (London: Routledge, 1988), pp. 168–80.

Macaskill, B. 'Charting J.M. Coetzee's Middle Voice', *Contemporary Literature*, 35.3 (1994): 441–75.

Marais, M. ' "After the Death of a Certain God": a Case for Levinasian Ethics', *Scrutiny2*, 8.1 (2003): 27–33.

——. 'Disarming Silence: Ethical Resistance in J.M. Coetzee's *Foe*', *Apartheid Narratives*, ed. N. Yousaf (Amsterdam and New York: Rodopi, 2001), pp. 131–41.

——. 'J.M. Coetzee's *Disgrace* and the Task of the Imagination', *Journal of Modern Literature*, 29.2 (Winter 2006): 75–93.

——. 'Literature and the Labour of Negation: J.M. Coetzee's *Life & Times of Michael K*', *Journal of Commonwealth Literature*, 36.1 (2001): 106–25.

——. ' "Little Enough, Less than Little: Nothing": Ethics, Engagement, and Change in the Fiction of J.M. Coetzee', *Modern Fiction Studies*, 46 (2000): 159–82.

——. 'Writing with Eyes Shut: Ethics, Politics, and the Problem of the Other in the Fiction of J.M. Coetzee', *English in Africa*, 25.1 (May 1998): 43–60.

Marks, J. *What it Means to Be 98% Chimpanzee: Apes, People and Their Genes* (Berkeley, Los Angeles and London: University of California Press, 2002).

Merleau-Ponty, M. *Phenomenology of Perception*, trans. C. Smith (London: Routledge & Kegan Paul, 1962).

Miller, J.H. 'The Critic as Host', *De-construction and Criticism*, eds H. Bloom et al. (New York: Seabury Press, 1979).

Monson, T. 'An Infinite Question: The Paradox of Representation in *Life & Times of Michael K*', *Journal of Commonwealth Literature*, 38.3 (2003): 87–106.

Mpe, P. *Welcome to Our Hillbrow* (Pietermaritzburg: University of KwaZulu Natal Press, 2001).

Mulhall, S. *The Wounded Animal: J.M. Coetzee and the Difficulty of Reality in Literature and Philosophy* (Princeton and Oxford: Princeton University Press, 2009).

Nabokov, V. *Lolita* (Harmondsworth: Penguin, 1980).

Ohmann, R. 'Prolegomena to the Analysis of Prose Style', *Essays on the Language of Literature*, eds S. Chatman and S. Levin (Boston: Houghton Mifflin, 1967), pp. 398–411.

Penner, D. *Countries of the Mind: The Fiction of J.M. Coetzee* (New York: Greenwood, 1989).

Plato. 'Cratylus', *The Dialogues of Plato*, volume 3, trans. Benjamin Jowett (London: Sphere Books, 1970), pp. 119–94.

——. *The Republic*, *The Dialogues of Plato*, volume 4, trans. Benjamin Jowett (London: Sphere Books, 1970).

——. *The Republic*, trans. Desmond Lee, 2nd edition (London: Penguin, 2003).

Riffaterre, M. 'Criteria for Style Analysis', *Essays on the Language of Literature*, eds S. Chatman and S. Levin (Boston: Houghton Mifflin, 1967), pp. 412–41.

———. 'Stylistic Context', *Essays on the Language of Literature*, eds S. Chatman and S. Levin (Boston: Houghton Mifflin, 1967), pp. 431–41.

Rose, A. *The Poetics of Reciprocity in Selected Fictions by J.M. Coetzee* (MA dissertation, University of Cape Town, 2007).

Rousseau, J.J. *Les Confessions, Oeuvres Complètes de Jean-Jacques Rousseau*. Vol. I (Brussels: Éditions Gallimard, 1959), pp. 1–656.

———. 'Préambule du Manuscrit de Neufchâtel' (www.lettres.org, accessed 6 May 2009).

Sanders, M. *Ambiguities of Witnessing: Law and Literature in the Time of a Truth Commission* (Stanford: Stanford University Press, 2007).

———. 'Disgrace', *Interventions*, 4.3 (2002): 363–73.

Saussure, F. de. *Course in General Linguistics*, trans. Wade Baskin (New York: Philosophical Library, 1966).

Schreiner, O. *The Story of an African Farm* (Harmondsworth: Penguin, 1971).

Sebald, W.G. *On the Natural History of Destruction*, trans. A. Bell (London: Penguin, 2003).

Sévry, J. 'Coetzee the Writer and the Writer of an Autobiography', *Commonwealth*, 22.2 (2000): 13–24.

Shklovsky, V. 'Art as Technique', *Russian Formalist Criticism: Four Essays*, trans. Lee Lemon and Marion Reis (Lincoln, Nebraska: University of Nebraska Press, 1965), pp. 3–24.

Smithson, R. *Robert Smithson: The Collected Writings*, ed. J. Flam (Berkeley, Los Angeles and London: University of California Press, 1996).

Tattersall, I. *Becoming Human: Evolution and Human Uniqueness* (San Francisco: Harcourt Brace, 1999).

van Niekerk, M. *Triomf* (Cape Town: Queillerie, 1994).

———. *Triomf*, trans. Leon de Kock (Johannesburg: Jonathan Ball, 1999).

Vice, S. '"Truth and Love Together at Last": Style, Form and Moral Vision in J.M. Coetzee's *Age of Iron*' (paper presented at the conference, 'J.M. Coetzee as Moral Philosopher', University of the Witwatersrand, Johannesburg, March 2009).

Vladislavić, I. *The Restless Supermarket* (Cape Town: David Philip, 2001).

Wicomb, Z. 'Translations in the Yard of Africa', *Journal of Literary Studies*, 18.3/4 (December 2002): 209–23.

Williamson, T. *The Philosophy of Philosophy* (Malden, Oxford and Victoria: Blackwell, 2007).

Wimsatt, W.K. 'Style as Meaning', *Essays on the Language of Literature*, eds S. Chatman and S. Levin (Boston: Houghton Mifflin, 1967), pp. 362–73.

Wittgenstein, L. *Philosophical Grammar*, trans. A. Kenny (Oxford: Basil Blackwell, 1974).

———. *Philosophical Investigations: The German Text, with a Revised English Translation*, 3rd edition, trans. G.E.M. Anscombe (Malden, Massachusetts: Blackwell, 2001).

Wittgenstein, L. *Philosophical Remarks*, ed. R. Rhees, trans. R. Hargreaves and R. White (Oxford: Basil Blackwell, 1975).

——. *Tractatus Logico-Philosophicus*, trans. C.K. Ogden (London and New York: Routledge, 1922).

Wood, M. 'In a Cold Country', *London Review of Books*, 29.19 (4 October 2007): 5–7.

Index

UNIVERSITY OF WINCHESTER
LIBRARY